COVENANT OF QUEENS

BOOK THREE : IMPERIAL RAND

SILVIA SHAW

Covenant of Queens

Cover design: M&J

Edited by Cath Walker

Contact: silviashaw@mail.com

This work is fiction. Any resemblance of characters to actual persons, living or dead, is purely coincidental.

CONTENTS

Synopsis	5
Acknowledgments	7
Also by Silvia Shaw	9
The Covenant	15
Chapter One	17
Chapter Two	29
Chapter Three	40
Chapter Four	52
Chapter Five	63
Chapter Six	74
Chapter Seven	84
Chapter Eight	95
Chapter Nine	106
Chapter Ten	118
Chapter Eleven	129
Chapter Twelve	138
Chapter Thirteen	150
Chapter Fourteen	161
Chapter Fifteen	170
Chapter Sixteen	182
Chapter Seventeen	195
Chapter Eighteen	205
Chapter Nineteen	216
Chapter Twenty	225
Chapter Twenty-One	236
Chapter Twenty-Two	245
Chapter Twenty-Three	260
Chapter Twenty-Four	270
Chapter Twenty-Five	281
Chapter Twenty-Six	293

Chapter Twenty-Seven   304
Chapter Twenty-Eight   317
Chapter Twenty-Nine   328
Chapter Thirty   339
Chapter Thirty-One   348
Chapter Thirty-Two   358
Chapter Thirty-Three   369
Chapter Thirty-Four   378
Chapter Thirty-Five   388
Chapter Thirty-Six   402
Chapter Thirty-Seven   414
Chapter Thirty-Eight   424
Chapter Thirty-Nine   435
Chapter Forty   445
Chapter Forty-One   454
Chapter Forty-Two   463
Chapter Forty-Three   473
Chapter Forty-Four   483
Chapter Forty-Five   494
Chapter Forty-Six   505
Chapter Forty-Seven   516
Chapter Forty-Eight   526
Chapter Forty-Nine   536
Chapter Fifty   549
Chapter Fifty-One   561

SYNOPSIS

The sweeping saga of Rand continues to its gripping conclusion ...

As the battle for Rand escalates, Savannah tries to unravel the secrets of the past to enable her to understand the future. Soon it becomes a race against the clock to solve the mystery of the third moon and to find the site of the enemy's time passage.

Although Commander Pela has organized the armies into a fighting force, she is unprepared for the attack that destroys a port on the Wide Sea of Mists. The enemy has air-power and bombs, something she hadn't foreseen. With the help of Countess Gladofin of the House of Amarim and Queen Lilybeth of Beria, Pela desperately tries to devise a military strategy to defeat the enemy.

As the fate of the Rand hangs in the balance, the Covenant of Queens gathers to close the Time Gateway. And while Savannah searches for her roots, an evil nemesis appears who won't stop until she is dead.

Danger and betrayal, secrets and myths, and new lovers, are mixed into a melting pot of magic in this electrifying finale of the Rand trilogy.

ACKNOWLEDGMENTS

To Duff McGhee, my Beta Reader who has an eagle eye for detail. Duff is studying for a career in editing, and I'm sure she will do very well in the industry. She was an invaluable help, very professional, and I can recommend her work.

To my friend Mary, who has been incredibly encouraging in my venture into self-publishing. As a Beta Reader, she has been there to discuss ideas and help with the plot.

To Cath, my editor, who as usual, with a firm hand has lifted the quality of my writing to another level. Her insight and expertise has been essential in producing a polished third book of the trilogy that I am immensely proud of.

ALSO BY SILVIA SHAW

Rand (Book 1)

A 2022 Winner of a Golden Crown Literary Award *Science fiction and Fantasy.*

"*A sprawling and majestic epic start to a fantasy new series, Rand by Silvia Shaw is an empowering and timely piece of fantasy fiction, bridging two worlds with grace and a whip-smart pen. Readers are drawn into a brilliant world with a detailed history that is unlike so many other carbon-copy realms in the genre*".

— SELF- PUBLISHING REVIEW

"*Must read. Amazing blend of destiny, magic, adventure, and romance in an epic fantasy world.*"

— REEDSY DISCOVERY

The Forgotten Realms (Book 2)

"This and the first one are such great reads. The tales are woven so well that it becomes more and more difficult to put the book down as the story progresses."

"Very calculating book feels like you're moving chess on a chessboard. Truly a good read."

For the girls

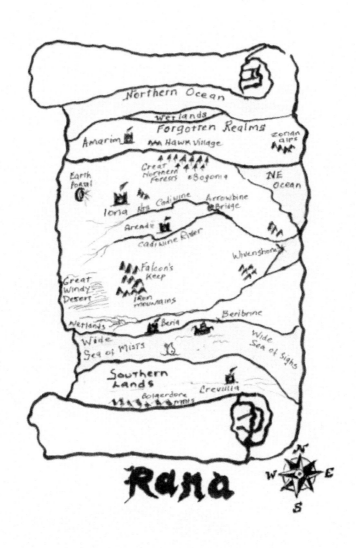

THE COVENANT

Valeria: Imperial Queen and Supreme Monarch of Rand

Jezzine: Queen of the Sirens and Consort to Queen Fern of Arcadia

Pela: Queen of the Bramble Hawks and Rand's Imperial Commander

Reagan: Enchantress and Queen of the House of Falendore

Tamasin: Mistress of Dreams and Consort to the Imperial Queen

Olivine: Queen of the Forgotten Realms and Head of the House of Amarim

CHAPTER ONE

THE REALM OF BERIAN

Savannah's stomach curled into a tight knot.

One moment, she was enjoying the brisk ride up the rugged Berian coastline on her Blue Fjord horse, Sunflower. The next, hundreds of winged creatures emerged from the rolling fog covering the headland in front of them. It was undeniably a military force — they were flying in formation, with armored riders on their backs.

And there was no mistaking their intention. This army was coming to attack the seaport of Beribrine.

Savannah looked down at the bustling port that she and the Elite Guard had just left. It would be an easy target for an invasion from the air. The city was gateway to the realms across the Wide Sea of Mists and had few fortifications. The harbor was full, ships tied up three deep, some in line to dock while others waited for the tide to turn to be on their way. The long-shoremen were busily loading cargo into the bellies of the squat merchant vessels bound for the Southern Lands: casks of spirits, sacks of fruit and vegetables, barrels of salted meats, and bales of cotton for weaving. The statelier sailing ships were loading passengers at a separate wharf further down.

To rest the horses, they'd stopped for an early lunch at The Black Barnacle tavern on the docks. She'd found the port area was clean but old, with draughty passage-ways and worn flagstones. It was a gray cloudy day with winds whipping in from the sea, and as they walked from the stable, the spray dampened Savannah's hair. They ate thick black bread filled with slabs of cheese and meat, accompanied by the sounds of the rumblings of the barrows over the stone floors and the squeals of the loading pulleys on the dock outside.

According to the publican, the Wide Sea of Mists was a fickle place, full of thick fogs and sudden squalls. The captains kept to the safe shipping lanes, for many who deviated off the established routes were lost forever in the mists.

They had no sooner collected the horses and started on their way to the Berian Palace when this strange and terrifying air force appeared.

Savannah figured for so large an invasion to get

here undetected, there mustn't be any warning patrols along the coast and inner islands. A decision Berian's Queen Lilybeth would regret. But Savannah could understand why she hadn't set them up. So far, there had only been assassinations in buildings under the cloak of darkness, and there were no indications the enemy had air power. Let alone in this proportion.

She fought down panic.

It was pointless trying to warn those below of the impending danger. She could do nothing now; the enemy was too close. The winged creatures had turned in the direction of the seaport and were racing across the cliff face to the harbor. Though she readied her magic, Savannah knew resistance would be fruitless against so many.

Time for flight, not fight. She must choose her battles wisely.

She waved to the Elite Guard to follow, then projected urgently to Sunflower, *"Go out to sea. Our only hope is to hide in the mists."*

As the creatures neared, the mare required no persuading. They were fearsome enough to make anyone's blood run cold. Though similar to the prehistoric pterodactyls of ancient Earth with their reptilian bodies and elongated beaked heads, they were longer and thicker. More dangerous as well, for their leathery wings were supported by arms with viciously clawed hands that looked capable of slicing a person open with one strike.

From their breast-plated armor, she could see the front riders were women. Then Savannah had no more time to study the enemy as Sunflower quickly banked into a sharp turn and began speeding toward the water.

Once clear of the shore, Savannah risked a glance over her shoulder. She snapped to attention when four riders broke off from the main force to chase them.

She quickly telepathed to Sunflower, *"Four are coming after us."*

The mare went immediately into the evasive tactics that they'd practiced at length.

As they dived and zig-zagged, an arrow zipped past Savannah's head.

She shot off a hurried bolt of magic then hunched down in the saddle. The fireball hit nothing, flaring harmlessly in the sky. A moment later, the Elite Guard uttered a strangled cry as an arrow struck her in the upper chest. Horrified, Savannah watched the warrior topple off her horse into the water below.

The horse squealed as one of the leathery creatures swooped down and ripped its belly open with its talons. As its entrails streamed out through the massive gash, the Blue Fjord frantically tried to flap away. The winged reptile struck again, this time slashing through the horse's neck. It dropped out of the sky into the water.

Furious, Savannah threw a flaming bolt at the beast. Its wing burst into flames, which sent it into a downward spin. The rider leaped off a second before it smashed into a cluster of rocks, but weighed down by armor, she disappeared under the waves.

Then the chase began in earnest.

As they headed out to sea, Sunflower ducked, dived, and weaved through patches of mist while Savannah sizzled out her magic. She knocked one more beast out of the sky, but she could tell by Sunflower's puffing and wheezing that she was tiring. They were miles out to sea, the Berian headland no longer visible. Yet the remaining two creatures clung close.

When Savannah felt something hit her leg, she looked down to see an arrow had nicked her upper thigh. Blood seeped through her breeches, and she feared if she didn't do something, they'd die out here. The next arrow could be fatal. To invoke the Death Vale would be the decisive blow, but she didn't know if she could do it on horseback, and even if she could, its violence might hurt Sunflower. Or deafen her. She couldn't take that risk. They'd try to kill them using their wiles.

"Drop down and see if you can get under them," she ordered.

The mare answered with a grunt, then dropped suddenly. Savannah was pleased she had prepared herself for the move, or she would have flipped over her head. The two in pursuit hadn't expected it. As they passed overhead, Savannah shot out a ball of magic. When the stream hit the leading creature in the underbelly, it burst into flames. Squealing, it plummeted into the sea.

As the other one circled behind them, Savannah noticed a blanket of dense clouds to the east. She jerked at the reins. *"Head for the fog,"* she urged.

Sunflower obeyed immediately, spinning sharply around. Before the enemy managed to get into a position to fire another arrow, they'd entered the fog. Savannah breathed a sigh of relief. It would be hard to follow anyone in here. It was as dense as soup, with no visibility whatsoever.

But after the euphoria of having avoided death by arrows, Savannah was presented with a far different problem, but one no less serious. They were flying blind into God knows where, and the plucky horse couldn't stay up indefinitely. Cautiously, Sunflower edged forward, stopping frequently to listen. The air was thick with the smell of fish and salt, and only the lapping of water could be heard. Further in, the cloud thinned, and a pale ray of sunlight revealed a line of jutting rocks in the sea ahead. They looked treacherous, the edges like jagged knife blades.

As Sunflower hovered to search for a safe passage through, Savannah grasped for the Farsight Stone she now wore permanently around her neck. Holding it up, she let the narrow beam of light show the way in, and quickly memorized the path in case the fog closed in again. But as she tucked the Farsight Stone back into her shirt, she heard the faint sound of flapping wings. She went cold — the enemy hadn't given up.

Then something strange happened. A wind boiled up, increasing to a violent squall that howled in rage. The sea became as capricious as the wind, whipping into foam-flecked white caps that crashed violently against the rocks. The sky darkened with rolling clouds as turbulent as the water. But though the wind snatched at Savannah's face, making her eyes smart and her cheeks burn, the full force of the squall remained behind them.

A waterspout formed in the middle, spiraling upward into the clouds. Through the shrieking wind, she heard the faint scream of a woman and the screech of the reptile.

Immediately, the squall died down from gale-force to merely a stiff wind, pushing Sunflower forward. When the horse was propelled through the rocks without colliding, Savannah knew magical forces were at play. And it certainly hadn't been an ordinary storm, though why the wielder of the magic spared them, she had no idea. She'd find out soon enough.

Once they were through the rocks, the water calmed and the fog lifted.

A dark body suddenly launched into the air, reentering the sea so near them they were splashed with water. Soon others joined in, spinning and vaulting through the air in an acrobatic display that made Savannah bubble out laughter. By the time the mare reached the beach, they were dripping wet. When she touched down, Sunflower sank to her knees, exhausted. Savannah crawled off, gave her an affectionate hug, then looked around curiously.

The beach was an inlet, sloping up to the base of a rocky cliff riddled with caves. The shore wasn't made of sand but finely ground shells that glinted in the sunlight. Brown sea creatures that looked like seals, waddled out of the water. From New Zealand, Savannah was used to seeing seals in the wild, but these were different. Though they had flippers, they also had short stubby legs to enable them to walk on land.

By the time every Seal was out of the water, Sunflower and Savannah were surrounded by them.

Savannah watched them nervously for any aggressive moves, but they simply stood watching. After a period of uncertainty when they seemed to be assessing her, they began to hum a soft hypnotic tune. She sank wearily against the horse and closed her eyes.

When she opened them again, it was mid-afternoon, the sea calm, the air clear. Children were playing with Sunflower on the beach, lining up for rides. Smiling, Savannah watched for a while — the mare was enjoying herself, taking them for short rides then tipping them into the sea as they squealed with delight. At a sound behind, she turned to see a heavy-set man striding down the beach.

From his expression, he didn't look happy. "The Madra wants to see you," he said in a strange guttural accent, then turned without another word.

Savannah got up and dusted off the fine shell from her pants, noting the blood on the breeches had crusted dry. Her thigh stung, reminding her she'd better check the wound soon before it became infected.

She followed him down the beach to the entrance of an underground cavern. Inside was a room with all the comforts of a well-appointed house. The woman sitting on the central chair was big-boned, with a slightly flat face, salt-and-pepper hair, and a dark complexion. When Savannah had a closer look, she could see her skin was a deep brown, the color of the Seals. She appeared pleasant, and intelligence sparkled in her eyes.

On the other hand, the man who had brought

Savannah in clearly didn't want her here. He pulled her forward roughly. "Bow to the Madra," he ordered.

Stiffening, Savannah carefully pried his hand from her arm. "Don't touch me again," she said quietly, embracing her power.

A cold smile played on his lips. "You're in no position to tell me anything, landlubber."

She looked at him disdainfully. Had the man any sense, he would have been able to feel the air about her crackling with power.

But then he must have felt it, for he backed away warily.

"That's enough, Dirk. Leave us. I wish to talk to our guest alone."

For a moment, he looked undecided, then nodded. "I'll be outside."

The Madra didn't acknowledge him again, instead focused on Savannah. "How can you speak our tongue?"

Savannah smiled. "I speak all languages on Rand."

"But how is that possible you know ours? Very few land people do."

Savannah didn't hesitate. There was no time to waste; secrets were at an end. "I wear the Circle of Sheda."

"It's back?"

Savannah pulled it out of her shirt. "It is. You've heard of it?"

"Of course. Every child in Rand knows the rhyme."
The Circle of Sheda was taken away
Into a faraway land.
When the dogs of war start baying again
It will come back to Rand."

Savannah listened with interest. It explained why everyone reacted with the same expression when they saw the medallion.

"I salute you, Chosen One. Tell me, why were you being chased by a Skeldach."

Savannah felt a stir of excitement. "You know what the flying lizards are?"

"I know everything that goes on in the sea. They live in the subterranean caverns under the chalky crags of the Isle of Misery. I've never known them to come out."

Savannah stared at her. The winged creatures weren't transported through time. If they lived here, then they could be destroyed in their home. "Why don't they come out?"

"They live their lives underground in darkness. On a dull day, they have a little sight, but are blind in bright sunlight."

"Do you know a way to get down to their lair?"

"Of course. The caverns reach the seafloor. We can go anywhere there's water." The Madra pointed to the seat opposite. "Sit down and tell me why they have come out and who was riding that one."

Savannah sat down heavily and grimaced. "The Crevlin are back. A large armed force riding the Skeldachs attacked Beribrine this morning. I was on my way to Queen Lilybeth's Palace when they appeared on the headland. I managed to get here, but my guard and her horse were killed. If it weren't for your intervention, they would have gotten me too. Thank you."

"You know what we are?"

"I've just come back from the Forgotten Realms, which is full of enchanted people and places. You're magical beings who turn into Seals. Are there any more shifters in the ocean?"

The Madra smiled. "Many. The seas are vast, Chosen One. Magic isn't confined to the land."

CHAPTER TWO

THE WIDE SEA OF MISTS

*T*hat the seas would be full of Magical Folk had never entered Savannah's head.

She cast the Madra a puzzled look. "Is it common knowledge that there are magical sea people? No one has ever mentioned it."

"We keep to ourselves, but people who live on the coast and the islands are aware there are enchanted folk and places in the sea. The Queens of Berian have always controlled these waters and protected us. We allow their ships to pass through, but they must stay on the designated routes. The mists can be treacherous in places, something we have no control over."

"You've met Queen Lilybeth?"

"We are friends, Chosen One. May I ask to what

Realm you belong? You are shorter than the Berian people."

"My name is Savannah, and I came through the portal."

"You're not from Rand?"

Savannah smiled ruefully. "No. Some of my ancestors must have been short, but I'm a descendant of Elsbeth."

The Madra stared at her. "Elsbeth had a child?"

"Twins. Queen Jessica sent her through the portal to protect the children."

"Oh!" The Madra chewed her lip while she digested the information. Then she bowed to her. "You are indeed welcome here, Savannah. My name is Nerin."

"Thank you, Nerin. Um ... will the Sea Folk help in the coming war?"

The woman shook her head. "We have little interaction with land people. What goes on outside our domain has no interest to us. We allow passenger and cargo vessels unrestricted access through the sea because they do us no harm. Anyone giving us trouble is dealt with severely. We sink ships carrying harpoons, and those wantonly killing us for sport disappear into whirlpools." Her lips peeled back into a mirthless smile. "Or fed to the Scaled Serpent Squids."

Savannah swallowed, hoping she wouldn't be

meeting one of those monsters. "But surely there are fishermen in the waters?" she asked.

"Fish are the staple food for everyone on the coast and islands. The people know what creatures to leave alone. We've always lived in harmony with them, especially the island people." She smiled. "There have been quite a few intermarriages."

Savannah turned that over in her mind. Fish weren't shapeshifters then. She wondered what type of marine animals were magical but didn't persist with her queries. It was something she'd ask Queen Lilybeth when she saw her. Or Winston. He mentioned he'd come from an island in the Wide Sea of Mists. "When this war starts, do you honestly think the Crevlin won't scourge the seas once they'd conquered Rand?"

"Why would they?"

"They hate magic."

"We keep our powers to ourselves."

"They'd have a motive for attacking the seaport," Savannah replied. "They must want unimpeded access to the shipping lanes to control who comes across. Which means either they want to stop the Southern Lands' armies from joining up with the rest of Rand, or their army is in the south."

Nerin shrugged. "As long as they do us no harm, they may sail their ships across."

"Will you come with me to see what happened to Beribrine before you refuse to help?" Savannah asked. There was nothing like seeing something first-hand, and her gut feeling told her the Sea Folk would be important in the future. "You can ride with me on my horse to give us time to look around before dark."

"I'm not going to change my mind," Nerin said dismissively.

Savannah looked at her with a gleam in her eye. "I'll strap you into the saddle. You won't fall off."

The Madra's brown cheeks grew a little darker. "I'm not afraid of flying. I suppose I could go for a look, although I think you have exaggerated the whole situation. To sack a city that size would call for Wizard's fire or a magic source, and you said yourself that this enemy hates magic."

"I hope you're right," muttered Savannah, but she had a bad feeling about it. Why would they come with such a force if they didn't intend to do more major damage? She stood up. "I'll get Sunflower saddled. She's giving the little ones rides."

†

What greeted them at Beribrine was far worse than Savannah ever imagined.

Sunflower hovered in the air to give them a view of the devastation, and it was confronting. The wharves were in ruins, and fires had gutted most of the warehouses and loading docks. Blackened husks of ships floated everywhere in the harbor; the only vessels intact were three fishing trawlers anchored off the point. Fire had already passed through the more populated areas of the city, and now the outer quarters were alight. It seemed that the harbor area had been the main target. She could only imagine how frightening it must have been for sailors and dockhands when they were attacked.

The air reeked with the stench of death and despair.

Cries of pain and grief echoed through the smoke that drifted in the wind over the dying city. Savannah could make out a few uniformed soldiers amongst people searching through the rubble for survivors. Hundreds had perished in the onslaught, for there were already bodies stacked into piles in the city square.

Savannah fought back her tears as she projected to Sunflower, *"Land somewhere on the wharf."*

When the horse did so without her usual cheery retort, Savannah patted her neck to soothe her. *"I know it's upsetting, sweetie, but I want to talk to someone about the attack."*

As soon as they touched down, Savannah's nose

twitched. The smell of ammonia was strong in the air. When she sniffed again and caught a faint whiff of sulfur as well, part of the puzzle fell into place. As she suspected, this enemy wasn't using magic but something lethal similar to gunpowder. Or perhaps it was dragon flames.

She turned to Nerin, who was looking around wide-eyed. "Can the Skeldachs breathe out fire, Nerin?"

"No. They kill with their talons and beaks." She waved a hand, her face a tight mask. "They couldn't have done this."

Savannah turned this over in her mind. "Then the Crevlin had bombs, explosive devices of some kind. Let's ask one of the survivors what happened."

Nearby, she saw The Black Barnacle amongst the ruins and headed for it. Surprisingly, though the tavern had lost the façade and half the roof, the bar was still intact. The publican, his salt-weathered face haggard, was cleaning up the broken bottles behind the bar. When they entered, he looked at Savannah blankly, then his eyes widened when they came to rest on the Madra. By his deferential nod, he was aware who she was. His gaze focused on Savannah warily. "You look familiar. Do I know you, Mistress?" he asked.

"I lunched here today."

"Ah, yes, you were accompanied by the Guard with the bird tattoo on her face."

"She was killed by the monsters who did this, and I barely escaped," Savannah said, not letting her emotions plummet. She had information to gather. "Tell us what happened here. I'm flying to the Berian Palace, and the Queen will want to know the details if she hasn't already heard."

He shuddered. "One moment I was serving ale, the next all hell broke loose. When I ran outside, I could see them throwing balls at the boats and ships, and they exploded on impact." He slammed a fist into his palm. "The poor blighters never had a chance. The wood went up in flames in an instant."

Savannah leaned forward, eyeing him intently. "How big were the missiles?"

"Small enough to fit in their hands. They had them in bags on their saddles. Some were throwing them, while others were archers, picking off anyone that moved." His voice dropped to an agonized whisper. "It was a blood bath. The people here aren't soldiers but merchant sea folk."

"I know," Savannah said sadly. "War has come to Rand and this was the first big strike. No one anticipated it would be here."

"Will they come again?" he asked fearfully.

"No. They've done what they came to do. Destroyed the fleet and crippled Berian's sea power."

He looked at her curiously. "Where do you fit into

all this? You don't look like a warrior. Are you from a Royal House?"

"I wear the Circle of Sheda, sir."

Relief flicked in his eyes. "Thank the Goddess, it has come back to Rand. We are going to need you, Chosen One. Those soldiers were beasts without honor, slaughtering everyone they saw. We carry no weapons."

Savannah dropped her voice to a whisper. "They were the Crevlin. The stuff of your nightmares."

He blanched, clearly brought up with the bogymen tales. "What shall we do, Chosen One?"

"Are there any troops from the Palace here yet?"

"No. The enemy destroyed the city stables, killing all the flying horses. We only have a garrison of eighty soldiers, and the Captain sent a courier on a land horse to Beria. She'll still have two hours before she reaches the city."

Savannah looked to the sky, estimating it was three hours before nightfall. "I'll get going then. You'll want troops here as soon as possible to evacuate the people."

The publican nodded grimly. "We'll require help to organize those alive and to burn the dead. We don't want animals eating their bodies. The wolves and bears have been restless in the hills lately." His expression remained unchanged, but moisture gathered in his eyes. "My brother died on the wharf."

Savannah's heart went out to him. It was going to be hard days ahead for the survivors. She squeezed his hand that rested on the top of the bar. "We'll get help as soon as we can." With Nerin at her heels, she strode quickly to the door,

"We'll give you a lift home," Savannah said as soon as they reached Sunflower, who waited patiently outside on the dock.

"There's a small beach around the point," Nerin replied. "Drop me off there. I'd prefer to swim home. The sea will wash away the stench of this evil."

"I hope after this you'll think seriously of helping in the war."

Nerin shook her head sorrowfully. "I'm sorry, Savannah, but my decision was final. As their leader, I cannot commit the Sea Folk to a war that doesn't involve them."

"No one will remain unscathed in this conflict," growled Savannah, feeling frustrated to the point of screaming at the woman. But she held her temper. She'd just try to find a way to convince her.

As soon as they climbed onto her back, Sunflower leaped into the air with a bound, clearly anxious to distance herself from the carnage. Around the headland, a sandy beach came into view. At first, Savanah thought it was littered with boulders, but when Nerin gave an agonizing cry, she realized they weren't rocks but bodies of Seals.

Sunflower hovered, reluctant to go down, and Savannah had to cajole her into landing. When she finally flew down, Nerin jumped off immediately. Kneeling at the first body, she keened out her grief. Around fifty Seals lay on the beach, all with their soft underbellies ripped open, and their innards devoured. As well, their eyes had been pecked out and cheeks and tongues eaten. Her stomach rebelling, Savannah forced herself to examine a corpse. From the look of the marks, two different carnivores had fed off the Seal. She hazarded a guess that the Skeldachs had eaten the offal and the Crows the face.

She knelt beside the devastated woman and took her hand. "I'm sorry, Nerin. This enemy is foul. If you like, I'll help you pull the bodies into the sea."

When the Madra turned to look at her, her face was like granite. "My people will care for their own. Go to your people and tell them the Sea Folk will fight with them. This enemy will not be allowed on the water."

"Is it possible to stop the Skeldachs from coming out of their caverns?"

"Everything is possible, Chosen One. Tell Lilybeth I will meet her at noon the day after tomorrow at our secret place. Now, I must go." She leaped to her feet and ran to the water's edge. With a final wave, she disappeared into the surf.

As Savannah watched her go, she wondered if the Crevlin would ever realize what a huge mistake they'd made today. Not only had they provoked Lilybeth, the ultimate warrior Queen, but worse still, they'd made a powerful enemy of the woman who ruled the seas.

CHAPTER THREE

THE BERIAN PALACE

*Q*ueen Lilybeth Vandersea strode down the passageway to the left-wing, trying to tamp down her temper.

As if she hadn't enough to do preparing her army for the coming war without also having to nursemaid a group of amateurs claiming to be military strategists. To house them in the palace was more than just an inconvenience, but when Tamasin, Consort to Imperial Queen Valeria, had asked her to accommodate them, she hadn't been able to think of a way to refuse. It was, after all, the best-fortified building on Rand. But it would mean she'd be going back to formal dining and court protocol, something she'd hadn't bothered with for years.

Once, it had been different. When Lilybeth was

twenty-five, she had wed a princess from a minor Realm bordering the Great Northern Forests. Though it had been a marriage of convenience and not a love match, they had liked and respected each other and had expected to spin out their lives in the quiet marriage. But it was not to be. Lilybeth had managed to bury, quite deeply, the agony of seeing her Consort drown four years after the wedding.

Since then, she'd been content or rather resigned to filling her time with her duties and raising their daughter, Maybeth, alone. But following in the tradition of the Berian warrior Queens, last turn of the moons on her twentieth birthday, Maybeth had become a recruit at Falcon's Keep. Lilybeth missed her dreadfully, which made her even more annoyed about the unwanted visitors.

And attending the royal Arcadian wedding had made her realize how empty her life had become. That Fern, Queen of Arcadia had chosen Jezzine, a courtesan and Queen of the Sirens, as her Consort had surprised the Royal Houses. Over the years, Lilybeth had watched with amusement while Rand's Royal Houses had jostled for Fern's attention, for there was no doubt Arcadia was the ultimate prize. She applauded Fern for having the backbone to pick the courtesan. Apart from it being an obvious love match, Jezzine was far more intelligent and versed in diplomacy than most aristocrats, who had become soft pleasure seekers. She would be a valuable asset to Arcadia's throne.

She paused at the door of the wing, listening to the laughter inside. After a momentary flash of guilt that she hadn't come up from the garrison to greet them when they'd arrived, she brushed the dust and salt off her work clothes and stepped inside. She hadn't bothered dressing formally, presuming they were imperial army personnel, but the group inside took her by surprise. The two women and two men had no military bearing whatsoever.

Charts were attached to the walls, and on the center table lay a raised map fashioned from clay. On close inspection, she recognized the map as Rand.

A dapper young man with a neatly trimmed beard gave a low bow. "Your Majesty. Thank you for taking the time to meet us. My name is Winston," he said, then introduced the others. Egwine, a thin woman with a large head who looked to be in her early fifties, Willowtine a younger attractive woman with mossy-green hair, and Limos, a middle-aged man with a thick mane of hair and yellow-tinged eyes.

Lilybeth acknowledged them with a nod, "You speak for your colleagues, Winston?"

He flashed a set of perfect white teeth. "No, Ma'am. The Countess is the boss."

On cue, the door opened and a striking woman,

with blond hair piled on top of her head, and wearing a fitting deep red gown which matched her lipstick, swept into the room. "Queen Lilybeth. Thank you for coming to see us."

Lilybeth glanced down self-consciously at her own dull coat and stained breeches, realizing too late her serious breach of protocol. By not being here to greet her, she'd insulted Countess Gladofin. She was the sister of Queen Olivine of the House of Amarim, Ruler of the vast Forgotten Realms, a powerful monarch, second only to Valeria, Imperial Queen of Rand. The Countess was a formidable woman in her own right, helping her sister govern the Magical Folk. Lilybeth had sat beside her at Fern's wedding banquet and thought she was one of the most captivating women she'd ever met.

She gave an embarrassed cough. "Countess. I'm sorry I wasn't here when you arrived. I was detained." Then added weakly, "I haven't had time to change. I had no idea it was you who was coming."

The Countess raised an eyebrow and murmured, "We don't expect to be fussed over. We're here to work."

Lilybeth flushed, catching the subtle chiding tone. She couldn't remember anyone managing to make her feel so small, so politely. "I trust my staff has made the wing comfortable for your stay. I enjoyed your company at the Arcadian wedding, and I'm looking forward to getting to know you." She cast her eyes around the room. "Perhaps you might tell me what exactly you'll be doing."

"Winston is our coordinator. I'll let him explain."

With a cheery grin, Winston gestured to the middle table. "Supreme Commander Pela sent a message that we're to start working out the likely routes the enemy will take and what strategic positions we must defend."

Pushing her etiquette blunder out of her mind, Lilybeth closely studied her Realm on the map. She pointed to part of the coastline. "There's another small headland after that bay, but otherwise, it's remarkably accurate. Oh … and there's a fishing village on an island here." She glanced at Winston. "Someone from Berian helped you?"

"I grew up on Oyster Island."

"Ah, that explains it. Your people are wonderful chart makers. In two days, we plan to set up a warning system along the coast and islands. Where do you suggest we put them?"

Winston stroked his beard as he gazed at the map model. "Well, for a start —"

At the sound of running footsteps and loud voices outside, he paused to listen. Lilybeth turned quickly when the door was flung open, and a figure burst into the room. The short woman was followed closely by a guard.

"Savannah," the Countess called out, hurrying forward. "What's happened?"

Recognizing the Chosen One, Lilybeth waved quickly to the guard. "Stand down, Lieutenant, and wait outside. I'll call you if there's any trouble."

The guard eyed Savannah warily, then thumped her chest. "I'll be in the corridor, Your Majesty."

When the guard closed the door behind her, Savannah gave a quick bow. "Thanks, Ma'am. I didn't want to hurt her." She smiled briefly at them all, then focused back on Lilybeth. "I've bad news."

Lilybeth studied her, noting her disheveled state, the soot covering her clothes and face, and the bloodstain on her breeches. "Sit down before you fall. From the look of you, I'm guessing I'm going to hate what I'm going to hear." She glanced at Winston. "Fetch her a drink of water, please, before we start."

When he returned with the cup, Savannah took a large gulp. "Thanks. I was parched." She gazed at Lilybeth sorrowfully then shivered. "The Crevlin attacked Beribrine from the air, Ma'am. They sank the ships in the harbor and burnt the city."

As Lilybeth listened, her heart sank. She'd been too slow getting their warning systems up and running. Commander Pela had warned her to take precautions as quickly as she could.

"The enemy has magic bolts?" asked the Countess incredulously. "We were told they feared magic."

Savannah shook her head. "Bombs made from minerals, similar to a substance called gunpowder in my world. I recognized the smell."

"Are there many dead?" asked Lilybeth, dreading the answer.

"Hundreds. The Beribrine people are desperate for help to find survivors before the carrion-eating beasts come out of the woods. The outer city still burns." Savannah took a deep breath. "They targeted the stables and killed all the flying horses. The survivors sent a rider on a land horse here to get help."

Lilybeth couldn't stop a few stray tears escaping over her lids. With an effort, she pulled herself together. "I'll dispatch my soldiers immediately. They can be there within the hour."

Savannah held up her hand. "Wait just a moment, please, Ma'am." She turned her head to look at Winston. "What do you think?"

"If I were the enemy, I'd wait until the troops were elsewhere and attack Beria."

"You think the seaport was a diversion?" asked Lilybeth quickly.

He shook his head. "No. I'd say their primary objective was to disable your sea power, but why leave it until after midday to attack. Early morning is the best time for a preempted strike. Everyone would be still in bed."

Lilybeth caught his line of thought. "They came that late so our troops would need to stay until tomorrow for the clean-up."

"Exactly. I think that the Crevlin may attack here either tonight or very early in the morning. They'll never have such an advantage again."

The Countess walked over to the map to study it. "I think you're right, Winston. Berian is a strategic position to control. To hold Beria would open up a route into the more populated lands to the North."

"May I make a suggestion?" Savannah asked.

"Go ahead. If I'd had my warning systems in place before this, the catastrophe could have been averted, or at least lessened," said Lilybeth bitterly. "I'd welcome advice."

"Send the strongest of your citizens with a small contingent of soldiers to Beribrine. They will be just as useful in the clean-up. Fit as many on horses as they can carry. Get there while the sun is shining, for the Skeldachs, the flying lizards, are blind in direct sunlight."

Winston looked at her curiously. "How do you know that Savannah?"

"I met someone who knows what they are. But I'll explain all that later."

Lilybeth strode to the door. "I'll give the order to the guards and be back shortly." When she stepped into the corridor, her army general was standing outside.

She saluted. "The guards called me, Ma'am. Is there trouble?"

"Beribrine has been attacked and the ships in the harbor sunk, General. Here's what I want you to do." After giving her orders, she added, "Come back here when you're finished. And hurry, please. They're in trouble. And General. Get one of the guards to find the Bird Master. We have messages to send."

After the soldier left, Lilybeth squared her shoulders before she re-entered the room. She couldn't shake the feeling that she'd failed them.

Savannah pointed to a seat. "Sit there, Ma'am. The Countess has just attended to my leg, and I'm resting it."

Lilybeth frowned at her. "Are you hurt badly?"

Savannah's eyes clouded over. "The arrow just grazed my thigh, but my Elite Guard wasn't so lucky. She was shot in the chest, and then a beast gutted the Blue Fjord. It was sickening to watch. This enemy is repulsive and without mercy."

"The Bird Master will be here in a minute. Write out what messages you want to be sent and to whom. We must warn the neighboring realms that there could be an air assault. Where is Pela?"

"She's still at Arcadia. I expect she'll come straight here when she hears what's happened," said Savannah.

"Good," said Lilybeth, feeling a sense of relief. Even though the Imperial Commander put the fear of Goddess into most of the Royal Houses, she admired the woman. Pela, a Bramble Hawk, was forthright, took no nonsense, and was a superb military tactician. The catapult on a turnstile for aerial fighting that she'd designed, was nothing short of brilliant. "We must prepare for the assault. Do you think they'll come tonight or at dawn?"

Savannah looked undecided then replied, "I think in the morning, but we should hedge our bets."

Winston smiled. "Spoken like a cautious gambler. What do you propose?"

"That we get a message out to the townspeople that no one is to use a light tonight unless the windows are blacked out. There'll be no beacons to guide the enemy here. And we must get the horses out of the stables. They'll target them. How many Bramble Hawks have you, ma'am?"

"Ten, and two Dreamers."

"The Hawks must patrol all night for Crows," said Savannah. "We found at Arcadia that the enemy had spies actually in the palace." She reached for a quill and drew the time symbol, a circle not fully closed. "They all have that tattoo on their upper arms. If your chancellor could gather the staff, including the stable hands, I'm prepared to check their arms one by one, in private. They must be executed on the spot if we find one. Otherwise, they'll tell any of the others, turn into Crows and escape."

"My word, Savannah, you've thought this through," exclaimed the Countess.

"I saw what was left of Beribrine, Countess. We don't want that to happen here. This enemy gives no quarter."

"I presume if they come in the morning, they'll hit at first light," said Lilybeth. "I'll get the troops to move the catapults into position tonight."

Savannah eyed her with delight. "You built Pela's revolving catapults?"

"Four. That's what I was doing all day. Testing and refining them for accuracy." She gave a broad smile. "They worked like a charm. We can fire off streams of arrows in seconds while they're rotating. One is as good as a hundred archers. I'll set them along the top of the cliff."

"If you do the right side and the middle, I'll stand on the left point," said Savannah. "All soldiers must stand well away from me. My magic is dangerous."

"Savannah," said the Countess disapprovingly. "You can't expose yourself like that. You're not immune to arrows." She frowned at Lilybeth. "You're the queen here, Lilybeth. Stop her."

Lilybeth cleared her throat. "Savannah knows her capabilities." The withering look from the Countess set Lilybeth's teeth on edge. The woman was acting as if it were all her fault. She couldn't remember when anyone had managed to make her feel so off-center.

"I'll be fine," announced Savannah with finality. "I was given the sacred medallion for a purpose, Countess. No one else can help me do this."

CHAPTER FOUR

*T*he two moons hung like purple lanterns in the sky.

Lilybeth stood on the second-floor balcony, gazing down at the raised walkway behind the stone battlement that fronted the Wide Sea of Mists. Naturally fortified at the back by the sheer cliff face, the city of Beria had always been considered impregnable. There was only one way in, which was in the front, an easily defended road. But against air power, Beria and her Royal House were vulnerable.

An hour off first light, all was quiet. Since a night attack hadn't happened, they'd never know if it had been planned and then postponed because they'd found and executed two Crevlin spies before they could get a message out. Or the blackout had worked. They waited for a morning assault now.

The four catapults were silhouetted against the sky, and she could just vaguely see the outlines of the soldiers catching their sleep in the shadows near the wall. She stirred uneasily. Were they prepared enough to ward off the invaders? She was brought out of her musings by the sound of footsteps and turned to see Savannah coming to join her.

She leaned over the railing beside Lilybeth and said softly, "It's different in my world, Ma'am. When we look at the night sky, we see stars. We have only one moon, and it's much smaller."

Lilybeth turned to her in surprise. "You're not from Rand, Savannah? I know very little about you or how you became the Chosen One."

"Tamasin brought me through the portal when she found I wore the Circle of Sheda and couldn't take it off. As soon as I discovered it, the medallion claimed me."

"It chose a stranger from another world?"

"Not quite a stranger. I'm a relation of yours, Ma'am. Queen Jessica sent Elsbeth through the portal to protect her unborn children. I am her descendent."

Lilybeth stared at her. "No one told the family that Elsbeth was pregnant when she left," she exclaimed, feeling a wave of hurt. "Surely Jessica could have trusted those who loved her?"

"It must have been important to keep it a secret," said Savannah.

"From whom was she hiding? Jessica destroyed the Silverthorne Witches' Coven."

Savannah fell silent as though turning the question over in her mind, then replied thoughtfully. "You know, Lilybeth, no one has ever said who she feared. Could she have been hiding the pregnancy from the father? A way-out theory, but one that shouldn't be casually dismissed."

"Who was the father?"

Savannah shrugged. "Ah ... that's the big mystery. If I knew that, it would explain many things."

Lilybeth smiled, noting Savannah had dropped her formal title. She wasn't used to court protocol, even treating the Countess casually, which most people wouldn't dare do.

Lilybeth studied her in the glow of the moonlight. She was smaller than average, with a pretty face and big blue eyes. Her face reminded her of Maybeth, who was more endowed with her mother's finer, attractive features. There was nothing delicate about herself. Lilybeth took after her mother who had been a strapping woman, with a warrior's body and strong facial bones. "Do you know what happened to

Elsbeth after she went through the portal?" she asked.

"No," Savannah replied. "I only found out she was my ancestor when I came to Rand, otherwise, I would have specifically traced her in our family tree. I discovered her body hidden in an underground cavern in a desert, which in itself was a mystery. She was in full armor, complete with her sword and shield, so I presume she was a noted warrior in my world too. I closed the tomb to leave her body undisturbed."

"You were alone when you found her?"

"Yes, I was caught in a sandstorm. There was no doubt that I was meant to find Elsbeth, because I found the way down to her resting place by magical intervention." She fingered the medallion through her shirt. "We don't have magic in my world."

"Extraordinary. Rand is full of enchanted beings and places."

"Which reminds me," said Savannah. "Nerin, the Madra, wants to meet with you at noon tomorrow at your secret place."

Lilybeth looked at her in surprise. "You've met her?"

"I told you we avoided being shot down by flying into a sea mist. What I didn't add was that the Madra saved us by conjuring up a squall to knock the Skeldach out of the sky," Savannah replied. "Afterward, she came with me to see the destruction of Beribrine."

"I doubt the Magical Sea Folk will come into this war, Savannah, so don't get your hopes up. They're my friends, but they stay strictly apart from the rest of Rand. They're only concerned with what goes on in the sea."

"Not anymore, Lilybeth. Around the point, we found a beach littered with dead Seals. The Crevlin had slaughtered them for food."

Lilybeth's stomach churned, "Oh, no," she breathed out hoarsely. "Poor Nerin. She must be devastated."

"Yes, and livid," said Savannah. "The Crevlin made a huge tactical error. They should have left the Sea Folk alone. Now they won't have safe passages for their ships. And as well, she's going to help us do something about the Skeldachs. Nerin knows where they live."

"I'll talk with her tomorrow about it," Lilybeth said, then looked to the sky. "But first we must win the war today... that is if they come."

"We'll know shortly," murmured Savannah. "There was one thing I've been meaning to ask you. Tamasin mentioned the Wide Sea of Sighs. Where is that one?"

"There are many different bodies of water, Savannah. The Southern Lands are about a third of the size of the rest of Rand, though the bottom third is an icy wasteland. At the eastern end of our Wide Sea of Mists are long strips of shifting sand bars, dangerous for shipping, and beyond that is the Wide Sea of Sighs."

"Why is it called Sighs?"

"Ah. There are worse things for sailors in those seas than mists. Parts are full of eddies, rips, and whirlpools that reverberate through the waters like sighs. Boats sailing that particular sea must be even more vigilant in keeping to the shipping lanes."

Savannah turned quickly to look at her. "There is another big port on that sea?"

"Beribrine is the largest, but there are many along the coastline. As I said, the Southern Lands are vast."

"Then I hope they attack us this morning," Savannah ground out. "At least we're in a position to cripple their force. Otherwise, they'll move down the coast, destroying the seaports as they go. Pela won't have time to move her armies to stop them."

Lilybeth nodded. "I hope so too. I want to make them suffer for what they did to Beribrine." She looked up. "First light will be here soon. I'll put on my helmet and join the troops. You had better get into position as well. I imagine as soon as they appear, it will be chaos."

"You intend to fight at the wall, Lilybeth?"

She gave a dry smile. "I am a warrior Queen, Chosen One. I stand with my soldiers."

To her surprise, Savannah thumped her hand to her chest. "I'm proud to be your kin, Ma'am," and then disappeared into the darkness.

✝

As the first rays of sunlight crept over the horizon, the Skeldachs and their riders appeared out of the heavy fog that blanketed the sea. It was a formidable force, over a thousand armored soldiers riding air-borne reptilian creatures. Lilybeth had never seen these winged lizards before, and they looked ferocious. Since Savannah had said they were blind in bright sunlight, her soldiers had gathered the largest crystals in the city and set them against mirrors along the outer sea wall.

As the enemy neared, they pulled the covers off the crystals. Bursts of bright light flared out, lighting up the sky in a dazzling display. The leading Skeldachs reared back, floundering against the second wave that flew close behind. In the bedlam that followed, the catapults launched their weapons. Hails of arrows streamed out, whistling through the sky in continuous waves. As they found their marks, screams and screeches sounded over the battlement. A third of the opposing force dropped into the foaming water far below before the rest rallied. Regrouping, their archers began firing arrows over the wall.

"Take cover," Lilybeth called, ducking down under the lip of the wall. She glanced at the catapults, silently thanking Pela for designing a protected compartment for the operators.

But as the catapults continued to rain down arrows on the enemy, more Crevlin poured out of the clouds to take the places of their fallen comrades. Gradually, they seemed to work out the patterns and heights of the catapult trajectories, and fewer were hit. As they advanced, thunderclaps began to reverberate off the eastern point. Lilybeth glanced across to see blasts of white fire shooting through the air.

Savannah had started her assault.

The Crevlin faltered, then retreated out of range.

After a few minutes' standoff, they reformed into ranks and advanced again as Savannah's fire blasted around them. Their front line pushed forward through the magic, and when they were within reach, they began to throw their bombs at the outer battlements. Blades of scarlet flames erupted against the wall, shattering holes in the rock and scattering pieces of stone into the air.

The soldier beside Lilybeth collapsed, blood spurting from her eye.

The Berian lancers ran forward, hurling spears at the Skeldachs. The winged reptiles reared back, many not quick enough to avoid being skewered. When the Crevlin advanced again, they reached a point close enough to lob their bombs over the wall. Explosions erupted along the walkway, forcing the Berians to take shelter. Following the blasts, over fifty Crevlin soldiers leaped off their hovering mounts onto the walkway. Savannah sizzled bolts of magic fire just outside the parapet, pushing the rest back.

"Attack," Lilybeth shouted, rushing forward with her sword raised high.

It didn't take her long to realize they were targeting her. A pack came at her swinging, separating her from the rest of the battalion. A group of Berian soldiers rushed through the rubble and smoke to help. The first collapsed from a blow to her neck, and then one by one, they fell by her side.

She thrust and parried, ignoring the ache in her arms and lungs. The real pain would come later after the heat of the battle. Gradually, she was forced down to the end of the wall until there was nowhere to go.

A broad-shouldered Crevlin came out of the pack and hissed, "She's mine."

As soon as the others stepped back, he pivoted, swinging his blade down hard. She flicked her sword up to deflect the blow. Then grasping the slim advantage, she swung low, nicking his thigh. Bellowing, he aimed slash after slash at her chest. She stumbled back under the onslaught and only just fended him off.

She fought on, until finally, unable to ward off a blow, the blade sliced her upper arm. She staggered as the arm dangled uselessly, blood running down onto her boots. With a last-ditched effort, she grasped her sword in her left hand. But as she swung it, her boot slipped on a pool of blood, and she crashed heavily onto the floor.

The Crevlin came forward, smiling down at her as he readied his sword for the death blow.

She lifted her anguished stare to the once pristine sky now tainted with smoke and death, then stiffened her shoulders. No Berian Queen would ever cry for mercy.

"Do your worst, vermin," she croaked out.

Suddenly, a flash of lightning shot through the air, accompanied by an enormous crack of thunder that shook the foundations of the palace. The Crevlin swung his head in the direction and cursed. Lilybeth followed his gaze. Savannah had launched an extremely powerful bolt of magic, blasting into the main enemy force. By the way they shrieked and scattered back into the clouds, she knew the bolt had crippled them. Berian had won the war, but she was also aware it was too late for her.

The Crevlin standing above her, peeled back his lips to bare his teeth. "Time to die, Queen."

But as he raised his sword to strike, a wind roared out of nowhere. It began to twirl like a tornado, gaining momentum until he was sucked off the stone walkway. The others followed him into the maelstrom, screaming as they shot into the air.

Lilybeth looked up to see the Countess, her body glowing white, hands outstretched as she weaved her magic.

Just as suddenly as the wind began, it stilled. The Crevlin dropped like stones over the cliff.

Lilybeth gazed at the Countess in awe, thinking how magnificent she looked.

Then all went black.

CHAPTER FIVE

*S*avannah hurried to Queen Lilybeth's bedchamber.

Berian soldiers waited in the hallway outside, and she could sense the air crackling with their anxiety and fear. She could imagine their distress when their Queen fell. Not only was Lilybeth held in great esteem as a warrior, she was also much loved by her subjects. They parted silently to let Savannah through, acknowledging her contribution to the battle with fist salutes. She returned the salutes solemnly before pushing open the door.

Lilybeth was asleep, stretched out on the four-poster bed with her bandaged arm supported by a pillow. From a chair beside the bed, the Countess contemplated Savannah.

"How is she?" Savannah asked, noting that the Queen's blood-stained armor and clothing had been removed from sight.

"The wound was deep, but thankfully the cut didn't sever any of her arm cords. She was lucky. I sewed her up, packed it with healing herbs, and gave her some numb seed."

Lilybeth's eyes flickered open, her mouth moving silently as if trying to speak. Then her lids fluttered shut, and she drifted back to sleep. The Countess wiped a wet cloth gently across her forehead. "The numb seed's working. By tomorrow she'll be much better."

"She's a very brave woman," murmured Savannah.

"A foolish one," the Countess replied sharply. "As Queen, she should have left the fighting to her soldiers."

Savannah gazed down at the big woman on the bed. Solid without an ounce of fat and well-muscled, Lilybeth obviously worked out regularly with her troops. "Look at her," Savannah said with a chuckle. "She's a warrior through and through. I can't imagine she would hide behind anyone."

The Countess pressed her lips together but said no more on the subject. "Tell me, Savannah, what did you do to rout the enemy after Lilybeth fell? The blast shook the palace's foundations. If you could conjure up so much power, why didn't you do it sooner?"

"It was the Death Vale, drawn from the very

heart of the ancient magic in the medallion. I can only do it sparingly, for once I invoke it, I'm drained for a time. I wasn't sure if there were more Skeldachs to come, and as it turned out, I made the right decision in delaying it. More were hidden in the fog."

"You saved the day. I can't imagine they'll return here after such a defeat."

"No. They'll pick a softer target next time," agreed Savannah.

"Do you think it'll take them long to regroup?"

Savannah shrugged. "I have no idea, for all we know, they might have a separate force somewhere else. As soon as Pela gets here, we must work out a strategy to hit the lizards where they live. If Lilybeth isn't fit enough, I'll meet with the Madra at noon tomorrow. Since Winston comes from a fishing village, he can join me."

"I've no doubt she'll drag herself from her sickbed to go," said the Countess with a ghost of a smile.

"I imagine she will," agreed Savannah with a chuckle. "I'll go with her. We must do something about those flying nasties. Airpower gives the enemy a big advantage."

"We'll marshal the Blue Fjords," the Countess announced firmly.

Savannah frowned, recalling how the Skeldach had

sliced open the horse's belly. "They'll rip them to pieces."

"Not with the Ice Elves on their backs. They're trained in aerial combat, and we have protective armor for the horses. I'll send my birds with messages immediately to Commander Jayden and Captain Leena to get the Ice Elves ready for action."

Savannah nodded and prepared to go. "I'd better tell the soldiers in the corridor that their Queen will be fine. They're anxious for news. Then I'll see what's happening at the wall."

By the time she reached the outer walkway behind the stone barrier, the soldiers had cleared away most of the debris and removed their fallen comrades. To her surprise, she could see the guards had a live Skeldach chained to a post, and in a distance were the bodies of two Crevlin. She could barely suppress her excitement. The Crevlin had to be still alive, or they would have changed into dead Crows. And they must be unconscious, or they would have turned into the birds and flown away.

What a coup!

She bent down to examine them, careful not to turn her back on the lizard. It was eyeing her like she was its next meal. The Crevlin were alive but knocked out. She called the Captain over. "Have you a fine net to wrap around these men. When they wake, they'll try to turn into Crows."

"Yes, ma'am. We've shrimp nets downstairs."

Leaving the soldier to organize the nets, Savannah turned her attention to the Skeldach. Tentatively, she sent out a telepathic feeler. Once inside its mind, she knew immediately there would be no reasoning with it. It was a savage beast with crude intelligence. She wondered how the Crevlin managed to control them, or how they even knew where the creatures lived. Fern had found an old diary in Arcadia from the last Crevlin war. It had revealed that they had used Skeldachs in that conflict.

She walked to the wall and gazed out over the sea. The thick morning fog had retreated to a mist which seemed constant. Shadows of clouds slipped across the water, appearing almost red as if stained by the blood spilled in the battle. Waves thundered over the rocks at the bottom of the cliff, a reminder that Beria was as much a part of this sea as the creatures that lived beneath its surface.

She was abruptly brought out of her thoughts when a voice echoed in her head. *"I have a message for Tamasin, Savannah."*

Savannah went still, relieved to hear the voice again. *"Hello, Grandmother. Where have you been?"*

"I'm never far away. You mustn't take too many risks, my girl. You were too exposed today," the old seer admonished.

"I know what I'm doing," Savannah replied firmly. *"What's the message?"*

"Tell Tamasin that Valeria must be taken somewhere safe before the fighting starts. Without her, the Circle cannot close the enemy's time continuum."

Savannah pricked up her ears. This was the first time the old girl had mentioned the Circle of Sheda in those terms. *"Why is she so important?"*

"Because the Imperial magic is the conduit for the power. Nothing must happen to her. If she dies, her eldest daughter, Rowan, becomes Queen and she isn't strong enough yet."

"Why don't we close the Circle now?"

"Because the moons need to be aligned," the old seer replied.

"What do you mean aligned?" asked Savannah mystified.

"There will be a sign you can't miss and you must be ready. It is still three turns away."

Savannah grimaced. *"Valeria's not going to like it."*

"No, I imagine she won't. But she has no choice."

"Are you going to tell me more about the Circle of Sheda?"

"No, Savannah. The threads are becoming much harder to see. I sense the end of this war will be different from the last. You will make a decision that the ancient magic hasn't foreseen."

"How do you know that?" asked Savannah with a touch of alarm.

"Because when the battle comes to an end, there are no more threads. The future hasn't been written yet. Not one that I can read anyhow. The time of the old magic will be at an end."

"Does that mean the Crevlin win?"

The voice began to fade. *"I don't know, Savannah. The future is in your hands."*

Savannah blanched. *"Don't you dare leave me hanging like that, Grandmother."*

But there was no answer, only the sighing of the wind. She shivered, not from the chill in the breeze but from the wave of fear that ran down her spine. To have the future of a world squarely on her shoulders was more than daunting, it was terrifying.

Knowing it wouldn't do any good to dwell on it, she turned to the problem at hand. How to make the Crevlin talk when they woke up. Then it came to her. She must send someone to get the Enchantress Reagan from the Forgotten Realms. With her magical ability to infiltrate minds, she can find out more about the Crevlin and what they intended to do next. The Countess should have something to keep the Crevlin comatose until Reagan arrived.

As she turned to go back, out of the corner of her eye, Savannah just caught a glimpse of a man in the shadows before he swung his sword. Lunging sideways, she barely avoided the blade that whistled inches from her cheek. The Crevlin kicked out and caught her knee with his toe, sending her sprawling to the ground. Her training automatically kicked in, and she leaped up into a fighter's crouch. A tall, thin man stood in front of her, wearing battered armor, and holding a single-edged sword with a curved blade.

When he came at her again, she zapped a burst of magic into his wrist. He stiffened, the weapon slipping out of his fingers. Savannah didn't hesitate. She leaned forward to press her fingers into his neck, letting out only enough electricity to paralyze him.

"Why have you come to wage war on Rand?" she asked, the old language rolling off her tongue effortlessly. Then she tamped down her magic to allow him to talk.

His eyes widened in alarm. "You speak our language?"

The words had a peculiar sing-song cadence, but she understood them well enough. "I do. Why do you come here?"

He ignored the question and stared at her. "You are another Time Walker?"

"Answer my question." She knew the Crevlin civilization ruled the Southern Lands and worshipped the God of Time.

"You think me a fool, mistress. If you speak our language, you must walk in the time dimension. You know we are doomed." He bared his teeth and spat at her face.

Involuntarily, she loosened her grip to wipe the glob of mucus off her cheek. Seizing the advantage, he jerked free and hit her in the stomach. When she doubled up, he turned and ran to the wall. Frantically, she raised her hand, but as she'd gathered her magic, he'd already leaped over the side. She reached the wall just in time to see him change into a bird. As she watched him fly off, she didn't zap him out of the sky, figuring it mightn't be such a bad thing that he'd escaped. The enemy would be nervous if they thought there was a Time Walker fighting on the other side.

Aware that she'd been lucky to escape unscathed, Savannah was more subdued when she made her way to the planning room. She vowed to be more careful.

She saw the Countess had left Lilybeth's bedside to join the group. They were circling the map on the center table, watching closely while Winston inserted a red pin into the moist clay.

At the sound of her footsteps, he looked up and grinned at her. "You were bloody brilliant, Savannah. You blew 'em out of the sky with that last burst."

"I don't enjoy killing, Winston. War is a senseless waste of life," she said sourly.

His smile faded. "I know it is, Savannah, but we still can enjoy a victory, so lighten up."

She acknowledged his rebuke with a lift of her shoulders. "Sorry. My nerves are on edge. I just had a run-in with a Crevlin on the wall. He jumped out of the shadows and nearly sliced off my head. If I hadn't seen him out of the corner of my eye, I'd be dead."

"Savannah," said the Countess. "You must be more watchful. Now the enemy knows what you can do, they'll be targeting you."

Winston drew an imaginary circle in the air, then poked his finger in the middle. "You've got a bullseye on your back now, Chosen One."

She ignored him and asked, "What are you doing?"

"I'm marking the best places in the sea for surveyance. Prior warning of a raid will be vital."

"I agree. But what sort of communication is there on Rand? Carrier pigeons will be too slow."

"The people near the sea blow large seashells to connect with each other. They have a sound language."

Like morse code, thought Savannah. "Do the Magical Sea Folk know it too?" she asked.

"Of course. The fishermen are their friends."

"How far can it be heard?"

"It depends on which way the wind's blowing. We'll set up outposts on the islands to relay the message to the mainland."

"Good thinking," said Savannah. "You and I will be meeting with the Madra tomorrow. She's promised to help." She turned to the Countess. "Have you a plant in that box of yours that can keep a person unconscious?"

"I have a vial of Foglorn sap. It'll keep someone in a coma indefinitely."

"Excellent," said Savannah with relief. One problem solved. "Is Reagan still at Amarim?"

"Yes. Why do you ask?"

"Because I want her to interrogate the two Crevlin we've captured. They're unconscious, and should be kept in that state until she arrives."

The Countess narrowed her eyes. "You can't seriously be thinking of bringing her here. Lilybeth wouldn't be able to handle her."

Savannah cast her an apologetic look. "Sorry. She's the only one who will be able to get anything out of them. I'll give the Bird Master a message to be sent to her immediately."

The Countess pressed her lips together disapprovingly though didn't reply.

As she went off to get her medicine box, Savannah wondered why she was so protective of Lilybeth.

CHAPTER SIX

*M*id-afternoon, Pela swept into the room.

After giving a curt nod to the Countess, she said without any preamble. "What happened here? Where's Lilybeth?"

Savannah hurried forward to placate her. Knowing Pela's tendency to be inflexible to the point of rudeness when faced with a serious situation, she gently stroked her arm. When Pela glanced at her with a flicker of a smile, Savannah kept her fingers lightly on her arm to show how much she'd missed her, and said quietly, "Sit down, Commander, and we'll explain."

By the time she'd given a summary of the destruction of Beribrine and the attack on the Berian palace, Pela's eyes had grown cold again with suppressed anger. "So they have air power and bombs," she ground out. "That puts another dimension to our preparations. More archers must be trained, and the Hawks and mounted Ice Elves mobilized."

Savannah frowned. "The Countess says the horses have armor, but the Hawks will be too exposed. They'll slaughter them."

Pela's voice had iron in it when she replied, "The Bramble Hawks are bred to fight. They won't get the better of us easily."

"I hope it won't come to that," Savannah said firmly. "If we move quickly, we can put an end to the aerial fighting. We have someone who can show us where the Skeldachs live. They're in underground caverns on an island in the Sea of Mists. If we can find a way to block their route out to the surface, the Crevlin won't have an air force."

"The sooner, the better," declared Pela. She looked around the room then scrutinized the map on the table. "I see you've wasted no time setting things up, Countess." She nodded to the others, stopping when her gaze rested on Winston. "We haven't met. You're the one who deciphered the Prophecy Chart and helped Savannah bring down the Wall dividing the Forgotten Realms from the rest of Rand?"

Instead of being intimidated, Winston smiled cheerfully. "I am. My name's Winston. It scared the living daylights out of us when it exploded into fireballs."

"So, Winston," said Pela eyeing him closely. "What do you think the enemy will do now?"

"Savannah has filled us in on the history of the events leading to this war. She explained the Crevlin had come before and were defeated." He stroked his beard absently. "Imagine you're playing a game of strategy, Commander, and you lost the first game. Would you make the same moves again?" Giving Pela no time to answer, he went on, "No, you wouldn't. You might start the same way to lull your opponent into a sense of security, but you'd change tactics before you got too deep into the play. Your number one priority would be to eliminate the key piece or hedge it into a position where it can't move."

"There's a lot of important people in this fight," said the Countess. "To defeat this enemy, it must be a combined effort."

"There's always a crucial piece, Countess."

"Do you mean Savannah?" asked Pela.

Winston shrugged. "Maybe, maybe not. What did our ancestors do to defeat them? I'm not privy to that information."

Recalling the message she had to give Tamasin, Savannah interrupted, "It's Valeria. The Circle of Sheda needs the Imperial Queen's magic as a conduit to close the exit of the Time Gateway to stop the Crevlin coming through."

Pela frowned at her. "How do you know that?"

"I'll tell you later," Savannah said, then went on, "Tamasin has to persuade Valeria to go to a safe place until she's called for. Will you tell her when you go back, Commander?"

Pela snorted. "As though Valeria's going to take notice of me."

Knowing how Pela and the Imperial Queen clashed, Savannah brushed a hand over her mouth to hide the small smile. "Tell Tamasin to say the order came from me."

"She won't go," stated Pela baldly.

"Impress on Tamasin that she must. Tamasin knows where to hide her. Valeria's daughter, Rowan isn't strong enough to take her place. Without her, the Crevlin will keep coming."

"If we know how to close the Circle, why don't we do it now?" asked the Countess.

"We can't until the moons are aligned."

Winston eyed her quizzically. "You lost me there."

Savannah grunted in frustration. "I'm guessing when the third moon appears, it will become plainer."

The big Mani with the yellow eyes called out from the back of the room. "Why do the Crevlin come into the future to fight us?"

Savannah looked over at him, thinking the shape shifter could be a cat of some sort in his other form. She hoped he wasn't going to shift into one of those intimidating Tigers she saw outside the Amarim Palace. "I asked the Crevlin who tried to kill me at the wall the same question. He replied *we are doomed.*"

The room was silent as everyone digested what she had said.

"Queen Fern of Arcadia is a historian and studied the ancient Crevlinian civilization," Savannah continued. "The people perished for some reason. What could have caused that do you think?"

Winston looked appalled. "You mean the whole lot of the Crevlin died?" he whispered.

"Apparently," replied Savannah. Even though this enemy was merciless, she still felt a measure of pity for them. "It explains why they have time travelled here and are going to such lengths to take over this future world. They're desperate for a safe place to live."

"To be told the future is wrong. Nobody should know when they're going to die," said the Countess indignantly. "Life is to be lived, not wasted waiting for death. I wonder what was coming that they feared?"

Savannah thought about that, casting her mind over her studies of the ancient people on Earth. "I was a historian in my world, and I imagine all worlds are much the same. Great civilizations are built, thrive, but eventually decline. It is the nature of things. While we have been able to track the rise and fall of most on Earth, some seem to have suddenly disappeared. Most theorists put the sudden demise of a race of people down to weather catastrophes or plagues. Perhaps it was a great drought or crop failure that destroyed the Southern Lands."

Winston eyed her skeptically. "Why wouldn't they have moved to the north?"

"Ah. That's the leading question," said Savannah. "I bet it has something to do with magic. At that time, the Northern Lands were full of Magical Folk and the Crevlin feared them. The Crevlin wouldn't have been allowed in."

Pela stared at her. "I'm getting where this is going, Savannah. After they were defeated the first time, you think the Crevlin orchestrated the Mystic Wars so that the Magical folk would be locked away?"

"And the slaying of the Sirens. There were probably more ancient houses as well we don't know about. But it couldn't have been the Crevlin, Pela. It appears they can only go into the future when the third moon is in the sky. No, it was the Time Walker they worship as a god who paved the way for this invasion. Then as soon as they raised another army, they came forward in the future to the next time the third moon was due in the sky."

"A race with nothing to lose is very dangerous," murmured Winston.

"How many Time Walkers are there do you think, Savannah?" asked the Countess.

Savannah groaned. "I have no idea." She glanced out the window, noting there weren't many hours of daylight left. She turned to Winston. "It's getting late. Show the Commander what you have planned so far, then when you're finished, bring her to the wall to see the Skeldach we have chained up. In the meantime, I'll check on those two prisoners to see if they require more Foglorn sap."

†

At the crunch of boots on the shards of rubble, Savannah turned back from the sea view. Pela and Winston had reached the Skeldach chained tightly to a stone column at the end of the walkway.

Winston eyed it curiously, then waved to Savannah, "I'll leave you to it," he said with a grimace. "It's one nasty son of a bitch."

As soon as he had disappeared down the steps, she joined Pela who was squatting near the beast. Though it was trussed up so tightly it could barely move, it still managed to menacingly hiss and flick its tongue. Pela ignored it, gesturing to Savannah to come closer. She sidled behind Pela to peer over her shoulder at the fearsome lizard.

Pela grinned at her. "It can't bite." She took a long knife out of her boot and pointed to the ridge along the leathery scales between the head and the back. "See there. There's a gap in the scales where the skull joins its back. That's where it's vulnerable. There, and the eyes. It has no eyelids, only a thin membrane to protect them. Living underground, the lids would have been bred out of them long ago." She tapped the beak with the blade. "It's as hard as iron and meant to rip things apart. The claws are deadly as well."

"They're vicious," said Savannah. "Your Hawks will be too vulnerable to go against them."

Pela gave a wolfish grin. "If we keep above them, they'll be easy to defeat. They won't be able to fight us." She sliced her finger through the air. "One sweep of our claws and their neck's severed. Then we peck out their eyes. If they don't go down, we tear at their wings."

"Don't forget they will have armed riders on their backs," Savannah said sharply.

"The Ice Elves will shoot the riders with their arrows, and we'll do the rest."

Savannah pressed her lips together. "Let's hope you won't be compelled to prove that theory. Tomorrow I'll ask Nerin to show us the way to the Isle of Misery to do something about their caverns."

"Do you know what you're going to do?"

"I'm forming a plan. It'll involve the Sirens and the Sea Folk." Savannah looked across at the Skeldach that was glaring at them balefully. "We'll take the Skeldach along to show us where they enter the caverns from above."

"When you're ready, I'll go with you. Now, I have one more thing to do. I want to see how the creature reacts to birds. Stand back."

Savannah had barely time to retreat to a safe distance before Pela changed into a Bramble Hawk. Savannah blinked, forgetting how huge she was in that form. As big as the flying lizard and just as lethal.

The Skeldach's reaction to the Hawk was extraordinary. It uttered a high-pitched shriek, straining frantically against its chains. As the Hawk danced in front of it, snapping its beak, the lizard went berserk. It's screeched and hissed, scraping its claws along the stone floor. When blood began to trickle from the excoriated skin beneath its chains, Pela ceased tantalizing it and morphed back.

She grinned at Savannah. "That got a reaction."

Savannah looked at the Skeldach curiously. "Why do you think it responded so violently?"

Pela looked baffled. "Either it's hungry and I represented a nice meal, or it was frightened of me."

"Hopefully the latter," murmured Savannah.

"Talking of food, dinner will be on shortly and we'll must get ready. Our room's the fifth door on the left from the top of the stairs."

"You go ahead," said Pela. "I'm going to get one of the Hawks to fly to the Forgotten Realms to ask my mother to send a battalion of Hawks to Berian. We must have air power."

CHAPTER SEVEN

*L*ilybeth's eyes flew open.

The room smelt of fresh herbs, and underneath, she caught a whiff of the Countess's fragrance of subtle wildflowers and sandalwood.

The Countess was sitting at the open window, humming to herself as she patched Lilybeth's torn shirt. Lilybeth watched her, unwilling to break the peaceful moment. The domesticity of the scene tugged at her heartstrings, bringing back the memories of all those lonely years. Had she been foolish not to find another consort? With her duties and Maybeth to rear, there had never seemed time for courting. But if she was honest, it had been only an excuse, for she'd been reluctant to put herself out there again. She was more at home with her soldiers than in a ballroom.

She continued to lie quietly, studying the Countess. Lilybeth had never seen anyone so alluring. The Amarim was statuesque and full-bodied, with a handsome face that was anything but commonplace. Her eyes were an unusual silver-green color, softened slightly with age, and when she spoke, her voice was well defined, almost musical.

She seemed untouchable, like a painting to be admired from afar.

Unaware she was being scrutinized, the Countess looked serene in the morning light.

Then realizing she was staring, Lilybeth gave a small cough.

At the sound, the Countess looked up from her needlework and said softly, "You're awake. How do you feel?"

"Much better, thanks. Whatever you gave me took away the pain, Countess."

"Please, call me by my name. It's Gladofin," she said with a smile. "I gave you numb seed which dulls the pain, but it makes you sleep. After I dress your wound, I'll give you another dose."

"No thanks. I have a meeting today with the Madra I must keep," Lilybeth said firmly.

"Savannah has offered to go in your place. It will be too taxing."

"I'll be fine. She may come along with me though."

Gladofin looked disapproving, though merely said, "That would be wise. Commander Pela arrived yesterday afternoon. I'll send her up after I change your bandage."

"I've no intention of meeting Pela in my bed," Lilybeth said, horrified. To be thought weak by the tough Commander wasn't an option.

"More pride than sense," Gladofin muttered. She gathered her bag from the table then settled in the chair beside the bed. "If you stretch out your arm on the pillow, I'll change the dressing."

After she unrolled the bandage, Gladofin coaxed off the poultice with measured, careful movements to cause as little pain as possible. "It looks healthy," she said. "There's no redness or swelling. I'll re-dress it with some more healing herbs. If you insist on getting up, use a sling."

As Lilybeth watched her tend the long gash, she was inordinately sensitive to the hand touching her. She wondered why she was reacting like that but ruthlessly quashed down the feeling. Gladofin was only here to dress her wound. She cleared her throat before she said gruffly, "Thank you for saving my life, Gladofin. You have great magical powers. I know so little of the folk in the Forgotten Realms. What are you exactly?"

"I'm a Guardian," she said. "In the magical world, we are the rulers. We have the power to manipulate the earth and air, though we do it sparingly. One cannot tamper too much with nature, or the equilibrium will be upset. Our role is to look after the natural world."

"Oh," replied Lilybeth, not really understanding. Hers was a much simpler life — the Countess's sounded complicated.

"You were married once, Lilybeth?" asked Gladofin as she carefully applied the bandage.

Lilybeth froze at the unexpected question. Even after so many years, she still had difficulty verbalizing what happened. The horror and guilt were an unhealed wound. "My wife drowned four years after we were married. She was swept off the point by a freak wave and taken out to sea," she said hoarsely.

Gladofin looked up quickly, her face radiating her sympathy. "I'm sorry. It must have been devastating for you."

"She came from a realm near the Great Northern Forests and feared the water. I couldn't save her." She gave a tired smile. "It was a long time ago, and I have our daughter, Maybeth, to remember our time together."

"Where is Maybeth? I haven't seen her here."

"At Falcon's Keep, training with the Elite Guard. The Berian Queens are warriors."

Gladofin smiled. "I noticed." She finished pinning the sling and stood up. "I'll help you dress now."

"No, no," Lilybeth said hurriedly, mentally visualizing her dreary underwear. "The maid can give me a hand. If you send her in, I'll see you at breakfast."

Gladofin gave her a stern glance. "Make sure you're careful of the arm. Otherwise, it'll start bleeding again."

When Lilybeth descended the staircase, the sight of the bowls of flowers scattered about the room brought a wave of pleasure. It had been years since her elderly housekeeper had bothered brightening up the place. For a moment, Lilybeth imagined a world where someone waited for her, listening for her footsteps in the corridor. It was so long ago, she'd forgotten what it was like.

Careful not to aggravate her arm, she walked to breakfast. She always ate in the smaller dining room, far more practical and intimate than the large formal one. The table there was so long that it was impossible to talk to everyone. She pushed aside the ache in her arm and opened the door. The atmosphere in the room seemed lighthearted, a reaction she guessed to the catastrophe narrowly averted.

Immediately, Pela rose to usher her to the chair at the head of the table, then took the seat beside her. "Queen Lilybeth, I came as soon as I received your message," she said, then added bitterly. "Not soon enough, though. I underestimated the fighting capacity of the enemy. I had no idea they would have an air force or bombs. You did well to ward off the invasion."

"Mainly thanks to Savannah and your catapults," Lilybeth said. She took a deep breath and continued in a voice laced with regret, "I should have had my warning systems in place."

Pela gave a little snort. "Don't beat yourself up about it. You're more prepared than any other realm in Rand except Arcadia. I had to speak very firmly to a few to get them to recruit more soldiers."

Lilybeth smothered back a smile. Pela speaking firmly would have put the fear of the Goddess into them. "This enemy won't surprise me again," Lilybeth said. "As soon as I speak to the Madra today, a warning system will be put in place."

"Good," said Pela. "I'll ask the planners to devise a system to relay the message across the land. In the meantime, I've sent a dispatch for a division of Bramble Hawks to come here, and the Countess has sent word to mobilize the Ice Elves on the Blue Fjords. The enemy mustn't be allowed to go inland."

From the chair opposite Pela, Savannah spoke up, "With luck, we may have depleted their force here. If we can still trust the information in that old diary, their main force will be in the City of the Dead. Have you heard of such a place, Ma'am?"

Lilybeth shook her head. "No. It's not around here. I know every part of the coast and islands."

"I suspected that," murmured Savannah. "We don't know exactly where it is either, but I think it's the spot where their time gate or whatever it is comes out. We're sure the City of the Dead was a metaphor for the exit." She flashed a look at Pela. "Have Tamasin's spies discovered anything?"

"Not yet."

"Humm. Maybe it's in the Southern Lands," Savannah murmured. "We won't dwell on it now. First things first. May Winston and I accompany you to see the Madra, Lilybeth? Having lived on an island here, he'll be an excellent liaison."

"Just the two of you, Savannah, no more. The Sea Folk are very private people."

"Of course. I'll let you do the talking."

Lilybeth nodded, then turned to her breakfast. Things were moving fast, and she had the distinct impression she wasn't in control anymore. Savannah and the Countess were two very formidable women.

✝

It was a benign day on the Berian coast. The sun shone brightly in a cloudless sky and only a gentle breeze blew in from the sea.

Knowing how fickle the weather could be, Lilybeth took advantage of the pleasant day and led her guests on a quick tour over the cropped fields before swinging back to the coast. When the secluded inlet came into view, she gave her bronze Fjord stallion, Banner, a nudge with her heel, and he descended gracefully onto the sandy beach. Savannah's little mare dropped down beside them, looking dwarfed beside the large warhorse. After Savannah and Winston slipped off, they helped Lilybeth dismount. Though it was demoralizing to be assisted, she was grateful for the helping hands. Her arm was beginning to throb.

The Madra was nowhere in sight, but they didn't have long to wait. Two brown Seals suddenly breasted the waves, morphing into people as they reached the foaming water's edge.

Lilybeth waved and called out, "It's good to see you, Nerin. Hello Dirk."

When Nerin reached them, Winston immediately sank to his knees. "Your Supreme Highness," he said reverently.

"Winston, you scamp," Nerin said with a chuckle. "I thought you went off to see the world." Her face filled with concern when she looked at Lilybeth. "We heard Beria was attacked and you were wounded."

Lilybeth gave a wan smile. "We managed to fight them off, but I got a slash in the arm. I hope you don't mind me bringing Savannah and Winston. If it wasn't for Savannah, their attack would have succeeded."

"We saw her magic fire," Nerin said, eyeing Savannah closely. "You are very powerful, Chosen One. Far more than I realized. You invoked the Death Vale, a rare talent."

"You know of the Death Vale, ma'am?"

"I have studied the ancient magic and all the spells."

"Have you heard of a Guardian?" asked Lilybeth.

"Of course," replied Nerin. "They are the most powerful of all the Magical Folk. They control nature. We've never met one."

"There's one in my palace. Countess Gladofin of the House of Amarim."

Nerin stared at her. "You are indeed fortunate to have such an esteemed guest. I would like to meet her one day."

"I'm sure she'd love to meet you too," Lilybeth said, then winched as a stab of pain shot through her arm. "Would you mind if I sat on the rock over there while we talk?"

"You should be in bed," Nerin chided. "Sometimes, Lilybeth, you should remember you are made of flesh and blood like the rest of us. You can't always be so strong."

Lilybeth gave a rueful half-smile. "I know, but my people rely on me. I do admit, though, that the wound hurts. Now, before I'm totally useless, let's discuss our defenses. We must have a warning system to alert us when the Skeldachs are in the air. Winston has prepared a chart of the strategic places for surveyance."

Winston pulled out a scroll of animal hide from his vest and spread it out on a rock. After pouring over it for a few minutes, Nerin nodded. "It should work. I'll send word to the Magical Folk and the fisherman to set up their surveillance sites immediately. They'll be in place by tonight." She looked at Winston. "We can relay it over the sea, but it'll be up to you to go from there."

He nodded. "We will have guards posted to listen for the sound of the shells."

She eyed him speculatively. "You have grown up, Winston. Your family would be pleased to see you."

He colored and replied a little reticently, "Since they didn't want me to go, I didn't leave on the best of terms, but I'll think about it."

She nodded, not pressing the issue. "Now, Savannah. Have you thought about how to get the Skeldachs into their underground caverns so that we can lock them down there?"

"I thought if we block off the top entrance, then you could devise a plan to stop them swimming out."

Nerin's lips peeled back into a grin. "That's no problem. The Scaled Serpent Squids guard the sea entrance. One remains there permanently."

"They sound terrifying," muttered Savannah.

"They're the most feared creatures in the sea, Chosen One, and the Skeldachs are a delicacy on their menu."

Savannah shuddered. "I hope they don't attack your people."

"I can manipulate the seas, Savannah. They know better than to aggravate me," Nerin replied in a matter-a-fact tone as if she was discussing the weather, not some ghastly monsters in the ocean depths.

"Right," Savanna muttered, vowing to never annoy this woman. She'd probably drown her. "I'll try to organize getting out to the island in a few days with my team."

"Good. Winston knows how to communicate with the shells. We'll be waiting for the call."

CHAPTER EIGHT

THE BERIAN COAST

While Nerin had a last quiet word with Lilybeth, Savannah gazed around. Surrounded by towering cliffs, the small cove was only accessible by air or sea. An ideal place for a secret meeting. She swept her eyes over the palms laden with odd-looking fruit and continued idly gazing up the sheer cliff face. On a ledge halfway to the top, she paused as she caught a flash of brown. Shading her eyes with her hand, she focused on it, trying to make out what it was. When she saw the outline of a wing, it clicked. It was a bird, a large brown one. And she didn't have to be a whizz to know who it was.

Pela.

Savannah gave a little snort. That Hawk had some

explaining to do tonight. Lilybeth specifically stated only two people could accompany her.

She turned back to see Nerin looking at the cliff.

"What's that bird?" she asked.

Savannah fidgeted with her sleeve, trying to think of an answer, but there was no way out. "It's a Bramble Hawk, ma'am. She's a friend."

"The fierce birds that live in the Forgotten Realms? I heard they were so antisocial they never came out."

"The Hawks have joined the fight," Savannah muttered, wondering how Nerin knew so much about the creatures outside her domain.

"Bring it down. I'd like to meet it."

Savannah hesitated for a second, then with a resigned shrug, waved to Pela to join them. When the Hawk glided down to the beach and changed, Nerin's darkening eyes were her only reaction to the intimidating hair and tattoos. Dirk, though, stepped hastily back and pulled out his knife.

Nerin immediately grasped his arm. "Put it away. The Chosen One has vouched for her."

Pela clicked her heels together, "I salute you, Madra. I am Pela, Queen of the Bramble Hawks, and Supreme Commander of the Imperial Army."

"You've come here uninvited, Commander."

A muscle in Pela's jaw twitched. "I have, but the time

for such protocol is at an end. We are at war, and I have a job to do."

Nerin looked at her for a long moment with hooded eyes and said sternly, "War or not, you are in my territory and must adhere to our customs."

Knowing Pela's temper, Savannah cringed. If she got the Madra angry, they were in trouble. And the woman wasn't someone Pela could boss around. Pela must have known this, for she bowed her head. "I apologize, ma'am. I'll go."

"You're here now, Commander, so we'll talk."

"Why do the Skeldachs hate birds?" asked Pela.

"Their natural enemies are the Great Black Sea Eagles of the Windy Isles. The Eagles hunt them, which is why the Skeldachs stay underground."

Her curiosity pipped, Savannah asked, "Are these Sea Eagles Magical Folk?"

"They are." Her eyes gleamed as they rested on Pela. "They rule the skies here. They're powerful and don't like intruders in their territory."

Pela haughtily lifted an eyebrow. "We will respect their domain," she said, adding with an answering gleam, "as long as we're not provoked."

Nerin didn't comment further, instead addressed Savannah. "Do you intend to kill the Skeldachs with your magic fire, Chosen One? You have the power to destroy them all."

Savannah frowned. "Of course not. I'm not a monster. They are creatures of Rand and have as much right to their lives as you and I. I only intend to make sure they can't come out until the Crevlin have gone."

Nerin nodded her approval. "The medallion has chosen its bearer wisely. I will take you out to the Isle of Misery when you are ready." She glanced down at Lilybeth, who was hunched over in pain. "She has to get home to rest. Nothing must happen to her. Berian and the Sea Folk will rely upon her strength in the times to come."

Lilybeth looked up and grunted. "Hey. I'm not dead yet, my friend, but can you help me to mount my horse, please."

"I'll ride back with you," said Pela in a softened tone. She circled an arm around her waist and lifted her effortlessly.

By the time they'd maneuvered her in the saddle, Lilybeth's face had turned a sickly gray. Pela sprang up behind her, cradling her arms and legs around her like a vice, then dug her heels into the stallion's flank.

"Go steady, Banner," Savannah projected to the horse.

"I will, Chosen One," he shot back and launched into flight.

Sunflower, with Savannah and Winston aboard, followed them into the air.

The Countess was waiting for them in the courtyard, her face set like granite. She glared at Savannah. "You took your time. Have you any idea how much blood she lost yesterday?"

Savannah winced. It was hardly her fault Lilybeth had insisted on going, but that logic seemed to be lost on the Countess. Pela and Winston quickly turned to help Lilybeth dismount, leaving Savannah to face her anger. *Cowards,* she thought.

"Don't fuss, Gladofin," Lilybeth croaked out. "I wanted to go. I'll be fine as soon as I get something for the pain and get to bed. I overextended myself a little, that's all."

The Countess pressed her lips together and gestured to Pela. "She'll want help. If you take one side, I'll support the other and we'll get her up to her bedchamber."

As they half carried her up the stairs, Savannah lagged behind with Winston.

"I've only seen the old girl as cranky once before," he whispered. "When she caught one of the players at The Pale Horse cheating, she gave him such a roasting he never came back."

"I think she likes Lilybeth," Savannah murmured.

"Of course she does. We all do."

"Don't be obtuse, Winston. I mean … you know… really likes her."

He blinked at her. "Don't be so fanciful. She's just met her. And besides, they say the Countess doesn't take lovers."

Savannah rolled her eyes. "If she did, she'd be discrete. She wouldn't want to be the subject of gossip in The Pale Horse." She looked at him pointedly. "Which she obviously is."

He grinned. "There are no secrets in that den of iniquity."

"I bet there aren't," said Savannah with a reluctant smile. She stopped at the door halfway down the corridor. "This is me. I'll see you at dinner."

By the time she had a wash and relaxed back with a wine in the small lounge, Pela came in. When she heard her emerge from the bathroom, Savannah called out, "You have some explaining to do, Pela. You were told only two people could go with Lilybeth to see the Madra."

Pela strode into the room and towered over her. "I'm not apologizing for my actions. I did what I had to do."

Narrowing her eyes, Savannah stood to face her. "That woman controls all the seas. You could have jeopardized our negotiations."

Pela glowered at her. "You have no right to question my decisions, Savannah. I'll do what I like."

Savannah glared up at her, then realized how ridiculous it must look. A chicken telling a rooster off. She reached over to place a hand on her arm and said more gently, "I know why you were there, Pel. But you can't protect me all the time." It came out as a plea.

Pela deflated. "I know, but I worry. You don't seem to have any concept of the dangers of this world. You acted as though you were going on a picnic, not to see one of the most powerful people in Rand. She's supposed to be ruthless with outsiders." She frowned at Savannah. "You keep too many secrets. You've never told me exactly who's this mysterious old woman you talk to."

"No, I haven't. I'm still filling in the gaps there, and it's quite complicated. I will when the time is right." Savannah eyed her thoughtfully. "But you can't lecture me. You have secrets too."

"Like what?"

"Like why didn't you fall sick with the curse when you were so long out of the Forgotten Realms. And how *did* you last so long under Ursula's cape? You've never been afraid of magic, not even Agatha's. Why Pel?"

Pela sidled up to her and stroked her hair. "Let's not fight. I'd rather be making love than arguing. I'll be going back soon so let's make the most of our time together."

Savannah gave in, knowing Pela had no intention of answering her questions. "Okay, but don't think I won't ask again," she said and then forgot about everything except the lips that were ghosting their way down her neck.

✝

Savannah stirred restlessly in the bed.

For a moment she didn't realize what had disturbed her until she got another zap from the medallion. Carefully, she slid out of bed, pulled on her breeches and shirt, then shrugged into her fur riding coat to ward off the night cold air. She decided to leave Pela sleeping until she found out what was wrong, knowing she would have gone out on patrol for a few hours before going to sleep.

Savannah padded out the door. All was quiet in the hallway, with no figures or Crows lurking in the shadows. She crept to the top of the staircase to peer over the railing. When she found nothing suspicious in the room below, she ran up the flight of stone steps that led to the outer wall outside overlooking the sea.

The sky was overcast, the moons barely visible through the layers of cloud. By the slight pink haze in the mist on the horizon, dawn wasn't far off. She stared out to sea, her gut feeling telling her something was happening out there. And then she heard it. The mournful sound of a conch over the sea. At first, it was so faint she could hardly hear it, and then gradually it became louder as it came nearer.

She didn't hesitate. With a bound, she leaped down the stairs two at a time. When she reached Winston's door, she banged on it loudly. By the time he poked his head out, Pela and the Countess were in the corridor. "The shells are blowing," she yelled.

Immediately, he raced up the stairs to the outer wall, then leaned over and cocked his head to listen. "A large force of Skeldachs and their riders left the Isle of Misery about ten minutes ago." He pointed to the northwest. "Heading that way."

Turning to Pela who was now at her elbow, Savannah asked her urgently, "What's in that direction, Pela?"

"Iona."

"Damnit," Savannah gasped. "They'll be slaughtered unless we do something. Where are the Bramble Hawks you sent for?"

"They're coming this morning. They would have left by now. I'll try to intercept them and take them to Iona."

"Would you know their route?"

Pela screwed up her nose. "With a bit of luck such a big force so should be visible from a distance."

"You'd better go. I'll head straight to Iona to warn them. I should beat them with a head start." When

Pela's face turned grim, Savannah leaned over and whispered. "Please, love. Don't argue. They won't have a chance without my magic."

Pela looked like she was going to argue, then nodded silently. She ran to the wall and as she vaulted over the parapet, she morphed into a Hawk. She circled once overhead, and with a screech, flew off into the northwest.

Savannah turned immediately to Winston. "Will you run down to the stables, saddle Sunflower, and tie on a waterskin, please. I won't be stopping. Then tell her to fly up here. I have something to do before I go."

As soon as he disappeared down the stairs, Savannah pointed to a recess in the wall. "Stand over there, Countess. I don't know what's going to happen."

The Countess frowned but didn't argue, catching the serious tone.

Savannah took a deep breath, praying it was going to work. She spread out her arms and called, "Manoak, can you hear me. Manoak, I need you."

At first, nothing happened, but then the air shuddered and shifted. The sky blurred, and time seemed to slow as a bubble formed around her. It was filled with such an alien hollow stillness, that she just knew she was in another dimension. Suddenly, the Blue Fjord King materialized in front of her.

"You called me, Chosen One and Mistress of the Fjora. You are in trouble?"

"Iona is on the verge of an air attack, Manoak. I want you to ask Queen Olivine if she would send Consort Prince Jayden and his mounted Ice Elves to ward off the attack. Tell her it's urgent. The enemy has a large force so he will require many riders. How long will it take you to get to the Amarim Palace?"

"I'm at the Palace now. I'll tell Queen Olivine immediately."

Savannah sagged with relief. All was not lost. *"Then go, my friend, and thank you."*

"Farewell, Mistress." Then he was gone, and the air shimmered back into perspective.

She looked round to see the Countess staring at her. "Where did you go, Savannah? You disappeared."

"I met with Manoak. He's going to get Olivine to send Jayden and the Ice Elves to Iona."

"You met with the King of the Blue Fjords. How is that possible?"

"I am Fjora, Countess." She looked up at the sky to see Sunflower flying over the turret. "Here's my ride."

She climbed into the saddle and called out as they took off, "Keep the Enchantress entertained until I get back. She's due to arrive today."

CHAPTER NINE

THE IONA PALACE

*T*amasin woke abruptly, her head throbbing, her mouth so dry she could barely swallow. The dream had left her trembling, and when she brushed a lock of hair out of her eyes, she wasn't surprised to find her face in a lather of sweat. The nightmare had been horrendous, so vivid that she could still see the fireballs exploding, the people screaming.

"Wake up, Val," she said hoarsely. "Something's going to happen, something really bad is coming."

Her eyes still heavy with sleep, the Imperial Queen shifted round to face her. "Wha ... what's coming?"

"Death and destruction. Iona is going to be attacked."

Valeria didn't question her premonition; she knew only too well that as Mistress of Dreams, Tamasin's dreams were to be taken seriously. Her brow wrinkled as if trying to get her head around what she had said. "How, Tam? We're invulnerable to an assault here. The guards would have seen an army gathering in the valley. Do you think they'll fly up here as Crows? That's the only way they're going to get here. We'll mobilize the Hawks."

"I'll order Jocose to do it immediately," Tamasin said and hurried into the corridor.

The two guards outside the door snapped to attention as soon as she stepped out. "Consort. Do you need anything?"

"Fetch Captain Jocose immediately to the Queen's chambers. Tell her it's urgent."

As soon as one of the guards sprinted off, Tamasin returned to the room and quickly dressed. She gnawed her bottom lip as she slid two extra knives into her belt. "It might have something to do with Pela not turning up yesterday."

Valeria turned to look at her. "Did she send a message?"

"No. I'll check with the Bird Master to see if one came in during the night."

The thud of boots in the corridor echoed outside, followed by rapping at the door.

Tamasin picked up her sword and called out, "Come in."

Captain Jocose quickly stepped into the room, saluting the Queen before she addressed Tamasin, "Is there trouble, Consort?"

"I've had a dream, Captain, one that can't be ignored. We are going to come under attack. And it'll be today sometime. It was too vivid to be far in the future."

She nodded. "I'll put the Palace guards on full alert and call everyone to arms."

"Do more than that, Captain. The townspeople as well must be warned. Blow the Great Horn."

Though Tamasin could see a measure of skepticism in her expression, Jocose saluted. "It's been a long time since it's been blown. What are your orders after that?"

"Shut down the pullies and detach the wagons that bring produce up the mountain. There'll be no way for them to get up here other than by air. All forty Hawks must patrol immediately and put as many archers as you can fit on the battlements. The enemy will fly in as Crows, and we must be ready for them. Send a squad downtown to order all citizens to seek shelter when the horn blows again, underground in cellars if possible. Shops and markets are to be closed today."

Frowning, Jocose asked quietly, "What did you see, Tam?"

"I saw explosions, fireballs, destruction on a scale that we've never seen here before, Jo."

Jocose swallowed, her eyes darting to the window.

"I'll go immediately." She bowed to the Queen and hurried out the door.

Five minutes later, the sound of the Great Horn of Iona split the air over the mountain. It reverberated over the Palace, the town, and down to the valley: long mournful blasts that hadn't been heard for three centuries. Tamasin shivered. The promised war was here, but was Iona prepared for what was coming? She had an awful feeling they'd completely underestimated the enemy, for if they weren't magical, what were the fireballs in her dreams?

She turned to see Valeria donning a thin chain mail shirt. "You can't join in the fight, Val. Rand can't afford to lose its Imperial Monarch."

Valeria pursed her lips, showing her irritation. "I'm not going to sit back quietly if we come under attack."

"I don't expect you to," Tamasin said gently. "But let's not get ahead of ourselves. Now we've been warned, we can prepare. They won't get past our defenses. Would you get the Council together and I'll slip up to the dovecotes and find the Bird Master. The Mistresses and Palace staff must be safe in the vaults before the fighting begins. Hopefully, there will be a message from Pela."

As she ran up the steps, the hairs on Tamasin's neck twitched upright. Even before she stepped out onto the roof, she knew what was bothering her. It was too quiet. Instead of the cooing of a hundred caged pigeons, there was an eerie silence. She slid a knife out of her boot before she slipped through the archway onto the flagstone floor. When she turned the corner, she sucked in a sharp breath. Every cage was empty. The doors were wide open, the nesting boxes had been tipped over and the roosting poles smashed.

As Tamasin rounded the first cage, she gave a startled cry when she nearly fell over the Bird Master lying in a pool of blood. She knelt quickly to examine him, finding his throat had been slashed from ear to ear. Since the blood had congealed, and his limbs were stone cold and stiff, she guessed he had been killed sometime yesterday evening.

Whatever the sent message contained, it must have been very important for the enemy to intercept. And it was obvious by letting the carrier pigeons out that they wanted to cut Iona off from the rest of Rand. She gazed over the wall at the dark clouds hanging over the mountain, uneasy that she was missing something important. Then it came. There was little point in going to such lengths to get rid of the birds if Iona had the horses.

Tamasin swallowed back a rush of bile. Had they done something to the horses? Clamping down her panic, she raced down the stairs and through the hallways until she reached the front door. The guards on duty eyed her in surprise, but she didn't stop to talk. Worry drove her on. By the time she reached the entrance to the royal stables, her heart was pumping wildly. She let out the painful breath she was holding when she found all was normal inside, the horses alive in their stalls.

Malkia, who was in the backyard with the young colts, raised his head inquiringly when he saw her. *"You want to go for a ride, Tamasin?"*

"No, my friend. I need you to do something for me. I'm putting all the horses into the two outer enclosures, except the mares and foals who will go into the small yard. If you see anyone come into the stables that you don't recognize, whinny loudly. I'll put two guards here to watch over you. If you hear the Great Horn again, get the horses out of here. Go off the northern end of the Palace to the back ranges. There are plenty of places to hide there. Do you understand me?"

"I'll get them to safety. But I will come back for you."

"Not this time, Malkia. Something bad is coming, an enemy that won't think twice about killing everything and everyone. I want you safe." She rubbed his muzzle. "Promise me you'll do what I ask. If I want you, I'll whistle."

He looked at her sadly with his big brown eyes then nodded. *"I will do what you ask."*

"Good man," she said then made her way inside the stables.

The two stable hands who were mucking out the stalls looked at her in relief. "We heard the Great Horn, Mistress. What should we do?"

"Take all the horses to the outer yards. Put the mares and foals into the small one, then go home. Get your families ready to go into your cellars … make sure you stock them up with food. Iona is going to come under attack. When you hear the next blast of the Horn, get to the cellar. Now hurry and lead the horses outside."

Satisfied the two had the stables under control, Tamasin jogged back up to the Palace. After ordering guards to the horses, she was heading for the Throne Room when Damia, the Dreamer assigned to protect Arcadia's historian, Mistress Moira, appeared in the passageway.

"Mistress Tamasin. I've been trying to find you. I had a disturbing dream early this morning."

Tamasin greeted her with a welcoming smile, liking the older woman who had been the chief tailoress for the Kasparian Royal Garrison. Damia and Moira were so well suited that Moira had been training her with the Palace historical research students.

"I had one too, Damia. Tell me about yours."

Damia's voice dropped to a whisper. "I dreamt Iona was under attack. The dream was disjointed, punctuated with explosions, arrows and screaming." She grasped Tamasin's arm, digging in her nails. "But just as I was wrenched out of the nightmare, I saw something in the sky, a shadowy thing with a beak and wings."

"A Crow?"

The Dreamer shook her head in frustration as she strained to remember. "It was only a glimpse, but I thought I saw a rider on its back."

Tamasin froze. If Damia saw it, then it could be real. She knew the power of the dream world — she'd lived in its shadows all her life. She took the woman's hand and squeezed it. "Thank you. I too dreamed we were going to be attacked, hence the Great Horn blowing. Come with me to join the staff."

When Tamasin entered the antechamber of the Throne Room, every Palace employee was assembled. Clearly puzzled at having been ordered there, they quietened as they waited for her to say something.

She did so without any preliminaries. Now was not the time to calm fractured nerves, it was imperative to spur everyone to action. "Iona will be coming under attack today. We must be prepared. Cooks and kitchen maids are to take food down to the underground shelters where you will all be hiding. There is a secret tunnel out to the back so you won't be caught down there. Your children and their minders are to be taken down now and settled in. When the Great Horn blows again, everyone is to drop what they are doing and go immediately to the shelters. Do not delay."

"Who is coming, Consort?" a voice called out.

Tamasin recognized it as the chief housekeeper. "The Crevlin are coming. The war has begun," she stated flatly, pleased to hear a collective hiss at her revelation She was past sugarcoating the situation — if they had the fear of the Goddess instilled in them, they'd obey her command without argument. "Now, go and prepare."

They dispersed without a word.

She continued into the Throne Room to find the Queen with her Ladies-In-Waiting and the ten Mistresses of the Imperial Council.

Valeria searched her face. "Did you find a message from Pela, Tamasin?"

"No. It's bad news. Someone killed the Bird Master and let the pigeons go."

"All of them?" asked Moira incredulously.

"Yes. We are on our own now. Members of the staff are preparing the underground shelters in the vaults. When the Horn blows, everyone is to go down there immediately," she looked pointedly at Valeria, "and I mean everyone."

Valeria merely frowned at her with pursed lips. "Can you hazard a guess when the enemy will arrive, Tamasin?"

Tamasin looked around the room, feeling every eye on her. "I figure it will be before lunch, so you must be ready to retreat to safety at a minute's notice." She looked across at Moira. "Do you have that transcript of the old diary? I'd like to look at it."

Moira nodded. "Come with me. It's in the library."

With the distinct feeling they hadn't paid enough attention to the diary, Tamasin followed her out. As soon as Moira produced Savannah's translation, she flipped to the second page. "Here," she said, pointing to a passage.

"*On the fifth turn of the moons, leathery birds with huge beaks and sharp teeth appeared in the sky.*

We haven't seen those things yet."

"Savannah and I didn't think we were going to," Moira replied. "That war was two millennia ago, and in all my research, I found no evidence those creatures still existed on Rand. We didn't think anything that size could be transported through time." She winced. "You think they're here?"

"I was just talking to Damia. She saw a creature similar in a dream this morning and thought there was a rider on its back."

"By the moons," exclaimed Moira, "was she sure?"

"She said she only caught a glimpse."

"But if it's true," whispered Moira, "it changes everything. If the enemy can fly, then Iona is vulnerable."

"Very much so," said Tamasin grimly. "We're ill-prepared for aerial warfare and Savannah isn't here with her magic."

"What shall we do, Tam?"

"We will fight, Moira." She leaned over and kissed her on the cheek. "Now go my friend and may the Mother keep you safe. I will organize the troops."

⸶

Two hours later, Tamasin stood on the battlement, trying to see into the gloom. The cloud cover was so heavy over the mountain that it was impossible to see any distance. A troop of Elite Guards stood beside her, looking fierce with their eye tattoos and single strips of hair running across the top of their heads into long oiled plaits.

She was just beginning to have a little hope that the dream had been nothing when Malkia's voice popped into her head. *"Savannah's calling me, Tamasin. She's over Chesterton now and a large enemy force is only ten minutes behind her coming from the south. The Crevlin are riding winged creatures. She says to empty the stables immediately. They'll bomb them first."*

"Get the horses in the air and head north, Malkia." Tamasin projected, then galvanized into action. She called out to the officer in charge, "Send the signal to blow the Great Horn, Lieutenant. The enemy will be here shortly." She then roared out to the troops. "Archers. Ready for battle."

She had just completed her rounds of the defenses when a horse appeared in the sky. Exhausted, Sunflower landed awkwardly onto the walkway. When Savannah jumped off, Tamasin strode forward and embraced her. "You're a sight for sore eyes."

"Not when you hear what I'm going to tell you." She looked around in surprise. "Your army is ready for war?"

"I had a dream, Savannah. How many are coming?"

"They have at least a thousand soldiers, riding ferocious winged lizards called Skeldachs. But there's worse to come. They have bombs in their saddlebags which will do a lot of damage." She looked over at the Palace. "At least Valeria has gone."

Tamasin frowned. "What do you mean? She's still here."

Savannah gazed at her, aghast. "I sent a message to get her to Kandelora. She'll be safe in their hidden city. They're here to kill her."

Tamasin winced. "They murdered the Bird Master last night. We got no message."

"Dammit, Tamasin. If something happens to her, we're all screwed."

CHAPTER TEN

*S*avannah pulled out the Farsight Stone and pointed it over the battlement wall.

Its beam cut through the layers of cloud, affording her a view of the southern skies. There were no Skeldachs visible yet, though she knew they wouldn't be far off. Sunflower would have lost ground when she tired at the end of the long ride.

As soon as she pressed the Stone against the medallion, the scene moved forward a minute. This time, at the far end of the valley the enemy were in the sky. She turned urgently to Tamasin. "They'll be here shortly." After she swept her eyes over the top of the Palace, she said quickly. "I'll be on top of the right corner tower. When I fire a bolt of magic, launch your arrows into the clouds." Then with a bound, she leaped back into the saddle. "Drop me up there, Sunflower."

The moment the horse landed on the roof, Savannah slipped off. "Now fly off the mountain, sweetie, and don't come back until I call you."

Defiantly, the mare clipped a hoof hard on the stone floor. *"I'm staying with you."*

"No, you're not," said Savannah firmly. "You know perfectly well you can't help here. Now go."

Sunflower gave a disgruntled snort before she rose in the air and disappeared into the north.

Savannah moved to the wall, keeping the Farsight Stone trained on the southern end. When she saw the first line of Skeldachs rise over the mountainside, she began her assault. Magic fire streamed from her fingers, lighting up the clouds in a dazzling display of pure power. As the misty cloud dissolved with the heat, she saw the first flight of arrows take a dozen riders off their mounts. The lizards reared back as arrows pierced their hides and squealed as their wings burst into flames. Again and again, she threw her missiles and the archers bent their bows.

But as more riders fell, others took their place. For a while, the arrows and magic kept them at bay, but gradually they gained ground. As line after line advanced through the fire, Savannah knew it was hopeless — there were just too many. After each wave came and went, their front had advanced a little closer. When the force eventually breasted the wall, they began dropping their bombs.

After the bombardment, the leading Crevlins leaped off their mounts, landing in front of the Ionian soldiers. As they rushed forward, the Ionians met them with swords. Ringing cries, clashes of metal, and screams echoed through the haze of smoke. The defenders held firm, but as they fought desperately to hold them off, more enemy soldiers poured over the wall.

Finally, Tamasin bellowed out, "Retreat."

Gathering her magic, Savannah raked the Skeldachs hovering at the wall with a rapid-fire barrage of bolts. In the bedlam that followed, to her relief, Tamasin and her remaining troops managed to clamber off the wall. They retreated to the big courtyard, where they joined the rest of the Palace guards who were shooting arrows from under the cover of the buildings. But once the main enemy force was past the outer perimeters, they began to bomb in earnest. The stables were the first to go, shattered into a million pieces by the blasts. After a run through the town with their bombs, they lobbed some into the courtyard, forcing the troops to retreat into the Palace.

Surprisingly, they left the main part of the Palace alone, but Savannah was under no illusion that they wouldn't come for her next. As she expected, a group soon swung her way, but then she lost them in the pall of smoke that now hung like a shroud over the mountain. As she prepared to flee, she swept the Stone around. Her pulse hitched — she had miscalculated badly. Another swarm was already swooping down from the back. She streamed out her fire. Three lizards squealed, flapping frantically as their wing membranes sizzled into flames. Immediately, the others retreated to a safe distance, wary now. She guessed they were waiting for the reinforcements before they tried again.

Furious with herself, Savannah quickly again pressed the Stone to the medallion. A minute into the future, no bombs had yet exploded on the top of the tower. There was time.

Abandoning her post, she sprinted to the door leading down through the tower, and when she reached the stairs, she didn't stop. Fear pushed her on. She hurtled down the steps, sliding on her heels in places but managing to stay upright as she waited for the tower to come crashing down around her. But when the first bomb exploded on the roof, she was already at the bottom of the long staircase and running along the corridor to the service entrance.

At a window, she stopped to peer out and her heart sank. The courtyard was filled with Skeldachs, and Crevlins were marching up the steps to the front Palace entrance.

Dead Iona soldiers were lying everywhere, Crows already feasting on their bodies.

Horrified, Savannah doubled back, heading for the Throne Room. She guessed any soldier left would be holed up there to make a last stand. She just had to hope Tamasin was amongst them.

She slipped out of the corridor into the antechamber and found a hiding place behind a large marble statue of the Goddess Iona in the corner. She flexed her fingers, readying the ancient magic. She had one chance. When the door opened, she was going to unleash the Death Vale. The last hope to turn around a disastrous defeat.

She held the Farsight Stone against the back of the statue to watch them enter.

When twenty Crevlin stepped into the antechamber, she knew she was defeated. There was no way now she could invoke her magic. Each held a hostage in front of them, women and children they had picked up in the town.

The Crevlin in the lead was in full battle armor, with a plumed helmet and a visor covering his face. His armor was made of zenphin, intricately carved and gleaming in the light. He was tall and thin like the others but strode forward with authority. She had no doubt he was their general. He also held a human shield, and this one Savannah recognized: Arwen, the

Queen's chief lady-in-waiting and a good friend of Tamasin.

Impotently, she watched as they walked to the great oak door of the Throne Room. With a flick of his wrist, the general pointed to the door. Two soldiers with battle axes began chopping through the wood. Splinters flew in every direction as the grand old door was shattered. When it finally fell apart, Savannah swung the Stone to look inside. Tamasin, Jocose, and about fifty Palace guards were lined up in front of the dais, swords in hand.

The General turned to a soldier and said, "Lock the door into the antechamber and put guards outside. There will be no one escaping from here."

When the enemy strode in with their human shields, Savannah saw Tamasin slump, defeat etched into her face.

"Bring me the Imperial Queen," the General ground out, "or I'll start cutting these people's throats."

That was enough for Savannah. Glowing with rage, she slipped out from behind the statue and strode into the Throne Room. "Touch one of them and I'll tear you all apart."

Startled, the Crevlins swung around. The next moment, one at the rear came at her with a knife. She sidestepped and jammed enough power into his side to kill him. When he dropped to the floor, the others gave her a wide berth.

She walked up to the General, who stood staring at her. "We're all going to die anyhow," she snapped. "But so will you. I'll make sure of that. I'll unleash enough power to blow the room to pieces."

Slowly, he removed his helmet and smiled. "You will condemn your friends to death for nothing, Savannah. I am a Time Walker. Your magic can't touch me."

She gasped, not believing her eyes. "Wayne McLaren," she spluttered as the memories of her boss at the Algerian dig flooded back.

"So you found the medallion, Savanna, and you never said a word."

"You knew about it?"

His face turned ugly, full of hatred. "Why do you think we went to that godforsaken place. After years of research, we discovered Elsbeth was buried on that hill. You weren't even supposed to get on the team."

"I had good credentials," she said huffily.

"You were nothing but a girl with limited experience. Absorbed with warrior women. But someone in the Algerian Government wanted you on the dig so we couldn't object."

Savannah pricked up her ears. So Grandmother had somehow influenced someone in Algeria. "We? Were the others in it too?"

"They were my employees." He glared at her. "And then you found that bloody ceramic bowl and you wouldn't shut up about it. The Algerians got wind of it, so we had to keep digging under their supervision."

She chuckled mirthlessly. "Ironic wasn't it, Wayne. You thought there was nothing there and the dig turned out to be an archeological treasure trove. The Algerians closed it down to foreigners and tossed us out. You couldn't go back. Now *that* must have hurt."

"And you're going to pay for it, Savannah," he snapped. "We were hoping you had died in that sandstorm." He eyed her speculatively. "I tell you what. I'll swap one hostage life for yours. That's a fair trade."

Casually, Savannah moved a finger to her chest and gently pushed the Stone against the medallion. When the room shimmered into the future, a battle horn was sounding outside. She sagged with relief, knowing what it was. The Ice Elves had arrived, and then at the end of the minute, she saw Pela coming through the Throne Room door. She had to keep him talking a little bit longer. "Arwen for me. I agree. But what will you do with the rest?"

His lips peeled back into a diabolical grin. "Kill them one at a time until the Consort here brings me her wife."

Savannah raised her eyebrows. "What do you want

with the Imperial Queen? You have Iona. She's a queen without a Queendom."

"Pah, You know nothing."

Savannah put her finger up in the air. "You're the one who knows nothing, Wayne. Listen... can't you hear it?"

He tilted his head to hear. "What."

"The Ice Elves have arrived. That's their battle horn."

He turned quickly, screaming at the soldier closest to the door. "Find out what's happening outside." But as the soldier swung around, a giant Hawk swooped into the room and clawed into his face. In the melee that followed, Tamasin and the Palace Guards moved into action. They leaped forward, Tamasin tossing her knives in rapid succession, each finding its mark. Arwen slammed her heel down onto Wayne's foot, and when he loosened his grip, Savannah launched at him.

As she grasped for his shoulders, the air about him swirled and he disappeared into thin air. Left floundering on the floor, Savannah heard his voice in her head. *"I was never McLaren, stupid woman. I am Borrentine, King of the Crevlinian Empire and Master of Time."*

Furious, she projected back. *"I'm not the stupid one. I was the one who found the medallion, you idiot."*

"And it will be mine."

"Like hell."

Shaking, she tuned out and dragged herself off the

floor. When she saw that bastard again, she was going to quash him like the vermin he was.

"Savannah," the old seer's voice popped into her head. It smacked of disapproval. *"Control your temper. He's going to work out what you are."*

Irritated, she flashed back, *"What I am? For God's sake, I don't know what I damn-well am, Grandmother."*

"Work it out, child." And then she was gone.

The feel of Arwen's hand on her arm brought her back to reality. "Are you all right, Savannah. You look confused."

Savannah patted her hand. "I'm fine. Just a bit stressed. Why aren't you with the Queen?"

"My old nanny lives in town. I went to help her into the cellar and got caught there."

"How are you feeling after that ordeal?"

"Pleased to be alive. Thankful to you. Wanting to see my husband."

Savannah smiled. "As soon as he hears, he'll be on his way."

"He'd better be," she replied. "Now I'll get down to Valeria and tell her what happened."

Savannah made her way to the front door, stepping over dead Crows as she went. They were littered everywhere in the foyer. Outside, the Elves were patrolling the skies and there were no Crevlin left in the air. The courtyard was full of dead Skeldachs, she presumed killed by the Bramble Hawks who were now circling the city looking for strays.

Tamasin appeared and gave her a wan smile. "Thank you, Savannah. Iona owes you a great debt." She looked up at the southern battlement. "We lost many good warriors today. War has indeed come, and for all the warnings I received, we were woefully unprepared."

"You weren't to know they had an air force."

"I never considered it and I should have."

Savannah shook her head. "There was no indication they had one. There's not much to be gained by blaming yourself. I'll head to Arcadia to see Jezzine tomorrow to do something about those flying lizards before they cause any more havoc." She looked up to see Pela striding toward her. "I'm about to get a lecture. I'll see you inside."

CHAPTER ELEVEN

"You expect me to run away. Abandon my people. You ask too much, Savannah."

Savannah frowned at her in frustration. Valeria being difficult was all she needed after such a traumatic day. "You'll be abandoning nobody, Your Majesty. You'll be doing the sensible thing. There's an old saying in my world: *Discretion is the better part of valor*. I've learned we can't shut down the Crevlin's time-travel warp without you. Therefore, you must go somewhere safe until the time comes for the Covenant of Queens to close the Circle."

Valeria's expression turned mulish. "I'll be quite safe here now. They won't come back."

"Of course they will," growled Savannah. "They know they must kill you to stay here. They'll assassinate you in your bed or plant bombs somewhere, but they'll be back."

The royal temper began to spike. "Don't push me."

"You're going, Valeria, and there'll be no argument," interrupted Tamasin. Surprised, Savannah glanced at her. As her Consort, she usually went out of her way to placate the Queen, but this time Tamasin looked worried. "The maids will pack your clothes, and I'll get Pela to organize an escort to Arcadia early tomorrow morning. Luna knows the way and has offered to take you from there to Kandelora."

Valeria looked like she was about to argue, then slumped back in the seat. "I shouldn't be deserting my subjects in this crisis, and I shall hate leaving you for so long, Tam. Will you take me?"

Tamasin looked upset when she shook her head. "I must stay here. The people will need help and reassurance, and it's my duty to bury our dead with the honor they deserve."

"I know," said Valeria with a sigh. "It was wishful thinking, that's all."

Savannah cleared her throat. "We must be smart about this. When the enemy finds you

went to Arcadii, it'll make that city a target. I have an idea. The guards can escort someone dressed in your clothes, with a hooded cape, and riding Marigold to the Berian Palace. They'll be reluctant to attack there again after the defeat last time. You can come with me to Arcadia, Ma'am, disguised as a guard."

Tamasin leaned forward in the chair. "That's an excellent idea, Val."

"They'll still recognize me," said Valeria dubiously.

"Not if we paint a bird tattoo around one of your eyes," said Tamasin looking amused.

Valeria glared at her, askance. "I'm not going to shave the sides of my head."

"No, no," Tamasin said quickly. "Plait your hair and wear a helmet."

After Valeria took a long moment to mull over the suggestion, she gave a nod. "The plan has merit. Jocose can pick one of her soldiers who has my build. I wouldn't be comfortable sending someone in my place who couldn't look after themselves."

Tamasin got to her feet and dusted off her breeches. "Then it's settled. I'll be the artist, the fewer people who know the better. Shall we join the others? Pela wants to address everyone, and Jocose has a damage report and the tally of lives lost."

†

Dinner was a dismal affair.

Savannah was pleased to get to bed, not only to get off her feet but to escape from so much anguish.

Though she was exhausted, her mind was so full of the day's happenings she couldn't sleep. Her thoughts drifted back to Algeria and the shock of finding Wayne McLaren heading the Crevlin army. What an asshole he turned out to be, and she'd really liked him back then. As the dig leader, he had been efficient, friendly, and a good boss.

Normally, her uncanny intuition would have given her some sort of warning that he was a fraud, but she hadn't had an inkling. There had been no reason to question his authority, his reputation was impeccable. Back in London, she'd been so caught up with all the post-dig hype that she hadn't given him another thought. And she hadn't heard anything of him since.

She flashed to the confrontation in the Throne Room, recalling that he'd said, *"Your magic can't touch me."* That was a real problem. Even if they closed the Circle, he'd keep coming back if she couldn't stop him. And Grandmother seemed worried about him. What were her words? *He'll find out what you are.*

Then it hit.

The old girl had said *what,* not *who.* This wasn't about Savannah's parentage — it was about her powers. While she and Wayne had argued, she'd heard him even though he'd vanished into thin air.

There could only be one explanation. She was a Mind Walker.

Well, no time like the present to find out.

"Are you there, Grandmother?"

"Yes, Savannah."

"I've worked it out. I'm a Mind Walker like you."

A soft chuckle came. *"Of course you are, Savannah. You've been initiating most of our conversations."*

"Is that why I can talk to the Blue Fjords?"

"Yes. Horses are intelligent, uncomplicated animals, very receptive to mind speak."

Savannah pondered that for a moment then asked, *"Can you talk to everyone?"*

"No. Only those with some ability. Many don't hear me. I talk often to the Dreamers in their sleep."

"It was you who commanded Tamasin to go through the portal?"

"Yes. Tamasin is the strongest Mistress of Dreams that Rand has seen in centuries. Smart too. Being half Ice Elf helps." The old seer lady went on with pride in her tone. *"You are a strong Mind Walker, Savannah, but you are also so much more. Be careful though. You're still vulnerable, and there's a powerful enemy out there. No more mistakes or they will realize what a real threat you are."*

"Are you talking about Wayne ... I mean Borrentine?"

"I have said enough. Your destiny must play out without interference. Too much knowledge and you may move too soon and break the thread. Now sleep tight."

Savannah groaned. The old girl was back to the cryptic threads again.

She'd just pumped up the pillow when she heard Pela come in and go into the bathroom. A few minutes later, she slipped under the covers. "You awake?" she whispered.

Savannah swiveled around to look at her. "I can't sleep," she moaned.

Pela pulled her into her arms. "I know. It's been a horrendous day."

Savannah sniffled, remembering the fallen soldiers in the courtyard and the Crows pecking their bodies. "I just want to be held tonight, Pel. To forget all the horrors."

When she felt the arms tighten around her, Savannah snuggled into the warm body. As she drifted off, she murmured, "I love you, my wonderful Hawk."

✝

While Savannah waited for Valeria to tour the town and say her goodbyes to the Palace staff, she visited the library. Moira was already at one of the desks, pouring over a scroll, a stack of books beside her. She put down her magnifying glass and pointed to a brown leather-bound book resting on a stand. "That's a book I found last week on the Southern Lands in the archives. It's too old for me to interpret."

Savannah settled into the seat and gingerly turned the cover. To her delight, there was a map on the front page with each landmark meticulously drawn, and the numerous towns named. From what she could see, most of this continent was made up of vast plains, the only substantial mountain range was at the bottom in the cold regions. For want of a better description, she labeled that area the Polar Cap. It covered at least a sixth of the south, and she saw the Bear Mountains where zenphin was mined were marked off in this winter wasteland.

The ink on the following page had faded, but she could still read the text except for an odd word here and there. Written over a millennium ago, the book turned out to be a reference book on the people and cultures. Then at the back, when she saw the appendage on the ancient civilizations, she knew she had scored. She read it eagerly.

The Crevlinian Empire had been the greatest in all of Rand, taking up the whole of the southern continent. After some unknown major catastrophe, the south fell into the shadow years. The author didn't know what happened but speculated that a freak winter may have been the cause. Gradually, the northern people settled the lands again. The map wasn't as detailed as the more recent one, but it was good enough for Savannah to get a rough idea of where the Crevlins' major city and the Imperial Palace was sited.

She pushed the stand over for Moira to look at the map. "Have you been to the Southern Lands, Moira?"

"A few times."

"What's it like?"

"Endless plains, wide rivers, and many lakes. It's colder than the north, and it snows in the winter. Plenty of deer and furry creatures. White wolves and bears roam the forests and periodically cause trouble with the livestock, but the homesteaders control them. However, there are creatures in the frozen wastes that are very dangerous. Only the zenphin miners venture into those icy mountains."

Savannah pointed to the drawing of a tower on the map. "Where do you think that is?"

Moira peered through the magnifying glass. "I can make out a lake near it. I think it's the Great Elken Lake … it's at the end of the Snakefish River."

"I intend to go down there to see if I can find something," Savannah said and jotted down the names.

"What could you possibly find after two thousand years?"

"In my world, I studied historical sites. There may be some ruins of their civilization left. I haven't time to dig, but there could be something on the surface."

Moira looked at her curiously. "Is there anything specific you would be looking for?"

Savannah pointed to the drawing of the tower. "That's what I'd be trying to find for a start. It's an odd sort of structure. It doesn't fit with any buildings I've seen in other books of that time."

"No, it doesn't," said Moira. "I wish you luck. You're going to need it."

"I guess I am," replied Savannah with a rueful smile, then carefully closed the book. "I'd better be going. I'll catch up with you when I can, hopefully in better circumstances."

When she walked outside, Marigold was just taking off, her passenger looking very regal in a hooded riding coat bearing the royal colors. Ten guards joined her in the air, and accompanied by four trumpet blasts, they disappeared off the mountain.

Savannah headed down to the back paddocks where the horses were grazing. Though the stables were in ruins, thankfully, some saddlery and tack had been salvaged. Sunflower was saddled, waiting beside Jocose and an Elite Guard who were already mounted. Savanna glanced around for Queen Valeria, then seeing Tamasin looking amused from the railing, turned her eyes back to the Guard. No one in their wildest dreams would suspect this was the Imperial Monarch — all she could see was the bird tattoo.

CHAPTER TWELVE

THE ARCADIAN PALACE

*A*fter the last traumatic few days, Arcadii was a welcome sight.

The city bustled with people going about their daily lives at the markets, shops, and trades. A steady stream of horse-drawn carts laden with produce came in and out of the city, and the big metallurgy plant was puffing out steam. Never had such a commonplace scene seemed so appealing to Savannah. Her mother had always said that you didn't value what you had until it was gone. With Rand on the cusp of a full-scale war, it was devastating to think that this beautiful city could be destroyed.

When they landed in the Palace forecourt, one of the guards disappeared inside immediately.

A few moments later, Jezzine appeared and ran

down the short flight of steps. "Savannah," she said delightedly. "We weren't expecting you until tomorrow."

"I've so much to tell you, Jezz. We'd better adjourn to a private room."

"Come on in then," Jezzine said and gestured to a soldier nearby. "Show these guards where to put their horses and then take them to the barracks for a meal, please."

Savannah flicked a look at Valeria who was standing ramrod-straight with a sour expression on her face. "My Elite Guard will accompany me," Savannah said quickly. "She has some news to relate."

"Bring her along then," Jezzine replied, barely glancing at the disguised Imperial Queen. "Come in."

Savannah smiled to herself, knowing how Valeria must hate having to walk two steps behind. She imagined the royal temper would be simmering.

Once through the front vestibule, Jezzine pointed to a small room off the side. "Go in there where we won't be disturbed. I'll fetch Fern."

"And Luna too, please. It concerns her."

"You need Fern's long-lost cousin? Now you've got me curious," said Jezzine with a quizzical glance.

When they returned, Fern hurried over and kissed Savannah on the cheek. "What's happened? We received word from Lilybeth about the attack on Beribrine, and Pela flew off immediately. We've heard nothing since."

"Sit down while I relate what's happened," said Savannah. She looked across at Valeria, who shrugged and took a seat at the door.

When she'd finished her story, Fern looked horrified. "They attacked Iona as well as Beria? It's hard to believe. Does Pela have a plan? If they have an air force, every realm will be vulnerable."

"That's partly why I'm here," said Savannah. "We found out the flying lizards live underground in an island in the Sea of Mists and we're going to try to stop them getting out." She turned to Jezzine. "I can't do it without the help of the Sirens."

"How many?"

"About ten if possible. Is that too many to find by tomorrow? I'll tell you later why I want them."

"You're in luck," replied Jezzine. "We have fifty training with the Cross Bloods from the Northern Quarter. Lieutenant Rhiannon and Ketra are the instructors."

Recalling she'd heard all the Sirens were gorgeous and knowing from her time at Falcon's Keep what a flirt Rhiannon was, Savannah said wryly, "That'd be a hardship for Rhiannon."

Jezzine chuckled. "I don't think she can believe her luck. And with her charm, she's popular."

A tap on the door interrupted their conversation and the maid bustled in with refreshments. She bowed to Fern. "Do you wish me to serve, ma'am?"

"The Elite Guard will attend to it, thanks."

When the door closed behind the servant, Savannah looked nervously at Valeria. Her face was inscrutable as she went over to the table and began to pour cider into the cups. Savannah noticed when Luna looked over at the guard, her eyes widened and she straightened abruptly in her chair. She flicked an enquiring gaze at Savannah, then rose to her feet quickly and said, "I'll help."

Without a word, Valeria passed over the tray. Her cheeks pink, Luna gave a half bow as she took it nervously. Her hands were trembling as she handed the cups around.

After taking a sip, Jezzine turned to Savannah. "We can provide labor to help with the clean-up."

She nodded. "I'm sure they'll be thankful for any assistance."

"How's Valeria holding up?" asked Fern solicitously.

"For God's sake, Savannah," the Imperial voice rang angrily through the room. "So much secrecy isn't necessary. It's not as though these two are going to rush off and tell everyone I'm here. They don't have the wit to recognize their Queen when she's standing in front of them."

"Your Majesty," gasped Fern.

The Imperial Queen pulled off her helmet and loosened her hair. "I'm glad to get that off." She frowned at them and continued scathingly. "It's no wonder the enemy has infiltrated every Palace in Rand. Doesn't anyone bother to look at the staff?"

Jezzine colored, bowing her head. "I apologize, Ma'am. But you do have a clever disguise."

"Tamasin's artwork. But it doesn't alter the fact that the royal houses must vet their staff more thoroughly. From now on, they are to search everyone for the Crevlin tattoo. And I mean everyone … down to the lowest stable hand. The time for complacency is over. All the royals need to step up. Iona lost half its soldiers yesterday, and the town sustained enormous damage. This enemy is so ruthless they won't stop until every last person in Rand is either dead or in chains."

Fern swallowed audibly. "We have been more vigilant since we found the Arcadian Finance Minister was a Wizard and that a Crevlin was working as a kitchen hand."

Valeria waved dismissively. "Not good enough. I would suggest you put an army checkpoint at the gates into the Palace grounds for foot traffic. Designate a manned landing pad for anyone flying in, and that should include members of royal houses. We are at war so let's act like it. Ask General Grogan to put more patrols into the city. An enemy is always wary of an armed presence."

Savannah looked at Valeria, impressed. The Imperial Queen was taking charge — it was a pity she had to hide. She was as much a force to be reckoned with as Pela.

"I'll give the order today," Fern said quickly.

Valeria took a chair and said more kindly, "How is your mother?"

Fern's face lost all animation. "Failing. She's bedridden now and finds it hard to even feed herself." She gulped back a tear. "The healer doesn't expect her to be with us much longer."

Valeria took her hand. "I would like to say goodbye to Wren before I go if I may."

"She'll be happy to see you, Ma'am. You have been a dear friend to her." She gazed perplexingly at her uniform. "Why have you come to Arcadia dressed as an Elite Guard?"

Valeria looked pointedly at Savannah. "I have been ordered to go into hiding."

"Oh," exclaimed Luna. "So that's why I'm here."

Valeria stood up. "While you two work out the finer details of my flight, I'll see Wren."

"I'll take you," said Jezzine jumping to her feet. "I know the way."

"It would be my honor, Ma'am," Jezzine replied,

then gave a small smile. "We do have Guards outside Queen Wren's chambers. You will be asked to explain your presence."

Valeria merely raised an eyebrow and swept out the door, leaving Jezzine to trail behind.

"Whew," said Luna. "She's intimidating."

"She lost a lot of people yesterday. Understandably, she's not in a good mood."

"I nearly had a heart attack when I saw who was serving the drinks," said Luna.

"You did well to recognize her," said Fern.

"Hunters notice everything. She didn't hold herself as a common soldier, more like someone expecting to be obeyed."

"I'm impressed," said Savannah, "I know she'll be in good hands."

"It's time?"

"Yep. She didn't want to go, but Tamasin insisted. They attacked Iona to try to kill her." She looked earnestly at Luna. "You'll have to go to Kandelora tonight. Are you certain you can find the way in the dark?"

"I have a good sense of direction, Savannah. Besides, I'll take Shade... he's been there before."

"Take another horse as well and leave it with the Imperial Queen. Be careful and hug the shadows. She is very important to us all."

Luna put her hand on her arm reassuringly. "I know how to be invisible."

Remembering the first time she'd seen her in the canyon, Savannah asked, "You still have your cape?"

"Yes, and Floris can give Valeria hers. Being a Faerie, she's small but it'll cover the Queen well enough. Even if someone follows us, we can vanish off the face of the world."

Savannah relaxed, happier now about forcing Valeria to go. "The Queen will be in good hands, my friend." She looked at Fern. "Could you spare me a session in the library this afternoon? I want to discuss your research on the Southern Lands. I'll head off to Beria around three to interrogate the two Crevlin captives."

"I'll be pleased with an excuse to get back to my books," said Fern. "Your old room is empty if you'd like to use the bathroom before lunch."

†

Fern unrolled the scroll, flattening it out carefully between four carved paperweights. "This is the oldest map of the Southern Lands I have. I found it buried in the lowest archive vault when I researched the Crevlinian Empire. It was under a pile of scrolls so encrusted with age that I couldn't even hazard a guess when they'd been disturbed last."

Savannah peered at it, trying to make out any markings that had been on the ancient map at Iona. She raised her head, disappointed. There were a few towns and geographical features drawn, but nothing detailed.

"It's rather basic," she remarked. "Have you any idea how old it is?"

Fern pointed to a symbol on the side. "That's how the Crevlin wrote their numbers."

"So you think it was from that era?"

"I do. I have other documents to substantiate the mark."

When Savannah ghosted her fingers over the scroll to feel for any indentations, a strange thing happened. The medallion reacted to the map by prickling her skin, and it wasn't a pleasant sensation. Something dark knotted inside her stomach, nearly causing her to heave up her lunch. She looked at it, bewildered. By now, she was familiar with all the magic scents of this world, the good and the bad. The unpleasant one was black magic which smelt like burnt tar. This was even worse: it was nauseating.

"Step right away," she said to Fern. "I'm going to do something, and I have no idea what the reaction will be."

Tentatively, she leaned over and touched the medallion to the parchment. Immediately, a cloud of noxious smoke burst out, followed by a crackling sound. When the air cleared, another map entirely was on the stretched animal hide, this one etched in sparkling detail. She waved urgently to Fern. "Let's analyze it quickly, in case it disappears again."

"By the moons," gasped Fern. "Where did that come from?"

"It was under a spell."

Her brow furrowed in concentration, Fern studied it closely. When she looked up, she said, "It's a map of all the lands south of the seas. It appears it was only one realm."

Savannah nodded. "That's consistent with the historical records from Iona. The Crevlins occupied the lot."

"Why did they bother putting a spell on the map?"

"I'm guessing because they didn't want future generations to see something."

Fern leaned over closer for another look. "What?"

"That tower," said Savannah, pointing to a section of the map. "I bet it's holding their pathway through Time, the Time Gateway."

"What would it be, do you think?"

"A door, a mirror, a machine — who knows. But whatever it was, it was built by the God of Time they worshipped." She snorted. "King Borrentine, Time Walker."

"You think he built something so they could time travel?"

Savannah shrugged. "They probably wouldn't have been able to do it on their own. There is something that really puzzles me though. If they feared magic, how could they turn into Crows? And when they die, why do they turn back into Crows?"

"It could have something to do with time travel."

"I was thinking that. Maybe it's the only way he can get them through time," Savannah said. She ran her eyes over the map. "Where do you think the City of the Dead could be?"

Fern looked at it thoughtfully. "The South is very flat and well populated. The only mountain range where an army could hide is in the ice regions. If I took a guess, I'd say it's not down there at all. Presuming the Time Walker had the power to put the exit anywhere, why choose to put it in the Southern Lands? His army would have to cross the seas."

"Good point. The Crevlin will be amassing thousands of soldiers as we speak. We need to find it and soon." Savannah took a piece of parchment and dipped the pen into the inkpot. "I'll jot down instructions on how to get there and make a copy of the area near the tower. Between the two of us, I shouldn't get lost."

"Why do you think they eat the bodies?" asked Fern. "I never found anything in my studies of the civilization that suggested they were cannibals. I've read some tribes think they gain special powers by eating their enemies."

"Maybe it's a simple answer. They could be just hungry."

CHAPTER THIRTEEN

THE BERIAN PALACE

*L*ilybeth watched with interest as the horse and rider flew into the courtyard.

This was the infamous Enchantress who had come to interrogate the prisoners. The woman the magical Guardians so disliked. Not that Gladofin said as much, but by the way her lips curled into disapproval whenever her name was mentioned, left Lilybeth in no doubt what she thought of the visitor.

Gladofin's voice cut through her thoughts as the horse's hooves hit the cobblestones. "Be careful of Reagan. She will enchant your mind and tie you in knots at the least provocation. She has no qualms when it comes to getting what she wants."

Lilybeth gave her a tolerant smile. "I'm not a callow youth to be taken in easily. And surely, as a guest, she will behave with propriety. It would hardly be in her interest to get me offside."

Gladofin gave a little puff of frustration. "Reagan plays by her own rules. Just be on guard — that's all I'm saying."

"I'll take it on board," she said, already pushing the warning out of her mind as she studied the Enchantress.

She was nothing like Lilybeth expected. Instead of a sour crone, she saw a striking woman, with high cheekbones, dark long-lashed eyes, and full lips painted scarlet. Her black hair was braided, piled high in an intricate design that accentuated her long neck. The blue riding dress was low cut and clung to her curves. Lilybeth wasn't an authority on fashion, but she couldn't help comparing the flashy outfit to the Countess's elegant gown. That one was all class.

As she ascended the stairs, Reagan scrutinized her with such blatant interest that Lilybeth felt her face flush in embarrassment. She schooled her expression and said pleasantly, "Welcome to Beria, Mistress Reagan."

"You have an impressive home, Your Majesty. I'm looking forward to my stay." She gazed around, surprise reflected on her face. "Savannah's not here?"

"She flew to Iona. I'll bring you up to date with the

situation after you've had a chance to tidy up after the trip. The Countess is also a guest."

Reagan's features set in an expression of haughty disdain. "So this is to where you disappeared, Gladofin."

The Countess eyed her with dislike. "I'm here to help in the war effort, as we all must do now."

Reagan merely raised an eyebrow and murmured, "Really?" Then she turned to Lilybeth with a smile. "Perhaps you'd give me a tour of your palace after I wash, Ma'am. My home is in the mountains, and I've never been to the sea before. I found it exciting seeing it from the air."

It had never occurred to Lilybeth that the folk from the Forgotten Realms would not have seen the sea. "Then what's at the top end of your Realms? I thought there was a great ocean."

"No ocean," Gladofin chipped in. "The north borders the wet wastelands. They say the gasses in the swamps are too toxic for anything to live there. But the Wizard's Wall blocked it off, so it was always just conjecture."

Lilybeth smiled at the Enchantress. "I would be pleased to show you our view over the Wide Sea of Mists, Mistress Reagan. The House of Vandersea is Guardian of the Waters." She chuckled. "I'm sure brine runs in our blood."

Reagan lightly touched her arm. "I can see you're

proud of your heritage. I admire that. May I call you Lilybeth?"

Though the fingers hadn't moved, Lilybeth felt as if they were caressing her skin, and even after Reagan removed her hand, the feeling still lingered. Resolutely, she quashed down the pleasant tingle and said a little hoarsely. "Of course you may. We don't stand on ceremony here, Reagan." She waved a hand toward the door. "Shall we go inside? The maid will fetch your valise and show you to your room. One of the grooms will stable your horse."

"Excellent," Reagan murmured, and with an exaggerated sway of her hips, she strolled inside.

Lilybeth turned from watching her climb the stairs, to find Gladofin gazing at her with pursed lips.

"She's not what I expected," said Lilybeth weakly.

Gladofin favored her with an enigmatic look. "And what did you expect?"

"Someone … you know … more like a witch."

"Have you ever seen a witch?"

"Only the Silverthorne Witch Ursula at Iona. She was a nasty old hag."

Gladofin just shook her head. "For a start, Reagan is not a witch. She's a very powerful magical being who can enchant minds, so beware. You have no idea what or who you're dealing with."

Lilybeth felt a wave of hurt. "I'm not a fool. I've been

154 | COVENANT OF QUEENS

ruling this realm since my mother died when I was twenty-three. I mightn't be as exciting as the people you mix with, but I take my duties seriously. And I'm considered a good judge of character."

Gladofin bowed her head apologetically. "I'm sorry. It wasn't meant to be a criticism. It's just that the people of Rand have not had anything to do with magic for centuries, and I fear some of my people from the Forgotten Realms are going to take advantage of that."

"The Madra says the members of the House of Amarim are the most powerful of the Magical Folk. Perhaps I should be warier of *you*, Countess."

Gladofin looked disconcerted. "And are you?"

"Maybe," Lilybeth replied with a shrug, but knew in her heart that this woman could be trusted. It was true what she'd said. She was an excellent judge of character, but it was an inherited ability passed down through her royal bloodline. Lilybeth could pick a fraud a mile away. It was recorded in their scripts that in a time before the Mystic Wars, the Madra of the seas had bestowed the gift on the Queens of Beria to help protect the Sea Folk. Her mother had cautioned her not to reveal their secret, for she would require the ability to rule effectively.

She was well aware Reagan wasn't to be trusted. But still, underneath that tough exterior, she also sensed the Enchantress was lonely.

When Gladofin said, "I'd better get back to work," Lilybeth felt a wave of remorse. The Countess hadn't been anything but kind to her, nursing her through her injury. And whatever herbs she'd put on the wound, Lilybeth had remarkably little pain now.

But before she could say something to mend the rift, a dumpy woman in her fifties with corkscrew curls burst into the hall. "I was reading one of the scullery maid's fortunes, Your Gracious … sorry, luv, I meant Majesty, and was in a trance to see who she fancied, when I saw 'em," she panted out.

"Calm down, Esme," Lilybeth said soothingly. "What did you see?"

"Crows. Five of the little black bastards. They were staring at a woman in a red dress."

"What did she look like?" Gladofin interrupted sharply.

Esme looked at her slyly. "She ain't got your class, Countess. She was fairly burstin' outa the dress. Let's just say she'd be more at home in one of them houses of ill-repute. A fancy one though. She wouldn't be cheap."

Lilybeth looked at Gladofin who mouthed, "Reagan."

To stop Esme bouncing from one foot to the other, she took her arm in a firm grip. "Come into the lounge and you can tell us all about your vision."

Strangely, Lilybeth had come to like the fortune

teller. When Tamasin had asked her to take a Dreamer who was one of the best but a difficult fit for the courts, she'd immediately known why when she met her. Esme was loud, talkative, and vulgar. She also had a crafty eye for money and had a side-line fortune-telling business up and running in no time in the kitchens. Lilybeth let her go, figuring she was harmless and her readings proved popular with the staff. But under all that, she sensed Esme would be loyal to her.

When they were seated, she said softly. "Now tell us what you saw. And, Esme," she added, "just call me Ma'am. It'll be easier."

Esme bobbed her head. "Well, Ma'am, I was telling that little scullery maid's fortune ... you know the one with the big —"

"Just the facts," Lilybeth answered quickly, conscious Gladofin was staring wide-eyed at Esme.

"Okay. I'd just gone into my trance when the picture of the head groom popped into my mind. You could have knocked me down with a feather. I thought she was keen on the blacksmith's apprentice ... he's younger and good-looking."

Exasperated, Lilybeth said sternly, "The facts, Esme, the facts."

"Oh, right. Anyhow, the scene suddenly changed and the Crows appeared."

"Could you tell where they were?"

"No. They were perched on a ledge somewhere. Then this woman in red came into view. She was kneeling doing something, but then the cook yelled for the maid and everything vanished." She clutched at Lilybeth's arm. "It's gonna happen tonight. It was too vivid. And there's more. I caught a glimpse of a man in a hooded cape watching too. I can't explain it, but there was something about 'im that sent shivers up my spine."

Lilybeth patted her hand. "You did very well, Esme. Run to the barracks and tell the Captain I want to see her. We'll mobilize all the Hawks immediately. In the meantime, I want you to stay in your room and go into a trance every half an hour. It'll help if we can pinpoint when they'll arrive."

When she disappeared out the door, Gladofin gave a little chuckle. "I can see you have your hands full with that one."

Lilybeth gave a rueful smile. "Nobody quite knows how to shut her up. But she's a whizz with the trance. She grows on you … she's not nearly as annoying as she used to be."

"Not many of the nobility would be so tolerant," remarked Gladofin.

"She's good-hearted and means well," said Lilybeth, then turned at the sound of running footsteps in the corridor.

After a quick tap on the door echoed, the Captain of

the Guard burst into the room. "You called me, Your Majesty."

"The Dreamer has forewarned us that Crows will be coming tonight. Unfortunately, we don't know where they'll appear, so get all the Hawks in the sky immediately to patrol the Palace and surrounds."

"Yes, Ma'am," she said, then hurried out the door.

She'd no sooner left the room when Reagan appeared from the direction of the staircase. She'd changed into a red gown, which brought to mind Esme's prediction. "Shall we take the tour before dinner, Lilybeth? I imagine the sea will be spectacular at sunset." Smiling sweetly, she turned to the Countess. "I'm sure you have things to do, Gladofin."

Unable to think of a way to include her, Lilybeth murmured. "I'll see you at dinner."

Now that she had her by herself, Reagan was all charm. As they strolled through the Palace, her comments were gracious and thoughtful. When they finally walked outside and leaned over the wall to take in the brilliant sunset, she seemed genuinely enthralled. "It's beautiful, with a wildness that stirs my blood. No wonder you love it so much."

For a long while, they stood gazing out over the sea in companionable silence. When the sun sank below the horizon and Lilybeth made a move to go, Reagan said softly, "Please, stay a while longer. Nights like this should be shared."

"Very true," Lilybeth agreed. It was nice to appreciate a view with someone by her side.

"You are alone, Lilybeth?"

"My daughter left this year to train with the Elite Guard. It's been lonely since she left."

Reagan sighed. "I am alone too. I've never lived with anyone for long."

Surprised, Lilybeth turned to look at her. "Why not, Reagan. You've much to offer a companion."

"No one can put up with me," she replied acerbically.

Lilybeth chuckled. "You should try keeping out of their minds. I can feel you rummaging around in mine."

"You can feel me?" asked Reagan in disbelief.

"I sense many things that few can."

"You're magical?"

"No. But I do have a gift." She looked curiously at the Enchantress. "How much did you discover about me?"

"I can read and manipulate minds, Lilybeth. I know you blame yourself for your wife's death even though it wasn't your fault. You are one of the few noble people I've met. But nobility has a price. You take too many problems on your shoulders and eventually it will kill you. You must take time out for yourself."

Lilybeth turned to study her in the moonlight. "I don't know you at all, Reagan, but something tells me you don't normally offer good advice."

Reagan gave a harsh chuckle. "No, I'm usually a sarcastic bitch and enjoy playing with people's minds."

Lilybeth touched her arm sympathetically. "That façade must be very taxing to maintain. I think you need to take time away from your inner demons more than I do."

"You're not what I expected, Lilybeth. I was under the impression you were a simple warrior Queen, more brawn than brains. A pushover. You're anything but that."

"And I thought you were dangerous."

"Oh, I'm dangerous. Make no mistake about that. But I promise that you are safe from me."

Lilybeth nodded gratefully. "Thank you." She pushed away from the wall. "I guess we'd better go to dinner."

But as she turned to go, Reagan suddenly grasped her by the arm. "Gad! Look at the moons. Can you see anything unusual?"

Lilybeth peered into the sky. "It looks like a shadow's coming out from behind the largest one."

"Not a shadow," exclaimed Reagan. "It's definitely another moon."

CHAPTER FOURTEEN

"That's strange," said Lilybeth. "I've never heard of a third moon. If it is one, from where would it have come? It doesn't make sense."

Reagan gazed thoughtfully into the sky. "Don't you think it's too much of a coincidence that it appeared the same time as the Crevlin?"

"You think it has something to do with them?"

"Maybe. It could help them move through time."

Lilybeth raised an eyebrow. "That sounds a bit farfetched. Iona's historian, Mistress Moira, may know if it's come before."

"The Iriwari will know," said Reagan.

"Who are they? I've never heard of them," admitted Lilybeth.

"Few have. They're a reclusive race of magical

scholars in the Forgotten Realms who spend their lives studying the stars. They live in isolation in the high Zorian Alps and were one of the ancient Magical Houses that disappeared after the purge. They're Sylphs, spirits of the air."

"Tamasin will be interested to meet them."

Reagan shrugged. "I doubt they'll give her an audience, but she can try."

"The Consort can be very persuasive," Lilybeth said, then gestured to the steps. "Let's go to dinner."

As they walked from the wall, Reagan's attention turned to a dark form near one of the stone posts. "What's that over there?" she asked, already striding to the Skeldach huddling in its chains.

Lilybeth hurried after her. "It's the winged creature that Savannah wants you to mind read. Perhaps we should wait for her."

"Nonsense. I'm here now," Reagan said firmly and leaned over to examine its scaly body from head to toe. "Hmmm ... aren't you an ugly one," she murmured.

When Lilybeth began to speak, she held up her hand. "Hush," she whispered. "I'm concentrating."

Then Reagan squatted down beside its head and stared it in the eye. The Skeldach went still as if mesmerized, its round lidless eyes focused intently on the Enchantress.

"What kind of creature are you?" Reagan hummed out in a lilting voice.

The Skeldach broke from its trance and eyed her sullenly. It opened its beak, exposing a mouth full of razor-sharp teeth. "So you can bite," said Reagan, changing her pitch to an even tempo. As her brow furrowed in concentration, the creature quietened.

Finally, Reagan looked up at Lilybeth. "Interesting. The creature has limited intelligence, driven mainly by instinct. This kind of animal is the most dangerous because you can't reason with it. However, these lizards are controlled, which is an anomaly."

"How do the Crevlin control them?"

"By sound," answered Reagan. "High pitched, in a frequency that's out of our hearing range. They must have whistles to get their commands across. Perhaps —"

Her words died away when a scream abruptly echoed from inside the stairway, "They're comin'."

Lilybeth whipped around to see Esme burst into view. And to her horror, four Crows sat on the wall, and one had already changed into a man. The Dreamer had only taken two steps into the open air when he was upon her. With a lunge, he plunged the knife into her side. Esme squealed, then fell to her knees.

When he lifted his arm to stab her again, Lilybeth screamed, "No."

As she leaped forward to help her, everything seemed to erupt at once. The assassin dropped the knife to clutch his head. When blood began to spurt from his nose and eyes, she knew Reagan was responsible. He staggered erratically along the stone floor as blood soaked his cloak. Finally, as he collapsed onto the ground, his body disintegrated into particles until only a dead Crow lay beside Esme. At the same time, three Bramble Hawks suddenly shot into view over the wall.

Cawing loudly, the remaining Crows tried to flap away, but they were too slow for the Hawks. They swooped down, snapping off their heads with their beaks. But when the Hawks came into land, something strange happened. Out of nowhere, a fierce wind blew up over the battlement. It began to twirl, spinning the big birds into its center, and one by one, they were hurtled into the distance out to sea.

Lilybeth flattened her body against a column, grasping it to stop herself from being sucked over the wall. Just as she thought she'd lost the battle, without warning, the wind dropped as suddenly as it had blown up. She looked around frantically. By some miracle, Esme was still on the ground. When she heard the Skeldach grunt loudly, she flashed a quick look at it. It went berserk, thrashing wildly against its chains. Then with a whimper, its eyes rolled back in its head, and it went limp. She knew it was dead, even without examining it. Whoever had conjured up the wind didn't want it alive.

Anxiously she searched for Reagan, finding her standing with arms outstretched, peering at something in the gloom. And then Lilybeth saw him too. A tall man was on the end of the wall, silhouetted against the glow of the moons. He was staring at Reagan, his face twisted in anger. She guessed then that Reagan had stopped the mini tornado somehow.

"So, the Enchantresses survived the purge of Falendore. We didn't foresee that," he ground out.

Reagan stiffened. "You are the Time Walker who slaughtered my people."

"We had help, witch. There were plenty who hated the power of the old magic."

"Then die, lover of demons," she hissed.

To Lilybeth, it appeared they were both just standing like statues staring at each other, but she knew that there was a momentous, yet silent struggle happening. Seconds stretched into minutes. The veins in Reagan's temple began to bulge, her face turning red with the strain. But in the end, it was the man who folded first. Slowly, he began to sway, clearly struggling to stand. Finally, he sagged.

"You're too powerful, witch," he panted, then vanished into thin air.

Her arrogance gone, Reagan's face was deathly

white when she turned to Lilybeth. "I barely held him off. He's strong."

"But you bested him, Reagan. That's what matters." Lilybeth looked over at the woman lying on the ground. "Rest for a moment. I must see to Esme."

The Guards and the Countess had already emerged from the stairs by the time Lilybeth reached the fortune teller. When she found a pulse, she breathed a sigh of relief. Gladofin knelt quickly beside her and helped Lilybeth gently ease the smock up to view the wound. Lilybeth stared in disbelief — the woman's undergarment was full of strips of thick leather. The cunning old fox had made herself a protective vest.

With a groan, Esme opened an eye. "By the moons, that 'urt. I would've made the thing thicker if I knew he was goin' to stab that 'ard."

"You knew what he was going to do?" asked Lilybeth.

"Course I did. I saw the swine do it in the last trance."

Resting back on her heels, Lilybeth gave a little chuckle, though it was more from relief than humor. "You're wonderful, Esme. Most people would have opted to stay in their room where it was safe."

"I ain't most people, Ma'am. Beria is my home now, and you are my Queen. I'll protect both."

Lilybeth felt moisture gather in her eyes. She put

her hand on Esme's shoulder and squeezed lightly. "I hope you'll stay with us when all this is over. Loyal subjects like you are invaluable." She gestured to the Captain of the guards. "Get two soldiers to help Mistress Esme down to her room, please." Then she turned to the Countess. "I'll see to Reagan. She battled the Time Walker tonight, and it's knocked her about."

Lilybeth ran over to Reagan, who sat on the ground, nursing her head in her hands. She knelt and put an arm around the Enchantress' shoulders solicitously. "Are you all right?"

"I'm fine. A headache, that's all. It's just about gone."

At the click of shoes on stone, Lilybeth glanced up to see the Countess looking down at them. She had no idea what she was thinking. Strangely, Gladofin was the one person she was finding hard to read.

Lilybeth stood and offered the Enchantress her hand to help her to her feet. Her color back in her face, Reagan dusted down her dress and then smiled at Lilybeth. "Thank you." She switched her attention to Gladofin. "It is time we put aside all animosity and worked together. I met the enemy tonight. No one can defeat him alone; he is far too powerful." She held up two fingers until they were nearly touching. "He came *that* close to defeating me. It was an unsettling experience; one I don't want repeated."

Gladofin's eyes widened. "Did you learn anything about him while you were in his mind?"

Reagan nodded. "He is capable of projecting much power with his mind but he can't read thoughts as I can. And he doesn't know how to shield his memories."

"Have you met anyone who can?" asked Lilybeth curiously.

"The Guardians can, to an extent, but there's only been one who could completely block me out. Savannah."

"She's an enigma," murmured Gladofin. "What did you learn about this enemy?"

"It was only quick glimpses while we were mind tussling. He's Borrentine, King of the Crevlin. Today, they attacked Iona."

Lilybeth looked horrified. "As we feared. What happened?"

"I saw flashes of fighting and bombs blasting the town. Dead Ionian soldiers lay in the Palace courtyard, and Crows were eating their bodies."

"Iona lost the war?" whispered Lilybeth.

"The Ice Elves arrived and defeated the Crevlin."

"And Valeria?"

"Safe. Savannah must have done something to him, for he was consumed with hatred for her."

"But why would he bother coming here with his assassins after he suffered a defeat?" asked Gladofin.

"Because he wanted to get the prisoners out before Savannah arrived back to interrogate them. And I'm sure he killed that Skeldach." Reagan's expression tightened. "They know you have them, Lilybeth. There is a spy in your Palace, and I suggest you investigate everyone tomorrow morning. Women as well as men."

Anxious now, Lilybeth called to the Captain. "Will you check on the prisoners, please. Then report straight back."

"Yes, Ma'am," she said and disappeared down the staircase.

"Perhaps it would be wise to hide them somewhere until Savannah gets here," said the Countess.

"I could go ahead with the interrogation myself," said Reagan, "but I'm not sure the questions Savannah wants answered."

Lilybeth smiled, noting Reagan's abrasive personality was nowhere in sight. She'd obviously found it very unsettling to find that she was not so invincible as she had imagined herself to be.

In this mood, people were actually going to find her likable.

CHAPTER FIFTEEN

THE BERIAN PALACE

From her balcony, Lilybeth gazed at the group of riders in the distance.

She had no idea who they were. Savannah was the only one due today, but she'd sent a message via a courier pigeon to let them know she wasn't arriving with the Sirens until tonight.

As they neared, Lilybeth took a sharp breath. The troop wore the imperial royal colors, and they were escorting someone riding the Queen's mare, Marigold. Since Valeria didn't allow anyone else to ride her Blue Fjord, Lilybeth galvanized into action. If the Imperial Monarch was turning up on her doorstep, she'd better be ready.

Once she reached the ground floor, she called loudly, and urgently, to her housekeeper.

A few seconds later, the woman appeared from the direction of the kitchens. "You require something, Ma'am?"

Lilybeth looked around the room, pleased to see fresh flowers again this morning. "Important visitors will be here any minute, Mistress Tiana. Tell the cook to put out her finest chinaware for morning refreshments. And I've been meaning to congratulate you on the flowers. You've spruced up the place."

Pink tinged the housekeeper's cheeks. "The Countess does the flowers."

"Oh," said Lilybeth, taken aback. "And is she responsible for the improvements in the meals?"

"Yes, Ma'am. She gives the cooks the day's menu every morning. She's taken to organizing the maids as well. She's helped me enormously. My old bones aren't what they used to be."

Lilybeth felt a flush of remorse. She'd been neglecting her household. By now, she should have given Tiana a cottage in town as a retirement gift and put on a younger housekeeper. It was a big job, and the maids needed a firmer hand. She'd have a word with Gladofin later, but now there was a more urgent matter.

As soon as she stepped through the front door, the horses appeared overhead, and the Queen and her entourage touched down in the courtyard. Valeria dismounted, drawing the cloak tighter around her face. Without a word, she was shuffled up the stairs by the commander of her escort.

Lilybeth recognized Captain Jocose, who saluted with an urgent, "Her Imperial Majesty asks to go somewhere private, Ma'am."

"Follow me," said Lilybeth without argument. Explanations could come later — something seriously was wrong, for Valeria hadn't raised her head or said a word. Filled with concern, she bundled them into the small sitting room before anyone else came outside to see who had arrived.

"Queen Lilybeth, I have a dispatch from Consort Tamasin to explain what's happening," Jocose said as soon as the door closed behind them.

She handed over a letter, then nodded to the robed figure who threw back her cape. "Meet Carmine, Ma'am. She's a member of my guard."

Lilybeth sucked in a startled breath. The woman who stood before her wasn't Valeria but someone with her figure and hair coloring. "You completely fooled me, Carmine. Well done," she said, then quickly broke the waxed seal.

My dear Lilybeth,
Valeria has gone into hiding, for the enemy intends to kill

her. She's been taken to a safe place, and this subterfuge is to throw them off the scent. As Beria is the best fortified place on Rand, I ask that you protect the woman I'm sending in her place, and I'd appreciate it if you kept our secret for at least a week. By that time, the trail will be cold. The fewer knowing she is not the Queen, the better.

Yours
Tamasin.

Lilybeth folded the page carefully, tucked it away in her pocket, and then bolted the door. "It was a stroke of luck that apart from the guards, I was the only one to greet you when you arrived. Now, tell me what happened at Iona. The Enchantress had glimpses of an attack there."

When Jocose had finished, so much emotion gathered in Lilybeth's chest that it felt like she was choking. For the enemy to inflict such destruction on the Imperial seat of power of Rand was unthinkable and horrific.

Jocose looked with concern at her. "You realize, Ma'am, that Beria will be a target now."

Lilybeth gave a harsh laugh. "The enemy turned up again last night, Captain. Their leader won't come back in a hurry — the Enchantress defeated him at his mind games. He knows she's here, and since he had spies in the Palace, he is aware the Countess is here too. The Guardians are to be feared as much as the Enchantress. Savannah is coming tonight with Sirens. He'll be a fool not to leave us alone."

Jocose smiled. "No one would dare go against all that magic power. You had a spy in the Palace?"

"Two actually. Both were women in the laundry. As soon as they knew the game was up, they turned into Crows but they didn't escape the Bramble Hawks. From now on, anyone entering the Palace will be examined for the Crevlin mark. We must be more vigilant."

"I'm going back to Iona shortly, Ma'am. Is there any message for the Consort?"

"Yes, Captain. Tell her we've made some progress with those flying lizards. The Enchantress discovered that the Crevlins control them with sounds that are too high-pitched for people to hear. Winston and his crew are trying to make some whistles that can reach the same pitch. It may confuse them."

Jocose leaned forward. "That's good news. Without an air force, they'll be on more of an equal footing with us."

"We're hoping Savannah may be able to do something about them," Lilybeth said, then stood up. "I'll put Carmine in a north wing suite. That wing is unoccupied, so visits to the privy will go unnoticed. I'm afraid you'll be confined there for at least a week, my dear, but

I'll make sure you'll be comfortable. I'll give an order it's off-limits to staff. Before you go back, Captain, take your squad to the barracks for a meal. Let them know you brought the Imperial Queen here and the enemy will soon hear. There will no doubt be a spy lurking downtown."

Jocose saluted, and after she left, Lilybeth turned to Carmine. "Cover your head with the cape and we'll sneak up the service stairs."

When they reached the room without meeting anyone, Lilybeth let out a long breath and willed herself to relax. So far, so good. Now she had to organize someone to bring Carmine her meals. She toyed with the idea of dressing the soldier as a maid, but her military bearing would give her away. As well, she'd be asked where she came from. A newcomer was always the subject of gossip in any household, and Esme, the eternal busybody, would discover her identity in two minutes flat with her trance.

No, it would be safer to keep her hidden in the north wing and find someone discrete to look after her meals. Only one name came to mind. After settling Carmine into the room, Lilybeth hurried downstairs to see the housekeeper.

"We have an important guest in the north wing, Mistress Tiana," Lilybeth said in a tone that didn't invite questions. "She is not to be disturbed. No

176 | COVENANT OF QUEENS

member of the staff is allowed in the wing. I will attend to her meals.

The housekeeper nodded though threw her a quizzical look. "Certainly, Ma'am. I will inform the staff."

"Good. Now tell the cook we will be in the dining room for lunch in half an hour. Get her to make up a tray for our guest. And Tiana ..."

"Yes, Ma'am."

"Our finest tableware on the tray, please."

As soon as she disappeared to the kitchens, Lilybeth made her way down to the planning room. They were huddled in a group, watching Winston blow a thin reed. Reagan was perched on a chair, looking on amused.

"How can we tell if it's making a sound?" asked the Countess.

"I can hear it," growled Limos. "It's extremely irritating."

"I can't," said Willowtine.

Limos flashed her a haughty glance. "You're a tree. What do you expect? Tigers have acute hearing."

"No bickering," ordered the Countess. "If it's annoying, then it will have the desired effect. Let's make some more."

When Lilybeth gave a discrete cough, they all turned to look at her.

With a smug smile, Winston held up the whistle. "It works."

"Good for you. Savannah can take some with her." She shuffled her feet, loathing she had to lie. "I've some news. A little while ago, the Imperial Queen arrived seeking Beria's protection. Her room in the north wing is off-limits to everyone." She paused, suddenly aware she'd miscalculated — she'd forgotten Reagan could read minds. By the look on her face, she was well aware it wasn't Valeria up in that room. Lilybeth held her eye, and when Reagan gave a tiny nod, she continued, "There have been some dreadful developments."

As she related the attack on Iona, the room fell deathly quiet.

When she finished, even Reagan looked distressed. "I should have fried his brain last night," she muttered, then added sheepishly, "But I guess I tried and failed."

Recalling their tussle, Lilybeth knew what it had cost the Enchantress to get any victory over this enemy. "You did well, Reagan, so don't admonish yourself about it. He is enormously powerful." She turned to Gladofin. "Could I speak to you in private, please, Countess?"

Gladofin got up without a word and moved to the door. "Let's go outside to talk. Rooms can be stuffy if one's used to the fresh air. "

Lilybeth nodded, feeling the same. The initial shock

of the attack on Iona had turned to anger, and she desperately wanted to cool off.

Once outside, Gladofin walked to the wall and stared out over the sea. Lilybeth joined her, and after a moment's silence, she briefly touched her arm. "I need your help. The woman in the north wing isn't the Imperial Queen; she's a lookalike sent in her place. Her name is Carmine. Valeria is somewhere safe, in a place no one can find. I have no idea where. Tamasin has asked me to keep the secret for at least a week, and I want someone I can trust explicitly to help me look after the woman. I've told the housekeeper to inform the staff the wing is out of bounds."

"Valeria left Iona?"

"The enemy is bent on killing her. Tamasin didn't give details in the letter, but Savannah can fill us in when she gets here tonight."

"You can leave Carmine in my hands. I can organize her meals in her room and see she has everything she requires."

Lilybeth sighed with relief. "Thank you. That's a weight off my mind." She reached over and took her hand. "I've been talking to Mistress Tiana. She's told me you've been helping her run the household. You must think me a poor excuse for a Queen, and you'd be right. I dispensed with proper court protocol years ago, and I should have provided Tiana with retirement by now and put on someone younger."

Gladofin didn't pull her hand away, seemingly content for Lilybeth to cradle it in hers. "In all those years, Lilybeth, why didn't you seek another consort? You had to have been lonely and raising a daughter by yourself must have proved a challenge. First love can't always be replicated, but companionship is important too." She smiled and said softly, "You would have had an easier life with someone to take charge of your household. Governing the realm would have taken up most of your time."

Lilybeth stood motionless, uncertain how to respond. She was unused to having a frank conversation about her life; no one had ever asked her such searching questions. And since she had only known the Countess for a short time, she knew she could easily avoid answering anything personal, and that would be the end of it. But if she was honest with herself, she didn't want to fob her off. Gladofin excited her, stirring something deep inside that she'd never felt before. She'd had plenty of royals trying to catch her eye over the years, for Beria was a prize for ambitious mothers of unwedded daughters and sons. But she was under no illusion that it was her Queendom and not her charms that attracted them.

They all paled in comparison to this Guardian from

the Magical Lands. Countess Gladofin was elegant, vibrant, and simply stunning. Why she was even letting Lilybeth hold her hand was a mystery.

She looked her in the eye and told the truth, "My marriage was comfortable, and we had a wonderful daughter together. We respected each other, but it wasn't a love match. I vowed if I ever married again, it would be for love. I'm afraid I've never found it. It was probably my fault because I lack the will to play courtly games." She made a rueful face. "I'm more comfortable with my troops."

"You never found a Consort from your army?"

Resolutely, Lilybeth shook her head. "As Queen, I cannot marry outside my class."

Gladofin tilted her head to study her. "My word, Lilybeth, you're such a traditionist." She gave her an inscrutable look. "Reagan is from Falendore, an ancient royal house."

Lilybeth chuckled. "You think I'm interested in Reagan? By the moons, Gladofin, I thought you were a better judge of character than that."

Gladofin's cheeks went pink. "She can be very charming when she wants to be."

"She can, and she's attractive, but we wouldn't suit at all. Reagan has a lot of issues that I wouldn't be able to solve. She has to be loved by someone who needs help."

Gladofin blinked at her. "You found out all this in a couple of hours? Reagan is notorious for putting people off-side immediately. Who *are* you?

"I can read people. It's a gift."

For once, Gladofin looked disconcerted. "Can you read me?"

"Strangely, no. And I don't know why."

"Well, that's a relief." She looked pensive. "I don't often underestimate anyone, Lilybeth, but I have misunderstood you. Now I'm doubly interested to learn more about you."

CHAPTER SIXTEEN

*T*he afternoon was coming to a close when Savannah saw Beria in the distance.

Dog tired after the exhausting few days and the flight from Arcadia, it was a very welcome sight. And a magnificent one as well. Bathed in the oranges and salmon pinks of the sunset, the Palace looked spectacular against the backdrop of the sea. The air was dead calm for a change, the purple moons reflected like glowing globes in the deep-blue water that was peppered with cottony mists. When she took a moment to appreciate the beauty of the darkening sky at dusk, something unusual caught her eye. As she focused on it, she realized what she'd first thought was a shadow was actually the curve of another moon peeping out from behind the larger one.

She gaped at it. The prediction that a third moon — the third eye in the old diary — would appear in the sky with the arrival of the Crevlin, had come to pass.

Then she recalled the old blind seer's words that they could only close the Circle when the moons were aligned. Well, it was here, and they hadn't a clue how long it would be before the moons were in position or where the Covenant of Queens was supposed to be to close the Circle. *Crap!* They were running out of time. Things were beginning to look desperate. They needed an astronomer, but that was someone they hadn't a hope of finding in this world.

"Where do you want me to land, Savannah?"

At Sunflower's query, she snapped her mind back to the present. *"Go straight to the stables. There're too many of us for the courtyard. We can walk up from there,"* she projected back, then signaled with a wave to the group behind that they were about to descend. The ten Blue Fjords, each carrying a Siren and her guard, swung immediately into a wide arc to form one line to follow her down.

One by one they touched down on the grassed area beside the stables.

Jezzine groaned as she dismounted. "I'm pleased to get out of the saddle."

Ketra, who had sat behind her on the double saddle,

nodded in agreement. "Me too. I haven't got used to riding yet."

"If you take the others to the Palace, Jez, I'll help the grooms settle the horses into their stalls," Savannah said. "Tell Lilybeth I'll be there shortly."

As she watched them walk along the side of the stables, she wondered how two races of people could be so different.

The genetic makeup of the Sirens was incredible. Every last one of them was beautiful, with bodies to match. As well, they were all intelligent and graceful, yet surprisingly, few were attached. Savannah couldn't understand why but figured that being creatures of emotion, it was their curse that they would find it hard to find a perfect match.

On the other hand, the Cross Bloods were a raggle-taggle lot, all shapes and sizes from the different Mani bloodlines. But they were all strong and fit, possessing the hybrid vigor of crossbreeding. They made excellent soldiers and guards for the Sirens. She wondered what manner of magical being had fathered Ketra, but she hadn't asked and the information hadn't been offered. She probably was ashamed of her magical heritage, not that Savannah blamed her. The Mani who had come to gamble and party at the Pale Horse Inn had sown their wild oats with the locals, then abandoned their bastard children.

As the last of the group disappeared around the corner, two grooms appeared in the yard to take the horses. She took Sunflower in herself, hoping to find the Countess's mare, Snow Pine. The stately white horse was in one of the larger stalls reserved for important visitors and whinnied when she spied them.

Sunflower pranced with excitement. *"Hello, Grandmother."*

"It's nice to see you, little one. Put her in my stall, Savannah."

"Thanks. She's been dying to tell you all about her adventures. We've had a hectic time since we saw you last."

Snow Pine shuffled over to make room. *"Then I shall be well entertained. The Countess hasn't been riding much lately."*

Savannah laughed. *"I'll tell her you're bored and want a ride. I'll see you both later."*

When she reached the Palace door, only Lilybeth was waiting for her. The Sirens and their guards were nowhere in sight.

"It's good to see you're in one piece, Savannah," Lilybeth said with a somber expression.

"It was horrendous, Ma'am." Savannah hooked two fingers in the air. "Did the *Imperial Queen* arrive?"

"She's safely tucked away in the north wing, which is now out of bounds to staff. Come into my office where we can talk in private. Captain Jocose told us the news of Iona, and I'll bring you up to speed to what's been happening here."

After she'd finished, Savannah said, "So Borrentine came here after he attacked Iona. How did he find out we had captives?"

Lilybeth made a wry face. "We found two spies in the laundry. Everyone coming in will be examined from now on."

"The prisoners are still alive?" asked Savannah anxiously.

"Yes. Borrentine mustn't have known where they were or he would have gone straight there."

Savannah breathed a sigh of relief. "We'll interrogate them tonight. It was lucky Reagan went ahead and examined the Skeldach. To know how they are controlled is a big advantage."

"Not only that, Winston has made a whistle with a high-pitched sound, which we're hoping will confuse them."

"Good. After Iona, we can't delay with the Skeldachs. We'll go to the Isle of Misery in the morning. The sun will be out and they should be underground. We've got the Sirens for back-up if a few are out. How to block the exits may be the problem, but we'll work it out when we get there."

Lilybeth stood up. "Let's go to the planning room. Reagan's there, and they're all anxious to see you."

Before she entered the room, Savannah paused briefly to look at the people inside. They were seated around a table, whittling holes in pieces of hollow reeds. Surprisingly, even Reagan had joined the activity, her face a study of concentration as she carefully smoothed off the ends of the pipe.

The Countess turned when she heard them step inside and rose with a smile. "Savannah. We were wondering when you'd turn up. Is Jezzine here?"

"She and her Sirens will join us for dinner," said Lilybeth. "But for now, Savannah wants to get on with the interrogation."

Savannah stripped off her riding coat then addressed the military operations unit. "Things have escalated. Arcadia received word before I left that King Gerard, Valeria's cousin, was assassinated in the early hours of the morning."

"Oh, no!" exclaimed Lilybeth. "That's a disaster. The Valley of the Pipers will be left with a very young sovereign. Gerard only had one heir, a son, Jonas, and he's just turned seventeen." Her brow furrowed. "Wasn't their General one of the first to fall under the assassin's knife?"

"Yes, he was," agreed Savannah. "It sounds like the Crevlin have a vendetta against that Realm."

Lilybeth's lips thinned into disapproval. "It's one of the poorest Realms, of no real consequence to the crown. The Windy Desert takes up half of its country. Gerard was Valeria's cousin, so I'd say Borrentine's showing her that he has the power to hurt her, the swine."

"Maybe he's trying to goad her to come out of hiding," said Winston.

"That's possible, but he won't succeed. Tamasin will appoint someone to help the young King," said Savannah. "But let's get on to the business at hand. Is it possible to wake the prisoners up immediately, Countess?"

"I have an antidote that works quickly."

Savannah looked over at Reagan. "How do we stop them from turning into Crows before you have a chance to read their minds?"

"I'll immobilize them as soon as they wake up."

"But will that stop them?" she muttered. She glanced at Egwine, Willowtine and Limos. "Can one of you explain how exactly you shift? Is it solely with your minds or do you move parts of your body?"

Limos got up from the table into a clear space. "Our bodies need to be in harmony with our thoughts for the shift to work. If I'm too stiff it's difficult, if I'm unable to move it's impossible. Watch me."

He began to flex his shoulders then stretched his torso and limbs to accommodate the extra body mass.

As his body began to grow, the air around him shimmered until she lost sight of what was happening. When it came back into focus, a Tiger stood looking at her. Savannah reared back nervously, eyeing it warily. It was huge, its muscular shoulders bunched and tail twitching back and forth as if it was ready to pounce. Its lips peeled back, exposing sharp fangs, and eyed her like she was a plate of food.

She ducked behind a chair, telling herself it was all in her mind but it didn't help. When someone tittered, she took no notice. The big cat looked like it could kill her with one swipe of its massive paw.

She was saved from further embarrassment when Reagan cried delightedly, leaping from her chair to stroke the sleek striped back. "Aren't you a pretty fellow," she cooed.

Savannah wasn't surprised — she knew the Enchantress preferred animals to people.

With a last look at Savannah with its yellow eyes, it morphed back into Limos. With a smug look, he returned to his seat.

She cleared her throat, ignoring Winston's snicker. "Thanks for the demonstration. Immobilize the Crevlin the second they come to, Reagan. Let's go."

✝

Though the block of underground cells was dreary and stank of dried seaweed and brine, Savannah wouldn't have described the place as a dungeon. That name brought connotations of the torture chambers of medieval Earth, where incarcerated prisoners were condemned to a life of pain and hopelessness. The Berian prison was clean and well lit, though being on the sea, it was impossible to stop the condensation. It seeped out of the stone walls and ceilings, keeping everything perpetually damp and made the air uncomfortably moist.

Savannah was pleased she'd put on her coat. While the humidity was high, the place was as cold as charity.

After the guard opened the door, the Countess entered first to administer her antidote. She cut a hole in the netting on the first Crevlin, just large enough to open his mouth and cautiously rubbed a liquid inside his gums with her finger. She stepped back, nodding to Reagan to come inside. "Be ready. He'll wake in a minute."

When his eyes fluttered open, Reagan placed her hand on his arm and he went stiff as a board. He remained like a statue, staring at the ceiling. Once the second Crevlin was in a similar state, the Countess exited the cell to allow Savannah to enter.

She knelt beside Reagan who had already begun to

probe. After a few moments, Savannah sent out a gentle feeler to see if she could walk with her through the Crevlin's memories. To her delight, she picked up the thread easily, though was careful to keep on the sideline to merely observe. If Reagan knew she was there, she gave no indication as she continued sifting through the brain. When she moved to the other Crevlin, Savannah crept in after her.

Finally, the Enchantress sank back on her heels and looked across at Savannah. "Did you get it all?"

She caught her Reagan's eye guiltily. "You felt me?"

"You were as clumsy as a hawk in a hen house."

"Oh!" said Savannah disconcerted. "I probably didn't get everything then, but I leaned some interesting facts, including the date he left the past. The Crevlins lived over two and a half thousand years ago. What did you find out?" She waved to Lilybeth and Gladofin. "Come in and listen to what Reagan has to say."

"These two have only been in the future for a few days. They were transported through some sort of time-tunnel funneling through a tall structure like a chimney," Reagan said.

Savannah nodded. "The Time Gateway, presumably. Fern had an old Crevilian map with a spire drawn on it. It was in a big city, which we believed was their capital."

"The countryside where they came from was so

barren it was nearly black," Reagan continued. "It was completely devoid of any grasses or crops, and most of the trees had died. The people were wearing thick coats and head coverings so it must have been very cold. That's why they're coming here. It looks like they're in a catastrophic drought, coupled with freezing temperatures."

Savannah gazed thoughtfully at the Crevlins. They were thin to the point of being gaunt. "They're starving to death."

"Why didn't they migrate to the north?" asked Gladofin.

"I'd say the two cultures hated each other and probably had been fighting for centuries," said Savannah, "Don't forget, the south disliked magic and all the ancient magical royal houses were in the north."

"Did you find out where they're accumulating their main army?" asked Lilybeth.

Reagan shook her head. "It was night when they exited the Time Gateway as Crows and immediately flew to join the battalion readying to attack Iona. I did get the impression they passed over mountains."

"Where was the battalion based?" asked Lilybeth.

"On an island."

Lilybeth nodded. "There are plenty of uninhabited islands in the Sea of Mists."

Savannah felt a flicker of excitement. "Did you get

any idea how long it took them to fly to the island from the time tunnel?"

"They flew all night. But don't forget they're only small birds, so it'd be hard to estimate how far."

"Still," said Savannah, "It's a long way from the sea if they took that long to get there. That's a start."

"There was another thing," said Reagan. "I got the impression they weren't used to being birds."

"I thought that too," said Savannah. "They hated magic, so I doubt they were born with ability to shape shift. They were probably somehow changed to move through time?"

"I agree," said Reagan. "And having been trans-formed, they are birds, not people. That's why when they die they turn back to birds."

"It would require very powerful magic to change a whole race of people," said Gladofin. "Borrentine must be strong."

"Not strong enough to defeat me," murmured Reagan.

"No, he couldn't," mused Savannah. "Maybe he had help to change them."

"I didn't get any vibes there was anyone else," said Reagan. She rose to her feet and looked at Lilybeth. "That's about all I found. What do you want done with them?"

"I'll get the guards to execute them. They're too dangerous alive."

"Don't bother calling the guards," said Reagan, then turned to stare at them. A minute later, both crumbled into dead Crows.

When Lilybeth raised an eyebrow, Reagan said defiantly, "That was for my people they slaughtered."

CHAPTER SEVENTEEN

THE ISLE OF MISERY

*A*fter Savannah shrugged into her flying coat, she arranged the eyeshade on her head.

"You all know the plan. Best of luck," she said to the Sirens, their guards, and the twenty Berian warriors who waited by their horses. Then she nodded to Lilybeth, who was already in the saddle. "I'll meet you and Nerin at the cove. The others will wait on the headland for us."

As soon as the warhorse, Banner rose into the sky, Savannah turned to Jezzine. "I don't expect there'll be much trouble. At noon, most of the Skeldachs will be underground. Hopefully, there will be a few on the outside to reveal the entrance into the caverns. If not, we'll find it ourselves. But please remember that the lizards can hurt the Blue Fjords, so no heroics. Ready the archers, Ketra, in case of trouble. The Hawks circling above will be a deterrent — the Skeldachs don't like big birds."

Satisfied she'd covered all contingencies, Savannah tugged at Sunflower's mane. "Off you go, sweetie. Fly first to that little cove where we met the Madra."

Nerin was waiting on the beach with Lilybeth, and after she greeted Savannah, her dark eyes fixed on her like a hunter's. "I have a couple of stipulations that you must adhere to, Chosen One. No Hawks. The Black Sea Eagles have agreed to stay close if you need them. Call them, and they will come. And do not invoke the Death Vale. That much power unleashed in the sea will make my people too nervous. I've held council with them, and they've agreed to help in the war, but they're still skittish."

Savannah inclined her head. "I understand. Will you be coming onto the island?"

"I'll show you the way, but this is your operation. I'll swim home if Lilybeth wants to go with you."

Savannah quickly shook her head. The Countess had insisted that Lilybeth's wound was too raw for her to be involved in another fight. "Queen Lilybeth will be taking you home." Savannah ignored Lilybeth's glare as she added, "Her arm hasn't healed yet. I trust you'll make sure she takes care of it."

A ghost of a smile crossed Nerin's lips. "Then I will accept a lift home."

"Um. I have a question about the Scaled Serpent Squids, ma'am. Exactly how big are they?" Savannah asked.

"Enormous. They are giant sea dragons with eight arms like a squid; ancient creatures that have lived in these waters from the very birth of creation and are invulnerable to magic. Pray you never meet one because the medallion would be useless against it."

Savannah looked at her curiously. "Then how do you control them?"

Nerin shrugged. "I can make their home very uncomfortable if they annoy me."

"Okay," Savannah said, digesting the information. They sounded terrifying. And if she was honest, Nerin did as well. She gave a glimmer of a smile. "I'll do my best not to fall into the water."

"Make sure you don't." Nerin pointed out to sea. "We'll meet you at that cluster of rocks in five minutes."

Savannah nodded then nudged Sunflower toward the headland. When they touched down, she waved to the leader of the Bramble Hawks. He descended quickly, morphing into a man as soon as he landed. "You have a message, Savannah?"

"Take your squad back to the Palace, Captain. The Black Sea Eagles will be helping us."

He looked uncomfortable. "Commander Pela specifically ordered us to guard you. She won't be pleased if we don't obey her directive."

"I know," she replied patiently, "but it's the Eagles' territory. If you go in there, they'll attack you. They're as possessive of their territory as the Bramble Hawks are of their mountains. Don't worry. I'll square it off with her."

Though he looked dubious, he thumped his chest. "Very well."

After he wheeled back into the sky, she nodded to her troop. "Let's go."

While the weather had been sunny and clear at Beria, it deteriorated the further they flew out to sea. By the time Nerin finally pointed toward an island in the distance, light rain had begun to fall. Though flying in the wet was unpleasant, the approaching island was far more daunting. Dark clouds formed such a heavy blanket over it that she could barely see its outline. Nearer, she could make out sheer high cliffs that were a dirty white color and recalled Nerin had mentioned the top was craggy chalk.

The sea had faded to a dull gray, and haunted by the images of the Sealed Serpent Squids, Savannah periodically peered down to catch any massive shadows beneath the surface.

When they passed over the buffs into a thick

clinging fog, goosebumps rippled across her skin. It was no wonder the place was called the Isle of Misery. It was grim and depressing. She hoped that the squad could keep the formation as they flew in blind — with visibility nearly zero, it would be easy to crash into the horse in front. Cautiously, Sunflower descended through the clouds, then hovered close to the land.

The small island was beyond bleak. With no vegetation, it was desolate, made up of rocks and crevices covered by some sort of black matter. As soon as the squad came through the cloud, Savannah called out, "Find a spot to touch down."

It was only when they were within a few yards of the surface, that she realized what a huge mistake she'd made. At the sound of her voice, the *black matter* began to move, and to her horror, unfurled its wings. The whole landscape became a seething mass of lizards.

Panicked, she frantically pulled at the reins to abort the descent, imploring Sunflower to gain altitude as quickly as possible. There weren't just a few isolated Skeldachs outside, the island was covered in them.

Savannah screamed out, "Sirens. Begin." Then yelled, "Cover your eyes, everyone."

She hastily pulled the heavy mesh over Sunflower's face to protect her eyes and slid the eyeshade over her own. The Sirens began to glow, becoming brighter and brighter until the whole island was bathed in blinding light. The Skeldachs went berserk, panic-stricken as they made a frenzied rush to get underground. Savannah peered through the mask, watching as they disappeared down three holes. There were obviously no more ways to get in, for quite a few were crushed in the jam in their haste to escape the light.

When the Skeldachs had eventually disappeared, Sunflower warily descended onto the island. Still shaking, Savannah dismounted just as cautiously. It had nearly been a disaster. If she hadn't brought the Sirens, Goddess knows what could have happened. They wouldn't have had a hope against so many lizards. There had been thousands of them, and there were probably just as many, if not more in the caverns.

The Crevlin had an unlimited air force supply.

Suddenly, shrieks echoed overhead, and ten large Black Sea Eagles swooped down amongst the cluster of rugged crags on the western and northern sides of the island. A handful of Skeldachs fluttered up from the crevices trying to escape, only to be ripped apart by the Eagles. When one lizard rushed their way, three arrows from the archers immediately took it out of the sky.

Finally finished mopping up the stragglers, the Eagles dipped their wings in an acrobatic display and vanished into the clouds.

When Jezzine hurried over to Savannah, her face had lost its usual composure. "That was frightening," she muttered. "We would have been in deep trouble if it hadn't worked. There were thousands of the ugly things."

"I'm sorry, Jez, I miscalculated badly," Savannah said.

"You weren't to know, and we're alive. Let's close the exits before they come back. I counted three holes."

"Me too. Come on. We'll work out where's the best place to blast to block them in."

The three exit holes turned out to be flaws that tunneled down through the layer of rock to the deep underground caves. Since the shafts didn't go straight down but were angled, she figured it would be easy enough to close them by blasting enough of the rock walls to clog the top sections.

Savannah flexed her fingers at the first hole, letting the electricity seep into her fingertips. "Mount your horses and stand well back. Take to the sky if anything untoward happens."

"I'll stay beside you," said Ketra, "in case you need help."

"Thanks," said Savannah. A backup would be handy if she was hit by any flying debris.

She zapped a burst of magic into the side of the fissure, pleased to see the side collapse into the gaping hole. After another blast at the other side, when the dust settled, the exit was completely covered in rock.

"It worked," Ketra cried out enthusiastically. "They're not going to get out of that one."

Savannah grinned, though more from relief than triumph. "No, they won't. Now onto the next." It proved as simple as the first, the fissure collapsing inward.

The third was different; a six-foot cleft split the limestone surface and fell straight down into some sort of chamber. She figured it probably veered off into passageways from there. When Ketra threw a small crystal into the darkness, Savannah could see it was at least a five-meter vertical drop. A sizable amount of dirt and rubble would be necessary to block it.

"Stand right back from this one, Ketra. I'll need to blast harder."

Savannah let fly again at the wall, watching in satisfaction as it caved in. But when the dust cleared, the hole was still open. "I'll give it another zap," she called out then shot off a bigger burst of power.

The wall exploded with a wrenching bang, but as it filled up the fissure, the earth beneath them began to move. It accelerated in seconds from a tremble to a full-blown quake. Savannah fought to keep her footing, automatically clutching hold of Ketra for support as the shaking and jolting intensified. Suddenly, the limestone cracked open and they plummeted through the hole into the chamber below. As she hit the bottom,

Savannah could hear the earth tumbling after them. As the avalanche of limestone poured down on top of her, Savannah began to choke.

Then Ketra had her by the scruff of her neck, dragging her out of the heap and into a tunnel off to the side of the cave.

Once they were far enough away from the flying debris, Ketra sank heavily beside her and pulled out another crystal. "Last one," she muttered.

Gasping for breath, Savannah wheezed out. "I've another in my coat pocket." She grasped her arm. "Thanks. You saved my life."

"Don't thank me yet," Ketra said grimly. "We're in a whole mess of trouble."

She shone the light around. They were in a wide passageway that ran down through masses of calcite crystal formations. If she hadn't been so worried, Savannah would have been able to appreciate its beauty. "The only way is down," whispered Ketra. "And the Goddess only knows where it's going to lead us."

"Right into the middle of the Skeldachs," muttered Savannah.

Ketra stood up, wiped the white dust off her clothes then said resolutely. "We can die here, Savannah, or we can try to find a way out."

"I know," Savannah said, struggling to her feet. "The Madra told me there is a cave at the bottom that leads out to the sea. If we could reach there, we may have a chance." She didn't mention the Scaled Sea Serpent. They'd overcome that hurdle when they came to it.

Ketra reached for her hand as they rounded the bend. "Careful, we don't know —"

The words dried up as they stepped into space.

And then they fell downwards into an abyss.

CHAPTER EIGHTEEN

THE BERIAN PALACE

*A*s Lilybeth neared home, she could see fog bunched up against the cliffs like ruffles of fine silk.

She felt a flicker of excitement at the thought of the Countess in the Palace, though she knew it was wishful thinking that Gladofin would be waiting for *her*. But she could always dream.

As soon as the groom took her horse, she hurried to the planning room. The group were around the center table, watching as Winston inserted different colored flags into the map. When Gladofin spied her in the doorway, a smile lit up her face.

Lilybeth returned it, suddenly shy, then looked at Winston when he said, "You're back already, Ma'am."

"I took the Madra home. We didn't go onto the

island with the others." She glanced down at the table. "What are you doing?"

Winston scanned the map as he absently twirled a flag in his fingers. "We're trying to work out what the enemy will do next. The colored flags represent various scenarios. You're an accomplished warrior, Queen Lilybeth. What would you do?"

She studied the model thoughtfully. "Presuming Savannah and the Sirens are successful, the elimination of the Crevlin's airpower changes everything. We'll have plenty of time to prepare — they wouldn't have foreseen the loss of the Skeldachs. They'll have to work out another way to throw their bombs."

"Catapults," said Gladofin.

Lilybeth nodded. "Yes. Or they could even float them over somehow. And don't forget Crows can fly. Since I doubt they could be in the air with that weight for long, all their options would require a short-range launch."

"Why won't they just throw them once they're close enough?" asked Willowtine.

"They undoubtedly will when the fighting begins," replied Lilybeth. "But it would be better tactics to fire them from a distance at first. Pela has been fortifying the outskirts of the cities with trenches and traps for weeks. They won't get near easily. If they try to fly in as Crows, the Hawks will pick them out of the sky."

"Would they attack without the bombs?" asked Limos.

"No," said Lilybeth. "They wouldn't give up that advantage."

Winston stroked his beard absently. "They've lost the southern route from the sea by failing to take Beria. With the Sea of Mists at their back, it would have been easy to defend their position. But they know now you have machines that can fire quantities of arrows quickly, Ma'am, which would make them wary of you. I think they'll go elsewhere to begin their assaults."

"I agree. They'll pick an easier target next time."

"As you said, to attack a city, they'll require catapults," said Winston. "And they'll require somewhere hidden to build them. Also, a secret place to gather their army." He pushed in a red flag. "The Great Northern Forests would be ideal. Parts are still wilderness."

"The very spot," agreed Lilybeth. "There are smaller forestlands scattered all over Rand. But except for a couple of the very isolated ones, they're all inhabited."

"Who would they attack first, I wonder," he mused.

"If I were them," said Lilybeth, "I'd try to capture the place Rand can ill afford to lose."

Winston jabbed a black flag into the map. "Arcadia."

"Exactly," said Lilybeth. "They've already crippled Iona. Not only is Arcadia the wealthiest realm, but it is also centrally situated, with a major river that has a network of tributaries to many other places. They don't want a protracted war. They must take and hold a city as soon as possible to feed their starving people."

"Don't forget Savannah and Tamasin are sure they'll be emerging at the City of the Dead. There must be food there," said Egwine.

Winston raised an eyebrow at her. "The whole civilization is coming through the Time Gateway. They'll require a lot to eat." He pointed to the map. "There's the Northern Forest. They'll be forced to move their catapults across the land, and we need to work out their most likely route."

"How many realms to the North of Arcadia?" asked Gladofin.

"Three minor ones. The Arcadian plains are vast." Lilybeth cleared her throat before she went on, "My wife came from Bogonia, a small Queendom which borders the forest. Her sister rules there."

"Great, then you're familiar with the land, Ma'am. Could you describe and point out the pertinent features of the countryside, please. We can formulate a strategy for Pela if the enemy comes that way."

Lilybeth nodded, settled comfortably on a stool and began.

†

Two hours later, Gladofin rose from her chair. "Time for a break. Lunch is in half an hour. By that time, Savannah and her crew should be back."

Lilybeth moved to join her. "Would you take a stroll outside with me? A breath of fresh air would be welcome."

"That would be lovely," Gladofin said with a smile. "I prefer the outdoors."

When they stepped outside, a cool breeze was blowing from the south that brought a hint of the winter months ahead. They leaned on the top of the wall, looking out over the water. Lilybeth took a deep breath, breathing in the scent of Gladofin and the sea. Surprisingly, they went together well.

As Lilybeth turned to study her, a warming sensation seeped into the pit of her stomach. A few strands of Gladofin's blond hair were loose, trailing in the wind. She reached over to brush a wisp from her face, then said without thinking, "Why haven't you ever married, Glad?"

For once, the Countess lost her composure. "It's complicated," she murmured. "I'm a Guardian, a ruler of the Mystical Lands. Though my sister, Olivine, is our Monarch, we Guardians have a duty of care to the people as well."

"How many of you are there?"

"Only fifty. Each presides over a section of the

Forgotten Realms. I've been assisting Olivine at the Amarim Palace, so I've never taken a spouse."

Lilybeth eyed her curiously. "Why did that preclude you from marrying?"

"It was easier to leave things as they were. Perhaps ...," Gladofin shrugged, "Perhaps if I had found someone who — " She cleared her throat, then closed the conversation. "I'm sure you're not interested in all that. Shall we go to lunch?"

Lilybeth could hardly say she was dying to hear *all that*, and reluctantly followed her to the stairs. She wondered how many lovers Gladofin had had over the years. Someone so accomplished and attractive could have had anyone she wanted, but she had the impression that wasn't the case. Maybe as she had said, it *was* complicated.

At the dining-room door, Gladofin said, "You go in. I'll take lunch to our guest."

Lilybeth watched her go, her emotions in a jumble. As they'd stood at the wall, she'd wanted to lean closer, just enough so their arms would brush together. To touch. She'd never had that urge before with anyone other than Maybeth. Her daughter had been an affectionate child, and though not so much as she grew older, sometimes she still hugged her for no reason whatsoever. She missed that closeness, that connection to someone.

Perhaps her feelings for this magical woman were a reaction to Maybeth's absence. After all, she hadn't known Gladofin long, certainly not time enough to form a solid attachment. But still, she couldn't ignore the pull. Desire wasn't reserved for the young. If anything, it was to be valued more with age.

When she entered the dining room, Lilybeth silently groaned to see Reagan sitting in the chair beside hers. One had to be in the mood to take the Enchantress's acerbic wit, and she certainly wasn't in the right frame of mind. And Reagan was looking at her like the cat who swallowed the canary. Lilybeth frowned at her, fully aware she was strolling around in her mind. She looked at her pointedly and said, "You promised."

Reagan chuckled. "Sorry. I couldn't resist. You were blaring out your thoughts. How's the Countess?" she asked slyly.

Leaning over, Lilybeth admonished her sternly. "Your meddling is going to get you into a whole heap of trouble. One day, you'll meet your match."

"Only Savannah is capable of blocking me," she replied, then added bitterly, "and the Siren, Jezzine."

"Everyone else isn't fair game, Reagan. We have a right to our privacy."

"Tch, tch, Lilybeth. You're so stodgy. When have you ever done anything remotely risqué?"

Lilybeth pursed her lips. "Not all of us have the

212 | COVENANT OF QUEENS

luxury of doing whatever we want without a thought for others. I have people relying on me."

Her face softening, Reagan squeezed Lilybeth's hand gently. "You're a fine woman. She's not good enough for you," she whispered, then chuckled. "None of us are."

At the sound of footsteps, Lilybeth looked up to see Pela. As usual, she strode into the room as if she owned it. She bowed briefly to Lilybeth. "Your Majesty."

"It's good to see you, Commander. Have some lunch with us."

"Thank you, Ma'am," she said with a nod, taking the seat on the other side.

Leaning back in her chair, Reagan eyed her with interest. "So, Pela, Queen of the Bramble Hawks, we meet at long last."

"I know who you are, Enchantress," Pela said. But as she bent to take a plate, she stiffened. A second later, she leaped to her feet. "Get out of my mind, witch."

Reagan stared up at her. "Oh my, aren't you an interesting one. You're more than just a Hawk — you have old magic in your veins," she said incredulously.

Pela's chin jutted out, her hand bunched into a fist on her hip. "I won't tell you again. Get. Out. Of. My. Mind."

Rising from her chair, Reagan gave a soft laugh. "You might be strong, Pela, but you're no match for me."

"Then bear the consequences," said Pela savagely and immediately morphed into a Hawk.

Lilybeth gaped at it. Inside this confined space, it looked enormous. Suddenly, a chair scraped back, and a huge Tiger shimmered into view. It padded over to stand beside Reagan and bared its teeth at the bird. When the Hawk, with its talons flexed, began to flap its wings, the Tiger let out a loud growl.

Lilybeth did the only thing she could think of to stop the looming fight. She stepped in between them.

"Calm down, both of you," she pleaded.

"No, Lilybeth," Reagan called out in alarm. "Get away. They've lost control."

But it was too late. The Tiger glared at her, bunching its muscles to pounce. Its massive wings outstretched, the Hawk rose with a shriek into attack position.

Suddenly, a crackling noise filled the air. Shards of powered ice materialized out of thin air. They formed into mini blizzards, lashing the animals, whipping around them until they were half-frozen and stiff. The Tiger sprawled facedown onto the floor, its fur thick with icicles. The Hawk vainly tried to flap away, then succumbed to the weight of the ice and crashed in an ungainly heap against the wall. They both went still.

Reagan fell with a scream to her knees, her face contorted in agony.

Lilybeth turned quickly around. Winston and the other two Mani were huddled in the corner while Gladofin stood on the threshold, her arms outstretched, her body glowing white with rage.

She marched into the room and said brusquely to Winston, "You three go back to the planning room — now."

They fled without a word.

Gladofin glanced briefly at Lilybeth, then stood over Reagan, who looked like she was about to be sick. "You went too far this time, Enchantress. We are here at Queen Lilybeth's invitation, and you nearly got her killed by your constant meddling. Now feel my judgment. You are banished until we call for you to close the Circle. I'll arrange with Tamasin to take you somewhere from where you cannot escape. I believe she has such a place. Once there, you will behave or by the Goddess, I will personally make you pay. Now get out of my sight."

Reagan staggered to her feet, then bowed her head in submission. "Of course, Countess." She looked across at Lilybeth. "I'm sorry, Your Majesty. I didn't mean it to go so far."

Only after Reagan had disappeared out the door did Gladofin turn to regard her, though didn't quite meet her eye. "I apologize for my people, Lilybeth. It was unforgivable."

Lilybeth blinked at her. She'd had no conception just how powerful the Guardians were. "It wasn't your fault," she said hoarsely, a little shaky now it was over. "I shouldn't have stepped between them."

"I'm sorry you had to see that. You and the rest of Rand have a lot to learn about the Magical Folk," Gladofin said wearily. "Even though the Mani are people, they still have the instincts of wild animals when they feel threatened in their other forms. We Guardians keep them in order. And civilized."

Lilybeth looked at her in awe. "And I thought Reagan was powerful."

"She is, but nowhere near as dominant as I am." She looked over at the Tiger and the Hawk. "I'd better wake up those two."

CHAPTER NINETEEN

*P*ela groggily sat up.

When she rose to her feet, for once, she looked ashamed. "I'm sorry, Your Majesty. It was unforgivable of me."

The Countess crossed her arms. "We are guests here, Commander. And not thugs. Queen Lilybeth is willing to forget the indiscretion, but it can't happen again. Since I know how aggravating Reagan can be, I will let the incident pass. Limos gets one last chance, but that pesky Enchantress does not. I'm sending her to Tamasin's safe place."

Pela raised an eyebrow. "Valeria is there."

"Yes. And the Monarch has a temper. Reagan would be well advised to watch her manners around her. The Imperial Line's magic is far stronger than hers."

Lilybeth hid a smile. She had never seen the much-feared Commander so meek.

Gladofin walked over to the Tiger and prodded it with her boot. "Wake up, Limos."

When his yellow eyes fluttered open, the Tiger stared in alarm at the Guardian towering over it.

"Change," she ordered.

Immediately, he morphed back into a man and shivered. "Sorry, Countess," he croaked out.

Gladofin narrowed her eyes. "Apologize to the Queen and go back to the planning room. Any more displays like that, and you can go back home."

He bowed his shaggy head. "I'm sorry, Ma'am," he said and shuffled out the door.

Gladofin rubbed her hands together. "Now that's over, shall we have something to eat. Have you any news, Pela?"

"Nothing new to report. The cleanup of Iona continues," she said and described the damage to the city.

As Lilybeth listened to Gladofin relate what they'd learned from the captured Crevlins, she was amazed at how easily the Mani involved in the almost disastrous confrontation moved on. It was as if the hostile events of the last half hour, once resolved, were forgotten or at least disregarded. It had taught Lilybeth that her preconceptions of the Forgotten Realms as an orderly, civilized place were way off the mark. And that the Countess wasn't as gentle and benign as she thought. When Gladofin wove her magic at the door, there had been a wildness about her that matched the two animals in the room. But instead of fearing her, Lilybeth's warrior blood had surged with exhilaration. Here was a woman worth fighting for.

As soon as the maid cleared away the dishes, Gladofin stood up. "Shall we adjourn to the others, Pela? We've been working on some strategies."

"I'd be interested to hear what you've come up with." She looked over at Lilybeth. "When are Savannah and the Sirens due back?"

"Any time now. It's been a few hours since I returned. After the Madra led them to the island, I took her back home."

"Right. Let's hope they were successful. My plans for the defense of Rand rest on the enemy having no air power. We'll go back to the Skeldach's island if they didn't manage to block their exits. But knowing Savannah," Pela added with pride, "she'll find a way."

"As long as there are only a limited number of entrances to the subterranean caverns, they shouldn't have any problem," assured Lilybeth.

When the Countess walked into the planning room, even Winston looked subdued. He bowed deferentially to her without his usual cheeky smile before he said to

Pela, "The colored flags are the various routes the enemy may take, Commander."

Pela studied the map, asking questions as she went. "Your best guess, Winston?"

He pointed to the red flags. "They'll gather their forces in the Great Northern Forests and try to take Arcadii. They'll make catapults, then carry them down in pieces, or barge them, and assemble them outside the city. As soon as they're ready, they'll begin to bomb." He pointed to a few strategic places along the way. "Their armies will be compelled to take those positions to get their main forces through."

Pela flicked a look at Lilybeth. "You agree, Ma'am."

"Yes. But foremost, we must hold the bridges. They'll be key to stopping them."

"And the three realms in their pathway to the river?" asked Pela.

"How can we defend so much countryside? It would be better to evacuate those realms and concentrate on keeping the enemy north of the Cadiwine," said Lilybeth. "Hawks can patrol if they try to fly over, but to move their weapons, they must march."

"What do you think, Winston?" asked Pela.

He frowned at the map. "I'm not so sure. My normal strategy is to exploit my opponent's weaknesses. We're playing the standard wargame here, which may or may not result in victory. Whatever way, many lives will be lost."

"I agree," said Pela. "As soon as I heard they were starving, it became clear how to defeat them. We will evacuate every person and all livestock north of the river. Towns will be stripped of all food stores, and we'll burn the crops. Our troops will keep niggling away at their perimeters with hit-and-run skirmishes, and night raids. Enough to slow them down. They'll find some food in the forest, but they'll find none when they march. We'll starve them into submission. I have no intention of losing many lives in this war if I can help it. Hawks will be mobilized ... there are thousands living in the mountains. No Crow will be safe in the sky." She smiled sourly. "We will do the same for every city they try to take."

"Brilliant," exclaimed Winston. "Now, all that's left is to find out if they are in the Great Northern Forest. How do we do that, I wonder?" he mused, staring at the map. "Its vast, with large tracts of nearly impenetrable wilderness."

Pela tilted her head around to address Gladofin. "Could your spy network find them, Countess?"

"Perhaps. I'll send my little birds to search — they can slip around unnoticed. However, the Gray Wolves would be better. That is if I can persuade them to go in."

Lilybeth threw her a surprised glance. "I thought you could control animals."

Both Gladofin and Pela laughed. "Not the Wolves. They're a law unto themselves."

"Are they Mani?"

"No. But they are intelligent creatures who can be very uncooperative," replied Gladofin. "And they hate the Hawks, so Pela can't go there."

"Can you speak to them?"

"To their leader," Gladofin said. "I'll leave tomorrow Pela. I promised Olivine I'd help with her preparations."

Lilybeth's heart sank. She'd thought Gladofin was staying for the duration of the war, but now it turned out she was going home to Amarim. "Are you coming back?" she asked in a small voice, then cringed. Dear Goddess, she sounded pathetic.

Gladofin raised her eyebrows at the question. "I'll only be a week. Jayden will be liaising with Pela about military matters."

"Oh, right," murmured Lilybeth, perking up.

"Where is Tamasin, Pela?" asked Gladofin. "I want to talk to her about Reagan."

"She went to Arcadii to say goodbye to Wren. The Queen is failing."

"Oh, dear. It's a sad time for Arcadia. Jezzine will be anxious to get back to Fern." Gladofin looked out the window at the moons and frowned. "It's past two. They should have been back by now. I wonder what's holding them up."

Pela's expression tightened. "How long did it take you to get to the island, Lilybeth?"

"Just over half an hour."

"And you left when?"

"After breakfast ... about eight," Lilybeth said.

Pela tapped her fingers impatiently on the table. "I wonder why they're late. My Hawks were under strict instructions to come back to tell us if anything was wrong, so I guess nothing serious has happened."

Lilybeth cleared her throat. "Um ... no Hawks went, Commander. The Madra forbade them entering the Black Sea Eagles' territory."

Pela thumped her fist down on the table. "I ordered them to go with Savannah. By the Gods, I'll rip the skin off their hides." She bounded off the stool and strode to the door. "Tell the Captain of the Hawks to get in here immediately," she yelled to the guard outside. The soldier took one look at Pela's face and raced off down the corridor.

Lilybeth, feeling pity for the hapless Captain, said softly. "Please, Commander, it wasn't his fault. The Madra rules the seas. They couldn't have gone."

When a tattooed man ran in a few minutes later, Pela bared her teeth at him. He flinched as if waiting for the axe to fall.

"You left your post," she ground out.

He snapped to attention. "Savannah commanded us to. We had no option."

"And it didn't occur to you that they are well overdue, and you should be in the air to find out why?"

"How can we, Commander? We were told the Black Sea Eagles would fight us to protect their territory. I didn't want to cause an incident with the sea folk."

Pela narrowed her eyes. "Having met the Madra, I'll accept that excuse. But have a few brains, God damnit. Don't go out there as Hawks. Get on some horses to have a look."

"Yes, Commander." He thumped his chest and ran out the door.

She shook her head in frustration. "The lot of them could do with some training at Falcon's Keep. They've been playing lords of the mountains with no real discipline for far too long. When this is over, there will be programs set up." She put on her coat. "I'll go and saddle my horse."

Lilybeth grasped her arm. "I'll come with you, Pela. We mustn't forget the sea is out of our control."

Pela nodded. "Very well. Let's go."

But before they reached the door, the guard burst into the room. "Riders are coming in, Ma'am."

"How many?" asked Lilybeth, the expression on her soldier's face lodging a feeling of dread in her stomach.

After a concerned glance at Pela, the guard said stoically, "They counted only nine, Your Majesty."

By the time Lilybeth turned to say something to Pela, the Commander was already racing down the stairs that led to the front courtyard.

CHAPTER TWENTY

THE ISLE OF MISERY

*a*s she toppled into the darkness, Savannah jammed her eyes shut.

Memories of her fall at Falcon's Keep flooded back, but she knew this time there would be no magic bullet to save her. She wasn't going to get out of this one. Her terror receded into a quiet inevitability as she braced herself for impact.

Then something unexpected happened.

A thought popped into her head, *"I've got you,"* and it wasn't the old blind seer's voice. It was Ketra's.

Immediately, a thick furry tail wound around her waist, abruptly halting her free fall as if a parachute had opened. They began to glide, though there was no flutter of wings from the strange creature that held her. Savannah awkwardly swiveled her head to look up, just able to make out in the gloom that the creature's skin was stretched like a sail from its wrists to its ankles. It mimicked the action of a paraglider as it floated from side to side in a gentle descent, skillfully avoiding all the jutting obstacles on the way down.

Savannah knew what it was — Ketra had shifted into a Squirrel Glider.

As they sailed down, the cavern walls looked like they were covered with glow worms but then she realized they were the eyes of the Skeldachs. As she began to panic when they stirred, she caught a thought, *"Blow the whistle."*

Annoyed she hadn't thought of it herself, she dug in her pocket for the hollow reed, not an easy task while swinging from the tail. When she managed to extract it, she blew it hard as she could. The glowing eyes wavered and came no closer.

They kept gliding through a network of four chambers in the limestone: two were steep and narrow, while the other two were larger, filled with stalagmites and stalactites. Between each cavern, they had to walk through rocky passageways until they could take to the air again.

Held by Ketra's tail, Savannah continuously blew the whistle furiously to keep the lizards at bay. Finally, when they entered a fifth cavern with a stream and a series of deep pools, she knew they had reached the bottom of the island. A light glowed in the distance, which Savannah hoped was the exit to the outside. She had lost track of time but thought at least two to three hours had passed since they'd fallen into the hole.

As they glided down, she could see they had a huge problem. Hordes of Skeldachs were perched on the towering stone columns and squatted like malignant melanomas on the floor. When they floated into their line of vision, the lizards stirred, then reared up and unfurled their wings. Though she readied her magic, she was aware that against so many that it would be hopeless. And she had promised not to invoke the Death Vale. Not that she could have anyhow in this confined space — the whole island would probably implode with so much power.

She dived back into her pocket for the crystal, holding it up to let the light stream through the cavern while she held the reed in the other hand. It had an immediate effect. With high-pitched squeals, the lizards cowered back and scurried into the shadows.

As soon as Savannah dropped to the ground, the Squirrel Glider landed beside her. In the light, she was able to get a good look at it. It was nearly her size and pretty as a picture with its large eyes, pink nose, soft brown fur, and enormous bushy tail.

With a twitch of its whiskers, it shimmered and morphed into Ketra.

Savannah smiled at her. "Your magical form is so cute."

Ketra cleared her throat and pulled out her crystal and reed pipe. "We won't be able to hold them off forever. What do we do now?"

Savannah pointed to the glow in the distance. "Head there. With luck, it will be the entrance to the sea. I'll call Sunflower when we get close." She swallowed back her misgivings. "That is if they're still up there. It seems we've been gone a long time."

Sidling close, Ketra held up her crystal. "Let's get out of this first before we worry about that. The damn things are moving toward us," she muttered. "The light isn't strong enough. There must be hundreds in here with us."

"I'll try to conjure up more light, then we'll make a dash for it," Savannah said. She let magic leak from her fingertips until she'd fashioned it into a ball of electricity. Bright bursts of pure energy radiated in waves through the cavern. When the Skeldachs retreated from the light, she ran.

Ketra sprinted after her, soon passing her with her long legs. Hearing the rush of wings behind, Savannah strained to keep up. Halfway to the entrance, Ketra turned abruptly and tossed her crystal into the Skeldachs. Savannah threw the ball of magic in amongst them as well and didn't look back. Seconds ticked away until finally, a cave with an ocean backdrop was within reach. Panting, they burst through the entrance, expecting the lizards to swarm over them. But all was quiet behind.

Taking a deep breath, Savannah turned to look. Not a Skeldach in sight.

Ketra gave a gasping whoop. "The rotten things are gone."

"Yes," said Savannah, knowing perfectly well why. This entrance was the lair of the Scaled Serpent Squid. "Um … Ketra. I hate to tell you this, but we're not safe yet. We've jumped from the cooking pot into the fire."

A frown furrowed Ketra's brow. "If you can't call Sunflower, I'll help you scale the cliff. Squirrel Gliders are expert climbers."

"We won't get that far," Savannah grumbled. "There's a monster guarding the entrance to the sea."

"What kind of monster?"

"A nasty one. And my magic won't work on it."

Ketra swore. "And we've got to get past it to get out of this place?"

"Yep." Savannah cocked her head, straining for sounds. "Listen. Do you hear it?" A gurgling sound echoed in the cave, followed by the swish of water. She peered into the sea that had begun to heave. A long tentacle suddenly emerged, whipping through the air.

"Duck," screamed Savannah, diving onto the ground.

It flew over their heads, then when another appeared, Ketra grasped her arm and dragged her behind a limestone pillar. "How many tentacles has it?" she gasped out.

"Eight. It's a sea dragon with arms like a squid."

"It must be an ugly son of a bitch," muttered Ketra. "I can't even visualize it."

A moment later, the water began to churn. When a monstrous head appeared through the turbulence, Savannah stared at it, aghast. It resembled neither a dragon nor a serpent but had a round head covered in scales with a single curved horn above a flat snout, though it was the enormous mouth bristling with rows of sharklike teeth that dominated the head. It looked like it could swallow them whole.

"By the Gods. How can we fight that thing?" Ketra squealed.

"We can't," said Savannah. "Maybe I can talk to it."

She sent a feeler into its mind, searching for its memories.

"Get out of my head, witch." The words were a succession of clicks and sharp squeaks, but Savannah had no trouble understanding them.

"We wish passage through to the outside," she said back in its language.

It uncoiled its body, dipping its head close to the pillar. "You can speak the ancient tongue of the sea? How is that possible?"

"I can speak all the languages of Rand, old and new."

It sniffed the air, then snorted, shooting out a spray of black inky glob. "I can smell powerful old magic. Who are you, and why do you come into my domain?"

Grimacing, Savannah wiped a streak of snot from her face. "I am the Chosen One. We came to keep the flying lizards permanently underground. We succeeded, but we're caught down here. I ask that you let us pass. We mean you no harm."

The Scaled Serpent Squid made a sound that Savannah interpreted as a laugh. "You cannot harm me, puny one. I am invulnerable to your magic." It circled the pillar with a tentacle and ripped it down.

Left exposed, Savannah quickly nudged Ketra behind her and forced herself to stand her ground. "I know that, but we are friends of the Madra. She won't be pleased if you kill us."

"Pah! This is my territory. She and I have agreed on that," it snarled.

Too late, Savannah realized her mistake in mentioning the Madra. It clearly didn't like her. "But why kill us?" said Savannah, desperate now. There was no way she was going to calm the beast down. But as that thought came, something clicked in her head.

Rozen, Pela's mother, had said those words when she had given her the vial before Savannah had run The Gauntlet. *This will calm down the beast.*

She grasped the lifeline. She slid her hand into her cloak pocket, nearly staggering with relief when she found the little bottle still tucked in the corner. She eased it out, pulled off the cork, and pressed a fingertip over the top.

"I'll kill you now, Chosen One, just to annoy the Madra." When it opened its mouth wide, all she could see were teeth.

With all her strength, she threw the bottle into its mouth.

As the violet-colored liquid splashed onto its tongue and gums, the Squid swallowed, and the vial disappeared into its stomach.

"Drop down," Savannah yelled, but whatever was in the potion worked immediately.

The beast reared back, its eyes widening, its pupils dilating. It began to hum, not in alarm but with what sounded like pleasure. When it swayed erratically, it looked like it was stoned. After a few minutes, its eyes began to droop, and the head fell to the ground. She gingerly poked it with her foot — it was out of it.

She pulled Ketra's arm urgently. "Come on before it wakes."

They sidled around the sleeping monster, careful

not to touch it. Once past, they dashed out of the cave onto the tongue of sand that jutted to the water's edge. With no hesitation, Ketra changed back into a Squirrel Glider, swung her tail around Savannah, and began to climb.

"Sunflower, can you hear me?" Savannah projected urgently.

Instantly, the reply came, *"Savannah. Where are you?"*

Relief swept through Savannah. *"Thank God, you're still there. We're climbing the cliff. Bring another horse without a rider to get us. I think it's on the north side."*

"I'm coming."

"The horses are on their way, Ketra," she called out.

The Squirrel Glider barked.

Just as Savannah was congratulating herself on their escape, she looked down. To her horror, the water was churning beneath them, and a long tentacle was swinging upward.

"Faster, Ketra, faster," she yelled frantically. "There's another one of the shitty things down there."

As the Squirrel Glider scrambled desperately up the cliff, Savannah kicked out with her boot at the tentacle. With more luck than good management, it knocked the end against a sharp rock. The Squid squealed, flopping the limb back into the water. As another tentacle snaked out, three horses, two with riders, dropped out of the sky beside them. The front Guard fired an arrow, piercing the top of the tentacle. The other Guard riding Sunflower grasped Savannah by the arm and hauled her onto the saddle. When the Squirrel Glider released its tail, it wound it around the spare horse's neck and swung onto its back. Safely aboard, Ketra changed back and wriggled into the saddle. The guards looked on bemused.

Savannah didn't need to hear the thoughts of the Scaled Serpent Squid to know it was furious. The sea was boiling. The last thing she saw when they reached the top, was a mass of tentacles writhing in the air.

As soon as they landed, Jezzine ran over and hugged them both tightly. "I'm so glad to see you. We thought you had no hope of surviving. We couldn't imagine how anyone could live with all that rubble on top of them, let alone make it through the Skeldachs."

Savannah glanced across at the Guards. They were covered in white dust and looked exhausted. "You tried to dig us out?"

The Captain gave a tired smile. "We had to try, though we knew it was hopeless."

"Thank you," said Savannah, her emotions raw. "We were worried everyone would have left by now."

Jezzine reached up to pat Sunflower who had her chin on Savannah's shoulder. "There was no way your horse was going to budge. The Sirens tried to help but they're not used to manual labor so I sent them back to

Beria to let them know what happened. They left half an hour ago. Ketra's people insisted on staying to dig with the Palace Guards. How did you manage to get through alive?"

"If it wasn't for Ketra, we'd still be down there. She saved my life. I'll tell you all about it when we get back to Beria." Then calmer, her heart back in place, she realized what they'd achieved. She broke into a smile. "We did it. The Skeldachs are stuck down there now."

CHAPTER TWENTY-ONE

*S*avannah climbed into the saddle, beyond relieved to be getting off the Isle of Misery, which certainly lived up to its name.

She'd never been in such a depressing place. It smelt of decay, and the limestone rocks looked like bleached bones. There were no sea birds nesting and chattering on the island, or any sign of the white gulls that forever wheeled over the Sea of Mists. Only an ominous silence, more frightening than the screeching of a thousand birds.

The blanket of fog seemed to be a permanent fixture, wet, thick, and cloying. It clung to Savannah's nose and infiltrated her clothes. Anxious to leave, she pointed the Farsight Stone to the northeast to check out the passage. No jutting rock formations were in their way, but the Sea of Mists lived up to its name. A squall twisted tightly like a corkscrew on the eastern horizon, and northward, a black cloud scudded across the white-capped water. On the verge of tucking away the Stone, her sixth sense trumpeted a warning. She took another look at the cloud, a much longer one this time. There was something not quite right about it — even for a storm, it moved too quickly.

Then she realized it was a large flock of black birds. Hundreds of them. And they were heading straight for the island.

She sucked in a sharp breath. Crows.

No wonder the Skeldachs had been out of the caverns when they'd arrived. They'd been waiting for their riders.

Crap! They couldn't be caught on the ground.

"Quickly. The Crevlin are coming in from the north. We must be in the air before they land," she called out and pulled the reins to the south. "Get off this place as fast as you can, Sunflower."

Requiring no urging, the mare leaped straight into the air while the others soared quickly into formation behind. Only when they were well clear of the island and had swung back to the mainland, did Savannah fully relax.

Halfway to the Berian coast, a squad of Blue Fjords appeared in the distance. As they neared, she had no trouble recognizing the tattooed faces or the imposing figure of Pela astride Lilybeth's warhorse, Banner, in front. Pela smiled broadly, touched her hand to her heart, and then turned her squad around to escort them in.

As soon as they dismounted at the stables, Pela strode over to Savannah and without a word, pulled her into a bear hug. She returned the embrace, rocking into the solid body. When they broke apart, they looked at each other silently. Savannah had never seen such raw emotion on Pela's face.

But then the anguish vanished, and her face tightened. "Why do you persist in taking so many risks?" she said sharply.

"We didn't foresee so much trouble," she said quietly.

"You must be more careful."

"I know," Savannah replied, knowing how worried she'd been. "I'll tell you all about it later, but first I want a hot bath to soak away the stench of that place."

Lilybeth and the Countess were waiting out the front, relief etched into their faces. Lilybeth strode forward with a smile. "You and Ketra are a sight for sore eyes, Savannah. The Sirens were convinced you were dead. You seem to have a knack for extracting yourself from impossible situations, but questions can be answered later. From the look of all of you, it's been a harrowing morning. The maids have drawn up baths, and we'll meet in the dining room in an hour." She saluted the officer of the Guard. "Take a few hours off, Lieutenant. You can give me your report later."

"Thank you, Ma'am," she said and disappeared with her soldiers to the barracks.

✝

Savannah was soaking in the bath when she heard Pela enter. Pela looked down at her, and said in a voice more wistful than censorious, "What am I going to do with you, Savannah? You have no concept of danger."

Savannah chuckled. "That's where you're completely wrong. I have the utmost respect for the places and people of Rand, but I wear the medallion so it comes with the territory. If I succumb to fear, I wouldn't be able to do anything." She splashed a little water on her. "Now stop glowering and get in the tub with me. I'll wash your back."

With a resigned shrug, Pela stripped off and eased into the water. Savannah lathered on the soap, running her hands lightly over the puckered scars. "Tell me, Pel, why was your father so cruel to you? You never talk about him, or why he gave you these scars."

When Pela tried to ease forward, Savannah wrapped her legs around her waist in a vice. For a long moment, Pela didn't reply, but then slumped back in resignation. "I think it was because he feared me, or he was just plain jealous. I was never sure. I only know he hated me. You see, my bloodline was much stronger than his."

"He wasn't your father?" Savannah asked in surprise.

"He sired me all right. But my mother's father was a Sylph, a magical being from the ancient House of the Iriwari, creatures of the wind. After the purge of the Magical Houses, the few Sylphs that were left retreated into the high Alps and never came out."

It seemed to Savannah to be a dreary existence living so isolated and never coming down to visit anyone. "What do they do up there?" she asked curiously.

"They're scholars. They study the sun, the moons, the stars, the Celestial Realms."

"How do they pay for things they can't make or grow?" she persisted.

"They formulate yearly weather predictions which they trade for essentials. Also, star charts."

Savannah felt a stir of excitement. If anyone would know about the third moon, these people would. "Have you ever seen them, Pel?"

"No. I was young when I left the Forgotten Realms. I never ventured that far."

Savannah pondered over this. It explained why Pela wasn't affected by the Curse the Magicians put on the Wall; people with old magic, like the Sylphs, were immune. And being from a scholarly race accounted for her intellect. More and more, she was realizing that this world was all about bloodlines.

"Where are these mountains?"

"They're the Zorian Alps, in the far Northern regions of the Forgotten Realms. They're the highest mountains in Rand, and inaccessible unless you know where you're going."

"Hmm," murmured Savannah. "The Iriwari should know the secret of the third moon. Its edge is already just visible behind the larger moon."

Pela swiveled her head to look at her. "I noticed it today. Don't for one minute think you're going up there. The Iriwari are reclusive, Savannah, and don't like visitors."

"Then how did your grandmother meet one of them?"

"She became lost in a storm, nearly perished, and was found by a Sylph who took her to their village to recuperate. They fell in love and she became pregnant. But because marrying an outsider was forbidden, and fearing the anger of the Iriwari ruling council, she returned home to her Bramble Hawk community. My mother said her mother never forgot her Sylph lover even though she eventually married one of her own."

"Oh," exclaimed Savannah, "that's so sad. Did your mother ever go up there to meet them?"

"I have no idea. Maybe when she was young she may have, though I doubt it. They probably wouldn't have welcomed her. And she wouldn't have gone after she married my father. He was a very jealous man," Pela said.

"You would think he would be proud to know his daughter had old magic in her veins," mused Savannah.

Pela snorted. "He hated anyone smarter than he was."

She rubbed Pela's shoulder soothingly. Being subjected to a life defined by rejection, it was no wonder she left her home. "After my experience with him, I can understand what you had to endure. My upbringing was so different. My father was a kind man, who never laid a hand on me. Even though I displayed some unusual talents when I was young, he never questioned whether they were genuine."

"What sort of things?"

"I had dreams that came true, and sometimes I had a premonition when something was about to happen. In my studies, I could easily pick out the important pieces in a long boring manuscript." She giggled. "I didn't tell him I could talk to the cat."

Pela looked at her quizzically. "Could you talk to any other animal?"

"Only the cat. It was a real fur baby, and Mum said it was a special breed. I suspect now it had magical qualities." Then Savannah sobered. "All I wanted was to be like the other kids. I began to resent my powers and ignored them. Perhaps that was the one place my parents failed me. They never encouraged me to embrace my gifts. It was as if they were terrified for me."

Pela climbed out of the tub and said as she reached for a towel, "They probably were."

"I guess. People can be cruel. In my world, anyone different usually gets a hard time. It's human nature to try to make everyone fit into the same narrow box. I'm finding Rand, with all its magic, is so much more tolerant," said Savannah, then added, "The Sylphs sound interesting."

"Forget about them," said Pela curtly. "The Zorian Alps aren't safe. As well as being tremendously high, savage unpredictable winds can blow up at any time without warning. And there are treacherous magical places that will tie you in knots."

"Okay," said Savannah, taking a towel off the rack. "I hadn't intended going up there alone."

"Good. Now let's get dressed and have something to eat."

Savannah followed her out of the bathroom, already planning when she'd go to see the Iriwari. She'd told Pela the truth. She had no intention of going up there by herself; she intended to ask Pela's mother, Rozen to take her there.

CHAPTER TWENTY-TWO

THE ARCADIAN PALACE

*A*s if the city was already in mourning, the streets of Arcadii were nearly deserted.

When Malkia soared high over the Palace spire, the largest moon caught Tamasin's eye. It appeared to be jumping out of the sky, but after she took another, longer look, she realized the shadow that gave it the three-dimensional appearance was the edge of another moon. Tingles of panic shot through her. The third eye was here, and she hadn't any idea where the Queens were supposed to be to close the Circle.

She figured, logically, that it must be where the Time Gateway emerged, but it was a puzzle proving hard to solve. Somewhere on Rand was a place so isolated that a whole race of people expected to enter undetected. But where remained a mystery. Her spy network had turned up nothing.

Her mind flashed back to the dream she'd had in the early hours of the morning. This one had been so vivid she'd wondered if she'd actually been awake and it was real.

A shadowy figure had formed in the mist, followed by a familiar voice.

"The alignment has started, Tamasin. You must find the City of the Dead."

"Where is it?" she gasped out.

"I have no idea. The Crevlin have hidden it well this time."

Tamasin tried to get her head around this. "Isn't it in the same place as last time?"

"No. The name is merely a figure of speech. It refers to a city that should have died." The Goddess of Dreams sounded as frustrated as Tamasin.

"Oh. We didn't know that." She tossed restlessly. "Why are you helping us?"

"Because the wielders of the old magic have interfered long enough."

Tamasin strained to see her, but, as always, she was only a floating wisp. "Are you talking about the ancient Houses like the Sirens of Sunhaven?"

"No. They will have a place in the new world. There is older magic than that. Darker, more powerful magic."

"Like yours?" asked Tamasin.

The answer was filled with sadness. "Yes, Tamasin, like mine."

"Are you a Goddess?"

"Ask Savannah," she said. "Now, there is something you must do. You are to take the Enchantress to Kandelora. Since King Borrentine is aware of her existence, he will send assassins to kill her. She's the only one of her kind — it's vital she's kept alive to take her place in the Circle. Go to Beria today."

"She won't go," said Tamasin, "and I wouldn't be able to make her."

A soft chuckle echoed in the dream. "Countess Gladofin has already banished her. Reagan is no match for a Guardian, especially an angry one."

After the dream faded, Tamasin had woken with a shudder. She'd lifted her head off the sweat-soaked pillow, beginning to think they wouldn't find the elusive City of the Dead in time. Especially since it turned out it wasn't even a city — it could be a hole in the ground for all she knew.

She drew her mind back to the present and put the dream aside for later. She was here to say goodbye to Wren.

Fern must have been keeping a look out for her, for she appeared on the top of the steps when Malkia touched down in the Arcadian Palace courtyard.

As soon as Tamasin dismounted, she hurried up the

stairs and pulled Fern into a tight hug. "How's your mother?" she asked softly.

Fern bit back a sob. "She took a turn for the worse during the night. She's barely conscious. I think she's only holding on to say goodbye to you."

Tamasin kissed her forehead. "Take me to her, love."

The walk to the Queen's chambers seemed longer than usual as Tamasin tried to ignore the pall hanging over the Palace. It felt like a morgue. Wren's bedroom, though, was peaceful. The lights were turned low, and the family sat around the bed, keeping vigil. Wren's youngest daughter, Clover, held one hand while Floris, Luna's partner, lightly stroked her other. Everyone nodded to Tamasin when she and Fern entered, and then they quietly filed out of the room to give her privacy.

As soon as Tamasin gazed down at the Queen, she had to force back the sudden urge to weep. After months of the wasting sickness, Wren looked like a wizened-up old lady in the bed. To see the once vibrant Queen reduced to this shell was confronting. She managed a smile. "Hello, Wren."

"I was hoping you'd come, Tamasin," Wren rasped out, her voice barely audible.

"I came as soon as I could, old friend."

Though it was an effort, Wren smiled. "Come, sit

down. I'm so tired, and there's nothing left to say except take care of my family."

Tamasin shuffled onto the closest chair and clasped the frail hand. She choked back a lump in her throat. This was much harder than she'd thought possible. "I will," she promised.

Wren whispered, "Thank you," and closed her eyes.

She never opened them again.

Tamasin took a seat at the back while the family members took turns sitting with their mother. An hour later, the Queen took her last breath. After extending her condolences, Tamasin slipped out the door to leave the family to their grief.

Fern followed her out, closing the door softly behind her. "Commander Pela requested we have a private funeral."

Tamasin put her arm around her shoulders. "I know it's upsetting, but she's right. A state funeral will only make the city a target. That can come later when this is all over. Meanwhile, quietly bury your mother with only family and close friends."

Fern sank into her, seeking her comfort. "I will. It's just so devastating we can't give her a proper send off. Will you stay the night?"

"I'm sorry, Fern, but I can't. I must get to Beria."

"Tell Jez to hurry home tomorrow," Fern said in a small voice. "I need my wife here with me."

"I won't need to tell her; she'll be up at the crack of dawn. She loves you very much."

Tears sparkled in Fern's eyes. "Mother was right ... I needed someone of my own. I can't imagine my life without Jez. She's wonderful."

"Your mother was one of the wisest women I've ever met. She will be sorely missed," Tamasin said. Her eyes also welled up as a feeling of acute loss swept over her.

"She will be remembered as a benevolent Queen," Fern said with pride. "It meant a lot to me that you came, Tam, especially under your own trying circumstances." Sniffling, she kissed her cheek. "I'd better get back to my family. They'll need my support, particularly Clover. She's not taking it well."

"Goodbye, Fern. Will you ask Luna to come out, please? I'd like a word with her."

"Of course," said Fern. She squeezed her hand before she disappeared back into the room.

Moments later, Luna greeted her with a nod. "I'm guessing you want to know how I got on with taking the Imperial Queen to Kandelora."

"Did everything go smoothly?"

"Very," assured Luna. "Nothing untoward happened on the way, and I'm certain we weren't followed. My people were thrilled to have such an important guest. They heard how the Imperial Queen brought the Silverthorne Witches to justice and made quite a fuss of her. She's in Floris's old rooms, which are very comfortable."

"Thank you, Luna. That's a load off my mind." Tamasin cleared her throat. "We've someone else we want the Kandelorian folk to hide. She … um … can be a little difficult."

"Oh? Who is she?"

"Her name is Reagan. She's from the Forgotten Realms, an Enchantress. She's the last of her line and is needed to close the Circle."

Luna stared at her. "Fern told me about her. She plays with people's minds."

"That's her. But don't worry, I'll ask Valeria to keep her in check," she said, then added, "My wife has a temper."

Luna gave a wisp of a smile. "Having seen the royal temper, Reagan would be foolish to provoke it."

"Exactly," agreed Tamasin.

Luna shuffled her feet. "Do you want me to take her?"

"No. I will," said Tamasin, amused at the relief on Luna's face. "Now, I must go if I hope to get back to Beria by nightfall."

After Luna returned to Wren's bedroom, Tamasin hurried off to the kitchen for a snack for the trip.

✝

Jezzine was the first to greet her when she arrived at dusk. "You've come from Arcadii, Tam?" she asked breathlessly.

"Yes, Jez. Let's go somewhere private to talk." Although Tamasin tried to smile, she failed miserably.

Jezzine studied her face, then winced. "Come into the side lounge." As soon as the door closed, she asked, "What's happened?"

"I'm sorry, Jez. Wren died this afternoon. I came straight here."

"Oh dear Goddess," Jezzine said, her eyes filling with tears. "Poor Fern. I'll go home at once."

Tamasin grasped her arm. "Wait until morning. If you're not used to night flying, it can be difficult to find the way."

"I have an excellent sense of direction, and Fern needs me. End of story. I'll let you tell the others while I get ready."

"Take Ketra with you."

"She's had a rough day and deserves a break." Jezzine shook herself as if to forget. "It's a miserable time for everyone."

"I'll ask Lilybeth for two soldiers to accompany you," said Tamasin firmly. "Do you know where the Queen is?"

"They're all in the big dining room for drinks before dinner. Lilybeth decided we needed to unwind. You'll be happy to hear the Skeldachs are confined to their underground caverns, but Savannah will tell you what happened."

For the first time in days, a flash of hope quashed down Tamasin's feeling of dread. It was excellent news that the Crevlin had lost their air power. She'd feared they would target Arcadii next, and the thought of that beautiful city being under bomb attack sent her stomach roiling.

As she walked through the corridors, she noticed the Berian Palace had lost its austere look. Vases of flowers filled every corner, and the drab gray curtains had been replaced with brightly colored fabric. Since someone was sprucing up the place, she guessed Lilybeth had at last retired Mistress Tiana, her old housekeeper. When she reached the dining room, she stood for a few moments on the threshold to watch the crowd of soldiers and guests mingling. They all looked cheery, and even Pela was drinking ale with Winston.

It was cruel that she had to be the bearer of bad news and burst their bubble. There wasn't much to be happy about in these times.

Savannah was the first to spy her. "Tamasin," she called out. "Have a drink."

Tamasin handed her riding coat to a maid, and Lilybeth came over immediately to greet her. "Consort. If there's anything Beria can do to help Iona, we are at your disposal."

"Thanks, Lilybeth. Beria has enough to do cleaning up Beribrine. Jezzine told me the flying lizards are now trapped underground, which will be a game changer. I'm interested in hearing Pela's plans for the defense of Rand, but that can wait." Tamasin touched her arm in a gesture of apology. "Unfortunately, I have some bad news. It'll be easier if I announce it to everyone at once."

Lilybeth nodded, giving a brief sigh, "Bad news has become commonplace these days." She signaled to the Master of the Staff. "Please inform our guests that Consort Tamasin wishes to speak."

The Master, a stooped man with a long face, thumped his staff three times. When the room fell into silence, he announced solemnly, "The Imperial Consort wishes to address the assembly."

Tamasin flashed him a smile, figuring it was probably many moons since he'd had to use the staff. Queen Lilybeth wasn't known for entertaining. She cleared her throat and called out, "I'm sorry, my friends. I've just flown in from Arcadii. Queen Wren passed away peacefully today. Arcadia is now in mourning."

A moment of serious silence followed her announcement. Ketra was the first to speak. "You have told Consort Jezzine?"

"Yes. She is flying back immediately. Since it's been a

tiring day for you all, she insists you leave your return trip until tomorrow," Tamasin replied, then turned to Lilybeth. "I'd be happier if two of your soldiers would accompany her."

"That won't be necessary," said Ketra sharply. "I will take her home. Wren was my sovereign, and Queen Fern will need our support."

"We will go with you," spoke up one of the Sirens. "Jezzine is our Queen."

"Good," said Ketra with finality. "Be in the stables saddled and ready in half an hour." She turned to Lily-beth and clicked her heels. "Thank you for your hospitality, Ma'am."

And then they were gone.

"The Arcadian Queens inspire great loyalty," said Gladofin.

Tamasin looked round to see the Countess at her elbow. "They do indeed," she agreed. "As does the Siren Queen. It's a long journey home and tired as they are, they didn't hesitate. I take it the attempt to keep the Skeldachs underground wasn't plain sailing."

"No, it wasn't. Savannah was nearly killed. If it wasn't for Ketra, she wouldn't have survived. I'll let her tell you the story."

"Savannah takes too many risks," growled Tamasin.

"Pela thinks so too. I overheard her giving her a lecture. Savannah has the feared Commander in knots,"

Gladofin said with a chuckle. "How long are you planning to stay? I have a favor to ask you."

"I know what it is. I'll take Reagan first thing in the morning."

Gladofin's eyes widened. "You're aware I was going to ask you to take her to your safe sanctuary? How?"

"I was ordered in a dream to hide her until the Covenant of Queens is called to close the Circle. Since she is the only Enchantress left in Rand and part of the Covenant, Borrentine will be desperate to kill her. It's ironic, isn't it, that such an annoying woman has the fate of the world in her hands." Tamasin eyed Gladofin curiously. "What did she do to anger you? It must have been serious if you're exiling her."

"She went too far, and it nearly had a grave outcome. The woman has no shame, digging intrusively in people's thoughts as if it was her right. She picked the wrong person when she did it to Pela. The Bramble Hawk vehemently objected to her prying."

Tamasin gaped at her. "Reagan's got gall poking in *Pela's* mind."

"Mad more like it," said Gladofin. "Reagan is a conceited busybody who needs to wake up to herself. I told her if she creates any trouble where you're taking her, she'll answer to me. And if I'm forced to speak to her again, she won't like it."

Tamasin looked at her with respect. Gladofin must

be far more powerful than she'd imagined. She wondered why the Guardian was so furious with Reagan, but any more information wasn't offered. She'd ask Savannah about it later. "Don't worry. I'll tell Valeria to keep an eye on her. No one messes with the Imperial Queen."

"That would be wise. I can't help worrying I'm sending a wolf into a flock of sheep," Gladofin muttered. "Lilybeth is the only one I've ever met who has a measure of sympathy for her. She says her anger stems from the fact that she's lonely and needs to be wanted."

"Bitter and twisted more like it," said Tamasin, recalling her own run-in with her. "Would you send Reagan a message to be ready at three in the morning, please Countess? We have a long way to go, and I'd like to be there by breakfast."

Gladofin signaled to the maid carrying a tray. "I will. Now have a drink. I'm sure you could do with one after your long day. I'll check to see if dinner is ready."

As Tamasin plucked an ale off the tray, Savannah wandered over and greeted her without her usual cheery smile. "Tam, it's good to see you, though it could have been under better circumstances. How is Wren's family holding up?"

"Clover is taking it hard, but the others are fine. They've had time to prepare for this day, though Fern will be very pleased to see Jezzine." She absently stroked down the side of the tankard. "It's all happening so fast, Savannah, one thing after the other. The attacks on Beria and Iona, and now Arcadia losing its long-standing Queen. In a way, I'm glad Wren didn't live to see war come to her beloved Arcadia."

"Pela has a plan that should prevent an attack on Arcadii. She'll explain it tomorrow."

"I'd be interested to hear it," said Tamasin, her spirits lifting at the news. Pela wasn't prone to flights of fancy, which meant the strategy had real merit. "Though it can't be in the morning. I'm taking Reagan to Kandelora."

Savannah nodded. "Winston told me what happened. The Countess was furious with her."

"Do tell," murmured Tamasin. "Gladofin didn't elaborate."

"When Reagan tried to read Pela's mind, Pela got cranky and turned into a Hawk. According to Winston, Limos has a thing for Reagan and morphed into his tiger form to defend her. Lilybeth stepped in-between them to stop the fight and would've been hurt if the Countess hadn't intervened."

"Okay. But that doesn't explain why the Countess was angry enough to banish Reagan."

Savannah leaned over and whispered, "She likes Lilybeth."

CHAPTER TWENTY-TWO | 259

Tamasin arched an eyebrow. This whole business sounded like one of Valeria's flights-of-fancy intrigues in the bedroom. *"Like* as in *more-than-just-a-friend like?"*

"Yep."

"Nooo. That's not possible."

"Why not? They're well-suited, both mature and powerful women in their own right. Just imagine if those two got together, what a boost it would give the plan for the integration of the Forgotten Realms into the rest of Rand now the Wall is down."

Tamasin turned this over in her mind. "What a boost indeed," she murmured and then added, "But don't get your hopes up. The royal mothers have been trying to get Lilybeth to notice their unmarried children for years. She's ignored them all."

CHAPTER TWENTY-THREE

KANDELORA

*I*n the glow of the moons, the Berian Palace was a ghostly sentinel guarding the dark sea beyond its walls.

With the Enchantress secured in the saddle behind her, Tamasin took one last look down at the coastline before nudging Malkia into the northwest. It was a pleasant night, only slightly chilly as if the land was reluctant to give up the last of the summer months. They soared over fields of crops, stands of tall trees, across the winding tributaries of the Cadiwine River, and when she recognized the village of Blossburrow in the moonlight, she turned Malkia west. Another hour passed before they rounded the first peak in the long chain of an austere mountain range.

CHAPTER TWENTY-THREE | 261

When they flew into the gorges, Reagan exclaimed, "What is this God forsaken place?"

"The Iron Mountains," Tamasin called back. She'd forgotten just how desolate the canyons were.

To avoid detection, they were forced to fly low through the succession of dismal gorges. The pitching motion of the horse helped to calm her nerves, for though the moonlight cleaved a pathway through the shadows of the overhanging cliffs, there were too many jutting rocks not to be anxious. She could tell Reagan was uneasy as well by the way she periodically clutched at Tamasin's belt. Only after they reached the wide smooth canyon below Falcon's Keep did Tamasin fully relax.

Although they had made good time, it was still well past dawn when they reached the entrance to Kandelora, the City of Outcasts. Aware how quickly and fiercely the heat settled at the bottom of the towering cliffs, she hoped they could get inside quickly.

When Malkia touched down, Reagan quickly pulled off her thick riding coat, then fanned herself with the collar. "Why are we stopping here? Isn't there a cooler place to rest?" she moaned.

"No. Now off you get," Tamasin said, climbing out of the saddle. "We're here."

"There's nothing here," said Reagan indignantly. She narrowed her eyes. "If this is a joke, it's not funny."

Tamasin pointed to the cliff. "Look over there." She knew they permanently posted a guard, but she still felt a measure of relief when a section of the cliff opened. Already the canyon's hot breath had begun to burn her lungs and scorch her eyes.

Two cloaked figures slipped out cautiously. When the leading man recognized Tamasin, he threw back his hood and clasped her hand. "Consort. It's good to see you. We weren't expecting you for a while." He tilted his head to look curiously at Reagan. "I see you brought someone with you."

"Hello, Eric. It's good to see you again, my friend. This is Reagan from the Forgotten Realms. I'm sorry to lob up with no notice, but things are escalating. We need a safe place for her. The enemy are out to kill her and Reagan has an important role to play in the coming war. Would you keep her hidden until I come back for her, please?"

"There's no need to ask, Consort. We have pledged our city as a sanctuary." He bowed to Reagan. "You are very welcome, Mistress."

Reagan must have realized she stared a little too long at the fur on his face, for a tinge of pink spread over her cheeks. "Thank you for your hospitality, Eric," she said quietly.

He ran a discerning eye over her exposed arms. "We'd better get you inside. It won't take long for the heat to burn your fair skin. We'll stable your horse inside, Consort."

As they followed him to the door, Reagan glowered at Tamasin as if to say, *you could have warned me.* She ignored her. The Enchantress was in for a lot more shocks when she met the rest of the Kandelorians. As soon as they entered the town square, a groom appeared to take Malkia to the stables. After the stallion trotted off, Eric led them to a table inside the Grotto Tavern. "While we have breakfast, Consort, I'll send someone to fetch the Imperial Queen."

"There's no need, Eric. I'd like to surprise her, but I'll have something to eat first. It was a long trip."

He grinned. "A reunion is always better in private."

"How is she going?" She was a little reticent to ask, having no idea how her wife would react to her forced confinement.

She let out the breath she was holding when he answered, "Really well. The people love her. She's teaching the little ones their letters."

Tamasin smiled. Valeria always said if she hadn't been born a queen she would have liked to teach. She glanced at Reagan who was looking wide-eyed at everyone.

Finally, Reagan turned to Eric and asked quietly, "What happened to the Kandelorian people, Eric?"

He glanced at her in surprise. "Didn't the Consort tell you our story?"

Reagan flicked a reproving glare at Tamasin. "No, she didn't."

"It was a spur-of-the-moment decision to bring Reagan here," Tamasin said hastily. The last thing she wanted was an angry Enchantress. Promises tended to go by the wayside when tempers flared. "Perhaps you might fill her in."

"Of course," said Eric. "We are also called the City of Outcasts." And as they ate, he related the history of the Silverthorne Witches' horrific experiments where they combined people with animals, and then the Outcasts escape into the mountain after the fall of the Prophecy Tower.

When he'd finished, Reagan's face was set hard. "Inhumane bitches," she muttered. "And you said the changes are passed down the family lines."

"Yes, though they lessen with each generation." Although clearly embarrassed about his appearance, he pushed on, "I'm covered in dog hair, but my father had paws which I don't."

Reagan reached over and squeezed his hand. "I love animals, Eric. Your appearance isn't unpleasant to me. Far from it. You are a handsome man."

Eric blushed. There was no doubt about Reagan, Tamasin thought. The woman could be charming when she tried. "Are there many people left with mental health issues from the change?" Reagan asked.

"Some do find it difficult to cope." He pointed to a child playing with a doll at a side table. As far as Tamasin could see, her only animal trait was her ears which were pointy like a cat's. "Zoey's mother was pregnant during the experiments. She died in child-birth, and the girl has never spoken a word."

Reagan gazed thoughtfully at the child, then abruptly got up and walked over to her table. She knelt beside her chair, took her hands, and gently rubbed her thumbs over the knuckles. The girl stared her in the eye as if mesmerized. As seconds turned into minutes, they remained locked together until finally, Reagan got to her feet. She leaned down and whispered in the girl's ear. With a nod, Zoey followed her to their table. When Reagan sat down, she climbed onto her lap and lisped, "Zoey."

Eric's mouth sagged open. "You made her talk?"

"Not made," said Reagan. "I removed the block in her mind that prevented her from speaking." She ruffled the child's hair fondly. "Zoey is a bright little girl. Her mind will heal, but it will take time. I will continue to give her sessions while I am here."

Eric gazed at her in awe. "There are others who need help. Would you be prepared to spend some time with them too, Mistress Reagan? We've never had anyone who knew anything about the workings of the mind."

"I'd be pleased to help them. And drop the Mistress, Eric. There's no need for a formal title." She shifted in the seat to allow Zoey to cuddle into her. "Maybe I could discover why the afflictions are passed on to future generations. I suspect it's something to do with black magic. I felt threads of it in Zoey's mind. Yes," she said, more to herself. "It'd be the black magic."

Tamasin blinked at her. The Enchantress had morphed from a the bitchy "witch" into a caring, compassionate woman. Who would have thought it possible? Noticing Eric was fixated on Reagan, Tamasin cleared her throat to get his attention. "I'll see you two later. Which way to the Queen's rooms?"

Memorizing the directions, she wandered down the labyrinth of passageways until she found the door.

A plump woman opened it. "Yes?"

"My name is Tamasin. I'd like to see the Queen, please."

"Her Majesty is having breakfast." After looking Tamasin up and down, she knocked on the bedroom door and called out. "A person called Tamasin is here to see you, Ma'am."

The door opened almost immediately, and Valeria ran into the lounge. Then as if conscious her haste would appear unusual, she slowed to a walk. "You may go, Hilda. I know her."

The maid nodded, cast one more look at Tamasin and vanished out the door.

Tamasin raised an eyebrow. *"Know her, Val?"*

"Oh hush," Valeria cried as she threw her arms around her. "Kiss me, then tell me why you're here."

Pulling her tightly against her, Tamasin kissed her thoroughly. When they came up for air, Valeria whispered, "I missed you."

Tamasin ran her fingers through her hair, tugging the strands lightly. "It's only been a few days. We've been apart longer than that lately."

"I know, but I can't see you when I want to." Taking her hand, Valeria led her to the chairs. "Now tell me why you're here."

"Borrentine is aware now an Enchantress survived the purge and will be desperate to kill her. The Goddess of Dreams ordered me to bring her to Kandelora."

Valeria jerked upright in her seat. "You've brought Reagan here. Are you crazy? These poor people have enough hardship in their lives without foisting *her* onto them."

"Calm down," said Tamasin soothingly. "The Countess has warned her not to cause trouble. All the Magical Folk, Reagan included, fear the anger of the Guardians, so she'll behave. I'll bet on it."

268 | COVENANT OF QUEENS

"How can you be so sure?" Valeria said grumpily. "She's the mind reader, not you."

"Because when she saw the people here, her attitude changed completely. Lilybeth had a word with me last night about Reagan. She said she was difficult for a reason. She had deep-seated issues and was lonely. But most of all, she desperately wants to be needed. And I'd say she's found what she's looking for here."

Valeria eyed her curiously. "That doesn't sound like Lilybeth."

"We have underestimated her, Val. We always thought that while she's an excellent military strategist, she had no other qualities. Savannah tells me the Berian Queens have always protected the Magical Sea Folk, and Lilybeth is a close friend of the Madra. She's regarded with enormous respect in her realm, and even Pela takes her advice."

"You lost me there, Tam. Do you mean to tell me there are Magical Folk in the sea?"

Tamasin nodded. "It's full of them. The Madra, Nerin, is the ruler."

"Extraordinary," murmured Valeria. "Berians know how to keep a secret."

"And they must be smart, considering how many have been chosen to wear the Circle of Sheda. And," she paused for effect, "Savannah thinks Countess Gladofin is interested in Lilybeth."

Valeria chuckled. "And you believed her? What fantasy world is Savannah living in? The Countess is extremely powerful, second only to her sister Olivine in the Forgotten Realms. Why would she be interested in a reclusive Queen who has no magic in her veins. Really, Tam, you'd believe anything."

Tamasin clasped her hand. "We shall see. Now no more talking and come to bed. I've a few hours before I need to head back to Berian."

CHAPTER TWENTY-FOUR

THE BERIAN PALACE

Savannah looked up to see Tamasin enter the room.

She looked relaxed, and Savannah guessed by her smile that the trip to Kandelora had gone without a hitch.

Winston dragged another stool over for her beside Pela. "Consort. Good timing. We were discussing the location of the City of the Dead."

Tamasin propped onto the stool and eyed him intently. "Have you any ideas, Winston?"

He pointed to a spot on the map. "Our best guess is here. It's a wet wasteland past the Wizard's Wall at the northern end of the Forgotten Realms. The Guardians have always believed the area was too toxic for habitation because of noxious marsh gasses, but Pela said that's not true."

"I went there years ago," said Pela. "It's a vast swathe of swamps, with an occasional thickly wooded stretch of dry land. I saw plenty of wildlife: black bears, large spotted cats, huge scaley reptiles, and lots of snakes. If there are poisonous gasses, they must be only in certain areas."

"Any people?"

"I didn't see any, Tam."

"I thought the Forgotten Realms went to the Northern Sea. So, it turns out there's a sizable uninhabited wilderness between them and the sea. Interesting," mused Tamasin. She studied the map. "The location would be perfect for the Crevlin to come through the Time Gateway undetected. It might be an ideal place to hide, but not a great location to move their army. The Bramble Hawks are too close."

"Perhaps that might be to their advantage," murmured Winston. "We'd hardly be expecting the City of the Dead to be so close to the Forgotten Realms." He trailed his finger across the map. "They could skirt the border, hug the coastline, and take the port of Wivenshore. It's on the mouth of the Cadiwine River."

"That could be why they attacked the ports first," said Lilybeth. "They wanted the coast in their possession."

"Maybe there was something in the old diary we missed," said Savannah.

"It won't do us any good. I had a dream that the City of the Dead isn't in any particular place," said Tamasin. "It's a reference to a city of people who should have died, but haven't."

"A metaphor," mumbled Savannah. "That changes everything. It could be anywhere and unlikely to be where they came out last time."

"Where else could a whole race of people gather undetected?" asked Savannah.

"I'll mark them off," said Winston, reaching for a box of colored flags. "Red for very likely, blue for less likely, and yellow, possible but highly unlikely."

When he finished, he stood back to admire his handiwork. There were nine reds, twenty-one blues, and six yellows. "Now we start whittling them down," he announced. "What do we know?"

"The Crevlin that Reagan interrogated said they flew all night over a mountain range to get to Beria," said Savannah. "Take off the flags of anywhere that doesn't have a mountain range to cross. Also, those places close to Beria."

Winston reached over and removed half the flags.

"If they're not in Wetlands, they'd most likely be in the mountains," said Gladofin. "More places to hide."

"Or a deserted island. There are plenty of those," said Lilybeth. "I'll get Nerin to scour the seas."

"Check the islands," said Savannah, "but I doubt it'll be in the sea. Too close. The Crevlin said they flew all night."

Winston stroked his beard, deep in thought. "I agree," he said, plucking out more flags.

Finally, there were only seven flags left: The Northern Wetlands; four forests; a wilderness area to the southwest; and the vast Great Windy Desert to the west. He took out the yellow flag in the desert. "Too dry. They'll need to find something to eat immediately. So that leaves six places to investigate. I'm thinking somewhere in those marshlands is the place. Plenty of fish for food. But we can't dismiss the mountains."

"I will visit the Gray Wolves tomorrow," said Gladofin. "And Tamasin might get her spy network to search the places we've marked off." She got up and dusted her hands. "That's enough for the day. We can't do anything more until the locations are investigated, Winston."

"The Garrison Commander has invited the four of you to the barracks for drinks," Lilybeth said to Winston and the Mani. When they jumped up enthusiastically and exited the room, she chuckled. "Knowing my troops, they'll have a hangover tomorrow, so it's just as well you're off in the morning, Gladofin." She gestured to the door. "Come to the lounge for a chat.

We're all dying to hear how you got on with Reagan, Tamasin."

As Tamasin related Reagan's interaction with the Kandelorian people, Savannah glanced over at Lilybeth. While the others looked amazed, her face showed not an ounce of surprise as if she expected it.

Tamasin turned with a nod to Lilybeth. "You were right. Reagan needed to be wanted."

"They will be good for her," said Lilybeth softly. "I suspect she has found a purpose in life at last. A family. She has been without anyone to call her own since her parents died. Those who are part of a family have no notion of what it is like to be without kin. She's the last Queen of the Great House of Falendore, a ruler without any subjects."

Gladofin looked at her oddly. "How do you know that's how she feels, Lilybeth?"

Lilybeth reddened, then cleared her throat as if she realized she'd said too much. "Just something I picked up."

While she sipped her wine, Savannah studied the Berian Queen. She'd already guessed there was more to her than met the eye, but she wondered why she was so astute at reading people. She was beginning to think she could read minds, not as Reagan could but in some other way.

Suddenly, the old seer's voice popped into her head. *"Get the Queen to touch the medallion, Savannah."*

Without argument, Savannah waited for a lull in the conversation and pulled it out. "Would you like to touch the medallion, Ma'am?"

Lilybeth hesitated. "I'm not worthy."

"If you're not, who is?" said Savannah. "It won't hurt you."

With everyone's eye on her, Lilybeth reluctantly stretched out a finger. As soon as the tip touched it, Savannah felt the metal grow warm, and as it heated, the room shimmered out of focus. When the air around her calmed, she was no longer in the lounge. She was on the top of a cliff overlooking the sea, and the old blind seer sat cross-legged on a flat rock, smiling at her. But this time, Savannah hadn't come alone. Lilybeth was by her side, looking bewildered.

"Hello, Grandmother," Savannah said delightedly. "I was wondering if you'd show yourself to me again."

"I wanted to meet Lilybeth. I have much to say to her."

"Who are you?" whispered Lilybeth. "And where am I?"

"Savannah calls me Grandmother. You may too, my dear. As for where you are, this place is the past … three hundred years ago to be exact. Look," she said, pointing a finger. "Elsbeth is waiting for her lover."

Savannah quickly swiveled her head. Her long blond hair blowing in the wind, a tall woman with an attractive face and a willowy athletic figure stood further down under a bristlecone pine. No man was in view.

"Will we see her lover?" asked Savannah hopefully.

"No. We can't risk it."

"Can I speak to her?" asked Lilybeth.

"I'm sorry. She won't be able to see you."

"Oh, that's a great pity. Elsbeth is a hero to my people," murmured Lilybeth. She turned and eyed the old woman curiously. "What did you want to discuss?"

"Secrecy is at an end for the House of Vandersea. The old days are gone, and you must embrace the new. It is time you stopped hiding, Lilybeth," the old seer said sternly. "Savannah must know who you are. War is here, and she will need you."

"What do you mean, Grandmother?" asked Savannah, looking from one to the other.

"The Queens of Beria are no ordinary folk. Their line is one of the most powerful in Rand."

Savannah gaped at her. "She's magical?"

"Yes and no. It's a different kind of magic, not in any sense you would recognize. Lilybeth was born of the sea, it runs in her veins, she's the Guardian of all the water. The Madra rules the seas, but she defers to the Berian Queen."

"You want me to declare our secret?" asked Lilybeth

horrified. "I've taken a sacred oath that it'll never be revealed."

The old seer huffed out a sharp breath. "We are moving into a new era. The very ancient magic and old secrets won't have a place in it. The future has yet to be written." She dropped her voice to a whisper. "But the Crevlin must be defeated, or there will be no future to write. Now goodbye, my dear, and do your best to help the Chosen One."

A second later, Lilybeth vanished, leaving Savannah remaining on the cliff. The old seer smiled. "I wanted a word with you alone, but we can't tarry. Elsbeth can't see you, but her lover will be able to." She uncurled her legs before she continued, "It would be ideal if Lilybeth married Gladofin. Do you think there's any chance of that happening?"

Savannah smothered a smile. So the old girl hadn't a clue they were interested in each other. She feigned disbelief. "Why on earth would the Countess look at Lilybeth?"

"Hmm. Perhaps you could give them a push somehow."

"Me?" squeaked Savannah. "No way. Why do you want them together?"

"It would cement the joining of the two cultures. And Gladofin needs a child."

"Olivine has a young daughter. She's the Queen, so the line is secured."

"For the Goddess's sake, Savannah, I thought you were astute. Gladofin, not her sister, is the most powerful Guardian in Rand and the strongest one the world has seen for centuries. Olivine rules well, but she is winter: cold, aloof, and predictable. Gladofin is summer: bold, vibrant and unpredictable. She has a wildness that needs someone strong and steady enough to guide but not stifle her. What an offspring that union would produce."

Savannah pressed her lips together disapprovingly. "Grandmother. You shouldn't interfere in —"

She stopped as a mist suddenly appeared in the distance. When Elsbeth gave a glad cry, the air shimmered around Savannah, and she was back in the Berian Palace.

Feeling the hard surface under her elbow, she realized she was on the floor. The room was silent as she climbed to her feet. She glanced over at Lilybeth who nervously plucked at a fabric thread on the armrest, and by the pleading look in her eye, she knew the Berian Queen feared she would divulge her secret. Savannah gave her a nod of reassurance.

"Where did you go?" asked Pela with a frown. "Lilybeth said you'd explain."

"We were transported back three hundred years,

before Queen Jessica waged war on the Silverthorne Witches. We saw Elsbeth in the distance, waiting for her lover."

Tamasin leaned forward eagerly. "Did you see him?"

"Unfortunately, no."

"Then why were you taken there, Savannah. Your visions always have a purpose," persisted Tamasin.

She toyed with the idea of fobbing her off, then thought better of it. It was time she divulged the name of the old seer who had been guiding her. "What we discussed, I can't say, but I think it's time I told you the name of my helper. She's an ancient Mind Walker, the one who talks to you in your dreams, Tamasin. She's Hola's sister."

"She's the sister of that nasty crone!" said Pela incredulously. "What's your Mind Walker's name?"

"I call her Grandmother, but she's never told me her name." She turned to Gladofin. "Do you know much about her, Countess?"

"At the Pale Horse — what seems so long ago now — you asked me about Hola. I said she is the Dark Spirit of Rand, and as everything has two sides, her sister is the Light. She is called Ronja, the great ancient Mind Walker, and the first Guardian of Rand."

Savannah felt a flicker of excitement — at last she was learning about her elusive seer. "So she's a Mind

Walker and Hola is a Time Walker. Do you know how long ago they lived?"

Gladofin toyed with the star pendant around her neck. "Well before the fall of the Crevlinian empire, but it was such a long time ago that the Guardians can't pinpoint exactly when. Some even believe the twins were a myth because no one since has inherited either talent." She grimaced. "It seems we were wrong. Borrentine is a Time Walker."

Savannah nearly revealed she was a Mind Walker but held back the information at the last minute. It might be wise to keep that secret for a while. She wondered, though, why she had a strong feeling that the period when Hola and Ronja lived was important.

CHAPTER TWENTY-FIVE

THE FORGOTTEN REALMS

*A*utumn had come to the Forgotten Realms, the forests and hills now decked in masses of reds, yellows, and browns. When a breeze sprang up, thousands upon thousands of the colorful leaves broke from their life support and fluttered into the sky. After Berian with its austere towering cliffs and windswept coast, Savannah had forgotten how pretty this part of Rand was in comparison.

When they reached the entrance to the Amarim valley, she looked across at the Countess on Snow Pine. Gladofin leaned forward in the saddle, her face alight with pleasure and anticipation as they neared her home.

Conscious of the time constraints, Savannah didn't stay long. After a stop for food and to rest Sunflower, and then with the Countess's stern warning in her head to be careful, she headed for the Bramble Hawks' domain in the mountains beyond.

Three Hawks appeared in the sky as they neared, dipping their wings in salute before they escorted them into the village. Savannah's stomach tightened. At the moment, she was more concerned about facing Rozen than the Iriwari. Whether the Sylphs would grant her an audience was in the lap of the fates, but she was going to ask an enormous favor of Pela's mother. She may think Savannah relied on her goodwill because she was her daughter's partner, and she wouldn't blame Rozen.

It was true.

As soon as they landed in front of the Royal Tree-house, Savannah led Sunflower into the shadows around the side of the building. "Stay here out of sight, and don't wander off."

She needn't have bothered with the instruction; the horse was a quivering bag of nerves amongst so many Hawks. *"Okay,"* Sunflower replied without her usual cheery retort.

Savannah patted her rump reassuringly. "I won't be long."

After three knocks, a maid appeared at the door and led her into the library. She didn't have long to wait. Rozen appeared, slightly breathless as though she'd been running, and pulled her into a hug. "Savannah. What a pleasant surprise. All's well, I hope?"

"As much as it can be. No doubt your Hawks would have told you of the outcome of the Iona battle."

"They did. Iona was lucky they arrived when they did, or it would have been a bigger disaster." Rozen patted her arm. "Why are you here, Savannah? Not that I'm unhappy to see you, but I'm guessing this isn't a social visit. Or is it?"

"No, it's not, Rozen." Savannah tapped her fingers anxiously on the armrest, wondering how to frame her request. In the end, she decided to just come right out and ask. "I want you to take me to the Iriwari."

Rozen's smile faltered. "How do you know about them?"

"Pela told me your mother's story. Since the Sylphs are experts on the celestial bodies, I need to see them, and I've no one else who can get me into their stronghold. I can't just lob up and expect an audience, presuming I can even find the place."

"You want me to take you into the Zorian Alps. That's a big ask, Savannah. I've only been there once but never actually entered the Iriwari city. Before I was married, I went up there because I was interested in meeting my relations. But the place was so well fortified that I lost my nerve. I flew around for a while and came back home."

284 | COVENANT OF QUEENS

Savannah eyed her curiously. "Do they know your mother had a child by her Sylph lover?"

"I have no idea," Rozen said. "She only mentioned him once because I nagged her to tell me. She preferred not to dwell on the past. She always said regret was a pointless emotion because it ate away your soul." As she went on, sadness dropped her voice to a whisper, "There are many reasons for regrets in our society. Arranged marriages are common and not always happy."

Savannah felt a wave of pity for the woman. Her marriage to the tyrant King of the Bramble Hawks had been fraught with violence. "I'm sorry, I shouldn't have asked it of you. If you draw me a map, I'll find my way."

"Why do you seek them out, Savannah?"

"Because they study the skies. The third moon is already visible, and we have no idea where the Circle of Sheda must be when the moons are aligned. We need someone who understands the significance of the third one and why it only appears in the sky every two thousand years."

"Why is it important?"

"Their alignment is the moment to close the Time Gateway. If we fail, the Crevlin will keep coming in, and there will be a long, protracted war."

Rozen's brows knitted together. "I understand the urgency, but you can't go up there alone. It's not safe.

People exploring those mountains have disappeared. The Alps are home to many savage creatures that wouldn't think twice about killing intruders."

"If I show them I'm the Chosen One, warrior of the Imperial Queen, surely they will defer to the Supreme Ruler of Rand."

"Oh, Savannah, you can't be so naïve to believe all the creatures of the Forgotten Realms swear allegiance to *that* Crown," Rozen said dryly. "They bow only to Queen Olivine, and some of the very fierce beasts in the Zorian Alps do so reluctantly, others not at all. And then, my husband didn't even bend his knee to the Amarim Queen."

"Unfortunately, I must talk to them, and I can't let that deter me. I'm perfectly capable of looking after myself with the medallion's magic, and besides, I'll be flying there, so I'll avoid any land beasts. All I require from you is a map."

Rozen looked undecided, then heaved out a sigh. "I'll take you. Pela would never forgive me if something happened to you."

"No," said Savannah firmly. "She'll never forgive *me* if I got you hurt. I promised her I wouldn't go up thereby myself, so perhaps we can compromise. If you take me as far as their city, I'll go in alone."

"Very well. Since the Iriwari are peaceful folk, you'll be quite safe once we get there, even if they refuse you entrance," said Rozen. She rose to her feet. "Come then. It will take the rest of the morning to fly there."

✝

It was no exaggeration that the Zorian Alps were wild and inhospitable. Savannah was relieved she was flying and not trying to climb them on foot. The range was steep, with narrow tracks that wound around the cliffs, where one wrong step would send her tumbling over sheer drops to the valley below. Every so often, the mountain would plateau into a terrain that was dark and forbidding. Things bellowed in the thick woods, and occasionally she caught a vague shape of some large beast through the foliage. Carrion-eating birds wheeled in the distance, but they left them alone, for none were as big or fearsome as Rozen, the Bramble Hawk escorting her.

Higher, the mild autumn weather changed, and the sky darkened. A storm began to brew in the north, forcing them to hug the other side of the mountain. Soon lightning streaked across the heavy black clouds, accompanied by rumbling thunder and sheets of rain that lashed the northern face. The storm was sharp and violent. Gale-force winds buffeted the mountain, and thunderclaps filled the air as the sky flashed white, leaving Savannah's eyes burning and ears ringing.

Eventually, the storm veered off down the range, but the remnants of the clouds became an indigo mist that settled like a blanket over the entire mountain.

Visibility had dropped to nearly zero when it happened.

One moment they were in the open, and the next, the Hawk blindly flew off course into a clearing covered with a high wall of foliage that curved around it like the green skin of a giant apple. When Rozen noticed the webs, it was too late. As she spun frantically to avoid them, its wing smashed against a thick branch. The bone snapped with a sickening crack, and the bird plummeted into the webs. Sunflower, who had followed it in, squealed, panic-stricken as she too floundered in the strands. Savannah toppled out of the saddle into the sticky web and found they held her like glue.

"Don't struggle," she projected urgently to Sunflower. *"You'll only make it worse. I'll burn you out."*

As the magic seeped into her fingers, she realized she'd better hurry. The webs weren't meant to keep the prey alive until the spider arrived — they were tightening, squeezing the life out of them. Icy tingles ran down her spine. If she didn't start immediately, she wouldn't be able to move. As it was, she could only rotate her fingers a fraction. Gritting her teeth, she let the magic sizzle out. The threads covering the fingertips sloughed off, enabling her to bend two knuckles. It was painstaking work as she burnt off the strands one by one until she had her hands free, and as soon as she could move her arms, Savannah quickly burnt off the rest from her body.

Immediately the last thread broke, she dropped heavily with a whoosh onto the ground. Ignoring the pain in her knees, she hobbled over to untether the Hawk first. When the bird was free, she gently eased her to the floor. After chopping Sunflower from her prison, Savannah angrily blasted the webs into oblivion.

When she knelt beside the Hawk to examine the wing, it only took one glance to know Rozen was in trouble if the bone wasn't set soon. It hung at an odd angle, though as far as she could see through the feathers, it wasn't a compound fracture. "If you shift, Rozen, I can do something about your broken arm," she said.

With a squawk, the Hawk morphed into Rozen. Her eyes clouded with pain, she looked up at Savannah and said hoarsely, "We must get out of here. These are the webs of the Or'orah, the giant tusked spiders of the Zorian Alps. They immobilize their enemies by spitting poison, and then they eat them. One splash is enough to paralyze, and you'll be unable to use your magic. They will have heard us crash into their webs, so we must leave immediately. Attend to my arm later."

"Okay. I'll put you on Sunflower, and then lead you out." She put her arms around her waist. "When I heave, stand up." As soon as Rozen struggled to her feet, Savannah pushed her awkwardly up into the saddle. After tightening the strap, she patted her leg. "That should keep you from falling off but hold onto the pommel with your good hand."

Savannah swept the Farsight Stone around to find the best way out. The front entrance was clear, but from the back, an enormous creature was moving through an underground tunnel littered with bones. She stared at it in horror. The thing was monstrous, as frightening as the Scaled Serpent Squid. It had the body and eight legs of a spider, but that was where the similarity ended. Its head resembled a wild boar, with two huge tusks and a wide mouth full of teeth that looked like they could rip a horse to pieces in seconds.

She lunged for the reins, dragging Sunflower toward the front entrance. "Run as fast as you can, and don't look back. When you're clear of the trees, wait there for me. There's one scary monster coming straight for us."

The little mare took off in a gallop. At the mouth of the hollow, Savannah turned, readying her magic. Instinct told her there would be no reasoning with this creature. The Or'orah had a reason to hate her — she'd destroyed its web. It wouldn't stop until it hunted her down. She'd have to kill it or be killed. And here was the logical place to make her stand — at least it was in a confined space. In the woods, it mightn't be the only predator wanting to pick her bones.

Though she was ready, Savannah didn't expect it to be quite so fast. When the spider sprang with a blood-curdling screech into the clearing, she flailed her hands wildly. Flashes of magic shot from her fingers, tearing up the dirt in front of it. As it jumped back, it spat at her. Ready for it this time, she ducked to the side, and the globs of poisoned saliva passed by harmlessly. She unleashed a burst of power, followed by a fireball. Fire engulfed it, blossoming into an inferno, but when it died down, the monster was still standing unhurt.

Savannah knew then she was in real trouble. The shell must be impenetrable to fire and impervious to magic; she hadn't a hope of killing it unless she invoked the Death Vale. And that would be impossible in such a confined space. As the monster lunged forward with its mouth open ready to spit, Savannah did the only thing she could think of. She drilled a magic bolt down its throat. The Or'orah screamed, clawing furiously at the ground.

Then something strange happened. Smoke began streaming out of its nostrils, ears, and lips. Then it opened its mouth, and flames gushed out from some-where deep inside its belly. Savannah guessed something inside was flammable, but whether it was the poison, she had no idea, nor did she care. As it began to stagger, she took off in a run and didn't look back.

Sunflower was waiting on the bank of a small stream and gave a happy nicker when she approached. Rozen leaned forward in the saddle, wincing in pain as she greeted Savannah. "You're a welcome sight. We were getting worried. What happened with the Or'orah?"

"I don't know if it's dead, but it won't be coming after us." She studied Rozen's broken arm hanging by her side. "I'll immobilize that arm with a splint, or it might be permanently damaged. You'll have to come with me to the Iriwari. Since they're scholars, they should be well versed in healing techniques." She continued gently, "I'll help you off the horse."

Rozen grimaced but nodded in agreement.

Savannah tapped Sunflower on the shoulder. "If you kneel, it'll be easier for her."

As soon as Rozen was on the ground, Savannah examined the arm. "Hopefully it is a clean break. I'll find something to splint it with."

She worked quickly, securing the arm between two pieces of bark, and then fashioned a sling out of a supple vine that snaked up an old fig tree beside the creek. When finished, she settled back on her heels to admire her handiwork.

And that was when she heard the ominous sounds. Snuffles followed by savage growls.

Savannah swallowed back the sudden rush of bile.

A huge wolf with a bushy gray coat watched them from the opposite bank. And it looked anything but friendly. Hackles bristling, its eyes glowed an angry red as its lips peeled back to show long sharp canines.

CHAPTER TWENTY-SIX

*S*avannah had learned years ago that wolves were dangerous.

In her final study year, the five archeology Ph.D. students had been sent by the university on a field trip to the Denisova cave in Siberia, a site rich in ancient bones and artifacts. They'd decided before flying home to spend a week hiking through the Taiga Biome in Russia's far north. Being money-strapped students, they did it on the cheap and hired a local village guide.

Though the forest was home to many predators — wolves, lynxes, foxes, and bears — they only ever saw the wolves. She remembered lying in her tent at night, listening to their mournful howls and then catching glimpses of them slinking through the trees in the daylight. At first, they kept their distance, but as the days went by, they crept closer. In a way, the disaster was as much the students' fault as the inexperience of the local guy. They had become complacent, failing to set up their camp properly at night to protect against wild animals, or burying their food scraps before they moved.

The last evening, as they ate dinner around the campfire, a pack of ten wolves had padded close and watched from the shadows. When someone stupidly threw a rock at them, without warning they attacked. One bit the arm of the guide who had leaped up first, while the rest of the pack rushed to the horses picketed at the side of the tents. One of the horses broke free from the ropes, taking off into the forest with the wolves after it. Savannah never forgot the sounds of the squealing horse or the savage snarling of the wolves echoing in the wintery night.

But for all that, they weren't as scary as this wolf staring at them across the water. It was a barrel-chested male, much larger than those Siberian wolves and looked twice as mean.

After a moment, it raised its muzzle, sniffed the air, and gave a series of little yips. Immediately, six wolves appeared from the underbrush and squatted down beside him.

"It's not the pack leader," whispered Rozen. "They have a strict hierarchy system. He'll be a guard."

"How do you know what he is?" Savannah muttered back, careful not to make any sudden moves to aggravate them. She wanted to get out of this peacefully, considering the Countess intended to ask them for help, though she had no idea if they even communicated with the other wolves in the Realms.

"You'll know the leader and his mate when you see them. They're always the largest in the pack. This one's not big enough."

"He looks pretty damn big to me," Savannah said nervously. "I suggest we get in the air as quickly as we can before they decide to cross the water. I'll help you up first." She edged over to Sunflower. "Are you ready?"

As Rozen raised her foot into the stirrup, a harsh growl sounded behind them, and she slowly brought her leg back down. When Savannah turned to look, her heart skipped a beat. Standing no more than three yards behind them was an even larger wolf. This one had a dark gray coat, with its face and ears streaked rusty red, and its yellow eyes flecked with orange. Savannah flicked a glance at Rozen, who nodded. She eyed him warily, readying her magic. If this was the leader of the Zorian Gray Wolves, he was the one with whom she had to reason.

Tentatively, she sent out a telepathic thought, *"I am Savannah, the Chosen One."*

By the way he tilted his head to study her, he under-

296 | COVENANT OF QUEENS

stood the message. But instead of mind-speaking back, he let out a series of yips. "What do I care. You are intruding on our territory."

"We mean you no harm. We were grounded by the fog and will go immediately," she answered telepathically rather than emulate the wolf sounds.

He stepped back a pace, regarding her with bared teeth then yipped, "Only an Enchantress can understand our language."

"I am not an Enchantress, nor am I a magical being. The sacred medallion gives me the ability to understand you. On behalf of the Imperial Queen, I ask that you give us safe passage to continue our journey."

He made a chuffing sound that sounded like a sneer. "You think we are servants of the Queen. If we have never accepted Olivine as our sovereign, why would we bow to the Imperial bitch."

Savannah stiffened her shoulders, not liking where this was going. *"It's time to put aside hostilities and work together. We are at war,"* she said but sensed her words were falling on deaf ears.

"You think we care?"

"You should. You're part of Rand."

"You wear the medallion, but you know nothing. Why do you think we Wolves live only in the most isolated forests?"

Savannah frowned at him, wondering what he was

getting at. *"I thought that's where you liked living so you can roam freely."*

He leaned closer until she felt his hot breath on her cheeks. She itched to step back, but she had no intention of giving him that satisfaction. "We were banished there," he snarled.

She blinked at him, not expecting that. *"Why?"*

"Work it out." This time he dispensed with the yip talk and spoke directly with his mind.

"How long ago were you banished?" she asked, dread sinking into the pit of her stomach.

"Long enough for everyone to have forgotten, including Gladofin and Olivine."

And then Savannah understood what he meant. *"The Wolves fought with the Crevlin in the last war, didn't they?"* Savannah said, horrified.

"Yes, and we will again," he said. *"We have been promised the Forgotten Realms. The Mani will be executed, and the wolf packs will have a vast hunting ground. Not like the slim pickings we exist on now."*

Savannah was so furious, that she began to glow with magic. She fought to control it — unleashing great power would kill everything in sight, including Rozen and Sunflower. *"You unfeeling bastard."*

He bared his teeth at her. *"Our war is beginning in two days. The Wolves in the Great Northern Forests will march with the Crevlin to attack Bogonia."*

"How can you know that from up here?" When his eyes suddenly hooded as though he knew he'd said too much, the epiphany hit Savannah. *"The packs can mind-speak to each other,"* she said flatly. *"Even to those on the rest of Rand."*

"Yes, and it doesn't matter you know. You'll be dead in a minute." He gave a series of triumphant yips. *"Just like the Countess will be."*

Savannah went cold. *"You have her?"*

"And her horse. We will enjoy eating the Blue —"

Abruptly, he ceased speaking, turned his head towards the woods at the back, then cocked his head and sniffed the air. Savannah followed his gaze into the shadowy trees, straining her ears for sound. The noise was faint at first, but it quickly increased to a roar. Something was coming, something big. The Wolves on the other bank immediately darted across the water to join their Alpha.

He yipped at them, "Kill them. The witch first."

Everything exploded into chaos. Three Gray Wolves launched at Savannah, teeth bared. She raised her hands, raking them with magic fire and electricity. As they flew howling backward, their coats alight, something huge crashed out of the undergrowth. She turned to see the Or'orah barreling down on them, its nostrils flared and mouth open. And it was heading straight for her. Caught between it and its prey, the Alpha had no option but to fight the angry monster. Immediately he bunched its muscles ready to pounce, the other Wolves left Savannah to fight beside him. When they launched an attack on the spider, it squealed furiously, striking out with the razor-sharp hooks on the ends of its legs.

One hook skewered the guard Wolf, its belly tearing open as the spider flung it away. The Wolf whimpered, crawling along the ground with its entrails trailing in the dirt. As the others sank their teeth into the spider's soft underbelly, it swung its head and gutted another Wolf with its horn. The rest of the pack continued to bite and rake with their claws, forcing the Or'orah backward. It tried to spit, but when nothing came out, it became even more incensed. It slammed its legs and gored with its horn. Though blood coated their pelts, the Wolves continued to sink their teeth into the spider.

The Alpha leaped onto its back, its massive jaws snapping down on the exposed junction of the head and the shell. The scent of both spider and Wolf blood thickened the air.

Now the focus was off her, Savannah ran over to Sunflower who had retreated to the side. "Get into the saddle, Rozen," she called out frantically.

As soon as she had her foot in the stirrup, Savannah grasped her bottom and thrust her unceremoniously up onto the saddle. But before Savannah could mount, the nearest Wolf rushed at Sunflower, sinking its teeth into her leg three inches above her fetlock. The mare squealed, danced to the side, and jerked her leg hard to dislodge her tormentor. The Wolf lost its grip, somersaulted backward, but regained its feet and charged again. This time, Sunflower lashed out earlier with her hoof, smashing its face. When it dropped like a stone onto the ground, she stamped down on its belly.

Though it was dead, it was too late for Savannah. The Alpha Wolf whipped around at the horse's squeal and bounded off the spider's back, leaving the rest of his Wolves to fight the monster.

"Get in the air, Sunflower," Savannah screamed. "I'll grab your tail."

Sunflower unfurled her wings immediately, already off the ground by the time the Alpha rushed at them. Savannah wound her arm through the tail, clutching on grimly to a fist full of hair. As the horse soared straight upward, the Wolf gave a feral snarl and launched into the air after them. Its teeth snapped down on the heel of Savannah's boot. For a while, they both dangled from the horse's tail while Sunflower desperately tried to climb with the extra weight.

She had just begun to flounder when the boot slid over Savannah's ankle, the Wolf flailing for purchase. When the boot slipped off, he tumbled down with it. Though he landed heavily on four feet, the Alpha still had enough energy to project his anger at Savannah.

"I'll rip the meat from your bones when we meet again, Chosen One."

"You can try, you mongrel," she shot back. Then she focused on keeping her hold on the tail as she swung precariously over the tops of the tree. "Land somewhere as quickly as you can. I'm losing my grip," she called out urgently.

Sunflower immediately headed for a gravelly hillock away from the dark woods. No animals were in sight. A foot from the ground, Savannah let go of the tail. When the mare touched down beside her, she gave Rozen a semblance of a smile. "That was close. Remind me never to piss off an Or'orah again. We'll be safe here to rest for a few minutes."

Rozen eyed her curiously. "What was going on between you and the Alpha, Savannah? You both looked intense."

"We were mind-speaking. I found I have the ability to talk to some animals that way."

"That's an extremely handy talent. What did you learn? He looked enraged."

Savannah pursed her lips. "The Wolves aren't our friends. They fight with the Crevlin."

"What!" exclaimed Rozen. "All the packs?"

"They can communicate to each other with their minds. And that includes the packs that aren't in the Forgotten Realms. We must get a message to Pela somehow. They've joined the Crevlin army in the Great Northern Forest and march in two days to take Bogonia, which is the Realm bordering the Great Northern Forests." She grimaced. "Somehow, the Wolves have captured Gladofin, and I don't know if Snow Pine is still alive. They went up into the mountains to talk to them."

"We're in the most isolated place in Rand, Savannah. How can we send a warning?"

"I've discovered I'm a Mind Walker, but I haven't time to explain that now. I'm a very inexperienced one, but I'll try. Maybe someone will hear me."

Rozen looked at her oddly but nodded.

Savannah sat down, cleared her mind, and projected a simple sentence. *"Can anyone hear me?"*

Nothing happened. She tried again, then again. Still nothing. She was just about to give up, figuring she probably would need to target someone specifically to be successful, when she heard the thought in her head. *"Come on, Luv, tell me who you like. I ain't got all day."*

Savannah straightened, then projected loudly. *"Who are you?"*

"And who the hell are you?"

"Savannah."

"Whatcha doin' in my trance?"

Savannah sat up straighter. *"Is that you, Esme?"*

"Course it is. I'm doin' a reading. Get out of my mind."

"No, no, no, Esme. Don't go. I need you to give Lilybeth a message."

"Hurry up then. The cook'll be here any sec."

"Tell her Gladofin needs help. The Amarim Wolf pack has her. And she must send a message to Pela. The Crevlin and Gray Wolves will be marching on Bogonia in two days."

"Gawd, Savannah. that ain't good news. I'll tell her. Now I gotta go ... the cook's on the warpath." And then she was gone.

Slumping forward, Savannah couldn't stop the tears dribbling down her cheeks. Rozen knelt beside her and put her good arm around her shoulders. "It'll be all right. You tried."

Savannah sniffled back her sobs. "I made a right royal stuff-up of everything. I nearly got you and Sunflower killed, and Pela will probably never speak to me again. And we're still stuck on this mountain without knowing if the Sylphs will even help us."

"Don't worry about Pela. She'll come around. As for me, except for this pesty broken arm, I've never had such an adventure. And with the Iriwari, I've something up my sleeve. I can shift into a Sylph as well as a Bramble Hawk."

Savannah began to laugh. "That's just the pickup I needed. And, Rozen, I got the message through to Queen Lilybeth."

CHAPTER TWENTY-SEVEN

THE BERIAN PALACE

The sound of running footsteps echoed through the workshop.

Lilybeth looked up from explaining the finer points of the catapult to Tamasin to see Esme burst through the door.

The Dreamer's round face was flushed bright red, her curls bouncing wildly into the air. She gave Lilybeth a hurried curtsey before panting out, "I gotta message from Savannah, Ma'am."

"She's back?" asked Lilybeth, surprised. "She only went this morning."

"She ain't *here*. She interrupted my trance."

Tamasin raised an eyebrow. "Savannah spoke to you while you were in a trance?"

Esme impatiently clicked her tongue. "I just said

that, Mistress. I was doing a reading, waiting for the second parlor maid to reveal her secrets, when blow me down if Savannah didn't pop into my head. She gave me a helluva fright. I nearly peed my pants."

"Calm down, Esme, and tell us what she said," said Lilybeth soothingly.

Esme bobbed her head. "When I asked why she'd interrupted my reading, she said I had to give you an urgent message. *Tell Lilybeth that Gladofin needs help 'cause the Amarim Wolf pack has her. And she must send a message to Pela. In two days, the Crevlin and the Gray Wolves will be marching on Bogonia.*" She looked at them seriously. "That's what she said, word for word."

Lilybeth felt a sudden surge of panic. Gladofin was in trouble. Forcing herself to be calm, she turned to Tamasin. "Pela must be notified immediately that the Wolves fight with the enemy. I'll send a courier pigeon to Bogonia."

Tamasin closed her sagging jaw. "I'll go. Pela will need help organizing the armies now the enemy is marching." She bunched her hands into fists. "Those traitorous Wolves will feel my anger."

"Wolves are sneaky bastards," piped up Esme. "My parents had a farm in the Southern Lands. My mother always said, 'Never trust a Wolf. They'd steal the food off the baby's plate if they could.'"

"Your mother was a wise woman," said Tamasin.

306 | COVENANT OF QUEENS

Esme nodded sagely. "She was."

"Tell the cook I gave you the rest of the day off," Lilybeth said. "Every half an hour, go into a trance. It'll keep some form of communication open for Savannah. And thank you, Esme."

When she disappeared out the door, Tamasin looked at Lilybeth curiously. "Why is she working in the kitchens? The Crown pays the Dreamers well."

Lilybeth chuckled. "She prefers to work. To quote Esme, 'I ain't a lady to put my feet up and do nuffin'. And the staff are gullible customers for her readings."

Tamasin smiled, but then her face lost its animation. "We'll send a message to Olivine about the Countess."

"I'll go myself," said Lilybeth firmly.

"You can't just lob up with a squad of soldiers to fight the Wolves. There'll be hundreds of them. I'll go."

"I know," said Lilybeth irritably. "I'll ask Winston to work out a plan. But how they captured Gladofin is a mystery. She's a Guardian and can control all animals. I've seen evidence of that — she bested even Pela." She leaned forward, dropping her voice as if the walls might tell her secret. "The old blind woman said she's more powerful than Olivine."

Tamasin blinked at her. "Really? The Wolves must have had outside help."

"No doubt. We'd better get going. Take six of my guards and two Bramble Hawks with you."

"Tell them to meet me at the stables," Tamasin said, then hesitated. "Let Olivine send in her troops. The Forgotten Realms is not the place for someone without magic."

"I've been around the Sea Folk all my life, Tam. I know my limitations when it comes to magic. But also," she shuffled her feet, not meeting her eye, "this is personal."

"I know, my friend," said Tamasin quietly. "She's worth fighting for." She patted her arm. "Now, I'd better be on my way. Best of luck."

Lilybeth watched her go, suddenly saddened. Nothing would be the same when they met again. The war was escalating. With a sigh, she hurried off to organize a detail to accompany Tamasin. Afterward, she made her way to the operations room.

Winston and his crew were busily placing names on the map when she entered. The model of Rand was nearly complete. Now virtually everything was marked, it was much easier to predict what military routes would give the enemy the most advantage.

Lilybeth sat down heavily on a chair beside the table. "I've got bad news," she announced solemnly.

There must have been something in her tone, for Winston's face paled. "Has something happened to the Countess or Savannah?"

"The Countess has been captured by the Gray Wolves."

The three Mani gasped, and after glancing at each other, Egwine nodded her large head at Limos. "You speak for us."

"The Wolves haven't the power to defeat a Guardian, Ma'am. Not even if all the packs together tried."

"I'm aware of that, Limos. We know the Wolves have her, so we can only assume someone else captured her. Who would have the power to defeat a Guardian?"

He was silent for a moment, deep in thought. "A demon perhaps, but they avoid the Forgotten Realms like the plague because the Ice Elves can kill them." His expression darkened. "They say that nothing on Rand is invulnerable to the dark magic of the Ancients."

Lilybeth frowned. "You're saying there's other magic more powerful than a demon's black magic?"

"So it is told. But whether it's only a myth, I have no idea."

"Hmm. Well, we can't dwell on that," said Lilybeth. "We must face the immediate problem — how to defeat the Wolves. Does anyone have any ideas?"

Limos bared his teeth. "They fear Tigers and Bears. They're also wary of the Bramble Hawks. I can organize an army of Mani to go in with us."

"You intend to come, Limos?"

"Of course. We all will. The Countess is loved in the Forgotten Realms."

"Good," said Lilybeth. "If the Mani handle the Wolves, I'll take a squad of my soldiers with me to see Olivine." She looked out the window at the moons. "If we hurry, we can reach the Amarim Palace before dark. We must move quickly. There'll be a reason they took the Countess."

"Probably to stop Olivine sending troops to help Rand's armies when the Crevlin begin their assault," said Winston. "Remember when you go in, there will be enemy soldiers with the Wolves. They would need someone to communicate their demands to the Queen."

†

The sun was low on the horizon when Lilybeth rode through the great stone archways leading into the Amarim valley.

The sky was a clear, cold, deep blue, so different from the wind-swept, often gray skies of the Berian coastline. The scene below was breathtaking, with a silver river running through green fields dotted with trees dressed in vibrant autumn colors. Further down, a regal white palace glittered like an exotic jewel in the afternoon light. Everything was beautiful to the point of being sublime but coming from a place where the landscape was harsh and the weather ruthless, Lilybeth found such perfection uncomfortable.

And she was nervous about meeting Queen Olivine. From all accounts, the Amarim Queen had a temper to rival Valeria's and wasn't as friendly as her sister. Since Gladofin had represented the Forgotten Realms at the Arcadian wedding of Fern and Jezzine, Lilybeth had never met Olivine. Now that she was lobbing up unannounced with a contingent of soldiers, she doubted the welcome mat would be out. As well, the three Mani had flown off to organize the rescue party, which left her to front up to the Palace alone.

Leaving her soldiers with the horses, Lilybeth walked to the front door.

The Guard eyed her military uniform in surprise. "The barracks are down the back, Captain."

Lilybeth ignored his blunder and saluted. "Inform Queen Olivine that Queen Lilybeth of Beria wishes to see her on urgent business, please."

The Guard peered over her shoulder. "Tell your Queen to come into the waiting room. I'll inform Her Majesty she's here."

"I'm Queen Lilybeth," she said shortly.

He snapped to attention. "Sorry, Ma'am. Come this way, please."

As she followed him through the front vestibule, she gazed around in awe. The place was so grand that by the time she reached the Throne Room antechamber, she felt completely demoralized. There was no way Gladofin would leave this splendor for the Berian Palace with its drafty halls and weather-beaten stone walls.

"Take a seat, Ma'am, and I'll inform the Queen you are here. She is busy with a deputation."

"Please tell her it's urgent, Captain."

He nodded and then disappeared through the door. Fifteen minutes later, a group of golden-tinged people with fluffy blue hair emerged from the room. When they eyed her curiously as they passed, she wondered what shapeshifters they were.

An elderly man appeared and ushered her through the door. "Whom shall I announce, please."

"Queen Lilybeth of Beria."

When he thumped his staff and called out her name, the Amarim Queen lifted her head from the paper she was reading to stare at her. She looked tired and irritable. "Where is Beria?" she asked.

Lilybeth cleared her throat. "On the Wide Sea of Mists, Your Majesty."

"What in the Goddess's name are you doing here, and why are you dressed like a soldier?"

Lilybeth lost her patience; all this carry on wasn't helping Gladofin. She straightened to full height and strode to the foot of the dais. "I am a Queen and, as such, demand respect. Shall we start again? I am Queen Lilybeth Vandersea of the House of Beria. Your sister Countess Gladofin is a guest in my Palace while working as a military strategist for the war effort. I told your guard that it was urgent, yet I was left to wait fifteen minutes like a common foot soldier."

Olivine's pale face turned a rosy red. With more ice than remorse, she replied, "I apologize, Queen Lilybeth, for our lack of etiquette. I've had a trying day. And usually, a visiting Royal dresses appropriately."

"Be as it may, Queen Olivine," said Lilybeth curtly, "but this is not the time to play courtly games. The Countess has been taken prisoner by the Amarim Wolves and I've come to help her."

Her eyes widening, Olivine rose abruptly from the throne. "That's impossible. Gladofin is a Guardian."

"I wish it were so. Savannah sent word that the Countess was captured, and the Wolves have allied themselves with the Crevlin."

"The traitors!" she exclaimed. "Do you know if it's only the Wolves in the Forgotten Realms?"

"The packs in the Great Northern Forests march with the enemy in two days."

"That's serious indeed. The Wolves have always been hard to control." Olivine walked from the throne and gestured to a room off the side. "It'll be more private in there."

Lilybeth followed her in, perching on the edge of the seat opposite her. Olivine studied her thoughtfully. "You brought troops?"

"A squad of thirty soldiers."

"Thank you for coming, Queen Lilybeth, but we'll take it from here. I'll know by morning where they're holding her. Consort Jayden and the Ice Elves will go in at dawn."

"Which will be playing into their hands. They would hardly have captured Gladofin and not anticipated that move."

Olivine lost her composure, her eyes clouding with worry. "What exactly is that supposed to mean?"

"There are darker forces at play. Whoever captured her must be very powerful to have bested a Guardian. Who would have that sort of magic?"

Olivine's voice faltered. "Only the Ancients. But they lived so long in the past that Rand has forgotten they even existed."

"But the Guardians haven't forgotten," said Lilybeth. It was a statement, not a question.

"No, we haven't."

"I met Ronja. When I touched the medallion, Savannah and I were transported back to Elsbeth's time. She's guiding Savannah on her quest."

Olivine looked at her in awe. "She is the one we call the Mother of Rand."

"And Borrentine must have old magic as well, for he is a Time Walker. Your Ice Elves can defeat the black magic of the demon world, but can they fight the ancient magic?"

"No," whispered Olivine. "They cannot. No one can."

"What about the Guardians together?"

"We will try."

Catching the waver in her voice, Lilybeth felt a wave of panic. "But you don't know if you'll be successful," she whispered.

"No, I don't. We are masters of nature, the air, and the earth. There is another element of the world."

"Water," said Lilybeth.

"We can control the rivers because we can move the earth through which they flow, but we cannot control the sea. All magic comes from a source, whether the magic's in a living entity or the natural world. If someone could control everything, they would be extremely dangerous." She searched Lilybeth's face. "Why do you think they took Gladofin?"

"Probably to stop you from entering the war. You should receive a demand from the enemy soon — tonight or early in the morning."

"I expect so. I'll ask Jayden to fetch the other Guardians."

Lilybeth remained silent for a few moments to marshal her thoughts. An idea was forming, and though it could backfire on her, it may work. "Our tactical group devised a plan to defeat the Wolves. The Mani are already gathering together the Tigers and the Bears to fight them. I expect when the rest of the Mani hear their beloved Countess is a hostage, they will all join them. Once the Wolves are out of the way, you and I can work out a way to free Gladofin."

Though her face looked drawn, Olivine managed a smile. "Thank you, Lilybeth. You have helped enormously. It is comforting to know Gladofin has such loyal friends. But there is no need for you to accompany us on the rescue mission. If she's been taken as we think by someone wielding ancient magic, the battle to free her will not be fought with swords."

"I know, but I'm coming."

Olivine looked at her in surprise. "You have no idea what —" She turned around quickly as an Ice Elf, carrying a box, hurried into the room.

After a salute, the Elf held out the box. "I'm sorry for interrupting, Ma'am, but we found this in the sentry post. The Guard's throat has been slit, and a note pinned to her shirt. With a bow, she passed over the piece of parchment.

"Thank you, Captain Leena." Olivine quickly broke the seal and spread out the page. After she finished reading, she swallowed visibly.

When Lilybeth said impatiently, "Well?" Olivine

read the contents aloud, "*We have Countess Gladofin. If you make one move to join Rand's armies, it'll be her head.*"

"Open the box," ordered Olivine.

Leena's hands were noticeably shaking as she untied the knot. When she lifted the lid, she sizzled out a small, distressed cry. Carefully, she placed the box at the foot of the Queen.

Snow Pine's ear lay in a cocoon of sawdust.

CHAPTER TWENTY-EIGHT

THE FORGOTTEN REALMS

They were high in the mountains when they saw the first Wolf.

It was squatting on a rocky ledge, and as soon as they flew into view, it loped into the trees. Lilybeth could see nothing pretty about this terrain. It was dry and rough, the trees bent and gnarled by the constant winds. Their leaves were a riot of cherry red, burning gold, and dying amber, a signal winter was approaching. The woodlands hugged the left side of the mountain; the right was slashed with crevasses and pocked with caves, affording plenty of places for the Wolves to hide.

Not far behind them, the Bears and the Tigers moved at a steady pace up the slopes while scores of Bramble Hawks circled in the sky. They had an army, but something in her bones told Lilybeth it would be useless against this enemy.

She irritably brushed away the insects that swarmed out of the trees and clustered around her face. Then a wind arrived, sending them scattering, but running icy hands along her skin. She shivered — the place was getting on her nerves. When Jayden finally signaled they were close, she sighed with relief. Thirty yards further on, he slowed, then hovered over a clearing in the trees at the base of a ridge. Lilybeth peered down, surprised no Wolves were in sight.

Gladofin was kneeling in the center, trussed tightly with thick black cords. Snow Pine, her wings bound with the cords and legs hobbled, was tied to a tree on the side. Rivulets of dried blood covered the left side of her head where the ear had been severed, and judging by the bites on her legs, she hadn't been captured without a fight. When Banner whinnied his distress at the condition of the stately mare, Lilybeth patted his neck reassuringly. "At least she's alive," she said in his ear.

Cautiously, Jayden and the squad of Ice Elves landed. When no enemy appeared, Olivine, accompanied by five Guardians, touched down. Lilybeth followed them in, leaving her soldiers keeping guard in the air. As her warhorse descended, she caught glimpses of the Tigers and Bears crouched low in the undergrowth around the clearing. The woods were steeped in shadows, broken by spots of light from a family of glowbirds nestled in the labyrinth of dying leaves. Magic hung around the clearing like fog in a valley.

The site secured, Olivine ran over to Gladofin, who stared at her, wide-eyed.

Before she could speak, Gladofin grated out hoarsely, "Get out of here *now*, Ollie, before it's too late."

"I've brought five other Guardians, Glad. We'll combine our powers." Olivine tugged one of the black strands on Gladofin's arm. When it sparked, she sprang back with a cry, "Ouch! That hurt."

"You don't understand," said Gladofin, desperation etched into her voice. "The ancient magic is too strong. Leave me and go."

"The enemy is prepared to spare you if we don't enter the war," said Olivine.

"Which is all lies. All it wanted to do was to get you up here. *Now go,*" Gladofin called out. "All of you, get out of here." But then her eyes widened when she caught sight of Lilybeth. "What are you doing here, Lilybeth?" she exclaimed.

"She insisted on coming," muttered Olivine.

"Savannah got a message to us that you were in trouble. So," Lilybeth tossed up her hands, "I'm here."

"You shouldn't have come."

"I had no intention of staying away when you're in trouble. The others are here too. Limos has gathered the Tigers and the Bears."

Gladofin's shoulders hunched in defeat. "It won't do any good. Leave now. Please."

"We can —" Lilybeth stopped as a whisper echoed somewhere deep inside the mountain. Moments later, a black cloud crested the ridge above and moved along its edge. As it went, it devoured the light until the woods became a ghostly shadowland. A deathly pall fell over the clearing as if the dead had arrived. With the darkness came a featureless Wraith dressed in a floating black material that swirled and twisted as it moved. Though the specter had virtually no form like a crudely constructed doll, Lilybeth sensed it was female.

Volatile energy rolled off the apparition as it settled on the ground in front of them, and when it spoke, it sounded as though the words came through a tunnel. "Kneel before me, Olivine, and feel the full force of my wrath. I have waited a long time to bring down the House of Amarim. The time of the Guardians is at an end."

Olivine turned to Jayden and said urgently. "Get the troops away now, Jay. You can't help in this fight."

Lilybeth ran over to her horse. "Go with them, Banner. And don't argue."

He bowed his head, and when the Blue Fjords with the Ice Elves on their backs bounded into the air, he rose with them.

The Wraith snarled as it watched them fly off. "You've only delayed the inevitable. I will deal with them later. It is you I want, Ice Queen, and when you're dead, I will raze your palace to the ground, stone by stone."

"You can try," snapped Olivine and gestured to the five Guardians. As soon as they moved forward to stand beside her, they linked hands and began to hum. As their tune increased, Lilybeth could feel a palpable manifestation of magical power engulf the clearing.

The Wraith raised bony hands, sending a wall of pure energy swirling around the Guardians. Lilybeth fought for control as the ancient magic, potent, and malevolent, invaded every sense in her body. She called on her ancestors for the strength to resist, to give her the power of the sea. If she had been the target of the rage, she may not have won the battle. But so far the Wraith had ignored her, and she'd managed to hold on, soothed by the undulating waves in her head and limbs.

But the Guardians were gradually losing the battle. One by one, they passed out until only the Queen was left standing.

When blood began to trickle from Olivine's nose, Gladofin screamed out, "Leave her alone."

The Wraith whirled to look at her. "You think you can order me around, Countess. Perhaps more pain will shut you up." Black tentacles shot from her fingers, coiling around Gladofin's neck. Tears sprang to her eyes, and she whimpered in pain as the strands dug into her flesh.

Lilybeth ran forward: *It was now or never.* She knelt in front of Gladofin before the Wraith could react.

"Who are you?" it hissed.

Lilybeth ignored it, took Gladofin's head in her hands, and whispered, "Open your mouth, Glad." Then she drew in a deep breath, pressed her lips firmly against hers, and blew in the power of the sea.

As their breaths merged, the air about them formed a bubble, crackling with an energy that they alone could feel. The scene changed. They were no longer in the woods but standing on a beach, white sand digging into their bare feet. Lilybeth took her hand, "Listen," she whispered. Long mournful blasts echoed across the expanse of water, and as the sounds drew closer, waves rose to the call of the conch. The sea swelled, climbing higher until it crested into white tips like a thousand galloping snow horses. The wave rushed forward, then curled around them in a tight embrace. With a roar, it released its magic.

The beach vanished, and they were back in the clearing, their lips pressed together, but this time in a lingering kiss. When Lilybeth pulled away, Gladofin began to glow a delicate shade of aquamarine. The black strands broke, sizzling and popping as they sloughed off.

The Wraith screamed out its rage, lashing its tentacles at them. Gladofin caught them before they hit, grinding them into dust.

She grinned a mirthless smile at it. "I have been given the gift of the sea, foul one. I now command all the elements. Your ancient magic can't touch me now."

The Wraith turned to stare at Lilybeth. "You can command the seas?"

"The Berian Queens are Guardians of the Waters. Go back to your master and tell him he was a fool. He should have left the Sea Folk alone."

The Wraith began to shake with rage. "You think I'm a servant? I have no master. Pray you never meet me again, Queen of Beria, for I will kill you if you do." And then she was gone, but not before Lilybeth caught a glimpse of black eyes glaring at her with hatred.

Immediately, Gladofin went over to Snow Pine and angrily stripped off the black restraints. She whispered something in her ear, then returned to Olivine who embraced her. "What was that thing, Glad?"

"Something born of the old magic. But whatever it was, it's had dealings with the Guardians before. It's helping Borrentine, though it's not his lackey."

"I sensed that it was a woman," said Lilybeth. "It's some ancient harpy that has a vendetta against you. Her magic was so foul-smelling I was nearly sick."

Olivine studied her a little warily. "I underestimated you, Lilybeth. You did my family a great service and I thank you. We are in your debt."

"There is no debt, Olivine. Your sister was in trouble, so I came."

Olivine looked from one to the other. "You haven't told me much about your work for the war effort, Glad, but I'm happy to see you've made good friends." When a howl reverberated from the mountain above, she stopped to listen. "We had better do something about those treasonous Wolves. I'll wipe every last one of them from the mountain."

"Please, Ma'am," interrupted Lilybeth. "Let the Mani handle it. They have come to fight for their Countess, and you cannot deny them that battle. It would be an enormous boost to their self-esteem if you'd trust them to defend her."

"You're telling me how to rule my subjects?" Olivine asked, looking more puzzled than offended.

Lilybeth moistened her lips with her tongue, meeting the pale blue eyes with a level gaze. "I meant no disrespect. I know they would welcome the opportunity to prove their love and loyalty."

Olivine regarded her thoughtfully, then flicked a

look at Gladofin, who remained silent. "Very well," She pointed upward, where hundreds of Wolves lined the top of the ridge. "I will call them to begin. Jayden will not be far away. When he hears the fighting, he will be here immediately."

The Tigers came in first, their muscles flexing as they padded out of the undergrowth to stand in front of the Guardians. When the Wolves began to howl in a chorus, the horses appeared in the sky, archers ready with arrows notched. The Berian soldiers vaulted off their mounts to join Lilybeth, who stood with the Tigers, her sword drawn. The Bears lumbered in, forming rows on either side. Then surprisingly, Willow Dryads formed a semi-circle of trees around the perimeter, which effectively blocked off the retreat. Behind them, Lilybeth glimpsed more animals in the brush: Foxes, Deer, and other species, some she recognized, others she didn't.

It seemed the whole mountain was covered with animals.

And then it began.

Wolves poured in a tide down the slope, growling and snapping as they came. The Tigers leaped forward, launching at the leaders. As the Wolves fell, more took their place, biting and mauling the big cats. The Bears rushed in, swiping with their massive paws and ripping with their jaws. The Bramble Hawks screeched above, diving to claw out the Wolves' eyes. Balanced on the horses, the Elves began to fire their arrows, picking off the Wolves as they ran down the hill.

Lilybeth waved her sword, crying out, "Follow me, my warriors," as she leaped into the fray. She slashed and hacked, driving the enemy back. Blood darkened their pelts, but the Wolves continued their assault. But as the air thickened with the smell of death, they eventually wavered. And when they finally turned to retreat, the way was blocked by a herd of enormous, scaley creatures that looked like giant Anteaters.

Olivine stepped forward, her body glowing white as her voice resounded like a foghorn over the cries of the battle. "Enough! I wish to speak to your Alpha."

The Wolves dropped onto their bellies as a huge Wolf trotted out of the pack.

The Amarim Queen shimmered, growing taller until she was towering over the animal. "You dare fight with our enemy. Now feel my vengeance." She shot a burst of magic into his chest.

With a keening whine, he shuddered, collapsing onto the ground. When he half rose. baring his teeth, she signaled to Captain Leena. The Ice Elf came forward, swung her sword down hard, and decapitated him.

The shimmering force surrounding Olivine dissipated, and she shrank back to her normal size. She cast her eyes over the cowering Wolves. "If I find any member of the Amarim pack in the enemies' ranks, I will personally hunt them down and strip off their pelts. Now get out of my sight."

When the last Wolf disappeared up the mountain, the Mani changed out of their animal forms. Lilybeth stood back on the sideline with Olivine while they came up to Gladofin, some kissing her hand, others content just to touch her dress.

Olivine looked on in bemusement. "I didn't realize she was so loved."

Lilybeth was lost for words, remembering the kiss. It had torn away all the barriers she had carefully woven around her heart. It had left her feeling vulnerable, excited, and hopelessly enamored with the magical woman.

"You seem to be on good terms with her," murmured Olivine.

Lilybeth's face flushed. "She's an honored guest in my house."

"And she'll be returning to her home when this is over," said Olivine with finality.

CHAPTER TWENTY-NINE

THE ZORIAN ALPS

Savannah gazed in awe at the houses built into the sheer cliff face.

They reminded her of her visit to Bhutan, when she and a friend took a tour of the Paro Taktsang Buddhist Monastery high up in the Himalayas. The Monastery was precariously perched on the side of a mountain, with a sheer drop of many hundreds of meters to the countryside below. It had been a fascinating place and the views spectacular. The vistas here in the Zorian Alps were as incredible, and the air just as cold and thin.

The Iriwari domain wasn't a cluster of monastic buildings but a sizable town spreading up the cliff and across a plateau on the top. There was cultivation on the flat section and herd animals in pens. Red-roofed stone houses circled an octagonal building with a winged platform on the outside and a domed roof.

As they flew nearer, the air began to vibrate gently, and if she hadn't been on the alert for trouble, Savannah would have thought it was only a small updraft caused by pressure changes at the higher altitude. When Sunflower began to flounder, she pulled back quickly on the reins.

"*Turn around,*" she projected urgently.

"What's wrong with her?" asked Rozen.

"There's some sort of magical force field around the mountain. Sunflower won't be able to get through it. And it might knock us out of the sky."

"The horse is tired, Savannah," said Rozen, her voice radiating concern. "She'll have to go back down a long way to find somewhere to land. We could run into the Wolves again."

Savannah let out an exasperated growl. "Then we'll land here whether the Iriwari likes it or not. I'm going to blast a hole in the shield."

"Do you think that wise?" asked Rozen dubiously.

"Probably not," said Savannah, "but we've come this far and we're not going back down." She patted Sunflower's neck. "*When you see an explosion, fly straight for it, sweetie. Now turn back around.*"

The mare circled until she faced the town, then hovered.

Drawing her magic, Savannah stood up in the stirrups and launched a stream of power into the atmosphere. Ten yards ahead, the air began to sizzle until a pale-blue shimmering force field materialized into view. When she let fly another burst, the magic blew a sizable hole through the barrier.

"Go," Savannah yelled and dug in her heels.

Sunflower leaped forward, soared through, then swooped down to land on a grassed area on the plateau.

The bang that accompanied the blast brought people out of their houses. They formed a circle around them, though they warily kept their distance. When a man strode out from a doorway of the central domed building, the crowd parted to let him through. He was past his prime: tall and stately, with thick eyebrows, a high brow, an aquiline nose, and a halo of silver hair that hung to his shoulders. Dressed in a flowing white robe and sandals, he looked like he'd stepped out of a Renaissance religious painting.

When he spoke, his voice had such a warm, deep timbre it was half hypnotic. "What power do you wield, little one, that can breach our defenses?"

Savannah pulled out the medallion. "My name is Savannah. I wear the Circle of Sheda, sir."

He stroked his chin, regarding her thoughtfully. "So it has come back to Rand as the prophets foretold. But that doesn't excuse your trespassing. We do not allow strangers here. Why have you come, and who is your companion?"

Taken aback, Savannah shuffled her feet. His reaction to her announcement was not encouraging, considering the rest of Rand venerated the sacred article. She exchanged a sidelong glance with Rozen. If she was going to claim her heritage, now was the time. It would also get them out of trouble. Rozen knew it as well, for she stepped away from the support of the horse's body and stood up straighter. She must have been in pain but gave no sign as she looked him in the eye and said proudly, "I am Rozen, mother of Pela, Queen of the Bramble Hawks. My father was a Sylph."

He blinked at her. "That's impossible. No Sylph has left the Alps for centuries."

"My mother was hurt, and a Sylph brought her here to recuperate," Rozen stated flatly. "When she left, she didn't tell her lover she was pregnant. She went home and married one of her own race."

His eyes narrowed. "Your story is a little too convenient. Two generations ago can hardly be proven."

Rozen pursed her lips, clearly annoyed. Without saying another word, she began to shimmer. When the air settled, an ethereal being floated a foot from the ground; a beautiful, slender air spirit with delicate wings, a creature of the wind. It swayed gently for a moment and then began to change again. As it grew larger, brown feathers appeared, until finally, a huge Bramble Hawk with a broken wing stood in the circle. A collective gasp echoed from the crowd as they backed hastily away.

The Hawk squawked, shook itself, and morphed back into Rozen. "Satisfied?" she gasped out.

Savannah ran forward to support her. Rozen, her face ashen, was fading fast. "She must rest. Her broken arm needs to be seen by a healer."

"Come this way," he replied and led them down the street to a house with potted vines trailing over the front door. "Mother Ulana is our healer and a seer."

A middle-aged woman in a red robe opened the door. After taking in Rozen's sling and drawn face, she said gently, "Take her through and lay her on the couch, then wait outside while I examine her."

"Would you look at my horse's leg as well?" asked Savannah. "She has been attacked by a Wolf."

"Put her around the side and I will attend to her when I finish here."

Savannah smiled at her gratefully. "Thank you."

As soon as Rozen was settled on the couch, the white-haired man ushered Savannah into the waiting room. "Sit down; we have much to discuss. My name is Victor,"

"Are you the King of the Iriwari?" asked Savannah.

He smiled. "Queen Cassine is our ruler. I am the

keeper of the Great Star Scroll and one of her advisors. Now tell me why the Chosen One has come here."

"I seek counsel of those who study the stars." She eyed him curiously. "If you don't have visitors, Victor, how do you communicate with the outside world?"

"The Blue Fjords transport materials we cannot get from the alpine villages and bring news of the outside. The villagers are our friends, but they are simple people who are as isolated from the outside world as we are. While we interact with them, no outsider is allowed into our city."

"Oh, no wonder everyone stared at us," said Savannah digesting this information. "You can communicate with the horses?"

"With the King and Queen of the Blue Fjords, and our Queen's Royal mount. Because we can fly and our laws forbid us to venture outside the Zorian Alps, we keep only a few horses."

"Manoak is my friend," said Savannah, adding with a measure of satisfaction. "I can speak to all the horses."

He looked astounded. "How is that possible? The Iriwari haven't that ability, and we are born of the wind."

"I am Fjora."

He frowned. "The Fjora were a very ancient race of people. How can you have their bloodline?"

Savannah sighed. "I'm trying to find that out."

"Talk to our seer later. She knows many things that ordinary folks do not," he said more kindly. "Now why are you here, Chosen One? I imagine it wasn't by accident you found our haven."

She gave a dry chuckle. "The Zorian Alps is hardly the place for a leisurely jaunt. We've already had a run-in with an Or'orah and a pack of Gray Wolves, and both encounters were very unpleasant. I came to find out from your scholars the secret of the third moon. I understand the Iriwari are authorities on the Celestial Realms."

"We are. But first, tell me where Rozen fits in with your quest."

"I knew her history and persuaded her to show me the way," Savannah said briefly, then, deciding there was no point not telling him, continued, "Her daughter Pela and I are together."

His eyes widened. "You are bonded to the Queen of the Bramble Hawks. She is supposed to be fierce."

"I can handle her," Savannah said with a smile.

Victor looked at her with respect. "You must be tougher than you appear."

Savannah smiled. "I am. Can I ask how many people live here? There aren't many houses in view."

"Nearly all the city is underground. Very few live outside because of the cold." He got up. "While our healer is working on Rozen's arm, I will introduce

CHAPTER TWENTY-NINE | 335

you to our people who study the stars, and to our Queen."

Savannah fist pumped as she followed him into the octagonal building. So far, so good — she had a foot in the door. The first floor consisted of a wide lobby with rooms off to the side, but the second floor was intriguing. The whole level was an observatory, with desks piled with books and scrolls, and walls lined with complicated star charts. In the center of the domed roof was a huge crystal that acted like a giant telescope.

The men and women at the desks were dressed in flowing robes, and like Victor, had long hair and the high foreheads. When Savannah entered, they stared at her in bewilderment.

Her expression registering her shock, a woman rose from the table at the end of the room. "You let a stranger into our city, Master Victor."

He cleared his throat. "I did not, Your Majesty. Savannah had the power to blow a hole in the force field. She was accompanied by a Bramble Hawk whose father was a Sylph."

Surprisingly, that announcement caused more of an outcry than a stranger blasting her way into their stronghold. When they all began talking at once, the Queen called out loudly, "That's enough. Did she know the name of her father?"

"No, Ma'am. The mother left without revealing her

pregnancy and married one of her own kind. I can remember there was talk years ago of a stranger in the city," he replied, his voice becoming deeper when he went on, "But there can be no dispute about her authenticity. She changed into a Sylph."

"Then she will be made welcome as our sister. I will meet with her later." She turned to Savannah. "Introduce us, please, Victor."

He bowed. "Queen Cassine, Guardian of the Stars and Ruler of the Iriwari, this is Savannah, the Chosen One and Consort of Pela, the Bramble Hawk Queen."

Savannah smothered back a smile. Ceremony was alive and kicking here.

After Victor's pomp, Cassine was a surprise. In her mid-thirties, she looked more like a scholar than a Queen. Her white hair was tied back in a ponytail, her sleeves rolled up, and her fingers stained with ink.

Savannah bowed low. "Thank you for seeing me, Your Majesty."

"The medallion is back in Rand?"

"Yes, Ma'am." Savannah dug it out of her bra and waved it in the air, satisfied with the gasps of wonder.

Cassine regarded Savannah with a pair of fine intelligent eyes. "You don't look like the usual one chosen to wear the medallion, but these are strange times."

"The Crevlin are back."

"So Manoak informed us. He also told me a warrior has come who has the old bloodlines. Is that you?"

"I'm yet to discover my full heritage, but I am Fjora, amongst other things."

"I sense the strength in you, but something foreign as well," said Cassine. "Tell me why you have come to us."

Savannah smiled. "You know perfectly well why I'm here."

A dimple appeared with the Queen's answering smile. "We have been following the trajectory of the third moon for some time now. It hasn't been this close to Rand for over two thousand years."

"The time of the first Crevlin war," murmured Savannah.

Cassine's eyes widened. "You worked that out?"

"With a lot of research and the help of an old diary. After Iona was attacked, I met Borrentine, King of the Crevlin Empire." After Savannah related everything that had happened, she asked the question she'd come all this way to have answered. "Can you predict where the Covenant of Queens needs to be to close the Crevlins' Time Gateway, Ma'am? And how will we know when the time is right?"

Cassine fell silent, deep in thought, then gestured to a map of the universe on the far wall. "I can answer your last question easily enough. Come over here, and

I'll explain." She pointed a stick at Rand's two moons. "We call them moons, but we suspect they're worlds like ours on the same path around the sun. The third is definitely a moon, so far away in outer space that it's only visible to the naked eye when it reaches our inner star system every two thousand and one years. They always align on the day before winter. You see it now, but we have been tracking it for a lot longer."

Savannah did a quick calculation. It would be four thousand and two years ago, Crevlin time. "What happens when they're aligned?"

Cassine looked at her apologetically. "If you're expecting a sign, Savannah, there won't be any that will pinpoint a place. As soon as the third moon fits between the other two, they will block out the sunlight. The world will fall into total darkness. That will be your sign."

"How long will it last?" whispered Savannah.

"Six hours only. You must find where they've hidden the Time Gateway, for it may take time to close."

Savannah went cold. There wouldn't be any magical sign or much time. They needed to find the City of the Dead before the third moon was in place. "Have you any idea why they require darkness to move through time?" she asked hoarsely.

"Because the pathway is through the Realm of the Dead."

CHAPTER THIRTY

*S*avannah had an awful feeling that everything was unraveling.

She pulled herself together. She'd faced problems before; it was just a matter of solving them one at a time. When Cassine asked if she had any more questions, she shook her head. "Not at the moment. You've given me a lot to think about, but at least we know what to expect."

"Then I'll show you our city," said Cassine, rising from her chair. "We'll have something to eat downtown, and afterward, I'd like to meet your friend."

"I'd like that," she said gratefully, pleased she wasn't going with the dour Victor.

He was hovering at Savannah's shoulder and said quickly, "I can take her, Ma'am."

"I've finished for the day, Master Victor, but thank you for the offer."

As soon as they exited the room, Cassine gave a soft chuckle. "He's so staid and pompous that he sucks all the joy out of a room." Savannah glanced at her in surprise — she certainly wasn't in the same mold as the other Queens of Rand.

Once they reached the street, Cassine led her down a flight of stairs leading underground. At the bottom, they boarded a small tram trolley connected to a wheel and pulley that automatically took off as soon as Cassine pulled a lever. Savannah could see by all the gadgets in the streets that the Iriwari were far more advanced mechanically than the rest of Rand. For a few hours, they traveled through the city which was much larger than Savannah had envisaged from the outside. The people were self-sufficient, growing their food underground, similar to the hydroponic farms of Earth. The lower level held deep water-storage units filled from the melting snows.

When they stopped to eat in a shop near the markets, Savannah ordered a meat dish that tasted like pork. "Why do the Iriwari cut themselves off from the rest of the Forgotten Realms, Cassine?"

"It's always been like this. We know no different. It's an ideal life, with no crime or poverty, but isolation does have its problems. Strict population control is required, so only a few couples are allowed children. And we have little idea how the rest of Rand lives." She smiled at Savannah. "I'm finding you fascinating."

Savannah felt her cheeks heat. "Rand will be united again. The barrier around the Forgotten Realms is down."

"We heard."

"Perhaps you might think about meeting other people once the war is over. That is," she said solemnly, "if we win it."

"I'll honestly give that consideration," Cassine said seriously. "Small steps at first, but it would be exciting. We are scholars, but sometimes I wish for more." She stood up. "Now, I want to meet your friend."

Mother Ulana greeted Cassine with a quick hug, then led them through to the sick bay. "She's in there, Cass." She nodded with approval at Savannah. "You know the healing arts?"

"My mother was a healer."

"I saw how you bound the break. It should heal nicely." When Savannah went to follow the Queen through the door, Ulana grasped her arm. "I sense you are not as harmless as you look. You have power, but you have questions. I am a seer, a descendant of the great Sylph Oracle, Pharen. I may be able to give you some answers."

Savannah frowned down at the hand that clutched

her arm. A sharp tingling sensation rippled into her skin where the fingers pressed. "I wear the Circle of Sheda, Ulana. That is the power you feel."

"No. What I am referring to goes deeper than the magic of the medallion." She tapped Savannah's chest. "It's in there ... part of you. When we finish in the sick-bay, we will talk. Yes?"

Savannah nodded, albeit reluctantly. "I guess I'll give it a go."

Rozen was sitting up in bed, her bandaged arm in a sling, and smiled when they entered.

"Feeling better?" Savannah asked solicitously, relieved to see her in such good form.

"Much. Ulana attended to my arm and gave me something for the pain. She assures me the break will mend without any lasting effects."

Savannah nodded to the healer gratefully. "That's a weight off my mind. I persuaded Rozen to bring me here."

Cassine perched on the side of the bed and took hold of her free hand. "I am Queen Cassine, Rozen. I understand your father was a Sylph. Did your mother tell you his name?"

Rozen dropped her gaze, hesitated a moment, then raised her head to look her in the eye. "It was Baden."

Ulana sucked in a loud breath, glancing at the Queen, who had stiffened. "Well, that was a surprise,"

Cassine said, ruefully twitching her lips. "It seems we're related. He's my grandfather."

Rozen's mouth formed into an O. "They were very young," she said apologetically. "Is he alive?"

"He is. We are long-living creatures," Cassine answered and added, "*Aunt.* Would you like to meet him?"

"I would if you're happy for me to," Rozen said softly.

"Of course I am. We do not dessert our own. I'll take you to meet Baden. If you can walk to the stairs, we have transport below. He lives in the Palace, three levels down."

Rozen's face lit up. "Thank you, Your Majesty."

Cassine smiled. "I think we can dispense with the title. You are family." She turned to Savannah. "Would you like to come?"

"It'd be fitting if Rozen met him without me. I'll stay here with Ulana for a while and come down later."

As they left the room, Savannah asked curiously, "If the elders in her family are alive, why is Cassine the Queen?"

"It is our law that Monarchs must retire at sixty. We believe a younger ruler brings vigor and new ideas. Her father reached that age three years ago, and since she is his only child, she inherited the throne."

"The measure of intelligence is the ability to

change," murmured Savannah. "That's a quote by a famous man called Einstein in my world."

Ulana looked at her in surprise. "You came through the portal?"

"When I found the sacred medallion, it claimed me. Imperial Consort Tamasin brought me into Rand."

"Yet I have a strong feeling you belong here."

"My ancestor was Elsbeth of the House of Beria. She was the Chosen One who took the medallion through the portal."

"Ah, that explains it," said Ulana, studying her thoughtfully. "Come with me. I have a room where I consult the Seat of Prophecy."

Savannah nearly rolled her eyes. Magic was one thing, but prophetic readings were mumbo jumbo in her book. Keeping her misgivings to herself, she followed Ulana into a small room. It was dimly lit, with heavy red drapes over the windows and a table and chairs in the center. Geometric shapes hung on the walls, but she had no idea what they represented or their significance. She wriggled self-consciously into the seat, then waited for the reading to start.

After sprinkling incense around the room, Ulana took a seat opposite and reached for her hand. "Relax. Close your eyes and embrace the force within you."

Savannah let her body go limp, trying to summon her inner strength as Floris had taught her to do in

Kandelora. Nothing happened at first, but then the room became darker, the smell of the incense more invasive. She could feel the first fluttering of her life force rise to embrace the magic of the medallion. It came tantalizing close before it receded into the dark recesses of her psychic.

"Be in tune with your body and mind, Chosen One. Let it come." Ulana's voice was strangely seductive as it wove through her thoughts. "You're still holding out, not accepting it."

"What aren't I accepting?" whispered Savannah. She was floating in something filled with wispy threads and pulsated to a steady rhythm.

"That much of your magic doesn't come from the medallion you wear around your neck. It's in you."

Savannah knew then that she was in the beating heart of Rand. She sang out exuberantly as her power rose, embracing every cell of her body.

Ulana dropped her hand with a cry, scorched by the heat. She began to shake. "You are much more powerful than I ever imagined. You may ask one question of my Oracle ancestors, Savannah," she said hoarsely. "You have caught their attention."

The incense fog receded enough for Savannah to grasp the significance of what she'd said. "Only one?"

"Yes. Use it wisely."

Savannah thought quickly. She could find out, at

last, the father of Elsbeth's children, but she had a more pressing issue. "Ask them how I can kill the Time Walker, Borrentine,"

The room suddenly faded, and Savannah stood in front of a raised platform. Five women sat on golden chairs, staring down at her. The Oracles. The one in the middle said in a solemn voice, "I am Pharen, the Great Oracle to the ancient houses of Rand. You want to kill the Time Walkers. There is only one thing that can do that. The Dagger of Yorn. It doesn't kill conventionally; when you stab, it extinguishes the life force."

"Where is Yorn?"

"It was a temple in the time of creation, but the Dagger is still in Rand."

"Do you know where?" asked Savannah.

"If you summon up all your power, it will show you the place. But beware. The secret is guarded by a very powerful spell. It will come at a price."

"Thank you," Savannah said with a bow of her head. She took a deep breath, calling forth her magic. As it rose from the depths of her body, it merged with the medallion's power. The warm tingling suddenly turned nauseating, and she fought not to gag. Excruciating pain shot through her. Screaming in agony, she dropped into a tight ball on the floor. Tears streamed down her cheeks as the black magic seared through every nerve in her body.

She called on her power, desperately pushing back the thick black cloak that threatened to suffocate her. She didn't know how long she writhed on the floor, but finally, the pain eased enough for her to see a set of stairs leading down to a door. As she stared at it, she realized she'd seen it before. She struggled to remember, and then it came to her. It was the room in the Prophecy Tower that she'd briefly looked at on her way through the Silverthorne stronghold.

As soon as she remembered, the black magic spell vanished, and she was on the floor in the healer's room, with Ulana staring at her, horrified. Savannah grimaced. "That was terrible."

"I've never seen that happen before," said Ulana, gazing at her in awe. "Where did you go?"

"To your ancestors. Phalen answered my question."

"Oh," said Ulana, then seemed lost for words.

"I've had enough for the day," muttered Savannah. "Let's go to the Palace."

As she accompanied Ulana underground, Savannah thought over the encounter with the Oracles. She didn't relish the coming tussle to break the spell to enter the vault in the Prophecy Tower and retrieve the Dagger of Yorn. But that wasn't what was worrying her. The Oracle had said Time Walkers. Plural.

Which meant Borrentine wasn't the only one.

CHAPTER THIRTY-ONE

THE REALM OF BOGONIA

*T*amasin studied the countryside from the air. One of the smallest Realms of Rand, Bogonia was only a sixth of the size of Arcadia and its Palace far more modest. It bordered the edge of the Great Northern Forests and was wealthy enough, being part of the rich black-soil belt of Rand. The Realm was ruled by Queen Clementine, a friendly, matronly woman in her late forties who was fanatical in her devotion to the Goddess Iona. Tamasin imagined Pela would have had a battle trying to persuade her to recruit soldiers, for funding their army had always taken second place to the many holy temples filled with the faithful.

She could see plenty of activity in the city, which made her wonder what pressure Pela had put on the

CHAPTER THIRTY-ONE | 349

Queen to make her move. After Malkia touched down in the forecourt, she handed him over to a guard and ran up the steps. The Queen must have been alerted of her arrival, for she appeared as soon as Tamasin stepped through the door.

She looked flustered and out-of-sorts. "Consort Tamasin, I'm pleased to see you."

"Queen Clementine. I'm sorry to come unannounced, but I have news that can't wait."

"I'm very relieved you're here. Commander Pela has been simply dreadful, bullying my General and criticizing my army," Clementine said, her ample chest heaving with indignation.

"I'll have a word with her about it," Tamasin said soothingly. "Please call your military officers and your advisors for a meeting immediately. Where is Commander Pela?"

"She's talking to them in the council chamber."

"Good. I'd like to see her before I address everyone."

Catching the urgency in her tone, Clementine nodded. "Wait in the library, and I'll tell her you're here."

Moments later, Pela hurried in. "Hey, Tamasin. I didn't expect you so soon. What's happened?"

"Savannah sent word that the Crevlin have gathered in the Great Northern Forests and intend to march on

Bogonia the day after tomorrow. And the Wolves have joined the enemy."

Pela swore, then narrowed her eyes. "Those traitors. I'll rip the pelts from their bodies." She frowned. "Where is Savannah? Is she safe? And how did she get a message to you?"

"She interrupted Esme's trance by projecting her thoughts. She didn't say where she was."

"Hmm," murmured Pela. "She's been keeping something from me and that's what it is. Apparently she's a Mind Walker."

Tamasin nodded. "She must be. But there hasn't been one for a thousand years as far as I know. The mystery of her bloodline thickens."

"It certainly does, but we can dwell on that later. We have a more pressing problem. I don't know how she discovered the information, but we're lucky she did. It's as Winston suspected; they're in the Great Northern Forests. We'll need to move earlier than I planned."

Tamasin cleared her throat. "You've upset Clementine."

Pela snorted. "That useless woman has let her defenses go to rack and ruin. Every time I mention the coming war, she assures me the Goddess won't let the city fall. As for the general of her army, he whores and drinks every night. Clementine's Consort, Hayden, is a sensible man but he's completely dominated by the High Priestess."

To ease Pela's frustration, Tamasin said quietly, "I've got your back. Whatever you order them to do in that room, they *will* obey."

Pela flashed a smile. "The Queen fears Valeria nearly as much as she does me. Mention her name."

"I'll do that. Let's go."

When they entered, the chairs around the long table were all occupied except for the two at the head. All rose to bow to Tamasin, then resumed their seats and looked at her expectantly.

"I won't sugarcoat this," she began. "The Crevlin have a formidable force in the Great Northern Forests, and I've been sent word that they intend to march on Bogonia the day after tomorrow. The Gray Wolves have joined them. We have one day's grace."

Queen Clementine opened her mouth to say something then shut it again. The General half rose, but catching Pela's eye, flopped back in the chair. The rest of the assembly gazed at Tamasin in horror.

"I expect you all to obey Queen Valeria's Imperial Commander without argument," Tamasin continued. "This enemy nearly destroyed Iona, and your army will have little chance against their might. Their bombs will blast your city to rubble, and many will die. I'll pass over to Commander Pela to outline her plan."

Pela stood up, frowning down at them. Her expression was so fierce that the tattoo seemed to jump off her skin. Tamasin smiled to herself; she frightened them witless. "We'll start the evacuation of Bogonia at first light tomorrow morning. Food stores will be loaded into wagons and taken into Arcadia. And I mean everything: bags of wheat, dried fruits, and fresh produce. There will be no food left in the city for their army. Livestock will be driven over the Cadiwine River. All citizens must leave tomorrow morning. Malkia will call the Blue Fjords to take out the elderly and the folk who can't walk."

Pela paused, then looked at the General. "Except for a small contingent of your best soldiers, I want the army in the saddle as soon as every person has left. Exit quietly — no trumpets, no drums, no shouts. March to the North Cadiwine and set up camps on the other side of the river. When everything is across, destroy the bridges bar one. The one left must be defended at all costs. Let no enemy pass over it."

She gestured to the Captain of the Bramble Hawks. "Send one of your squad tonight to the Forgotten Realms to bring a large force of Hawks from the Eastern mountains to patrol the skies over the river. Kill any Crows who attempt to fly over. I want four more soldiers in the sky tonight to relay a message to the four Realms further along the North Cadiwine.

They're ready to evacuate when I send word. Another one is to fly to the Arcadii garrison. General Grogan waits for word to send troops to join you at the river."

Tamasin glanced across at her, impressed. Only Pela could have pulled them all together in so little time.

The High Priestess, a sour, pinched woman, exclaimed sharply, "You expect us to abandon our homes to the enemy without a fight?"

Pela glared at her. "Yes, I do. We have no hope of defending anything against their bombs. And when everyone has left Bogonia, we'll set all the crops alight. There will be no food for their soldiers who are already wasted from hunger."

Pela pulled a map off the wall, stretched it out on the table, and pointed to three spots on the parchment. "Send small patrols to these places to hide, General. Hit-and-run tactics at night only. Instruct them to retreat if they're compromised, but they will not engage the enemy in the open."

"Why such stealth?" grumbled the General. "My troops are seasoned warriors."

Pela's expression turned dark. "The enemy will not eat any fallen soldiers either. Let the bastards starve!"

The Bogonians fell silent, horror reflected on their faces.

✝

By mid-morning, the outer farms had been evacuated, the crops in the fields abandoned, the flourishing market gardens poisoned, and the country folk had joined the long exodus of people fleeing the city. When Pela had arrived in Bogonia, she'd commanded all livestock to be driven at once to the river plains. A timely order, for there was no way that the herds could have reached the river in a day.

The loaded wagons and carts had left at first light, fresh harness horses tied behind to replace those tiring in the traces. The convoy wouldn't stop until the last wagon crossed the bridge, a journey that would take them well into the night.

By late afternoon, the streets were empty except for a few mangey dogs scavenging for scraps in the deserted marketplaces. Finally satisfied the city was clear, Tamasin strode into the Palace drawing room where the Queen and her husband were waiting with the High Priest and Priestess. "Time to go, Clementine," Tamasin said gently.

A stray tear trickled down the Queen's cheek. "It's hard to abandon my home to the enemy. I expect the brutes will destroy everything I cherish."

"I know. But you'll all be alive, and Valeria and Fern will help you rebuild. Beria has offered aid as well. Fern has sent word that you and Hayden are welcome to stay in the Palace. The Arcadii Priory has offered accommodation for the High Priest and Priestess."

"That's kind of Fern," Clementine murmured. She took Hayden's hand. "Shall we go, dear."

As they trailed out the door, Tamasin couldn't help thinking that it would do Clementine good to be away from the influence of those domineering spiritual leaders and have a chance to reconnect with her husband. From the way the High Priestess frowned at the offer of the priory, she had expected to be invited to the Palace as well.

Pela came to join Tamasin as she stood on the balcony, watching them fly into the distance.

"Even though Clementine annoyed me to distraction," said Pela. "I can't help feeling sympathy for her. The enemy will trash the city looking for food."

"And if they don't find anything, they'll destroy her Palace out of spite," Tamasin said. She pushed away from the railing. "Have the Ice Elves arrived?"

"Jayden landed with two squads an hour ago. He's brought news of the Countess. She's safe. He'll tell you all about her rescue at dinner. The Ice Elves are in the barracks and will mount at daybreak."

"That's excellent news about the Countess," Tamasin replied. "We'll eat with them. The cook left enough for the last supper."

It hardly felt like her head had touched the pillow when Tamasin began to dream. And then the familiar voice spoke in her ear, "*You only have one turn of the moons left to find the City of the Dead, Tamasin. The third eye has begun to close the gap.*"

She writhed in the bed, straining to see the face, but, as always, it was only a shadow. "*Tell me where it is.*"

Even though it was a dream, she sensed the aged voice sounded frustrated. "*I don't know. There is only a faint thread of the future left, and they have hidden their exit well this time.*"

Desperate, Tamasin cried out, *Can you see anything? Is it where their army is now?*"

"*No. The Crows flew there. Now it is time to wake up. The enemy is on the move. And remember, you must hurry to find the Time Gateway.*"

And then she was gone.

After wiping off the lather of sweat, Tamasin quickly pulled on her clothes. Her knives sheathed in her boots, she ran down the corridor. When she banged on the doors, Pela opened hers immediately, and because she appeared fully dressed, she guessed she'd slept in her clothes. "There's still two hours 'till daybreak. What's wrong, Tam?"

"I had a dream. The enemy is on the move."

Jayden and the Ice Elves were already in the hallway.

CHAPTER THIRTY-ONE | 357

"There's a fireplace burning in the stables. Light your lanterns and get into the saddles."

When they sprinted off, Tamasin turned to Pela. "I hope they've put enough pitch on the arrowheads. We don't want them snuffing out before they hit the ground."

"Don't panic. Jayden knows what he's doing."

"I know," she growled. "I just can't help worrying."

Pela grinned. "Come on then. It's no use sitting here wondering what's happening. Let's look."

"Okay. I'll saddle Malkia and meet you at the stables."

By the time they were in the air, long shadows were lengthening across the ground. When the Hawk wheeled in the sky heading north, Tamasin followed. Two miles on, they passed over a hill that overlooked a plain of golden wheat ready to be harvested. In the distance, wisps of smoke spiraled upward, which soon increased to billowing clouds.

And then bright orange and red flames spurted into the sky, hungrily devouring the crops and tinder-dry autumn leaves piled under the trees on the slopes. As the fire licked the countryside black, the howls of Wolves reverberated through the smoke.

CHAPTER THIRTY-TWO

THE FORGOTTEN REALMS

*L*ilybeth picked her way through the gardens to the Amarim stables in search of Gladofin.

She found her with her medical box, kneeling in the straw beside Snow Pine. The smell of pungent herbs hung heavy in the stall. The mare was shivering, and Gladofin's bottom lip trembled as she attended to the Wolf bites.

At the sight of their distress, Lilybeth had an overwhelming urge to ease their pain. She dropped to the floor beside Snow Pine, then wriggled closer to cradle her head in her lap. "Pass me one of those wipes and a bowl of water, Glad," she said softly, "and I'll clean her face."

Gladofin passed them over without a word and continued smearing a thick brown ointment over the bites on her legs. Careful to avoid touching the open wound at the ear, Lilybeth took her time as she gently worked off the dried blood set hard in the hair. When the mare's face was completely white again, she gave a hum of satisfaction. "There you go, my sweet. You're pretty again."

She looked up to see Gladofin studying her. "I see my maid supplied you with clean clothes."

Lilybeth plucked at the material self-consciously. "The top is a little tight around the shoulders. I'm not as slender as you."

"No, you're not. You're so superbly fit, you put us all to shame." She slid her gaze away a fraction, not meeting her eye. "Why did you come, Lilybeth?"

"Because I heard you were in trouble."

"But you knew the Forgotten Realms have many powerful Magical Folk to help me. You weren't to know about the Wraith."

Lilybeth squirmed, then caught Snow Pine looking up at her. By the gleam in her big brown eyes, the mare knew perfectly well why Lilybeth had dropped everything and rushed here like some smitten knight in shining armor. She squared her shoulders and took a deep breath; it was now or never. "I came, Glad, because I've become fond of you."

Gladofin arched an eyebrow. "Fond?"

"Well, a bit more than fond." She cleared her throat

self-consciously. "A lot more, actually. I'm ... well ... quite taken with you. You're the most exciting woman I've ever met, and I know we haven't been formally courting, but I want to," she said in a rush.

Gladofin smiled. "Oh, Beth, you're such a stickler for convention. At our age, I think we can dispense with those formalities. I've been interested in you ever since I saw you at Valeria's reception. When I sat beside you at Fern and Jezzine's wedding, you captivated me. I thought I made that clear."

Lilybeth gazed at her shyly, inordinately pleased at the shortening of her name. That this stunning woman would even give her a second glance was a miracle, let alone reciprocate her feelings. "I haven't had a lover for years, Glad. I'm rather rusty."

A chuckle burst out of Gladofin. "The matrons of the Royal Houses must have been so frustrated trying to get you to notice their children. They would have tried everything. A single Queen of a prosperous Realm is a great prize."

"I told you before, I find balls and social events a strain, nor does court gossip appeal to me."

"Nor me," agreed Gladofin. "I found your company refreshing at the wedding banquet." She reached over and touched her face. "We will do very well together."

"You still haven't told me why you never married. And what you meant by, *it's complicated.*"

"I will, but first things first. After I put a dressing on Snow Pine's head, we'll get her on her feet. Lying down won't be good in her condition. Then we'd better clean up and get to dinner. Olivine likes to eat on time."

"Um … about Olivine. I don't think she approves of me."

"No, she doesn't," said Gladofin blithely. "She's aware I'm interested in someone, and since you rushed here to help me, she now knows it's you. She's one of the *complications*. I've been helping her rule since our mother died. I've always let her think I chose to stay and to be fair, I've been content to do so and accepted the privileges that came with the position. When I needed a break, I went to the Pale Horse to relax."

"Everybody must be blind. Someone should have snaffled you up years ago."

Gladofin smiled. "I thought you didn't know how to flirt, Beth."

"It's the truth."

"Which makes your words so precious," replied Gladofin. "When Savannah first appeared at Amarim, she had a message from the Mother. She said that I was to step out of my sister's shadow. Ollie and I discussed my going then, but we never really believed I would. I guess we were both too settled to think about change." Her voice took on a serious tone. "Ollie has guessed I intend to leave the Palace, and she's not happy about it,

but she'll come around." She squeezed Lilybeth's hand
and said softly, "I know you can stand up to her, so it's
no longer a problem. After dinner, will you come to my
room, Beth?"

Lilybeth's pulse leaped. "I'd love to."

†

Dinner began badly.

Since Queen Olivine had informed her staff that she
required a quiet dinner to recuperate, only the three of
them were at the table. Jayden had no more arrived
back at the Palace than he was off again. An enemy
force was marching out of the Great Northern Forest
the following day, and Pela had requested two squads of
Ice Elves. After a hurried goodbye, he flew off to Bogonia, leaving Olivine without his comfort after the trying
day. When Lilybeth appeared wearing Gladofin's gown,
her mood darkened even more.

Her silence was ominous through the soup. Gladofin seemed unconcerned when the main course
arrived, but Lilybeth wasn't so sure. Olivine was keyed
up like a coiled spring, stabbing at her food with her
knife. Halfway through the dish, she dropped it with a
clatter and shoved the plate into the middle of the table.

Sitting back on her chair as if she was on the throne,
she folded her hands on her lap and eyed Lilybeth criti-

cally. "I trust you're leaving first thing in the morning, Lilybeth."

"No, she's not," said Gladofin casually. "I'm taking Beth for a trip around the Forgotten Realms tomorrow." She smiled at Lilybeth. "Would you like to do that?"

"Very much. I'd love to see your homeland."

"And I'll enjoy showing it to you." Gladofin glanced across at Olivine, a challenge in her stare.

The wintery eyes focused on Lilybeth, ignoring her sister. "I believe your Realm is on the sea. Does it have any beauty, or is it a dull place, gray and windswept most of the time like I imagine?"

Lilybeth shrugged. "Beauty is in the eye of those who look. I love everything about the sea: its tranquility, its mercurial nature, and even its cruelty."

"I'm not surprised. You're keen to fight like a soldier. Strange behavior for royalty."

"I come from a long line of warrior Queens, Olivine. Far more Berians have been chosen to wear the Circle of Sheda than any other Realm."

"Brawn not brains," Olivine muttered, though not softly enough not to be heard.

Lilybeth studied her thoughtfully. She had thrown down the gauntlet, pushing and shoving for Gladofin's loyalty. The Countess had really underestimated how badly her sister wanted her to stay.

When Gladofin began to speak, Lilybeth grasped her hand. "This is between your sister and me." She turned to see Olivine frowning at them. "We can jostle all day for Glad's commitment and love, Olivine, but ultimately, it's about what *she* wants, not what we want. And it mightn't be me she eventually picks, though I hope it is."

"Never," snapped Olivine.

"If you force her to choose, you would be foolish. Like it or not, now the border is down, there's another world for her to explore. Let her stretch her wings."

"You know nothing about us. So don't act like you do."

Lilybeth tilted her head to look at the Queen, catching the uncertainty, or perhaps it was fear in her eyes. "I have a gift, Olivine. I can read people. I will tell you what I see when I look at you. You are proud, accepting the homage you receive as a Guardian as your right, without any humility. As firstborn, you inherited the crown. But Glad has always been the strongest, the boldest, the forward thinker, the one who made the hard decisions. You fear to reign without her by your side, yet you must when she goes. You should lean more on your husband, for he must be tired of waiting in the wings."

Shaking with anger, Olivine glared at her. "How

dare you speak to me like that. You have abused my hospitality."

Lilybeth stared back. "And no one has ever trodden on my name as you have done. I won't be treated like a common servant, and I intend to see more of Glad, whether you agree or not. She needs someone of her own so let her go with your blessing."

"You expect my blessing?"

"It would be better if you accepted it. My gain doesn't need to be your loss." She smiled apologetically at Gladofin and said softly, "Sorry. That sounded presumptuous. We're hardly attached."

"Yet," mouthed Gladofin.

"I meant it," Lilybeth whispered.

"That's all I wanted to know." She looked at Olivine sternly. "That's enough, Ollie. You've been rude to Lilybeth, so apologize."

"You want *me* to apologize?"

"I mean it. Lilybeth is my guest, and by the Goddess, you will treat her like one. Your fight is with me, not her. We both know I've been ready to go for a while, and meeting Lilybeth only hastened me to make that decision. I'll always come back to help if you call, but you haven't needed me for a long time. You're a fine Queen with an excellent Consort in Jayden." She stood up. "Now, if you'll excuse us, we're going to bed."

Lilybeth quickly got to her feet to follow, pausing at

the door to glance back. Olivine sat brooding in the chair, staring into space. She wondered if the Amarim Queen would ever forgive her. She hoped so, for she'd hate to come between the sisters who loved each other. But when they reached the suite, she forgot about everything except the woman who smiled at her with shining eyes.

The bedroom was elegant, tastefully decorated, but still felt as comfortable as her favorite warm coat.

Gladofin looked at her shyly and kissed her on the cheek. "I'll wash first. I won't be long. Clean towels and sleep clothes are in the wardrobe."

As she watched her go, it occurred to Lilybeth that Gladofin might be as nervous as her. She wondered how many lovers she'd brought home, or had she avoided inviting anyone to the Palace, knowing how Olivine would react. The Queen was hardly a cheery welcoming committee. Taking a towel and nightshirt from the rack, she looked out the window while she waited. It was a cool night, with showers of rain blowing in on the breeze, too wet for most of the animals, except for a few Deer wandering about the gardens. But it was a good omen for her; she loved the rain.

At the sound of the door opening, she hurried in to wash.

When she exited the bathroom, Gladofin was

stretched on the sheet, naked except for the star pendant around her neck. With her blond curls tumbling over her shoulders and her blue-green eyes the color of water, she looked like one of the Sea Goddesses in the tapestry above the Berian Throne. Captivated, Lilybeth swallowed, slightly breathless.

When the Countess shook back her silken hair and said in a throaty, low voice, "Take off your clothes and come to bed," her heart flipped.

She stripped off and crawled in beside her. Soon she forgot about everything except what this wonderful woman was doing to her. As Gladofin brought her to such heights that she had never imagined possible, Lilybeth didn't think, only felt. And as she climaxed, the waves of exquisite pleasure brought a wrenching cry from somewhere deep inside her.

When she flopped back, spent, Gladofin leaned over her and said softly, "You're the first lover I've ever brought to my bedroom, Beth. And you fit just right in here. Now, go to sleep. We won't hurry the first time; we have our whole lives together."

Lilybeth opened her eyes to regard her. "I might be rusty, but I'm not dead," she replied huskily.

With a quick movement, she flipped her onto her back. "Now, my love, I intend to make you forget any lovers you've had in the past."

And she proceeded to do so, letting the tides of

passion rip through her as she made up for all those years of loneliness.

Gladofin writhed, moaned and begged until finally, she screamed and collapsed back onto the bed. She looked at Lilybeth shyly and with a little awe. "What a wonderful lover you are, Beth, and how lucky I am to have found you."

Lilybeth stroked her face. "I'm the lucky one. Are you going to tell me what you meant by the other *complication?* It's not going to frighten me away."

"All right. Be prepared." She stepped from the bed, and the air around her began to shimmer. As it whirled into a kaleidoscope of colors, a form took shape in the center. When the air stilled, an exotic being stood facing Lilybeth, a creature like none she'd ever seen. It had the upper torso of a woman, a floating lower body with a long-fanned tail, and a head that faintly resembled a unicorn with a horn sparkling with stars. It glowed a soft golden color. The parts complemented each other so well that the creature was beautiful.

Then the air shimmered again, and Gladofin reappeared. "The Guardians are shapeshifters too, Beth. Don't let it frighten you away."

Lilybeth burst into laughter. "You have to be joking. Your other self is lovely. You forget I'm used to the Sea Folk. Seals aren't pretty, but the Skeleton Octopuses are seriously ugly."

CHAPTER THIRTY-THREE

*S*avannah gazed down at the Amarim Palace as Sunflower prepared to land.

The showers had cleared away, leaving droplets clinging to the high tower like a cape of diamantes. It was an hour before sunset, late to be lobbing up unannounced, but it couldn't be helped. To give Rozen more time with her long-lost family and although it put Savannah's schedule a day behind, they hadn't left the Zorian Alps until after midday. Her father had been delighted to see her, holding an impromptu dinner in her honor. After all the death and destruction of the last few weeks and, with a full-scale war looming, it was nice to find a feel-good story.

Despite her broken arm, Rozen had never seemed

happier. As they left the snow-tipped mountains behind, Savannah couldn't help thinking that things probably wouldn't be the same for the Iriwari. Strangers had reached the reclusive city, and the young Sylph Queen had discovered another world out there waiting to be explored. Cassine had talked to them well into the night about the people and places in Rand, and no doubt when the time came, Rozen would help her niece bridge the cultures.

As Sunflower touched down behind the stables, Savannah concentrated back on the present. The Countess's plight was foremost in her mind as she led the mare under the archway into the main stable. She prayed Lilybeth had relayed the message of her abduction in time. Halfway along the corridor, Sunflower suddenly whinnied, jerked free of the reins, and trotted over the flagstones to the end stall. She stood outside, pawing at the floor. Savannah ran after her, horrified when she looked over the door.

"Oh, shit, Snow Pine," she exclaimed. "What have they done to you?"

The elderly mare stood trembling in the corner, a sorry sight, with an ear missing and angry bites covering her legs. Sunflower was keening in distress, trying to get into the stall.

Savannah stroked her neck soothingly. "Calm down.

I'm going in to see her. I want you to stay outside in case you knock her by accident."

The little mare struck the stone floor hard with her hoof to show her annoyance but shifted to the side to let Savannah past. "Good girl," Savannah murmured. "I'll see if I can help her."

Snow Pine summoned up a welcoming nicker. *"Hello, Savannah. The Countess dressed my wounds this morning which has dulled the pain."*

"Who cut off your ear, dear one?"

"There was a black ghost with the Wolves. She sliced it off with magic, then put it in a box."

Savannah blinked at her. She thought it must have been Borrentine — as far as she knew, he was the only one capable of besting the Guardian. "Are you sure it was a woman?"

"Yes. And while the Wraith fought the Countess, the Wolves attacked me."

Savannah angrily pressed her lips together. If this witch could defeat Gladofin, she could have controlled the horse easily without setting the Wolves onto her. Savannah touched her muzzle gently. "I'm going to give you a gift, Snow Pine. I can't replace the ear, but I can get rid of your pain and help you heal." Taking the mare's head in her hands, she let a sliver of the medallion's magic leak from her fingertips into her facial crests. As the magic seeped in, Snow Pine began to glow until her skin turned a healthy color and her mane brightened. Though the bites on her legs were still visible, the wounds no longer looked raw and inflamed.

"How does that feel?" she asked softly.

"Wonderful. The pain is gone."

"The bites will heal quickly now. Would you allow Sunflower to come in with you?"

Two tears trickled over the lids of the big brown eyes. *"I would like that, Savannah. I've been lonely since the Countess and Banner left this morning. He has the adjoining stall, and we became friends at Beria."*

"Queen Lilybeth is here?"

"She came to help the Countess."

Savannah pricked up her ears at this. The romance must have moved to another level if Lilybeth rushed halfway across Rand to her aid. Grandmother would be pleased. Smiling as she visualized how smug the old girl would be, Savannah moved out of the stall to let Sunflower enter. Giving a soft nicker, she sidled up to the taller Snow Pine and touched her muzzle with hers. Savannah gave a last fond look at them before walking to the exit. She was anxious to hear how the Countess escaped and the identity of the black witch.

The guard at the door saluted in welcome before he showed her through to the library. In a comfortable chair in front of a fireplace, Queen Olivine was reading a book. Her eyes widened and quickly closed the book. "Savannah. This is a surprise."

"I'm sorry to arrive so late, Ma'am, but we didn't leave 'til noon."

Olivine smiled at her pensively. "The lateness of the hour doesn't matter so long as you achieved what you wanted to. We owe you many thanks for warning us that the Wolves had Gladofin."

Savannah eyed her in surprise. The woman looked preoccupied and sad, nothing like an Ice Queen.

Olivine nodded at a chair. "Sit down and tell me where you went."

Savannah glanced down at the book title on her lap, *Beria and its Seas.* She looked up to see Olivine watching her.

"You've been to Beria, Savannah. What's it like?"

Savannah struggled to put her thoughts into words. "Windswept, imposing, austere, but it has such a wild beauty that it's captivating. Not for the faint-hearted. The Palace is huge, plain in comparison to others, and sits on a cliff overlooking an expanse of sea. The people are hardy but are the kindest, most welcoming of all the Realms. Don't be fooled by Queen Lilybeth either. Underneath that tough exterior, she's one of the most astute people I've met. She inspires great loyalty; her subjects adore her."

"So I've learned," muttered Olivine. "And it's not only her subjects who admire her."

"Countess Gladofin?"

"It would seem so."

From her expression, Savannah guessed that she didn't approve. Well, time to give Lilybeth a helping hand. She leaned forward and said conspiratorially, "This must remain our secret. The Mother told me she wants Lilybeth and Gladofin together to close the gap between the Magical Folk and the rest of Rand. They're destined for great things in the new world."

Olivine stared at her, her mouth sagging open. She uttered a long, "Ohhhh," then blushed. "Perhaps I've been a trifle hasty. I have a few bridges to mend."

Savannah smothered a smile. From the Queen's guilty look, she guessed *trifle* was an understatement. "Never mind," she said reassuringly. "Lilybeth will be only too willing to be friends. She knows how close you are to Gladofin."

"Huh! Not too willing. She was very rude."

Savannah was saved from replying when the sound of voices echoed in the hallway. Olivine hastily put the book away, and moments later, the two women stepped into the room.

"Savannah," cried Gladofin, hugging her. "I can't thank you enough for what you did for Snow Pine. She was so depressed when I left, it was very upsetting. She's back to her old self, well enough for the groom to take her for a walk in the yard."

"I gifted her a little magic from the medallion. I couldn't leave her in that condition, and Sunflower wouldn't forgive me if I had."

Gladofin chuckled. "That mare has you where she wants you. Now tell me. Did you manage to see the Iriwari?"

"I did. I've so much to tell you all." She raised an eyebrow at Olivine, who cleared her throat.

"Sit down, please, Lilybeth. We got off on the wrong foot last night. Since Gladofin thinks so highly of you, I would like to know you better."

Lilybeth flicked a glance at Savannah, then took a seat warily. "Thank you, Olivine. That would be nice."

"Good, then that's settled," said Olivine briskly and turned to Savannah. "Do you mean to tell me you went into the Zorian Alps and gained entrance to the Sylph's stronghold? Even I have never seen it."

Savannah nodded and launched into her story. When she'd finished relating the events in the alps, she asked, "Snow Pine told me you were captured by a Wraith, Countess. What was it like?"

Gladofin winced. "Very nasty. It was dressed in black, with little form, though we could tell it was female. It floated but was solid enough. And when it spoke, its voice was hollow." She shrugged. "That's all I can tell you. It was probably something Borrentine conjured up from the underworld."

"Can spirits from the underworld come into this world?"

A frown wrinkled Gladofin's brow. "I've never heard that any have, but it was the only explanation I could come up with. Demons have come into our world and that thing wasn't one."

"What's the difference? I thought they were the same."

"The underworld is a place for the dead. The Demon world is another realm entirely, one where they don't die."

"But I've killed demons," persisted Savannah.

"Destroyed. There is a difference. They don't fall sick."

Like robots, mused Savannah. But she pushed the thought aside to puzzle out later. "We'd better get on to the pressing issue. Finding the City of the Dead. While we're here, we should investigate those Wetlands north of the Forgotten Realms. Would you and Lilybeth accompany me there tomorrow on Banner, Gladofin? More eyes with three of us. And safer."

"Take a squad of Ice Elves with you," said Olivine.

"Too many horses will be like waving a red flag."

replied Savannah. "Two should have a better chance of slipping in without being noticed."

Gladofin looked across at Lilybeth, who nodded. "We'll leave first thing in the morning. The Wetlands are extensive, and not everything is visible from the air."

CHAPTER THIRTY-FOUR

THE NORTHERN WETLANDS

*J*t didn't take Savannah long to conclude the Crevlin would be crazy to exit their Time Gateway in these Wetlands.

It was a harsh environment, part land and part water. The wet areas were bogs, marshes, and winding canals; the drier parts were thick woodlands, and plains covered with mountains of plumed grasses and tall reeds. Nearly impossible to trek through. Trees clogged the swamps, half their roots above the water, vines snaking up their trunks, and long gray veils of moss hanging from their branches. Small plants and lilies floated on the water, while cattail reeds grew in dense clumps on the edge. And as the waterways spread out nearer to the Northern Ocean, they became thickets of mangrove roots and branches where only crabs and small crustaceans could live.

As Sunflower skimmed the tops of the trees, Savannah craned over her neck for a better view. Periodically, she pointed the Farsight Stone at the thickest woodlands to see what was beneath their canopies. She glimpsed a few big cats plus other strange large animals in the undergrowth and imagined the water would be filled with strange aquatic creatures as well. So far, she hadn't seen any people or Crows.

When she noticed a clear patch, she signaled to the others to descend to give the horses a rest and to have a closer look.

As soon as Sunflower touched down gingerly and folded her wings, Banner landed beside her. Cautiously, Savannah dismounted, keeping an eye out for any unexpected predators.

"From what I've seen of this place, a whole race of people couldn't come here without some of them being eaten by something," Lilybeth said, her voice hushed as if she feared any noise would alert whatever was lurking in the trees nearby.

Gladofin pointed to four birds circling in the sky. "Nor would they be safe as Crows. Those Velokites hunt small animals, including birds. They've been tracking us for miles."

Savannah shadowed her eyes to catch a glimpse of

them through the glare of the sun. They were unusual birds, resembling large kites but with much longer beaks. As she watched, one shot by overhead. With wings stretched wide, it let out a shriek as it banked into a tight turn, circling once before joining the others who had flown off into the east. "Do they come into the Forgotten Realms?" she asked curiously. She'd never sighted any there.

"No. The Bramble Hawks would kill them."

Savannah turned her attention to a swampy stretch of water at the bottom of the slope. It was a brooding place, with a jumble of dirty white rocks scattered like bleached bones at the edge. Brown scum covered the water, and though the surface was calm, occasional bubbles popped up, emitting gas. It formed a mist over the water, which was caught by the breezes, wafted up the hill, and dispersed over the nearby land.

Savannah sniffed. The air was heavy with a smoky musky scent that made her feel wonderful. It was so seductive, that she jogged down the slope closer to the edge to take in more.

"Savannah," Gladofin called out, alarm resonating in her voice. "Come back. We must get out of here. *Now*."

"Why," she asked, eyeing Gladofin in a new light. She really was a very attractive woman. She smiled at her as her libido spiked. "You're gorgeous."

Gladofin, who was covering her nose with her

handkerchief, rolled her eyes. "For the Goddess's sake, Savannah, snap out of it and get on Sunflower. The gas is a strong erotic stimulant." She looked over at Lilybeth, who was staring at her, mesmerized. "You too, Beth. Get on the horse and put something over your nose."

Lilybeth shook herself, pinched her nostrils reluctantly, and turned to Banner. Ignoring Sunflower's whinny of protest, she shunted the amorous mare away from the stallion and crawled up into the saddle.

Savannah continued to gape at Gladofin, captivated.

But as the Countess hurried down the hill to fetch her back, the water exploded into a torrent of spray.

Savannah whirled, then stumbled backward with a cry as an enormous creature arched out of the water and launched straight at her.

She crashed in an ungainly heap onto a cluster of the white rocks, sending shooting pain up her spine. The Countess was beside her in an instant, glowing white as she forced the creature back with magic. Savannah's stomach lurched. The thing was terrifying. It looked like one of the prehistoric crocodiles she'd seen in the London Natural History Museum, with a long head that ended in a big snout bristling with teeth like a T-Rex, and a mouth capable of swallowing her in a few gulps.

She shuffled back, finding the *rocks* she'd landed on

were thick bones. Perspiration blossomed on her face as she staggered to her feet. Then to her horror, she could see two more creatures churning through the water toward them from the far side of the swamp. And judging from the strain on her face, the Countess was having some difficulty holding this one back.

As Savannah readied her magic, she called out frantically, "There're more coming."

"Get on your horse," Gladofin ground out through clenched teeth. "This thing is so strong I can't hold it much longer without conjuring up a storm. And from the size of it, that mightn't work either. Hurry."

Savannah didn't argue — she ran up the slope and vaulted into the saddle. "When I fire a bolt, run Countess," she called out.

Not waiting for an answer, she let fly a powerful zap. When the crocodile-like beast shuddered, Gladofin scrambled into a run. But to Savannah's dismay, the medallion's magic barely made a dent in the creature's scales. It bared its teeth, roared, and raced up the hill in pursuit. Panic stricken, Savannah drilled another burst at it and then another. Though it slowed it down, the magic didn't stop it completely, just enough to give the Countess time to reach Banner.

The two other beasts reached the edge of the water, settling into a fast canter as soon as they crawled onto dry land.

Lilybeth hauled Gladofin into the saddle, then dug her heels into Banner's flanks. He darted immediately into the sky, Sunflower following close on his tail. The front crocodile roared in fury, snapping uselessly in the air as they soared out of reach.

But then it forgot about them when a large furry animal darted out from the trees into the clearing. The others rushed in to kill it, and the last glimpse Savannah had of the monsters was of them fighting over the carcass. She sank back into the saddle, waiting for her heart to stop pounding. The croc had been just another in the line of scary things in this world.

After flying in a zigzag pattern for two hours, it was time to rest the horses again. Using the Farsight Stone, Savannah deemed a patch of short grass in the woodlands safe to land.

She eased off Sunflower with a half-hearted, "I suppose we should have a look around." After her their recent nasty encounter, she would have preferred to wait with the horses.

"If the Crevlin are going to be anywhere, we know now it won't be near the swamps," said Gladofin. "We should look to see if there are any signs they could be in the woods. Footprints or old cooking fires,"

Lilybeth replied in a no-nonsense voice, "The sooner we look, the sooner we can get in the air again."

Then she walked into the trees before they could protest.

They pushed their way through the undergrowth, ducking under low spreading branches of firs and birches, and through thickets of huckleberry. Oversized spider webs crisscrossed every bush. The air was close and humid, the accumulated moisture pattering down on their heads in fat drops. The ground was littered with forest debris: decaying leaves, bark, moss, and lots of bugs. Savannah bent down to examine the insects. They were all larger than normal. She slapped at a bloodsucker on her arm that looked like a mosquito, but the size of a grasshopper.

When the brush thinned, a small stream came into view. They looked about uneasily, then waded through shallow water to the other side.

Nerves stretched to breaking point, Savannah said testily, "I think we've seen enough. There's no sign of anyone having been here, so let's go back."

Lilybeth drew her sword. "Stay here, and I'll have a quick look up further. I think I saw something move on that rise."

"You're not going up there by yourself," Gladofin said sharply.

But Lilybeth, nimble for a big-boned woman, had already vanished into the trees.

Savannah sat on one of the rocks to wait. "Let her

go. Lilybeth is more adept at merging into the habitat than we are."

Gladofin snorted, but as she turned to join her, she froze, staring at the overhanging limb behind the rocks. "There's a snake on the branch behind you. Don't make any sudden move, or it might bite."

"Big?" Savannah squeaked.

"Huge."

Panicked, Savannah forced herself to slide off the rock slowly, inching away until she was ankle-deep in the murky water. Once far enough away, she readied her magic.

Gladofin grasped her arm, and she said in a voice carrying a thread of panic, "No, Savannah. No magic. This is an ancient place, too old for the medallion's magic or mine to work effectively. Let's wait on the other side of the stream."

"Okay, though I —" She stopped, gaping as Lilybeth bounded toward them.

"Run," Lilybeth called out. "A leopard is coming, and it's enormous."

Savannah didn't hesitate. She took off, and though her legs were shorter than the other two, fear gave her enough speed to keep up. But they were losing the battle. The snarls and growls were getting closer at each step.

She looked back to see the big cat bearing down on

them. As was the crocodile, it looked more like a prehistoric creature than a leopard: a cross between a spotted big cat and a wolverine, with massive front limbs and razor-sharp saber-like teeth.

Suddenly, Ulana's words popped into her head: *"Much of your magic doesn't come from the medallion you wear around your neck. It's in you."*

Savannah had sensed then that the magic in her was ancient, far older than the medallions.

Taking a breath, she swung around to face the beast. It was only a few yards away; she could already feel its hot fetid breath in the air. She dug deep inside, calling forth the ancient magic in her bones. It rose to the surface, not as the Death Vale in a violent flash of lightning, but more subtly. Threads spun from her fingers, twirling around the leopard, binding it in such a tight cocoon that it crashed to the ground. Leaving it sprawled helplessly, she turned to find the Countess up ahead, staring at her wide-eyed.

Savannah only shrugged and said, "Let's get out of here."

Both Gladofin and Lilybeth eyed her thoughtfully without a word before she climbed into the saddle.

They flew on, heading east until finally the Wetlands petered out, and the country rose into the line of hills bordering the Forgotten Realms. They touched down on a ridge for a break.

Savannah looked down at the Wetlands in the distance. "It's as though the place hasn't evolved like the rest of Rand."

"It hasn't," said Gladofin. "That's why the creatures were impervious to magic." She glanced sideways at Savannah. "Mine and the medallion's, that is. They've been cut off for thousands of years and are best left alone. The Crevlin couldn't live there for even a day."

"No, they couldn't," agreed Savannah. "We'll just have to keep looking for the City of the Dead elsewhere." She shuddered. "That was a seriously scary place."

"It was indeed," said Gladofin. "I've never seen anything like those creatures. We'll need a drink when we get home."

Though Savannah smiled, underneath, she felt a little sick and panicky. The magic she had conjured up was the same as the old witch Hola's.

CHAPTER THIRTY-FIVE

THE NORTH CADIWINE RIVER

*T*amasin gazed down at the line of tents, stained a dirty gray by the ash and smoke blowing in from the north.

She'd be pleased to get out of the saddle; she been on and off it all day. The North Cadiwine was a long river, beginning in the Chesterton Hills and winding across the northern Realms to Wivenshore on the Eastern Ocean. It was the largest river in Rand, too wide and deep to cross except by bridge, boat, or ferry. There were few bridges, and most foot traffic used the numerous ferry barges along the river. It had taken all morning to destroy the bridges, to remove the cables from the ferries, and to tie all boats on the southern shores.

Once the armies were in place, all they had to do

was wait. The combined forces of the ten smaller Realms were already at their posts. They blocked the passes through the Chesterton Hills on the western side, and a few miles past the junction of the tributaries of the Cadiwine, two divisions guarded the roads into the Myrtle Vine Valley on the eastern perimeter.

It effectively left the enemy one way to go — down the center. The Arrowbine Bridge was now the only way to cross the river, and being in open countryside, easy to defend.

Ignoring the acrid smell of the smoke, Tamasin made her way to the command tent. She pushed aside the flap, finding Pela studying a map on the table. After stripping off her gloves, Tamasin took a long draught from the waterskin, and perched on a stool at the table.

Pela looked up, acknowledging her with a preoccupied nod. "Did everything go as planned?"

"Yes. No one will be crossing the river."

"Good," she tapped the map with a finger. "My Hawks reported the enemy was only a mile off the Bogonian capital, Bogant."

Tamasin frowned. "They're moving faster than we anticipated. The fire didn't slow them down much. How many soldiers have they?"

"Their best estimate was ten thousand. The Hawks couldn't tell how many Wolves, but the place was teeming with them."

"Damnit, Pela. That's far more soldiers than we'd anticipated."

"It is," replied Pela. "But the size of their army doesn't worry me as much as their speed. They must have been collecting horses for a while, because their officers were mounted, and some were pulling wagons."

"Probably commandeered from travelers and farm stables," said Tamasin.

"It's making their progress faster, something we didn't factor in. At this rate, we'll have a fight on our hands at the bridge. Borrentine would have sent Crows to investigate our defenses and will find a way to get his bombs across the river. If I were him, I would make rafts to slip some troops over at night. There's plenty of wood to make them in the city."

"Then we have to increase our surveillance of the river. We're going to need more Hawks."

"Already organized, and Jayden has sent for more Ice Elves."

"How do we fight the Wolves?"

Pela curled her hands into fists. "We must delay their march until they're mad with hunger. The Wolves will turn on the Crevlin in the end. They're loyal only to their packs, and a ravenous wolf is extremely dangerous."

"Increase the hit-and-run tactics."

Pela gave a sour smile. "Yes. Only this time, it will be

with special forces who will do real damage. The Bogonian soldiers we ordered into the field to carry out night skirmishes will be reassigned to fight here. I've sent for fifty Elite Guards, all knife experts, and thirty Weyfire Assassins."

Tamasin raised her eyebrows. The Assassin Guild of Weyfire was a legendary all-male order of killers hired by anyone who could afford them. Five centuries ago, turmoil was rife within the Royal Houses, and after an irreparable spate of political killings, the Imperial Queen outlawed the Assassin Guild. "Do you mean to tell me they still exist?"

"Didn't Iona learn anything from the Witches and Wizards? Banning a society only sends them under-ground," said Pela with a shake of her head. "They're alive and kicking if you know where to look."

Tamasin threw up her hands. "I won't ask where they are. Did they come willingly?"

"Yes, after I negotiated their payment."

"How much?"

"One hundred gold Proton pieces each."

Tamasin pressed her lips together. "Take it out of the war fund. Mistress of Finance will have a fit."

"Right."

"How did you organize it so quickly?"

Pela grinned. "You're not the only one with a spy network."

"Huh! When do they arrive?'

"The Elite Guards are already here. We'll have a round-table conference when the Assassins turn up." When a trumpet call resonated across the camp, she rose from her stool. "That'll be General Grogan with the Arcadian Army. He's bringing four divisions; Fern knows how important it is to stop Borrentine here. If he crosses the river, he'll spread out and be hard to contain. Arcadii will be sitting like a plum ripe for the taking."

At the sound of someone outside the tent, Tamasin fully expected to see the Arcadian General. Instead, Savannah appeared, smelling of smoke and flecked with ash. She smiled widely when Pela bounded over to hug her.

After she planted a soft kiss on Pela's lips, she whispered, "I missed you too." She smiled at Tamasin. "Hi, Tam. I've lots to tell you both."

"You'll have to fill us in later, Savannah," Pela said. "General Grogan will be here any minute and we'll have a discussion. You smell like a fireplace, so I presume you've come from the Forgotten Realms. Did you see Borrentine's army?"

"I did. They're in the Bogonian city. The Realm is burnt black, with hardly a blade of grass left on some of the plains. It must have gone up like a bomb."

"Good," said Pela with satisfaction. "We're lucky it's

the dry season. We'll light up the other side of the river when they're on the move again." At the sound of footsteps, she turned to the door. "Here's General Grogan now."

The Arcadian looked weary as he strode in. He acknowledged them with a gruff, "Commander Pela, Consort. Good to see you again, Savannah."

"Hello, General," Tamasin said, eyeing his travel-stained uniform. "You didn't fly here?"

"I marched with my troops, Consort."

Tamasin would have liked to reply, *good for you*, but merely said, "I'm glad you're here."

As they discussed their military plans, she could see the threat of war had tempered Grogan. No longer the affable sociable commanding officer she'd met months ago, he was leaner, harder, more astute, and had licked his soldiers into a fearsome fighting force.

When they finished, Pela called out to the guard at the door. "Send in the heads of the special envoys, please."

The two women and two men were poles apart. The women with their distinctive hair style, bird tattoos, magnificent physiques, and wearing their blue uniforms arrogantly, were as dangerous as they looked. The Elite Guards were the best fighters in the country.

In comparison, the men seemed nondescript, with wiry, lithe bodies and forgettable faces. Their clothes were brown with pale green streaks, camouflage which blended into the surroundings. But there was something about the way stood watching her, that sent the hairs on the back of Tamasin's neck twitching. Like hunters stalking their prey. When they caught her gaze, their eyes were as cold as death.

Pela didn't seem intimidated, giving her instructions firmly and precisely as she pointed to the map. When she finished, she reiterated, "Remember, do not openly engage the enemy. Create as much havoc as you can under the cloak of darkness. And don't get caught. They're starving and will eat you."

One of the Elite Guards swallowed, but there was no reaction from the Assassins. They stood up, bowed their heads briefly in gestures of politeness that were almost mocking, and melted out of the tent. The Elite Guards smartly saluted before they vanished through the flap.

General Grogan cleared his throat. "I wouldn't like to meet those fellows on a dark night."

Pela gave a mirthless grin. "Your throat would be cut from ear to ear before you realized they were there."

Grogan harrumphed. "I almost feel sorry for the enemy." He stood up with a sigh. "I'd better get to my quarters. After two days in the saddle, I need to wash. I'll eat with my officers tonight, so I'll see you in the morning."

Savannah wandered over to the wooden cupboard. "Anything to drink in this place?"

"There's a bottle of mead on the second shelf."

"Great," she said pouring out three cups. "You going to need this when I tell you my news."

Tamasin took a drink, and said with an encouraging, "Go ahead."

"Firstly, Tam, the City of the Dead isn't in the Northern Wetlands."

As Savannah described their ordeal, Tamasin felt a wave of alarm. Time was running out. "There're not many options left," she growled.

"I know," said Savannah. "I'm heading off tomorrow for the Southern Lands. I'll make a detour at Beria and talk to Winston. He'll come up with something." She went on, "Um … there's another thing I learned while in the Forgotten Realms. It's about the third moon. There is no actual sign that'll tell us the position of the enemy's Time Gateway. When the moons are aligned, they'll block out the sun for six hours. If we don't close the Gateway then, we've lost the battle. It will stay open."

"It doesn't give us even a hint where it'll be?"

Savannah shook her head glumly. "Nope. And with that timeline, we'll have to be in the right spot when the light disappears."

"Where did you find out all this information, Savannah?" asked Pela.

Savannah forced a smile. Pela must have guessed where she had gone, for she didn't look happy. "I went to see the Iriwari," she said offhandedly.

"You promised you wouldn't go there."

Savannah wriggled in her seat self-consciously. Pela wasn't going to let it go. "I said I wouldn't go up there alone. I had someone with me."

"Oh. Who?"

"Your mother."

Pela narrowed her eyes. "I trust you got her home safely."

"Um … she broke her arm when we had a run-in with an Or'orah, but I'll tell you about that later," she said in a rush.

Tamasin, seeing Pela's face turn red, quickly intervened, "Who are the Iriwari, Savannah?"

"They're Sylphs, They study the stars and are experts on the Celestial Realms," she said and relayed Queen Cassine's explanation for the third moon.

When she finished, Pela rose abruptly. "I have things to do," she said curtly and walked out the door.

Savannah fiddled with a thread on her sleeve, avoiding Tamasin's eye. After a long moment, she muttered, "I might have pushed her too far this time. I promised I wouldn't go up there. *Alone* was just a technicality. And then we had a fight with the Wolves as well as the giant spider, and I nearly got her mother killed."

"She worries about you."

"I know, Tam, but I was chosen for a purpose. And she can't organize a war effectively if she's worried about me. Perhaps we should cool it for a while," she said miserably.

"Is that what you want, Savannah?"

"No … of course not. I love her, but I'm not being fair to her."

Tamasin reached over and rubbed her shoulder. "Hey, you've both got jobs to do. Pela hasn't come to terms with the fact you aren't one of her recruits to be told what to do. She's a natural leader so you have to work out a way to get what you want."

"Is that what you do with Valeria?" asked Savannah curiously.

Tamasin laughed. "Of course. Valeria's twice as bossy as Pela. Now let's have another drink, then you can tell me everything that happened in detail."

"There's one thing that's been puzzling me about the Time Gateway, Tam. As far as I can see, the Crevlin have already brought thousands of their people here. They've still time to get them all through before the moons are aligned. So why are they worried about us closing the Gateway?"

Tamasin stared at her. "I don't know. Do you have a theory?"

"The only logical answer I can come up with is that it's not fully opened yet. Birds can come through, but nothing bigger yet."

"So you're saying some large animals might be coming through as well as the birds."

"They're really not capable of defeating us now without a protracted war. Even with their bombs. And they'd hardly have come all this way to die on the battlefields. I think they must have something more lethal yet to come," Savannah said with a shudder. "Imagine if they brought thousands of Skeldachs here. Or something worse."

†

Savannah woke to the sounds of coughing and thumping boots. The camp was stirring.

Pela wasn't in the tent — had she come back during the night? Savannah got up and stretched her sore back — the sack filled with straw wasn't the most comfortable bed. She pottered around, waiting to see if Pela would turn up. When she didn't, Savannah hauled on fresh clothes and packed her bag, feeling hurt. Pela had overreacted, and if she was going to be snarky about it, there was no point hanging around the camp. She

CHAPTER THIRTY-FIVE | 399

would head off straight after breakfast. She had enough things to do.

It was a chilly morning with a light frost coating the grass, forcing Savannah to pull up the collar of her riding cloak and slip on her gloves before she ventured outside. Amidst the smell of smoke was the scent of fresh pine from the trees felled to erect fortifications around the camp. Soldiers crowded around the campfires, cooking slabs of meat and stirring pots of a thick lumpy porridge. Flasks of watered-down sour wine, the standard drink for the army camps, were lined up beside stacks of bread loaves.

She wandered through the rows of tents until she found Tamasin eating a bowl of cereal.

As soon as she saw Savannah, she wriggled over to make room on her log. "Grab something to eat."

When Savannah put the bag down, Tamasin looked at her in surprise. "Are you going already?"

"After breakfast," said Savannah, spooning out a bowl of cereal.

"I thought you'd spend some time here. Pela will want to show you around."

"I must go, Tam. I have a long ride ahead of me. Tell Pela — no, don't bother, it doesn't matter."

"She's still mad at you?" Tamasin asked.

"I haven't seen her since last night. She didn't sleep in the tent."

Tamasin looked at her sympathetically and tactfully changed the subject. "You're off to the Southern Lands?"

"Yes."

"Why? The south is too vast to attempt to find the City of the Dead."

"I'm not going down there for that, Tam. I'm interested in the site of the Crevlins' capital city."

Tamasin's eyes widened. "That was over two thousand years ago. What could you possibly find after all that time?"

"I have no idea. Probably nothing, but I know as an archeologist, sometimes there may be subtle clues in the landscape," Savannah replied, then added with a smile. "I won't be digging."

Tamasin just shook her head. "I have no idea what you hope to achieve — it seems like a wild-goose chase to me. When will you be back?"

"Four or five days. It'll be a day and a half flight from here. I'll stop at Beria to rest Sunflower and to see Winston, then fly on to the halfway island for the night. According to Lilybeth, it's a rest stop for anyone flying over the Wide Seas, with accommodation if you need to stay the night."

"Eat up. You'll need something in your stomach to see you through. The porridge might be bland, but it'll stick to you."

After Savannah ate the first mouthful of the thick mush, she poured more honey into the bowl. Tamasin was right — it was tasteless.

She lingered as long as she could over breakfast, but when Pela still failed to appear, she made her way to the horses. They were picketed at the far end of the camp, the small herd of Blue Fjords standing apart from the land horses. The army's flying horses were for the officers and scouts, not the common soldier.

As she put on the saddle, Savannah brushed away a few stray tears.

She'd really ruined things with Pela this time.

CHAPTER THIRTY-SIX

THE SOUTHERN LANDS

*T*he Southern Lands were nothing like Savannah expected.

Though she didn't know why, she had visualized an untamed frontier, not orderly, picturesque country. The fertile plains were vast, with extensive cultivation, grazing paddocks, and stands of cedars, pines, and various species of spruce. From the air, the wild animals in the woodlands were deer, bears, and larger beasts that looked like bison. By the number of villages dotting the landscape, the country was well-populated. The many rivers formed an inland network of navigable waterways, draining into lakes formed in the hollows and troughs of the otherwise flat countryside.

After a while, although it was pretty, Savannah

found the landscape monotonous. Since crossing the coast mid-morning, she and Sunflower had taken a sight-seeing tour, stopping at a few villages on the way. As they flew south, the colder it became, until finally, with the Bolderdore Mountains on the far horizon, and freezing to death, they turned north again. Once they hit the Snakefish River, they followed it to the Great Elken Lake.

It was late afternoon when Elkendale, a quaint village nestled on the banks of the clear blue water came into view. After paying two coppers to stable Sunflower, Savannah made her way through the town to find an inn. At the end of the main square, The Blushing Bear was a charming tavern lit up brightly and humming with laughter. She booked a room for the night, made her way to the lounge and took a seat at the end of a wooden table near the fireplace. Flames danced in the hearth, the warmth feeling like heaven after the cold ride.

She ordered a cup of wine from the serving girl who was bustling through the room, expertly carrying tankards in both hands without spilling a drop. When a young man in an apron appeared with plates of fish and vegetables, Savannah handed over a coin. She looked down the table, smiling at the merry drinkers downing their ales.

"I ain't seen ye here before, girl. What brings ye to Elkendale?"

At the question, Savannah glanced over at the man sitting opposite. He looked in his late forties, with a weather-beaten face dominated by deep-set eyes. He smelt of fish but judging from his coarse home-spun clothes and rough hands, he was a fisherman rather than a fishmonger.

"I study history," she replied, figuring it was better to stick closely to the truth. She pulled out a copy of the ancient map from Fern's library and pointed to the spot where the Crevlin Tower was marked. "I came here to search this area, sir. My mistress thinks it was the site of a very ancient city."

His jaw muscle tightened. "No one goes up there. It's cursed, and ye best stay away."

"Really? What do mean by *cursed*?"

"It's haunted."

"I don't believe in ghosts," she replied firmly.

He eyed her sourly. "Well, ye should." He raised his voice to address his four friends. "This woman wants to poke around Deadman's Knob."

The woman sitting beside him muttered, "The locals leave that area well alone, miss. Strange things happen there."

Ignoring the prickle of apprehension, Savannah

forced a smile. "I've come a long way, so I'd like to see it. How far is it from here?"

The woman shrugged. "I wouldn't go if I were you, but it's your funeral. Six miles to the northeast. You can't miss it — it's a small hill without a blade of grass."

"Thanks," replied Savannah, grateful for the directions. "I'll fly to the spot in the morning. Whatever is there isn't likely to appear in broad daylight."

"Don't bet on it," mumbled the fisherman. "Them things —"

His words were lost when the publican bustled over, greeting her with a loud, "Welcome to the Blushing Bear, young Mistress. Have you come far?"

Savannah looked around, finding a Sithe Dwarf, renowned publicans throughout Rand, his prominent belly covered by a beer-stained apron, affably smiling at her. She returned the smile. "I'm from the north, sir. I know Publican Gert from the Pale Horse in Arcadii. I presume he's your relation."

His face brightened. "Then you are very welcome indeed. He's my cousin. I'm called Hagget."

"I'm Savannah."

He looked at her curiously. "You flew here, Savannah?"

"Yes. It's an interesting part of Rand for a historian. I'm researching the ancient Crevlin civilization, and their capital city was supposed to be in this area. I know it was a very long time ago, but do you have any historical documents, or anything about that era?"

He eyed her thoughtfully, then gestured with a hooked finger. "Come with me. Being a history buff myself, I have an interesting collection I've gathered over the years."

She followed him past the bar to a room at the back. "Wow!" she exclaimed as soon as she stepped inside. It was a mini-museum chocked full of memorabilia, artifacts, and tapestries. "It's wonderful."

He beamed at her proudly and pointed to the front section. "I laid it out in chronological order. At the back is the really old stuff, so we'll start from the front and work our way through."

Curbing her impatience, Savannah listened to him give the history of the artifacts as he moved down through the years. It was fascinating, and soon she became enthralled in the life and times of the eras. The collection of seashells was like nothing she had ever seen, rare and beautiful, from huge pink conches to tiny periwinkles.

When they reached the oldest section, he said almost apologetically. "This is the last. It starts after the Shadow Years."

"Those were the times after the Crevlin empire fell?"

"Yes. After two hundred years, they resettled the south."

"Do you know what happened to the Crevlin?"

"No, but I have old scripts from the first settlers after the Shadow Years. Our teacher translated it as best she could, but there are gaps. What she could gather, the Crevlin just disappeared."

Savannah froze. "Suddenly, or over a few years?"

"She thought it happened quickly."

"Would you allow me to read the scripts?" Savannah asked hopefully.

"You can read the old language?"

"I can."

He studied her closely. "Who are you exactly, Savannah? You said you flew here, but only important people ride the Blue Fjords, not apprentices. You can read an ancient language long since dead and forgotten, something no one else can do."

She watched him search her face, waiting for her to respond. He was astute, a valuable ally if they needed someone in the Southern Lands. It was time to out herself, though she didn't know if the medallion was as revered here. "I am the Chosen One, Hagget. I wear the Circle of Sheda."

She needn't have worried, for he answered with the familiar cry, "It has come back to Rand. I salute you, Chosen One."

"Yes, it's back."

His face darkened into a frown. "But that means a war is looming."

"It has already begun in the north. The Crevlin are back."

"But how is that possible?"

Savannah grimaced. "They have a passage through time, which is the reason I want to look at the site of their capital. May I read those scripts?"

"Of course, Chosen One. I'll find a light crystal for the table."

"Thanks," said Savannah, taking a chair.

When she carefully turned the first page, she was thankful it was made from an animal hide, tough enough to withstand the impact of time. The ink, however, was very faded, and she brought the lamp closer to read the text. Most of it referred to the hardships the pioneers faced: the climate, and the need to grow food and build shelters. Standard troubles for any settlers. The only reference to the Crevlin was that there weren't any. The author surmised there had been some cataclysmic event that wiped them all off the face of the planet.

When she closed the book, Savannah couldn't help but fear the worst. Even with harsh winters and famine, it wasn't logical that none had survived. People were more resilient than that. She hoped it didn't mean that the Covenant of Queens had failed to close the

Time Gateway, and every Crevlin had come into the future.

"You look worried," said Hagget. "Were you able to translate it?"

She nodded, giving him a summary of the text, but didn't mention her fears about the Time Gateway. There was no need to panic him. "I'll stay another night to record the writings before I go."

But as she stood up, she noticed a tapestry in the shadows on the back wall. Most of the color had faded out of the threads — it looked like an old black-and-white photograph. "What have we here?" she murmured, holding up the crystal to examine it. It was a rural scene with towering trees, birds, and large animals. When she swept the light into the sky, she sucked in a sharp breath. They weren't birds, they were Skeldachs. Slowly, she brought the light down the tapestry, illuminating the animals imprinted in the cloth. Many strange creatures were roaming about, none she'd ever seen in Rand.

She turned to Hagget, who had moved to her side. "What's this scene all about?"

"It was found locked in a watertight trunk under a ruin by the lake. We're sure it's a genuine tapestry from the Crevlin era."

"Any of those creatures still about?"

"They're all extinct," he replied, then pointed to an

animal that looked like an elephant with a scaley body. "Except that one. The miners have reported seeing some in the Bolderdores. But they keep to the mountains and don't bother anyone."

Savannah swallowed the bitter taste in her mouth. If the large creatures came through the Gateway when it was fully open, Rand was in trouble. They were monsters.

†

Savannah scrutinized the bare country below, trying to identify some landmark where the Crevlin Time Tower could have stood. Judging by her constant quivering, Sunflower was nervous, and she didn't blame her. There was something *off* about the place. The hill was a hummock, with a jagged fracture in the top and a pile of rocky rubble beside it.

As they touched down, the stench hit. It smelt foul like something had died and was in the ripest stage of decomposition. With an agitated whinny, Sunflower pawed at the dry earth.

Savannah patted her neck soothingly. "Get right away from this area and wait under those trees. I want you fresh when we have to go back."

The mare didn't argue, trotting off immediately until she was well out of range.

Forcing herself to ignore the putrid smell, Savannah circled the split in the ground. But when she crept closer, the dirt under her feet became spongy as though trying to hold its form. She stepped back hastily, then shuffled to the side until she found a more stable surface. Inching forward, she reached the edge of the crack without sinking and peered over the lip. It was no more than a sliver wide, too dark to see anything inside.

But when she straightened, everything suddenly turned weird. An intense cold descended over the hummock, followed by a shift in the air that sent everything out of focus. The fetid smell intensified until she gagged, and the air of despair that hung like a cloak couldn't be ignored. Somewhere close, she heard screams, throat-searing screams so heartrending that they could only be heard not described. She couldn't see any forms or ghosts or whatever was in there, but she could feel them clawing at the earth beneath her feet.

Memories began to stir uneasily. A collection of horrifying fragments in her mind: the grief for loved ones long since dead; washing blood off her hands; blasting the Silverthorne Witch Agatha to pieces. She dropped to her knees as they kept coming: grief, death, destruction, and worst of all, guilt. With her head clutched in her hands, her screams resounded with all those of the lost souls.

"Savannah. Get up."

She kept screaming.

"Savannah, Get out of there. Now."

When the voice didn't let up, she finally stopped to listen. Now calmer, she became conscious the medallion was going berserk, zapping frantically into her chest. *"What's happening to me, Grandmother?"*

"You are a hair's breadth away from the Realm of the Dead, girl. Get away from that crack."

It took every last bit of her willpower, but she rose to her feet and staggered off the hill. She had no idea where she'd been, but it had certainly been on another plane of existence.

"Thanks, Grandmother. That was dreadful."

"You were nearly lost to the dead. I don't know how that crack got there. I hadn't seen it in any thread. Be more careful next time," she admonished, and then she was gone.

Savannah eyed the hill with hatred — it was no wonder the locals avoided it. There was no doubt in her mind that this was where the beginning of the Time Gateway had been, and the Crevlin Time Tower must have fallen hard to leave such a deep crack. She couldn't even imagine, over such a long time, just how many

CHAPTER THIRTY-SIX | 413

poor people had been driven mad by the screams of the dead. She flexed her fingers — time to close it forever.

Raising her hands, she called forth her power. When it streamed out, she swept it over the hill and flattened it until satisfied the crack was buried under tons of dirt and rocks. As she turned to go, something glittering in the newly disturbed ground caught her eye. She picked it up to find a large, fossilized seahorse, perfectly preserved and quite spectacular.

Ideal for Hagget's collection.

CHAPTER THIRTY-SEVEN

THE NORTH CADIWINE RIVER

*T*amasin squinted, trying to see through the haze of smoke.

The morning of the fifth day and the enemy had yet to arrive. The fires and the night raids had slowed them down, and the Ice Elves had launched an arrow attack by air. By the fourth day, their army had slowed to a crawl. She wondered how many Crevlin the night raids had killed and if the Weyfire Assassins and Elite Warriors had suffered any losses. They hadn't come near the camp, still out there, using guerilla tactics to pick off the enemy in the darkness. The fires would have helped guide them — logs were still alight, the smoke lingering over the countryside.

Yesterday afternoon, the scouts had reported that the Crevlin army was six miles from the river and was in dire trouble. Dead Crows littered the sides of the roads, and the Wolves had abandoned them, heading back to the forest to hunt. It was now or never for the Crevlin army to retreat or they would perish from starvation. Though the Arcadian soldiers were impatient for action, this was one battle not fought by the clash of swords or thrust of spears.

Footsteps sounded behind Tamasin, and General Grogan appeared at her elbow. "They'll turn into Crows and go back after dusk," he muttered.

"They will, General," agreed Tamasin. "If Borrentine doesn't go now, he'll lose the lot. They're too weak for a full-scale assault. The battle is over." She looked around to see Pela talking to the division of Bramble Hawks. "Pela knows they'll go tonight. She's organizing her Hawks to catch the Crows."

"She's an astute military tactician," said Grogan with admiration in his voice.

"She is indeed. Borrentine will lick his wounds and know he'll have to be more cunning in the future."

"I'll see you at dinner tonight, Tamasin. I have a few things to organize."

Grogan had just bustled off when a guard on the bridge shouted, "Rider."

Tamasin shaded her eyes to look to the sky. A horse came into view, circled the camp, then swooped down to land. Savannah climbed out of the saddle, greeting her with a broad smile.

"How was your trip, Savannah?" Tamasin asked, pleased to see her.

"It was worth the long ride. After I tether Sunflower, we can talk."

Tamasin signaled to a soldier who hurried over. "Put this mare with the Blue Fjords and give her some oats, please."

Savannah patted Sunflower, then glanced over at Pela. She hadn't looked her way. With a resigned shrug, she mumbled, "Let's go."

They had no more sat down in the tent when Pela appeared, wearing a frown. "So you're back, Savannah. I trust you had a good trip."

"It had its moments, Pela. But I learned a few things, though not all good."

Tamasin leaned forward in her chair. "You found the site of the Crevlin city?"

"I did. It was near a town called Elkendale. The publican of The Blushing Bear tavern was a Sithe Dwarf who'll be a valuable contact if we need one in the Southern Lands." Savannah looked almost apologetic as she continued, "I saw no signs that the exit to the Time Gateway was in the south, Tam. It's so heavily populated that any strange people would be noticed."

"I didn't think it could be there, but where the hell is it?"

Pela interrupted abruptly, "What's the bad news, Savannah?"

"The publican had an old tapestry from the Crevlin era. The animals on it were monstrous, and there were Skeldachs as well. If they come through the Time Gateway, we're in trouble."

"Why do you think they will?"

"I'm working on the theory that it only fully opens when the moons are aligned. At the moment, Borrentine is bringing the people through as birds because it's only a fraction open. He didn't come here to lose the ultimate war. The huge animals will be his secret weapons."

After turning this over in her head, Pela replied, "If that's the case, I doubt he'll try another offensive until the Gateway is open enough to get them through. How much time have we, Tam?"

"The last turn of the moons starts shortly."

"Four weeks," whispered Savannah. "Take out the six days when they're aligned, and it's only three weeks. How are things going here?"

"They'll turn tail tonight," said Pela with satisfaction. "Because there's a smoke haze, they'll get some to safety, but they must fly if they hope to reach the forest. My Hawks will be hunting as soon as darkness falls."

"So your strategy was a success."

"It was. We won without a battle." She eyed Savannah speculatively. "I suppose you'll be off again tomorrow without a word."

"You stormed off and didn't come back, Pela. What was I to think?"

"I go on patrol every night."

Savannah looked at her from under her eyebrows and chewed her bottom lip. "You could have told me you wouldn't be coming back to the tent. I had a long way to go and waited as long as I could."

"Not long enough."

Tamasin jumped in quickly to halt the argument. Both were as proud as the other. "It was a misunderstanding, so settle it later," she said firmly. "I've some more questions, Savannah. Did you find anything at the site of their city?"

Savannah looked sick. "The locals claimed it was haunted. And it was. I was nearly sucked into the Realm of the Dead. It was a shitty experience, one I never want repeat. Cassine told me their time passageway was through the Dead Realm, and she was right. Maybe that was another reason they had to go as birds. People probably wouldn't be able to leave."

"What do you mean *sucked into?*" asked Pela sharply.

"When the Crevlin Time Tower fell, it caused a fracture in the earth. Using magic, I flattened the creepy hill when I got away," said Savannah with satisfaction.

Tamasin smiled at her with sympathy. "You did well. Where do you plan to go from here?"

Savannah shifted uneasily in the chair and glanced at Pela. "I need to go to Falcon's Keep to get something from the Prophecy Tower. I was hoping you'd go with me, Pel. We need time together. I know you're busy, but this war is pulling us apart."

Pela's face softened. "I'll come, Savannah. There's nothing I'd like better."

†

For the first time in days, Tamasin felt relaxed. When the last report from the scouts confirmed the enemy was in full retreat, the cook had prepared a victory dinner for the officers in Pela's tent. After the days of waiting, everyone was in fine form. The first course had just been served when two Assassins strode into the room. They were filthy and smelt atrocious but faced the assembly unapologetically.

They nodded to Tamasin and bowed to Pela. "Imperial Commander, we have fulfilled our contract."

Pela got up and saluted. "We thank you for your services, soldiers. Did you lose any men?"

"Two wounded only."

"Excellent." She walked over to the cupboard and pulled out a box. "There are thirty bags of gold Protons inside, as was our arrangement."

The Assassin opened it, then took out fifteen bags and placed them on the table. "For the women who fought with us. It would not sit well that we received more. It was an honor to fight by their sides."

The muscle in Pela's jaw twitched, the only sign she was touched by the gesture. "Did they all survive?" she asked.

"Yes. Three wounded but not gravely."

Relief flittered across Pela's face. "Where are they?"

He grinned, the only emotion he'd displayed in the time they'd entered the room. "They wanted a bath."

Then they bowed and disappeared out the door.

"They're odd fellows," said Grogan. "I didn't expect them to have a code of honor."

"Don't be fooled by that gesture, General," said Pela. "They're mercenaries, hard men who have no loyalty except to their sect. They kill without a qualm and only value money. The Elite Guards must have acquitted themselves very well to earn their respect."

Tamasin looked up from her plate. "I balked at paying them so much but in the long run, they were cheap. A battle won without a fight is rare."

Moments later, a cold wind whistled through the tent flap. As the temperature plummeted in the room,

Grogan called out, "Tie that door, please, Captain. We haven't had wind for days, and it's like ice."

The Captain rose to her feet, hurrying over to the entrance. She was nearly there when a dark man came out of the shadows. Before anyone could react, he plunged a knife under her ribs. After he yanked the knife from her chest, she gurgled and slumped to the floor.

The air rang with the sound of crashing plates as Pela vaulted over the end of the table. Magic streamed from his fingers as the man whirled to meet her rush. She halted abruptly, then fell to her knees and her face contorted in agony.

When the hood was removed, Borrentine stood glaring down at her. "If anyone moves, I'll kill her now," he said in a measured tone.

The muscles in Tamasin's jaw tightened as she gritted her teeth. "Get back to your army, or what's left of it, King."

He stared at her with hatred. "Imperial lapdog, you think that this is the end of it? You will be begging me for mercy when the real war comes. But it won't be with this Hawk bitch."

When Grogan stood up to protest, Borrentine shot a blast of magic into his belly. The General sprawled backward with a cry.

Borrentine looked contemptuously at the four officers scrambling for their weapons. "Sit down, or I will kill you all. He's not dead."

He turned to Pela, gripped her braid with his fist, and pressed her face against his cold cheek. "Prepare to die, Hawk."

"Let her go, Borrentine," a sharp command rang out.

He whirled at the sound of her voice and growled, "Savannah. What are you doing here?"

"I said *let her go*."

"And you'll do what? I'm going to kill her, and it'll be much more satisfying having you watch."

Savannah's eyes turned to ice. "I've come into my full power, Borrentine. You will not best me this time. I won't tell you again. Let. Her. Go."

"You can't kill me, Savannah," he snapped and swung the knife at Pela's throat.

Long blue threads immediately streamed from Savannah's fingers. They curled around his hand before his blow was complete and kept winding until his arm was tightly bound to his torso. As he struggled to escape, the knife slipped from his fingers, clattering to the floor. He gaped at her in disbelief. "That is ancient magic. The medallion does not have that power. How do you command it?"

"That is my secret."

He looked at her with loathing and gave up struggling. "We will meet again, Savannah, and I will be more prepared. You will not best me again."

With a hiss, he vanished into thin air.

As soon as he left, his magic disappeared with him. The General stirred and sat up. When Pela climbed to her feet, Savannah gave a shaky laugh and hugged her tightly. "Are you all right?"

"I'm fine. Check on the Captain."

Tamasin was already kneeling beside her and shook her head. "She's gone. She lost too much blood." She suddenly felt tired and afraid. "How can we defeat an enemy who can walk in and out of places at will?"

Savannah looked thoughtful. "Although he'd like to let us think he can flit through time at will, I don't think it's easy at all for him. Otherwise, he would have turned up to kill Pela before this. I think it takes a lot of magic to do one jump. He possesses the very ancient magic, but he didn't have enough left to fight me."

"Was that what you have, Savannah?" asked Tamasin.

"Yes, Tam. It's not the magic of the medallion. The magic is in me."

CHAPTER THIRTY-EIGHT

FALCON'S KEEP

*S*avannah felt a surge of excitement when they reached the battlements of Falcon's Keep. The Elite academy was as austere as she remembered, with stone houses jutting up like extensions of the mountain, a large amphitheater occupying all the far end, and a green common giving the only touch of color. But it felt like home. At eleven in the morning, the streets were largely deserted, the recruits still at the morning training session. Their regimen hadn't changed, Pela insisting the Keep remain away from the fighting unless absolutely needed.

A Guard appeared from the post house, eyes widening when she caught sight of Pela. She snapped to attention. "Imperial Commander. We weren't expecting you."

"At ease, Sergeant. It's an impromptu visit. Tell the Commander we have arrived, and we'll join her at lunch."

When the soldier hurried off, Savannah chuckled. "The whole Keep will be in a tizz getting ready for lunch. The cook will be cranky because she's probably dishing up left-overs from last night's dinner. And the recruits will have to wash and change into fresh clothes before dining."

Pela smiled, then glanced at the amphitheater, plainly eager to see the training.

"Off you go," said Savannah. "After I put Sunflower in the common to catch up with her mates, I'm going to the kitchen to see Lyn."

Once the mare was happily amongst the horses, she found the service entrance leading to the lower level beneath the great mess hall. She ran down the ramp into the bakery, where three men in smocks were baking bread. They didn't give her a second glance as she passed by. Lyn was peeling potatoes on the wooden bench, and when Savannah appeared in front of her, she squealed in delight, "Savannah. What are you doing here?"

"Pela and I are just visiting. Since we're staying for a

426 | COVENANT OF QUEENS

night, we can get together later. How are you going? I've missed the place," said Savannah wistfully.

"We've heard of your exploits. You're making quite a name for yourself, Chosen One."

Savannah gave a little giggle. "I often wished I was back eating with you in the kitchen. No airs and graces here." She looked up to find everyone staring at her. She smiled and waved, "Hi, folks."

The portly chief cook came over and folded her into her ample chest. "Welcome back, Savannah." She held her out and eyed her closely. "You could do with more meat on those bones. Haven't they been feeding you?"

"I've missed your cooking, Mistress Dora. Pela and I will enjoy lunch."

"The Supreme Commander is here?"

"Yes."

The cook whirled around, galvanizing into action. "Right. No leftovers. You, girl, stop picking at those turnips and get the chickens ... "

Chuckling, Savannah whispered to Lyn, "See you tonight," and left them to it.

When she entered the library, the old librarian looked up from a book and her face broke into a smile. "Savannah. It's so good to see you. How long are you here for?"

"Only a fleeting visit, Glenda. How have you been?"

"To be honest, lonelier since you left. I missed your

visits to the library. It's the last place the recruits want to be."

Savannah settled down in the chair opposite, ready for a gossip session. "What's the new Keep Commander like?"

"She isn't too bad, but not Pela by a long shot. Her training regimens are excellent, but she has no interest in history. She's only set foot in the library once." Glenda sighed. "I'm too old for change; that's my trouble."

"Nonsense. What you need is more to do. With your wealth of knowledge, you're wasted here. I have a proposition if you're interested."

Glenda blinked at her. "Oh?"

"Queen Lilybeth is looking for someone to record the history of the Berian Realm. I suggested you. It would be necessary to move there, but the Queen is well-liked, and I'm sure you'll be happy."

Glenda's face brightened. "I know her well. I trained Lilybeth when she was a recruit at the Keep. She was one of our best. We have her daughter Maybeth here at the moment."

Savannah nodded, imagining Lilybeth would have been one of the Keep's stars. "Then you'll think about it?"

"I don't need to. I'd be thrilled to do it. You're a good

person, Savannah. Being the Chosen One hasn't gone to your head," she said shyly.

Savannah reached over and squeezed her hand. "You were kind to me when I needed a friend, Glenda." She blinked back a tear. "Now, while I'm here, I was wondering if you have any tapestries. There must surely be a catalog of the great art and who acquired them. I've ignored them in favor of books, which was silly because they are a graphic history of Rand."

"How far back?"

"Whatever you have," Savannah replied. It had been nagging her for a while that she was missing a vital piece in the puzzle. "Are there any of the Goddess Iona? In my world, there are many religious paintings of our gods."

"There are paintings, tapestries, and statues all over Rand of her, Savannah. She is the creator."

"What about the Demon Prince Dazorak?"

"He's in many tapestries at the head of his army. The Great War of Creation, the battle for Rand between Iona and Dazorak, is a common theme for artists."

"What kind of demon was he, Glenda?"

"Oh, he wasn't a demon. He was a man."

"A flesh-and-blood man or a god?" asked Savannah, confused.

"There are various interpretations. Some say that

Dazorak was a god, others that he was a demi-god." Glenda shrugged. "But it's only supposition."

"What was the war about?"

"Power, or so the legends would have you believe. He was jealous of Iona and wanted her crown."

"So she was a Queen as well as a Goddess?"

Glenda nodded. "She was supposed to be the Imperial Queen."

"That's interesting," murmured Savannah. "Now, let's look for some books on tapestries."

†

"This place gives me the creeps," said Savannah after they flew into the ruined landing bay in the Prophecy Tower. Three crystal lamps had survived, illuminating with a muted glow the destruction in the cavern after the blast from the Silverthorne witchcraft. It was a mass of rubble and ash, but it wasn't the wreckage that was so chilling, it was the oppressive silence as if the ghosts of the witches lurked in the shadows.

"It was put off limits after we evacuated everyone," said Pela. "No one has been here since."

"The black magic still lingers like a malignancy," murmured Savannah. "I can feel it in my bones.

Pela shivered. "Where to first?"

"I want to look inside the Silverthorne Palace."

Pela didn't argue, though Savannah could see by her dour expression that she would have preferred not to go in there. They hurried up the staircase to the royal floor, then down the corridor and past the kitchen until they entered the small courtyard in front of the Palace steps.

Pela eyed her doubtfully. "You sure you want to go in there? We didn't clean up. There would be nothing left in the Throne Room after Valeria brought down her Judgement and you unleashed the Death Vale."

Savannah didn't reply, stepping past the pile of green marble in the corner that was the remains of the Helva Hounds. Once she reached the antechamber, she stopped and looked around. "Here's what I came to see, Pel," she said, pointing to the tapestry of the Battle of Creation.

"I don't know why," Pela muttered. "That was one thing I hoped never to see again. Don't get too close. There might be some of Agatha's spell left and we don't want to be caught again in the tapestry."

Ignoring her, Savannah walked forward until every part of the picture was clear. It was a huge tapestry; she couldn't even imagine how long it would have taken the artisans to embroider it. Or how many had worked on the project. As she continued to study it, her senses heightened until she could smell and hear the war: the rush of combat, the clash of steel, the whistle of arrows, the curses and groans, the metallic odor of blood, and the unrelenting screams.

She was acutely aware of the fear, and worst of all, the rage.

Though it was hard to ignore, she forced aside the sensation to concentrate on the picture. It was a sweeping panorama, set in an open field with undulating hills on either side. Demons and warriors filled the whole tapestry in a bloody battle, though it was impossible to tell who was winning the war. The Goddess Iona was on a white horse on a rise overlooking a cavalry charge. While a man, whom she presumed was the Prince, was seated on a brown horse, watching from a hill on the other side of the picture. He looked a lot like Iona in facial structure and coloring, but she figured that didn't mean much. Many artists painted people in the same style, but it did confirm that Prince Dazorak was a man.

Though she could hear Pela fidgeting behind her, she moved nearer to look closely at Iona. She was decked out in a suit of silver armor but wore no helmet. A thin silver and gold crown was entwined in her braids. As Savannah gazed at her eyes, the air appeared to shimmer slightly and Iona turned to look directly at her.

The Goddess bent her head to acknowledge her and smiled. "You are so like him, dear one."

The voice was so low that Savannah could barely hear the words. She moved closer, stretching out her hand to touch her leg, to connect, feeling an over-whelming affinity for this lovely woman.

A hand descended on her shoulder with a thump. "Savannah! Don't touch it. Step away," Pela hissed in her ear.

The air immediately shimmered again, leaving Iona caught in the threads, staring at the battle. Savannah nearly wept with frustration — she had been so tanta-lizingly close to solving the puzzle of her bloodline. "I was fine," she growled.

"No, you weren't. You could have been sucked into the battle again if you had touched it."

Savannah threw up her hands. "Okay. Maybe you're right," she conceded. "Let's see if there's anything else of interest here."

There were statues of long-dead witches and two tapestries of the Prophecy Tower in its heyday. When she spied a small tapestry depicting a blacksmith at his forge, she stopped to examine it.

"Why do you think this is here?" she asked. "It looks incongruous amongst the other works."

Pela peered at it. "Perhaps it has something to do with what he's making. It has a small blade like a dagger."

"The Dagger of Yorn," whispered Savannah.

"What's that?"

"The weapon I've come to retrieve from the vault on the top floor."

Pela frowned at her. "How in the Goddess's name do you know it's in there?"

"I learned where it was while in Iriwari city. The Oracles told me it was the only thing that could kill the Time Walkers."

"You'll have to fill me in about your trip there," said Pela. "You're still keeping secrets."

Savannah just shook her head. Pela seemed to have conveniently forgotten her hissy fit when she heard she'd gone there. "I'll tell you tonight. I need to get the Dagger and get out of this place. The taint of black magic is making me sick."

Without another word, she hurried out of the Palace and up to the last floor. When she reached the landing at the top of the staircase, she pressed Pela's arm. "You'll have to stay here, Pel. The magic is very powerful and could kill you."

Pela began to argue, then nodded reluctantly. "I'll be outside if you need me, love. Be careful."

As soon as Savannah stepped inside and closed the door, she felt the spell. An evil so intense it took her breath away. Cautiously, she approached a door on the far wall that reminded her of a bank's security vault. Its handle was surrounded by a circle of symbols that she presumed was the spell. She inched closer until she stood a foot away, then called forth the ancient magic embedded in every fiber of her body. It seeped through the pores of her skin, cocooning her in a protective barrier.

Confident of its ability to withstand the witchcraft, she put her hand out to grasp the handle. Even before she reached it, she triggered some sort of phantom thread. A shock of searing pain shot through her spine from the base of her skull. As her back arched, she nearly lost consciousness. Savannah worked her tongue around her mouth, which had gone numb, desperately trying to work up some saliva. A second later, the symbols began to pop, rocking the room. She smelt something so vile it was beyond anything she could have imagined. Her face twisted in shock as black smoke engulfed her.

The ancient power within her raged to be released, and as she fought to control it, a blast of hot air knocked her sprawling onto the stone floor. She closed her eyes and fell into a black chasm.

CHAPTER THIRTY-NINE

*T*ime twisted.

No matter how much Savannah struggled, she couldn't stop the slide into the darkness.

She could hear creatures crawling around, growling and snapping ferociously. Something brushed against her legs, something slimy and cold. She flinched, shrinking away. Voices began whispering vile things in her ear that turned her stomach. A war scene flooded the void, bloody and brutal, accompanied by the screams of dying soldiers.

In the middle of the chaos, the blacksmith stood at his anvil, striking a piece of steel with hard, sharp blows. Sweat dribbled down his neck, coating his chest and bulging biceps. After he finished, he grasped the blade with tongs and dipped it into the tub of water.

Steam gushed into the air. When he pulled it out, Savannah knew what had been forged in the heat of battle that surrounded him.

The Dagger of Yorn.

Her eyes popped open. She reinforced her protective shield, unleashed her power, and allowed the ancient magic to take over. It streamed out, eating away at the spell that tried vainly to claw back its form. Minutes later, a twang sounded like a guitar string breaking, followed by a flare of bright red light. Immediately, the appalling smell dissipated, and the symbols surrounding the lock crumbled into dust.

Savannah took hold of the handle, turned it, and cautiously pulled. The door swung open, exposing a room with reinforced metal walls. She put a hand over the threshold and found no resistance. When she stepped inside, her eyes widened. The shelves were filled with coins, artifacts, gemstones, and precious metals. The pile of zenphin alone was worth a fortune. The accumulated wealth of the Silverthorne Coven was sitting in front of her, a huge windfall for the Imperial Queen. Putting aside her desire to examine the artifacts, Savannah searched for the Dagger. Tucked away in a corner, she found a small plain iron box that seemed out of place amongst such riches.

She fiddled with the lock, her shield warding off the sparks. When it finally opened, a blast of magic shot out, so powerful that if Savannah hadn't been protected, she probably would have lost her head. A small dagger with a marble handle was inside. There was no doubt this was the weapon she sought — a red glow engulfed it. When she touched it with her fingertip, she could feel the power, but strangely, it had lost its hostility. All it gave off was a feeling that it was there to serve her.

She closed the lid, tucked the box inside her deep coat pocket, and went outside.

Pela, pacing up and down, breathed an audible sigh. "Are you all right. There was a lot of noise coming out of there."

Savannah flashed a wide smile. "I found the Dagger of Yorn, but you're not going to believe what else is in there. Go in ... the spell is destroyed."

"Gad," gasped Pela when she entered the small room. "There's a fortune in here. We won't have to worry about funding the war."

"It'll hardly make a dent in all this. We'll have to get it to Iona somehow."

"It'll be safer left here until the war is over," said Pela. "Very few people in the Keep know what stone to press to open the window into the landing pad. We'll tell only Tamasin it's here. Have you anything more to do?"

"No. I want to leave. That spell has left a bad taste in my mouth. It was vile."

"I won't be sorry to get out into the fresh air either. The place stinks of evil," Pela muttered.

They hurried down through the levels, not stopping until they reached the exit. Savannah urged Sunflower forward, then waited to shut the window after the Bramble Hawk had flown out. As they soared into the open sky, Savannah could see the canyon far below, a wasteland as barren and hot as the Sahara.

It was late afternoon when they returned to the Keep, still two hours until dinner. When Savannah emerged from the stables, Pela took her hand and said softly, "We could go up to my special place and watch the sunset. It'd be nice to be alone where we won't be disturbed."

Emotion welled up in Savannah's throat. "There's nothing I'd like better," she murmured. "It's my favorite place in Rand."

As she climbed to the top of the rocky outcrop at the end of Falcon's Keep, Savannah recalled the first time when Pela had to guide and cajole her up the sheer face. And when they'd reached the top, how it had reminded her of an eagle's nest. She hadn't a clue then that Pela was a Bramble Hawk.

They settled into the small recess, Pela behind Savannah with her arms and legs cradling her. Savannah sank back into her warm body, pulling her arms more tightly around her. And then she began to talk, relating in detail her trip to the Iriwari city and Rozen's reunion with her father. She finished by saying, "The Sylph bloodline is yours too, Pel. It would be nice if you could meet your other family."

Surprisingly, Pela agreed with the suggestion. "I will. For my mother's sake."

"I've learned this world is all about bloodlines," Savannah mused.

"Have you discovered anymore about the mysterious father of Elsbeth's children?"

"I have a theory, but to prove it will be impossible unless I can persuade Grandmother to tell me. And she's being very close lipped about it."

"Grandmother, as in Ronja the Mind Walker?"

"Yes. She likes the name."

"It must be odd to mind-speak with someone from the past," Pela remarked.

"At first, it was, but now it's become second nature."

Pela dropped a kiss on her shoulder. "Tell me about your theory."

"There are two puzzles here," Savannah began, pleased to have someone to bounce her thoughts off. "One Grandmother could verify, but the other will remain an educated guess. It was too long ago. But that's what historians do, form a theory, then analyze historical sources and evidence to support the argument."

"What's the first one?"

Savannah closed her eyes, organizing the facts in her head. "I've always wondered why Queen Jessica sent Elsbeth through the portal. It seemed an extreme way of hiding her — there must have been plenty of places in this world. Change her appearance and give her a role where no one would think to look. And then there's the third line of that little rhyme about the Circle of Sheda ... *When the dogs of war start baying again.* How did Jessica know there would be another war?"

"I've no idea. This world is so steeped in legends and myths that no one questioned it," said Pela.

"Exactly. There's so much magic here that anything seems possible. But I doubt Queen Jessica was the one who sent Elsbeth through the portal. I think it was Grandmother. She probably gave the order in her dreams, just like she did to Tamasin. And through the dream world, the rhyme was well circulated so people wouldn't forget the medallion existed. Then when Elsbeth went through, Grandmother kept an eye on her. That's how she knew where Elsbeth was buried."

"I see where you're going with this," said Pela. "The puzzle is now why Ronja sent her there. So there was someone powerful enough to find her in Rand."

"Exactly."

"Borrentine?"

Savannah shook her head. "I don't think so. True, he would have liked the medallion, but why would Elsbeth's children be a threat to him?"

"Why did she take the medallion with her when she went? She could have buried it somewhere." Pela sounded confused.

"Because she couldn't take it off," said Savannah with a dry chuckle. "I know that firsthand."

"There's one flaw in your theory. Why did Elsbeth agree to go? She was leaving her family and everything she held dear."

"Ah ... I'd say she had an attempt made on her life or a fright that scared the daylights out of her. Don't forget she was pregnant, and a mother will do anything to protect her children."

"It sounds feasible," Pela acknowledged. "And I'd say you're probably right. Have you any idea who was trying to kill her?"

"Not yet, but I'm working on it."

Pela moved into another position, then pulled Savannah close again. "Sorry, my legs were going to sleep. So what's the second puzzle?"

"Iona. She's revered as a Goddess, but you saw her in that tapestry. And we know the War of Creation was real because Agatha, the Silverthorne Witch sent us there. Did you notice Iona's crown in the picture? It's the same one Valeria wears, so she must have been the Imperial Queen."

"What's your point? She could be the Queen as well as a Goddess."

Savannah took a calming breath, telling herself to be patient. "I know, but what was the war all about? I think Rand was created long before the battle of Creation."

"You've lost me, love."

"I know, but I'm sure it has something to do with my bloodline. Or bloodlines, as it's turning out. My heritage seems to be a potpourri of magic, and it only could have come from the father of Elsbeth's twins. By a freak of nature, I inherited all his magic."

"You think he was a magical being?"

"Undoubtedly. There's no dispute about that." She paused, wondering how to phrase her theory. "Though I couldn't possibly prove it, my theory is that Iona didn't create Rand, she created the Magical Folk. And they evolved into the Great Houses of the ancient world."

Pela pressed her arm. "I wouldn't be going about expounding that theory. Iona is a Goddess in Rand. People like Queen Clementine would call it blasphemy."

"I know," said Savannah with a sigh. "I'll keep it to myself. Glenda was the one who told me Iona was the Imperial Queen."

"What would Glenda know?" huffed Pela.

"Don't underestimate her. She has had nothing to do for years except read history. She has an enormous wealth of knowledge. It would do the recruits good to study some history as well as physical training."

"Having met you, I can see the merit in that," Pela said with a chuckle. "But what's the significance of Iona being the Imperial Queen *and* a divinity?"

"The Queen must have an heir to carry on the Imperial Line. She would have had a consort."

"Hmm. I suppose you're right, but there's never been any suggestion she was married."

"No," replied Savannah, "because that would make her mortal, and people don't want to hear that."

"They don't. I'm afraid that theory will remain one, so it's time we got off the subject and looked at the sunset."

Savannah gazed out over the Iron Mountains, now turning red and orange with the setting sun. The mountains were so barren they effectively isolated the far west from the rest of the world. She'd always thought the Valley of the Pipers must be the loneliest Realm in Rand and the worst economically. Half the Kingdom was taken up by the Great Windy Desert, a place that sounded as cruel and harsh as the Sahara.

As she looked into the distance, black specks in the sky caught her eye. "What are those birds, Pel?"

Pela was silent for a long moment, then muttered, "Crows."

As they watched, more came into view, all heading west. "If I'm not mistaken," Pela ground out. "They're the remnants of Borrentine's army."

"The only place that way is Realm of the Valley of the Pipers," Savannah said, knowing what it meant.

"Exactly. Damn, we've been so stupid. It was one of the first Realms to lose its General and then later its King. We should have asked ourselves why they went to all that trouble when they weren't a threat. Borrentine must have taken over Wynfield when he killed Gerard. The City of the Dead, or as we know it now, the Time Gateway, has to be in the Windy Desert."

CHAPTER FORTY

THE BERIAN PALACE

*A*s she walked outside, the chilly morning air pinked Lilybeth's cheeks.

Gladofin turned at the sound of her footsteps and smiled in welcome. "The sea's so peaceful this morning."

Lilybeth leaned on the wall beside her, closing her eyes as she drew in her delicate scent that felt like a sweet caress. She felt suddenly shy as she gazed at the beautiful, beguiling face. "I have a gift for you."

"You're spoiling me, Beth."

Lilybeth watched her unwrap the package, feeling inordinately pleased to see the Guardian's reserve melt as she held the necklace up to the light. "It's lovely," whispered Gladofin in awe. "I've never seen pearls quite like them."

"The light-green color is extremely rare."

Gladofin turned her gaze away from the necklace to focus on Lilybeth. "It's a wonderful present. You're very good to me."

Lilybeth looked into the expressive eyes that regarded her warmly and said softly, "I want you to know I think you're the best thing that has ever happened to me. The moment I saw you, I couldn't keep my eyes off you. Your touch never fails to excite me, and your laughter is music to my ears. You have become my friend, my lover, my home. After the courting period, I intend to ask you to marry me."

Gladofin's eyes grew moist as she lightly stroked Lilybeth's face. "And I shall accept with all my heart."

Lilybeth pulled her into her arms, feeling that physical closeness spoke more than any words. "You don't think I'm old-fashioned to want to get to know each other properly before we commit?"

Gladofin gave a soft laugh. "You're such a romantic … I expect nothing less of you." She pulled out of the embrace and said hesitantly, "Would you like another child, Beth?"

Lilybeth blinked at her. She'd hadn't thought that far ahead, but now the question was asked, she knew the answer without even having to think about it. "I'd love another little one," she said, then looked anxiously at Gladofin. "Would you?"

"Oh, yes … it would be wonderful."

Lilybeth smiled. "Then we'd better make it a quick courtship … we're not getting any younger." She took her hand and squeezed it. "I have an appointment with the Madra shortly. She's expressed a wish to meet you. Would you like to accompany me?"

"Very much, and Snow Pine will appreciate an outing." She handed her the necklace. "Put it on me, Beth. Something this beautiful should be worn."

After Lilybeth closed the clasp, she brushed aside the blond strands of hair and feathered a kiss down her neck. She lingered for a moment, then pulled away reluctantly and said, "We'd better go. Tamasin sent a message that she'll be arriving at noon."

As they walked down to the stables in companionable silence, Lilybeth was acutely aware of the woman beside her. Then when Gladofin slipped her arm through hers, Lilybeth wished the warmth by her side would never leave.

Snow Pine gave a happy nicker when she spied them approaching. Gladofin rubbed her muzzle gently. "Are you up for a ride, dear one?"

Lilybeth fondly watched the two interact. She wasn't privy to the mare's telepathic reply, but from Gladofin's chuckle, Snow Pine had regained her sense of humor. She also looked much better: her coat had a healthy shine, the bites on her legs had healed, and the shoemaker had fashioned a leather ear to replace the missing one, which Savannah had fixed on with a little magic. When they had flown to Beria from Amarim, Gladofin had ridden with Lilybeth on Banner so as not to put any strain on the mare. Now, judging by the way Snow Pine was prancing, she was ready for a rider.

Once they'd saddled the horses, the Countess swung onto her back with effortless poise. Lilybeth mounted, then regarded her with a smile. "Let's go."

When the secluded inlet came into view, she gave Banner a nudge to descend onto the sandy beach covered in the light morning fog. When Snow Pine landed beside him, Gladofin exclaimed, "This beach is lovely."

"It's more secluded than most of the coastline, and the hills shield it from strong winds. A pocket of tranquility. Life is different by the sea, Glad. We are at the whim of the elements. We plan by the tides and currents and work by the moods of the weather." Lilybeth climbed out of the saddle and helped her dismount. "We're a little early ... she'll be here shortly."

Gladofin slipped off her sandals, digging her toes into the sand. "That feels so good," she murmured, then sniffed. "For all its unpredictability, I love the sea: its salty smell, its wildness, its vastness. One could get addicted to it."

Lilybeth smiled. "I know what you're saying. The

ocean is in my blood." She pointed to the sea, where two Brown Seals were riding the white-tipped crest of a long breaker in the distance. "Here they come."

The wave rolled to the shore, and after it crashed onto the beach, the Madra and her guard waded out of the water. Lilybeth stepped forward to greet them, then led them to Gladofin, whose body language had subtly changed from a lover to a woman in authority. She stood regally on the sand, regarding them with a steady gaze. After Lilybeth introduced them, Dirk retreated to the horses to let Nerin speak to Gladofin alone.

"Countess Gladofin, it is indeed an honor to meet you. Welcome to my domain," Nerin said with a deep bow. It was the first time Lilybeth had seen the Madra bow to anyone.

"It's a pleasure to be here, Nerin. Lilybeth has told me about the Magical Sea Folk. I'd love to meet them all one day."

"You intend to stay for a while then, Countess?"

Gladofin smiled, turning her head slightly in Lilybeth's direction. "Yes. I am a member of the military operations' team currently in the Berian Palace. Queen Lilybeth has kindly provided accommodation for the war effort."

"I've met Commander Pela. A formidable woman indeed."

"And a very clever tactician," replied Gladofin. "We

received word that her army has won a battle north of the Cadiwine without engaging the enemy in hand-to-hand fighting. She starved them into submission." She scanned Nerin's face. "Savannah informed us your people have promised to help in the war."

"No enemy will be allowed to pass over the sea. The Black Sea Eagles are patrolling the skies for Crows."

"Good. The only way over for them now is to fly. The days are running out. If the time door can't be closed, the war will begin. Women and children from the northern Realms may need to be evacuated to the south, and you will be called upon to help the people to cross the sea."

Nerin pursed her lips. "I agreed to keep the shipping lanes open to the people of Rand, and to block the Crevlin. Are you asking for more?"

"If there's an exodus, we will need more than boats."

"We can only do so much. The seas are treacherous in places, something I have no control over,"

"Then we must hope it doesn't come to that," Glad-ofin murmured. She looked up at the sky. "Thank goodness the sun's come out at last." She took off her riding cloak and threw it on a boulder. "That's better."

Lilybeth watched her, thinking she looked simply stunning, like a Sea Goddess, with her white gown blowing in the breeze, flowing blond hair, and bare feet.

Nerin took a sharp breath as she focused on the

pearls. She raised an imperious eyebrow and asked, "Where did you get that necklace, Countess?"

Smiling, Gladofin fingered the string. "It was a gift."

"Those are the Sacred Pearls of Nessalia, the Coral Goddess who is venerated by the Sea Nymphs. Whoever wears the pearls is under the protection of the Goddess."

"Protection against what, or whom?" asked Gladofin quietly.

"The ancient black magic," replied Nerin. "I've never known the Nymphs to give them to anyone."

Lilybeth inwardly groaned. So much for making sure Gladofin was protected from Borrentine. Knowing Nerin, she wouldn't leave it alone until she had ferreted out who gave her the pearls, for as the Madra, she liked, or rather demanded, to know everything that went on in her Realm.

Gladofin eyed Nerin thoughtfully before she replied, "Then I'm lucky to receive such a gift," and deftly moved on. "Tell me about the species of shape shifters who live in the seas. They're called the Mani in the Forgotten Realms."

There was an awkward silence while Nerin seemed momentarily struck speechless. But now aware the Countess had no intention of divulging who gave her the necklace, she didn't press the issue at the risk of annoying the powerful Guardian. Lilybeth stood back while they talked, contributing little to the conversation. She hoped they'd become friends, for both women were dear to her. By the time it came to go, the two were on such good terms that Lilybeth relaxed.

But as they readied the horses, something unexpected happened. Ten figures suddenly materialized from the surf and stood on the water's edge, watching them silently.

"Good Goddess!" muttered Nerin. "I've never seen a Nymph outside the Coral Isles."

Lilybeth turned to say something to Gladofin, but she had already left her side and was walking to the water. When Nerin went to follow, Lilybeth quickly grasped her arm. "No, Nerin. They've come to see the Countess, not us. I think the necklace is calling them to her."

As she watched them circle and touch her, Lilybeth realized that Gladofin looked a lot like them. They were blond, with pale blue-green eyes and willowy figures, and moved with a natural grace and poise. She figured one of the Countess's ancestors must have mated with a Nymph, for this likeness was too pronounced to be random. Then it struck Lilybeth that this was probably why she had such an affinity with the sea. After talking for ten minutes, Gladofin hugged each one, and they disappeared into the water.

When she returned, tears glimmered in her eyes.

"They're beautiful and so innocent," she whispered. "When this is all over, they have invited me to the Coral Islands to spend time with them."

Nerin eyed her curiously. "They're timid and rarely seek my council. Lilybeth has more to do with them than anyone." She gave a self-deprecating shrug. "I think I frighten them, but I make sure that they're left alone and unharmed."

"They know, and are grateful," Gladofin said with a smile. "Now, it's time we went."

"Till we meet again," said Nerin, then nodded to Dirk. They jogged to the water's edge, waved, then vanished into the sea.

"You have a Nymph ancestor," said Lilybeth. "No wonder you like the sea."

Gladofin nodded. "As soon as I saw them, I knew. And they think the world of you as I do."

CHAPTER FORTY-ONE

THE BERIAN PALACE

*S*hortly after they arrived back at the Palace, Tamasin walked in.

Lilybeth hurried forward to greet her, noting how tired and worried she looked. "Tamasin. Can I get you something to eat?"

"Just something to drink, thanks, Lilybeth. I'm anxious to hear if Winston has come up with any ideas on the possible sites for the City of the Dead."

His usual grin missing, Winston sounded frustrated when he replied, "Since the Countess has assured us it couldn't be in the Northern Wetlands, we're running out of ideas. There are few possibilities left."

"We've just spoken to the Madra, and it's not on an island anywhere."

"Savannah's been to the Southern Lands," said Tamasin. "She can't see how it could be there."

Winston studied the map, then muttered, "It has to be somewhere in the Great Northern Forests."

"But they would need to feed their people," said Lilybeth. "And we're talking about a whole race ... millions, not thousands. They'll have to occupy a city to do that." She turned at the sound of footsteps hurrying down the corridor outside and frowned. Visitors would be a giant inconvenience today.

When Pela and Savannah swept in, Lilybeth breathed a sigh of relief. The presence of the Commander and the Chosen One went a long way to calm strained nerves.

Pela glanced around the room, acknowledging them with a brief nod, and declared without any preamble. "We've news."

"Something good, I hope," said Tamasin wearily.

Pela's face broke into a smile. "It looks like the City of the Dead is in the Windy Desert. While we were at Falcon's Keep, we saw the remnants of Borrentine's army flying west to the Valley of the Pipers. I've only seen an odd Crow so deep in the Iron Mountains before, certainly not in those numbers. Ironically, after our searching and strategizing it was under our noses all the time."

"We missed the signs," said Savannah. "It was one of

456 | COVENANT OF QUEENS

the first Realms to lose its General and later its King. We should have wondered why they went to all that trouble when the small, isolated Realm was no threat. They have no resources anyone would need."

"The enemy must occupy Wynfield," said Tamasin.

"That's their capital, Savannah."

"How many more towns are there?"

"Six villages — Wynfield is the only town of any size. The River Wyn runs through the valley and empties into the Wetlands bordering the Sea of Mists. The valley is fertile, but further west is the Great Windy Desert. It's full of sand dunes and home to only a few nomadic tribes."

Lilybeth stood back to watch them, pleased to see the mood in the room had lightened as they crowded around the large clay map on the center table.

"It has to be a remote place where the Time Gateway comes out, which means it's in the desert," declared Winston. "They would have to gather a force in secret before they captured the Valley of Pipers, otherwise Gerard would have gotten a message to Iona."

"I've brought someone along who knows the desert. He's waiting outside. I'll fetch him," said Savannah. She returned with a heavyset man in his middle years, who looked around the room warily. "This is Leon. Before he was a guard in the Prophecy Tower, he was a foot soldier in King Gerard's garrison." She nodded encouragement at Leon, "Go ahead."

He shuffled his feet, then nodded to Lilybeth. "By your leave, Ma'am. I was a sergeant in the Wynfield garrison for ten years. My troop patrolled the desert to keep the tribes under control. They were fair bastards if we didn't keep a tight rein on them, raiding the outlining farms and stealing their livestock. I know the desert like the back of my hand. It's a dry, harsh place and hot as hell."

"What's beyond it?" asked Savannah.

"Salt flats and then the ocean. No one would last a day on the flats."

Tamasin motioned him forward. "Can you point out where there's water in the desert? Enough for a lot of people."

Leon touched his finger on the map. "There are a few small wells and springs scattered about, but there are only two watering places of any size. The Windy Well in the deep desert, and the Oasis of Wydola, in the third line of dunes. Both have a good water supply, but travelers who don't know the desert wouldn't last very long, even at the Well. The Oasis is the only place with shade. The pool of water is a fair size, fed by a permanent underground spring. There are trees, and the Valley's army has built a few huts for the patrols."

Pela studied it carefully. "How often are the soldiers at the Oasis?"

"Not often," replied Leon with a shrug. "The Nomads tend to confine most of their activity further down south where they can disappear into the line of hills that skirt the dunes. They hide there, but if we get too close, they vanish into the desert. If there are frequent raids, we go in."

"Firstly, we have to ascertain that the Crevlin are at the Oasis. The Nomads would be aware of any strange activity," mused Pela.

Leon snorted. "Forget it. You've no hope of finding them if they don't want to be found."

"Then we'll have to work out a way for someone to get into the place, preferably long enough to find out what's happening there. They will see us if we fly over. We need to find a way in for the Queens without alerting the enemy." Pela looked around the room. "Anyone with any ideas?"

"Even one of my spies will be noticed," said Tamasin. "How many trees are in the oasis, Leon? Enough for a hiding place, that is presuming we can sneak someone in?"

He shook his head. "There are clusters of palms and olive trees, and on the edge of the pond, sycamores, willows, and tall grasses, but they're not thick enough."

"If you can get me in, I can join the willows," said

Willowtine. When every eye turned toward her, she added shyly, "What better disguise than a tree? I can stay there as long as I have to."

Winston flashed her a smile. "Good thinking."

"I could verify if the Crevlin are in the Realm," offered Egwine. She pointed to the Wetlands south of the Realm. "I could fly up through the swamps. I'm a Praying Mantis, and no one notices an insect."

Savannah stared at her. "How big is your other self?"

"I'm the smallest of the shape shifters. I'm adept at blending in with the greenery, so don't worry, they won't even notice me."

Lilybeth nodded approvingly. "You could check out the south but take a few friends. By now, I imagine the Crevlin would have overrun the entire Realm. I could ask Nerin to send some Sea Otters up the River Wyn to look at Wynfield. They're quick, slippery little fellows and hard to catch."

"Right," said Pela. "Once we have verification the Crevlin are indeed in the Valley of the Pipers, we'll move our armies into place. There is one route through the Iron Mountains, and the Moaning Pass takes it down to the valley. It'll be easily defended, but to march an army through the ranges would be virtually impossible. It's like a furnace in the gorges." She scanned the map, then pointed to the cliffs on either side of the pass. "We won't put troops there. The Falcon's Keep recruits and trainers can wait high in these mountains with their horses. We'll get more Blue Fjords to the Keep to provide a mount for everyone." She turned to Gladofin. "An army of Magical Folk can defend the southern end. There'll be plenty of places to hide in the Wetlands down there. Will Olivine be agreeable?"

"Jayden runs the army, Pela. There will be no argument from him."

"Excellent." She stabbed a finger on the map. "Tamasin and General Grogan will organize the armies of Rand to barricade the way from the north." She gave a wolfish grin. "You, Winston, will devise a way to get Willowtine into the Oasis and out again. And you have two days to come up with the plan."

Winston shot Savannah a grin. "You can't make an invisible cape, can you, Chosen One?"

Savannah fell silent for a long moment, then said thoughtfully, "There's an old saying in my world, Winston. 'Many a truth is said in jest.' What we need is a spell to make her invisible. Are there any sorcerers left in Rand or anyone capable of casting a spell?"

He stroked his beard idly. "My team will work on it. There are other ways to make yourself invisible."

Pela stood up, glancing at everyone in the room. "This time, we must engage the enemy in combat. The Queens need unimpeded access to the Time Gateway to close it, which means we keep the enemy busy elsewhere. I'll be relying on your group, Countess, to form a battle plan. The Crevlin will blow us to pieces with their bombs if we get too close."

Lilybeth stood up. "We'll adjourn to the dining room for lunch. Take a stroll with me, Tamasin. I have something to discuss."

When the others had moved off, Lilybeth walked out onto a balcony overlooking the side gardens.

Tamasin joined her at the railing and asked, "You seek my counsel, Lilybeth?"

Lilybeth glanced her way, hoping she wouldn't object. "Would you be happy if my army fought with the Magical Folk, Tam? The Wetlands are nearly on our doorstep. Sailing there will be easy, as opposed to a long march to the northern end."

"I was going to suggest to Pela that your soldiers be kept in reserve to defend the coast in case we can't close the Time Gateway."

"I intend going, but your plan has merit," said Lilybeth. "I will only take a squad of fifty, leaving the rest on battle alert."

"If you really want to, then by all means go, but the Magical Folk will have a formidable army."

Lilybeth cleared her throat self-consciously. "I just can't sit here twiddling my thumbs while everyone is fighting."

"Everyone, or just Gladofin?" said Tamasin, sounding amused.

"Okay … Glad. She's become important to me and I have no intention of letting her go into battle alone."

Tamasin reached over and touched her hand. "I know how you feel, Lilybeth. Go and fight beside her with my blessing."

"She's my family now and mine to look after," said Lilybeth softly but firmly.

CHAPTER FORTY-TWO

THE ARCADIAN PALACE

*P*rince Delvin entered the Throne Room and saluted.

Savannah barely recognized him in his uniform; his time as Pela's aide had altered his appearance considerably for the better. Fern's brother no longer had the affected manners of a court dandy but looked stronger, confident, and every inch a soldier. Savannah knew from experience that Pela would have made him train with the Elite Guards and pushed him hard to whip him into shape. She wouldn't tolerate anyone unfit on her staff, and he had proven his mettle by lasting the distance. He would make some lucky royal a fine consort one day.

"Princess Luna and Mani Willowtine are waiting outside, Commander."

Relief flitted across Pela's face. Waiting for this news had been a strain, for it was only two weeks before the eclipse began. "Show them in, Sergeant."

From their smiles, Savannah knew the operation had been a success.

After tossing ideas around about how to get Willowtine into the Oasis of Wydola, they'd decided, in the end, to ask Luna to make a hooded cloak to blend in with the sand. A reversible one, the other side the same dark color the Crevlin assassins had worn. As soon as she reached the perimeter, she was to turn the cloak and slip into the crowd.

Willowtine looked around shyly, bowing to the Queen before she focused on Pela. "It worked, Commander. After Luna flew me to a place well out of sight, it took me about a half an hour to reach the dune behind the Oasis. The sun was setting when I came down the dune. If someone had looked west, it would have been too difficult seeing anything in the sand because of the haze and shadows. You were right; the Crevlin are there. The Oasis was packed, and no one gave me a second glance. I went from tree to tree until I reached the water, then crept into the middle of a group of willows and changed."

"When I flew back to the pick-up point two days later, she was waiting for me," said Luna. "The operation went without a hitch."

"Well done," said Pela. "Where exactly is the Gateway?"

"On the northern outskirts of the Oasis," replied Willowtine. "Streams of birds came out continuously. They changed immediately into men and women and were taken for a meal. The strongest changed back into Crows and flew off in the direction of Wynfield, while the weaker ones remained until they could fly to the city."

After chewing this over for a moment, Pela asked, "Were you able to see the size and shape of the Gateway?"

"On the way out, I had a look. Nobody took any notice of me. It was chaos, with Crows changing as soon as they exited the Gateway and everyone talking at once. The Gateway is a hole with seven distinct sides and is roughly three-quarters the size of this room. There is a small gap where the birds are coming out."

"Which will open fully when the moons are aligned," muttered Savannah.

"We were expecting a circle, not a seven-sided shape," mused Pela. "Since the Covenant has five Queens, plus Valeria, who would occupy the seventh place?"

"I imagine the bearer of the Circle of Sheda would take the last," said Savannah. "Maybe the Queens' powers are channeled through it into the Imperial

Queen, or it's a catalyst for the magic to work. I don't know, but the medallion was made for a specific purpose."

"You will need to be at the Oasis with us, though the General will sorely miss your magic fire." Pela turned to Fern. "The armies march tomorrow. General Grogan is waiting with the men in the camps for the order. I'll see him before Savannah and I head off to Amarim."

"Have you decided where you want the Sirens, Pela?" asked Jezzine, who had been sitting quietly beside Fern.

"They can come to the Oasis with us, along with a contingent of Ice Elves and Hawks."

Jezzine shot her a worried frown. "Borrentine will have access to the Blue Fjords in the King Gerard's royal stables and have airpower to drop his bombs. The Ice Elves will be reluctant to kill the magical horses."

"I can answer that," said Savannah. "The Blue Fjords will never let them mount them, for they won't side with the enemy against their own. They are not like ordinary horses, who obey whoever is holding the reins. They choose their riders ... I'd be surprised if they haven't escaped into the mountains by now."

"I want all the Covenant Queens at Falcon's Keep in three days, Jezz. The Sirens and their Guards as well. You'll be safe there until it's time to move. Tamasin is fetching Valeria and Reagan, and I'm going to see Olivine."

"The last stand has begun," whispered Fern, leaning over to grasp Jezzine's hand, "and there's no turning back."

For the first time, Pela looked subdued. "We're committed now, Fern. May the Goddess keep us all safe."

As Pela turned to go, a Berian soldier hurried into the room. She bowed to the Queen, then, with a troubled expression, addressed Pela, "Imperial Commander, Queen Lilybeth wishes to inform you that the Mani undercover agents have returned from the Valley of the Pipers. The enemy has overrun the whole of the Realm and they occupy the capital. They found evidence that soldiers and many citizens were slaughtered. The able-bodied people have been put to work on the farms to harvest the crops."

Pela gritted her teeth. "I'll quash that bastard King under my boot. Inform the Queen Lilybeth I'm mobilizing the armies, please, Captain. I'm heading now to see Prince Jayden, and they can expect the mounted Ice Elves and the Hawks tomorrow. The rest of the Magical Folk will be shipped there."

"As soon as our horses are rested, we'll go back, Commander," she said, saluted, and hurried out the door.

⸸

Sunflower nickered excitedly when the Amarim Palace came into view. Fluffy clouds floated in the sky, the occasional ray of sunlight enough to release a flash of sparkles like diamonds across the valley. After the Berian coastline, Savannah thought this place seemed like a fairy-tale world. She imagined it would be a winter wonderland in a few months when the Palace and gardens were adorned with thick pillows of snow.

As soon as they touched down in the front court-yard, Pela morphed back into her human form. After a groom took Sunflower off to the stables, they hurried up the stairs to the front door where they were met by the elderly Master of the Staff.

He led them at a snail's pace to the Queen's private sitting room. "Her Majesty is anxious for news," he said solemnly.

Olivine rose to her feet, and after a brief greeting, came to the point. "Any news, Commander?"

"Yes, Ma'am. It has been confirmed the enemy has taken the Valley of the Pipers, and the exit of the Time Gateway is three miles west in a desert oasis. I'm mobilizing the armies immediately. Countess Gladofin is waiting for Prince Jayden at Beria. When your troops arrive, a guide will lead them through the Wetlands."

Olivine blanched. "So soon. I was hoping for a few more days."

"It will take the boats three days to get upriver and around the sea," said Pela gruffly.

Savannah's heart went out to the Queen. All signs of her usual arrogance were gone and she seemed a little lost. She stepped forward and said softly, "Your people will be fine, Ma'am. The Crevlin fear magic."

Olivine gave her a wan smile. "I can't help worrying. We have been at peace for so long that it's hard to comprehend having to march to war." She hesitated, then asked, "Is Countess Gladofin going with them?"

"Yes. She's leading the ground forces. All the Guardians will be needed."

Olivine made a little huffing sound. "Now she's with that warrior Queen, she thinks she's a fighter."

Savannah smothered a smile. Olivine hadn't yet fully come to terms with her sister's romance or her choice of partner. Lilybeth was going to have to learn to handle her in the future. Out of the corner of her eye, Savannah could see Pela stepping from one foot to the other, a sign she was getting impatient.

Before Pela forgot who she was talking to and was overly abrupt, Savannah stood up quickly and said, "Pela and I are going into the hills to see her mother now. We'll be back to take you in two days to Falcon's Keep."

Olivine blinked. "So soon?"

"The Queen's must be ready to move a day before the moons align," Pela said in a no-nonsense tone. "There will be darkness like we've never seen on Rand, so we have to be in place. We don't want to be stumbling around when we get there. And it could even be earlier than predicted."

Olivine stiffened her shoulders, morphing back to her old self. "Then Hyacinth and I will be ready, Commander. Prince Jayden is in the stables, waiting for orders."

"Then we'll be off, Ma'am."

†

As soon as they reached the Bramble Hawk village, Savannah was excited to be seeing Rozen again. After giving Sunflower a reassuring pat and leaving her around the side of the house, she joined Pela at the front door. Rozen answered at the first knock, and after hugging them both, led them into a comfortable sitting room on the second floor.

She eyed Pela thoughtfully. "I take it you're not here on a social visit, Pela."

"No, Mother. We're preparing for battle. Are all the Hawks gathered here?"

"Half. The rest are waiting at Red Rock Peak. A

force of twenty thousand all told, and more if you want them."

Pela nodded, looking well satisfied. "We'll keep some in reserve. That'll be enough to frighten those Crows witless."

"You're staying the night, I hope?"

"Two days. I have business to catch up with." She eyed her mother's arm closely. "How's the broken arm?"

"Feels fine. The Iriwari healer knew what she was doing." Rozen flicked a look at Savannah. "You told Pela what happened?"

"Yes. When all this is over, she wants to accompany you to meet the Sylphs."

Rozen's face lit up. "They're dying to meet you." She gave a sly smile. "Queen Cassine was quite taken with Savannah. You'd better hurry up and marry her, Pela."

"Rozen!" exclaimed Savannah aghast. "We haven't discussed marriage yet."

"Oh. Why not?"

Pela squirmed in her seat and glared at her mother. "Because when this is over, Savannah might want to return to her world. I don't want her to feel she's trapped here."

Savannah stared at Pela. "You think I want to go back?"

"I don't know, that's the point. You never talk about it."

"That's because I'm happy here, Pel. I had good friends and an excellent job when I left, but no real ties … no family, and no lover."

"But you must want to go back for a visit."

Savannah suddenly felt sad as the reality of her situation hit. "Maybe in a few years but not now. I just can't lob up after being away for nearly a year and expect no one to ask questions. Imagine the third degree I'd get from the police. I've a high public profile, and I disappeared without my phone, credit cards, and personal items. I'm a missing person, a possible homicide. The Mayor's wife knew Tamasin saw me that night, and I'd have to explain who she was and what she wanted. What would I say? If they did a strip search or send me for a medical, I can't take off the medallion."

"So you *are* trapped here," stated Pela cautiously.

Savannah shrugged, then broke into a smile. "None of us are completely free, Pel. Responsibilities tie us down. The truth is, if I went back, I'd be busting to get back to you because I love you. Wherever you are, I want to be."

"You would be happy living up here? At least part of the time."

"Of course. But there is one stipulation."

Pela raised an eyebrow, "What?"

"Our house has to be only three stories, max."

CHAPTER FORTY-THREE

THE IRON MOUNTAINS

*A*t the sight of Falcon's Keep, Olivine wrinkled her nose.

Savannah smiled inwardly — the remote training school and the beautiful Amarim Palace were poles apart. She recalled her first impressions of the stony Keep when she thought it was the end of the world, and she could see Olivine was thinking the same.

"It grows on you," said Savannah reassuringly. When she heard a squawk, she looked up to see a Bramble Hawk fly over the top of the battlement.

After it landed, the bird fluffed up its feathers and shifted into Pela. "I'll take Olivine to her quarters, Savannah, if you'd like to attend to the horses."

Savannah took the reins, pleased to remain with the horses and not Olivine. She still felt a little intimidated by her icy tongue. As she watched them walk off to the Commander of the Keep's office, she imagined what a flap the poor woman would be in. To host the Covenant, two of whom were the Imperial and the Amarim Queens, would be more than daunting — it would be a nightmare. Accommodation was basic, offering no luxuries or comforts, and while Olivine and Valeria would be too well-bred to comment, Reagan would undoubtedly make some snide remarks.

They had already begun bringing more mounts in for the recruits, for horses packed the common, spilling over into the Amphitheatre. After she removed the saddles, Savannah took the two mares out into the fresh air. The presence of the aristocratic Hyacinth created quite a stir amongst the Blue Fjords, who had never seen a pure blood except for Malkia. Sunflower pranced beside her with her nose in the air as the horses greeted Hyacinth like royalty.

Savannah dug her in the ribs. "Behave, Missy. I'll see you later."

Tamasin and the Sirens were already in the recreation room. Tamasin pulled her aside and said in a low voice, "I'm picking up Valeria and Reagan after lunch. Would you like to come with me to say hello to the folks?"

"It's a date."

╪

"We'll take the long route around the mountain to Kandelora and avoid the wind tunnel in the east," Tamasin called out as she swung into the saddle.

Though it was a mild day at the Keep, as soon as they touched down in the canyon, a blast of hot air hit like a slap.

"Doesn't it ever cool down in these damn mountains?" growled Savannah, then found her irritation slip away as she regarded Tamasin's smiling face. She smiled back, knowing how much she must be looking forward to seeing Valeria.

They were only there a moment before a flicker of motion caught her eye, and the cliff face opened. Eric stepped out, waving them inside as he called out, "Bring the horses in with you." Immediately the door closed behind them, he clasped their hands warmly. "You are most welcome, Consort, and you, Savannah, though I fear you're here to take our guests away."

Savannah regarded him with a measure of compassion. It was undoubtedly going to be a wrench removing the only visitors the city had ever had for any length of time. From his expression, the women were going to be missed.

"The order has been given for the armies to march, Eric. It's time for the Queens to send the enemy back where they came from," said Tamasin. "How is the Imperial Queen?"

"She's well. We're going to be devastated to see her leave. She has won all our hearts."

"After this is over, my friend, we will discuss how we can help your people," said Tamasin softly, then cleared her throat. "How is Reagan handling it here?"

Eric gave an odd smile. "She too will be sorely missed but come ... see for yourself. She's officially our counselor and will be in her office."

Savannah raised an eyebrow at Tamasin as they followed him past the water reservoir to the door leading to the city square. A young boy came to collect the horses, nodding shyly before taking them off to the animal enclosures.

"We'll drop into Reagan first; she's just down the passageway," Eric said, moving down the corridor until he reached a brightly colored door with a plaque, *Reagan Falendore, Mistress of Minds*. Savannah gave a soft chuckle — trust Reagan to be so flashy — then smothered a smile when she saw Tamasin gaping at it.

As soon as Eric tapped on the door, a voice answered, "Come in."

When he entered, Reagan called out, "Hi, love, I was just ready to take a lunch break. Would you join me?"

Eyebrows twitching, Tamasin mouthed *love* at

Savannah before she stepped over the threshold. "Hello, Reagan."

Reagan's eyes widened then she flushed. "Tamasin. I didn't realize you'd arrived." She glanced over her shoulder and said even less enthusiastically, "Hello, Savannah."

Savannah acknowledged her with a nod, noting with surprise that she was dressed in a flowing casual dress, not her usual low-cut gown. With her hair down and only a touch of lipstick, she looked ten years younger.

Tamasin seemed almost apologetic when she said, "We're here to pick you up, Reagan. It's time for the Covenant to close the Gateway."

After a glance at Eric, Reagan answered with a resigned shrug, "I'll get my things and meet you in half an hour at the Grotto Tavern."

With a sigh, Eric stood up. "I'll help Reagan, Consort. You know the way to the Queen's rooms."

Tamasin stretched over and squeezed his shoulder. "I'm sorry, Eric, but the final conflict is about to begin. We'll take the Queen and Reagan back on our horses and give you the one here."

"Thank you, Tamasin. We've never had a way out before."

"That's going to change, Eric," said Reagan sharply. "When this is all over, anyone that wants to leave will be welcomed at my home, Falenbriar. Your people will never feel rejected again. I'd especially like my patients to come to continue their treatment."

When Eric remained silent, looking at Reagan with shining eyes, Tamasin tugged Savannah's arm. "Let's go."

As soon as they were in the corridor and the door closed behind them, they exchanged incredulous glances. "Now *that* was a surprise," whispered Tamasin.

Savannah nodded, feeling a nearly overwhelming desire to laugh at Tamasin's expression. Reagan and Eric were never a pairing she would have envisaged, but from what Lilybeth had said about the Enchantress, it made sense — Reagan wanted somewhere to belong, and she had fit in here like a glove. There was no doubt Eric loved her, and the feeling looked mutual.

"Love can sometimes find people in the strangest places," Savannah murmured, recalling her burgeoning love for Pela at Falcon's Keep.

"That it can," agreed Tamasin. "Valeria chose me, a soldier in her garrison, over all the Royals. Eric has given Reagan love and a purpose in life." Then added, looking amused, "Though I bet she can be still annoying."

Savannah chuckled. "Undoubtedly. A leopard doesn't change its spots."

When they arrived at the Queen's suite, Savannah exclaimed with delight, "These are Floris's old rooms."

A plump woman answered the door, greeted Tamasin with a brief nod, and beamed at Savannah. "Chosen One. It's so good to see you again."

"Hello, mistress Hilda. It's good to be back. I'd like to catch up with Sanyo and Pablo while I'm here."

"I'll tell them. Where will you be?"

"At the Grotto in ten minutes."

"I shall tell them. Her Majesty is in the sitting room readying for the afternoon lessons," she said and bustled out the door.

Without bothering to knock, Tamasin pushed open the door and walked inside. Valeria, who was writing at a table with a stack of books beside her, looked up at the sound of their footsteps. "Tamasin," she said delightedly, then caught sight of Savannah behind her. Her face clouded as understanding dawned. "It's time to go?"

"Yes, love. We're gathering the Covenant at Falcon's Keep. You and Reagan will be the last to arrive."

"Then I'd better pack," said Valeria. "I shall hate to leave. I've really enjoyed my stay here, the first time I've been free from my royal duties." She shook her head disgruntledly. "Never envy those who wear a crown, Savannah, for responsibilities weigh heavily. An ordinary citizen has more freedom to choose their way in life."

Savannah gave a wry smile. "Nor should they envy a Chosen One. The medallion sometimes feels like an anvil around my neck."

Valeria chuckled. "Point taken. Now I'd better pack."

"I'll take my leave, Ma'am. I have a few people I'd like to catch up with before we go," Savannah said, then slipped out of the room, leaving the two to their reunion.

The twins were waiting at the tavern, eager to hear what was happening in the outside world. Savannah studied them thoughtfully as they chatted and laughed. Pablo and Sanyo had the eyes and ears of a cat though the cross was cute, not repugnant. They were so bright and good-natured, it would be a shame if they didn't have an opportunity to leave if they wanted to. "Would you like to see the rest of Rand one day?" she asked quietly.

"We would be mocked looking like this," said Pablo.

Savannah patted his hand. "No, you wouldn't, not now the Forgotten Realms are open. Many strange folks are living there, as well as odd animals, and once they start spreading over our world, no one will give you a second glance. For a start, I'll see Countess Glad-ofin about integrating those who desire to leave the

Forgotten Realms. Believe me, you'll fit in very well there."

Sanyo gazed at her with tears in her eyes. "We would like that very much, Savannah. Our soothsayer's prediction was right when she said 'the Chosen One would lead us out of the darkness.' We just never understood what it meant."

"Now Queen Valeria and Mistress Reagan are aware of the burdens you carry, they will help in any way possible. Mistress Reagan intends to open up her castle in Falendore to the people of Kandelora, especially those who need counseling."

"We all love them both and we'll miss them when they go."

"When this war is over, they will be back," reassured Savannah.

She looked up to see Valeria and Tamasin approaching and behind them Reagan and Eric. By the time they reached the tavern, a crowd had begun to gather, swelling rapidly until the city square was full.

Eric raised his hands to address them. "Friends. It is time to say goodbye to our two guests. They will be sorely missed, but they have promised to return to see us. They now go to fight the enemy and we wish them — "

A thin wail erupted from somewhere in the room, and a small girl dashed out of the crowd and clutched

Reagan around the waist. "You can't leave," she sobbed out.

Reagan looked like she was also going to cry as she gently stroked the girl's back. "Hush, Zoey love, I won't be gone for long."

Zoey sniffled then hiccupped. "You promise to come back?"

"I promise. When I return, I'm going to show you my home in the woods. Lots of animals live there." She hoisted her into her arms. "Come and see me off. Savannah might let you pat her horse before we go."

Savannah's heart went out to the child. "I'll do better than that, Zoey. I'll ask Sunflower to give you a ride."

"Does your horse have wings?" Zoey asked shyly.

"She does, and she loves children."

Zoey clung tighter to Reagan and smiled.

As the people filed past to say goodbye, Savannah felt the love and respect in the room.

A bright spot in a world on the brink of war.

CHAPTER FORTY-FOUR

FALCON'S KEEP

*W*inston was waiting for them when they arrived back at the Keep.

Savannah regarded him in surprise, wondering what was so urgent for him to come. He hurried forward, bowing to the Imperial Queen before he addressed Tamasin, "Consort, I'd like to talk to you, Savannah, and Commander Pela in private."

Catching his serious tone, Tamasin, without argument, signaled to a recruit to fetch Pela.

"Tell her we'll be in the study down the corridor," said Savannah.

"Yes, Ma'am," she said, then hurried out.

Savannah led them to the small room she'd used when she'd sought quiet time to read her books. Winston placed a scroll on the table and took a seat. "I'll explain why I'm here when the Commander arrives," he said.

Pela didn't take long, slightly breathless as though she'd been running. As soon as she sat down, she asked with narrowed eyes, "Is there trouble?"

Winston ran a finger over the scroll and began haltingly, "Well…"

"Out with it, man," ordered Pela impatiently. "You didn't come all this way for nothing."

He resolutely looked her in the eye. "No, I didn't. I've been rethinking our tactics, turning things over, playing out the various outcomes if we proceed with our strategy."

"And what did you find?" The words shot out like bullets.

Without flinching, Winston replied calmly, "We can't win. We haven't paid enough attention to the most important fact — Borrentine knows from the last war that the Queens can close the Time Gateway. We'll never get near it; they would have made catapults to throw the bombs and booby-trapped the dunes. He'll halt the migration temporarily, and it won't matter if he blows up the whole Oasis. The Gateway will still be there when the dust settles." He gestured to Savannah. "Play the game with me, Chosen One, and use the medallion to help."

When Pela opened her mouth to speak, Tamasin

grasped her arm. "Let them play. I'm interested to see what they come up with."

After a nod to Savannah, Winston carefully unrolled the scroll onto the table. A map of Rand was on the parchment, with lines forming it into squares. He tipped out red and white playing pieces from a box, then lined them up at either end. "I'll be red, the enemy," announced Winston. "My pieces are Borrentine's army, the Wolves, bombs, weapons, Skeldachs, and other large creatures that will come through the portal. Your move first."

Savannah drew on her magic and began. She played the first game as they'd planned the war and lost her Queen in record time to a bomb. Six games later, Savannah looked up at Winston and said solemnly, "We can't beat him unless we take the Oasis of Wydola, which is nearly impossible with the pieces we have."

He nodded. "Exactly. An attack by air will fail. Arrows will be useless if they build shelters, and the Elves will be vulnerable in the sky. He'll mine the dunes to stop a land assault."

"There will be thousands of Hawks above," said Pela.

"Borrentine will fight them with his magic," said Savannah. "According to Lilybeth, he conjured up a wind in Beria and blew the Hawks out to sea."

"We can do a few things," Winston said. "Change the

timelines, and everything's altered. The Queens can go earlier to close the Gateway."

Savannah frowned. "The Iriwari said it had to be when the world falls into darkness."

"How exactly did they phrase that?" persisted Winston.

Savannah strained to remember. "Cassine said when the third moon fits between the other two, it will block out the sun, and there will be no light. That will be the sign the Gateway will open."

"But did she say you had to close it then, or *by* then?"

"I see what you're getting at," said Savannah. "We always presumed it was time to close the Gateway when the sign came. Should it be closed earlier?"

"I think you interpreted it the wrong way. If it only stays fully open for six hours, it would be logical to lock the gate and plug the gap beforehand. Once a door starts opening, it's harder to shut," said Winston. "At some stage, they'll need to move everyone out of the Oasis to prepare the ambush."

Putting aside her rising concern, Savannah concentrated on the problem. "We must stop the enemy planting their bombs in the Oasis ... that's the crux of the matter."

"Exactly. That's where we add another piece to our side, something that he won't have considered," said Winston. "We find another player to stop them at the

Oasis, someone who is used to killing with stealth," said Winston.

"The Weyfire Assassins," Pela exclaimed.

"We can't afford them," said Tamasin quickly. "The soldiers and extra recruits have to be paid."

"Money isn't a problem anymore, Tam. We can hire as many as we want," said Savannah. "We haven't yet told you what we found in the Prophecy Tower. A vault containing the wealth of the Silverthorne Witches. It's a fortune. We'll take you and Valeria to see it tomorrow morning."

Tamasin blinked at her. "Really?"

Winston tapped her finger on the table to get their attention. "We need to be synchronized to ensure victory. Once the Assassins successfully kill the soldiers planting the bombs and disable the catapults, the Queens must go in immediately. That's the only window they'll have. Borrentine knows he must hold the Oasis, so as soon as he realizes what's happened, he'll scoot there at once with his soldiers. They'll have to fly there, and the Bramble Hawks will stop some of them before he intervenes."

"Meanwhile, it'll be easier to take the Oasis with him busy elsewhere," said Pela. "By now, their spies would know our army has left Arcadii and is marching south-west to circle the Iron Mountains. Their catapults and soldiers will face the north." She stabbed a finger on the map. "We halt the army below the Moaning Pass out of reach of their catapults and let the Forgotten Realms army attack from the south. With Borrentine out of the way, they won't have any defense against the power of the Guardians."

"I hope it doesn't take too long to close the Time Gateway," muttered Savannah. "He's sure to come up with something."

"We have the Elite Guards in reserve," said Pela. "They'll fly to the Oasis at the first sign of trouble."

"Just one last thing," said Winston. "All officers and riders need a supply of light crystals, for once the sun is covered, the world will fall into total darkness. It will come as a shock to everyone on Rand."

Pela stood and nodded to him. "Thank you for coming, Winston. I'd like you to stay as my advisor when the battle begins. We'll set you up in a safe place close enough to be on hand to discuss tactics."

Winston pondered the suggestion for a moment, then flashed a smile. "I'd be honored, Commander."

"Good," said Pela. "I'll organize my man to take me to the Assassin Guild immediately. How many shall I ask for, Winston?"

"If money's not a problem, then ask for forty or fifty. If the Assassins are as good as you say they are, they'll have the place clean in ten minutes." He looked over at Tamasin. "How long before the moons are aligned?"

"Eight days."

"They'll need to start clearing the Oasis soon to set up their defenses," said Pela. "The Assassins must be in place as soon as the last of the new arrivals have gone. We have a problem, though — how to get the message to the Queens when to go in. They can hide some-where close, for speed is essential." She perused the map. "The northerly mountain on the western side is out of sight and it'll take them about fifteen minutes. They'll need to fly low in a wide circle to avoid being noticed. But to make sure, General Grogan could move the army closer with a few trumpet blasts to distract them."

"That's all very well, but how will we notify the Queens?" asked Tamasin.

Winston flicked a glance at Savannah, who gave a resigned shrug. "I'm the only one who can do it. I can send Malkia a mind message."

"You're not going in with the Assassins, Savannah," Pela said sharply. "They work alone."

"I'm not suggesting I accompany them. Give me Willowtine's camouflage cape, and I'll wait on the top of the dune behind the oasis. Once they've disposed of the Crevlin soldiers, one of the Weyfires could send me a signal. Say flash a light toward the western dune."

"It has merit," said Tamasin, ignoring Pela's scowl. "They'll go in any time after dark. Though you'll have to be there every night waiting, you must fly to somewhere cooler during the day. You'll bake in the heat."

"With only a limited time left before the alignment, it won't be for many nights," said Savannah. She hoped it wouldn't, not relishing waiting in the lonely desert, night after night.

"Just be careful, Savannah, and no heroics," said Pela sternly, then stood up. "I'd better get going. I'll leave you to show Tamasin and the Imperial Queen the vault in the ruins of the Prophecy Tower."

✝

Valeria sniffed the air. "This place still has the revolting taint of black magic."

"It's seeped into the stones after so long," said Tamasin, looking uncomfortable.

Savannah didn't blame them for being wary; she hated the place. She wondered how Valeria was going to take her next request. "Um … Ma'am. I dislike asking, but I have some questions about the tapestry. Could we have a quick look as we go past the Silverthorne's Palace, please?"

Valeria eyed her in horror. "Why do you want to go back in there. Remember what happened last time, Savannah."

"The spell's long gone," she replied calmly. She

didn't mention that Iona had spoken to her from the tapestry — that would alarm them both.

"Okay," said Valeria grudgingly. "But at the first sign of magic, we run. Understood?"

"Yes, Ma'am."

Tamasin led the way, gingerly giving the remains of the Helva Hounds a wide berth. When they entered the antechamber, she remained at the door, poised like a gazelle ready for flight.

Valeria, displaying more fortitude, moved into the room in front of the tapestry, though she didn't stand too close. "What do you want to know, Savannah?"

"Iona wears your Crown. Is she an Imperial Queen?"

Valeria didn't answer immediately, instead studied the scene with interest. "I've never seen anything like this, even in Iona. It's magnificent, and so detailed. Most tapestries and paintings depicting the War of Creation were made centuries later and were only the artists' interpretation."

"But we know this is real because we were there," persisted Savannah.

"Yes, it's a true picture."

"Who is the man on the brown horse?"

Valeria hesitated then muttered, "It's Prince Dazorak."

"You haven't answered my question, Ma'am. Was

Iona an Imperial Queen?" asked Savannah, watching her closely.

Valeria went still, seemingly in two minds about answering. Finally, she said reluctantly, "Yes, she was."

"Then she had to have an heir to continue the line. Was Prince Dazorak her Consort?"

Valeria stared at her, then dropped her voice to a whisper, "You're interfering in things you don't understand, Savannah."

Savannah bowed her head but not before she caught the look of shock in Valeria's eyes. The Imperial Queens had their secrets, and Savannah had just uncovered one. "Sorry. I was just curious."

"You're never *just curious*. Let's go. We've dallied here long enough," Valeria said quickly and swept out of the room.

Pleased with herself, Savannah trotted after her, taking the lead when they reached the next floor. On the landing outside the small room, she said, "It's inside."

When Savannah pushed open the vault, Valeria gave an audible gasp. "There's a fortune in here," she said in awe.

"Enough to fund the war and rebuild all our cities," said Tamasin, running a hand through the gold coins. "Thank you, Savannah."

"Perhaps some could be given to the Kandeloran

people," suggested Savannah. "They've paid for it with their suffering."

Valeria looked up from examining a large red jewel and smiled at her. "I've talked to their elders about relocating. Many of the older generation are content to stay, but the younger ones and single people are keen to see the world. I'll set aside a fund for them out of this wealth." She held the precious stone up to the light. "This alone is worth a Queen's ransom."

CHAPTER FORTY-FIVE

THE WINDY DESERT

*S*avannah wriggled her body into another position in the sand to relieve her aching back.

She rearranged the pale orange cape around her shoulders, resting her chin on her folded arms to peer over the top of the dune. It was only two hours before sunrise, and at the first blush of dawn, Sunflower would be back from her hiding place two dunes behind to pick her up.

After her third night in the desert, Savannah was beginning to despair that they had miscalculated the enemy's plans. In three days, the eclipse would begin — already half the third moon was visible and only a few inches away from the sun. Borrentine had to move soon, for the armies of Rand had rounded the mountain range, and the first waves of soldiers had marched yesterday afternoon as far as the Moaning Pass. She figured he must be leaving it to the last minute to get as many soldiers here as possible, for the earlier losses north of the Cadiwine must have seriously depleted his fighting force.

Then it happened. Midway through another sweep of the dark Oasis, she caught a flutter of light amongst the cluster of palms on the northern section. When another three flicks came, she knew it was the signal she'd been waiting for.

Tamping down her excitement, she projected a thought, *"Are you there, Malkia?"*

The answer came almost immediately. *"Yes, Savannah."*

"It's time for the Queens to come."

"I'll tell Tamasin."

She quickly sent another message. *"The Queens are coming, Sunflower. When you see them fly in from the west, follow them to the Oasis."*

As soon as the mare answered, Savannah tied the tabs on the cape and pulled the hood down over her face, then crawled over the top of the dune. Although it was slow going, she remained on her hands and knees until she reached the first line of trees. Once in the shadows, she carefully stood up and reversed the cape. There was no movement anywhere, but before she took another step, the cold blade of a knife pressed against her windpipe.

"I'm a friend," she squeaked in alarm.

A hissing whisper sounded in her ear, "You're lucky I realized it was you, Chosen One. It's just as well all the enemy are dead — you sounded like a herd of wild animals."

Only when the knife was removed from her throat did Savannah fully relax. *Crap!* That fright had taken ten years from her life. Though she couldn't hear him breathe, she knew the Assassin was still behind her. She remained frozen to the spot and said in a low voice, "The Queens will be here in five minutes. Will you stay until they've finished?"

"We're here until the Gateway is closed. Then our contract is ended."

Savannah felt a wave of relief that they would be there to protect the Covenant, for once the ritual started, she imagined it had to continue without stopping.

"Come," he hissed. "I will show you the Gateway."

When she turned to follow him, she found it so difficult to make out the camouflaged form that she trailed after him more by instinct and her sense of direction.

The Crevlin soldiers wouldn't have stood a chance. Dead Crows littered the way, most decapitated. She swallowed, visualizing how close she'd come to losing her own head. At the end of the tree line, the mercenary gestured toward a large hole in the ground some meters away. On closer inspection, she found it was a seven-sided polygon, the inside sunken like a crater. A circular hole pierced its center, too small for anything to pass through except something the size of a bird. An atrocious stench wafted out of the hole, the same putrid odor of decomposition she'd smelt at Deadman's Knob in the Southern Lands. The Iriwari had been right — the pathway was through the Realm of the Dead.

Thankfully, the hole was far enough away for the screams of the damned to be faint, but she still felt the sense of the inevitability of death warring against her desire to stay alive. She noticed the Assassin kept his distance; she guessed a cold-blooded killer would have far more reason to be terrified by the screams.

When she stepped from the edge, she heard a flutter of wings in the western sky, and six horses appeared over the treetops. After they touched down, the riders dismounted and waited for the Hawk to land. As soon as Pela shifted, dark-robed figures appeared from the shadows and circled the hole. Savannah could barely see them in the dim light, but she was acutely aware they were there.

The Weyfire leader approached the Queens, bowed, then addressed Pela quietly, "We destroyed the enemy,

Commander, before they had time to place their bombs. I suggest you hurry ... dawn isn't far off."

Pela nodded. "Tell the horses to wait on the western edge of the oasis, Savannah, and we'll take our places." She turned to the royal women, "Let's go. We'll stand in the Sheda sequence, with the Chosen One next to the Imperial Queen. Siren, Hawk, Enchantress, Dreamer and Amarim."

As soon as the horses disappeared over the treetops, the Queens moved forward, the air around them crackling with such power that even the silent men stepped right back as they passed by. One by one, the Queens, representing the Earth, Skies, Emotions, Minds and Dreams took their places on the heptagon. Lastly, Savannah as the bearer of the Circle of Sheda, joined them. Valeria raised her hands while the others closed their eyes to concentrate on projecting their magic.

Immediately, a surge of power rushed around the crater, gathering momentum as Valeria began to glow. She lit up the whole area as if daylight had already come. But as Savannah watched in awe when the most powerful magic in Rand was unleashed, she sensed a pervasive odor. The hairs on the back of her neck began to twitch, her sixth sense telling her something evil was here with them.

Suddenly, a Black Wraith materialized in the air above the edge of the Oasis, its formless body dressed in a floating material that swirled and twisted even though there was no wind. For a long moment, it hung there, watching them. When no Queen reacted, Savannah realized they were focused solely on their task and hadn't yet noticed the apparition.

When it began to move toward them, Savannah whispered to Valeria, "Don't stop. The Black Wraith is here. I'll handle it."

Valeria shot a glance over at it, then nodded, the slight trembling of her hands the only indication of her apprehension.

The Assassin must have been aware this wasn't something he could kill, for he hastily stepped aside as it approached. But not quickly enough. The Wraith pointed a finger at him, and long tentacles curled out, strangling him in an instant. It turned to look at Valeria. "You think we would leave the Gateway undefended, idiot Imperial bitch. Now feel my fury."

With a bound, Savannah left her post to confront it. She summoned the ancient magic deep inside her and called out, "Come no further, ghoul, you aren't welcome here."

When more tentacles shot out, she met them with her own. The threads twisted together, coiling and writhing, struggling in a silent battle for supremacy.

Finally, the Wraith dropped its hand and said sourly, "You are strong, Chosen One. You command more than the power of the medallion ... there is ancient magic in your bones." It cackled. "But there are other ways to win a war." It waved its hands at the dunes. "One sting will kill a horse."

At first nothing happened, the pall of silence that fell was as oppressive as the parched land stretched endlessly before them. The sand began to shimmer, and images danced like a mirage, accompanied by a hissing sound. The scene sharpened, and to Savannah's horror, scorpions poured out of the northern dune by the hundreds, skittering along the ground straight at them. The nearest Assassins rushed forward, quashing them with their boots, only to be engulfed by them. They screamed in agony as the poisonous stingers plunged into their flesh.

Savannah raked the ground with a burst of magic fire. But even as the leading wave of scorpions sizzled and popped, more scrambled over their bodies like an endless tide. She continued to sweep the ground with flames, but she knew it was a losing battle. There were just too many. Even though the Queens' faces were strained, they continued to pour their power into Valeria. Her glow increased — it was only a matter of time before she had enough strength to lock the Time Gateway.

Savannah desperately tried to think of a way to give her those minutes. The Wraith hadn't moved, content to let the scorpions do their dirty work. Savannah racked her brain to recall the facts about scorpions she'd read about in preparation for the dig in the Sahara. After frantically straining to remember, it came to her. The predators that ate scorpions were owls, geckos, and bats. She homed in on the bats. According to the book, with their big ears and pig-like noses, they were well-adapted for battling scorpions, as well as being immune to their venom.

She called out frantically, "Reagan, bring the bats. They eat scorpions."

Reagan turned her head to look, then immediately waved a hand. Thousands of bats appeared in the sky, crying out high-pitched squeaks as they swooped down to the oasis. They trawled along the ground, picking up their prey in their claws and mouth. For a start, the streams of scorpions kept coming, but as the flocks of bats ripped them apart, they eventually wavered and scuttled back to the dunes. The Wraith screamed, waved a hand and the scorpions disappeared. As soon as they were gone, Reagan made a quick gesture with her fingers, and the bats vanished too.

Its black robe billowing in the air, the Wraith moved within a yard of Savannah. "You think you've bested me, Savannah, now feel my fury," it said, its hollow voice dripping with hatred. Plucking up a handful of sand, it swept it over the bare ground behind.

Savannah readied her magic for whatever was coming next.

The grains of sand crackled, then began to grow. She watched horrified as they formed into strange soldiers: hellish creatures, with squat muscular bodies covered in wiry fur and with the heads of tusked boars. They wore plated armor to their knees and carried double-edged swords and axes. There were hundreds of them, too many for the remaining Weyfire Assassins, yet they silently lined up beside her, ready for battle. As the creatures began to advance toward them, Savannah streamed out her magic, pushing the first line back. Many fell, but it did little to stop the advance. The Assassins leaped at them, ducking and weaving as they slashed out with their knives.

They fought on, seconds becoming minutes until ten had passed.

Though Savannah kept up the flow of magic, she was tiring. When she stumbled trying to avoid a sword thrust, she knew it was only a matter of time before they all fell, for though most of the Assassins were still on the feet, many had blood streaming from their limbs and faces. Frantically, she cast a glance at Valeria. She was glowing so white that she should be ready to unleash the magic soon, but Savannah doubted they would be able to hold on to give her the vital time she needed.

As she reached the end of her tether, something unexpected happened. The dune behind the creatures erupted and hundreds of bodies leaped out of the sand. With blood-curdling cries, an army of Nomads wielding curved swords raced into the clearing. On the defensive now, the enemy turned to meet the onslaught. Catching the Black Wraith moving quickly toward the Queens, Savannah lassoed it with the ancient threads.

The Wraith spun to face her, but before it could react, a blinding light shattered the darkness, followed by a roar as the heptagonal crater exploded. Rocks spewed into the air, chased closely by a gush of thick molten liquid like black lava. When it fell back down into the hole, the black liquid spread over the surface and solidified immediately, leaving it as smooth as glass. The foul odor in the hole dissipated until only a faint smell of smoke remained.

The tusked creatures crumbled back into sand.

Furious, the Wraith screeched, wheeled in the air, and cried out, "You won this encounter, Imperial Queen, but you won't win the war. We have another Time Gate hidden, one you will never find now. The third eye is nearly in place, and soon the world will fall into darkness. And what comes through the gate will rip your armies to pieces."

With a swirl of black mist, it was gone, but not

504 | COVENANT OF QUEENS

before Savannah saw a pair of black eyes glaring malevolently at her.

Eyes she'd seen before.

Valeria flinched, her shoulders slumped in defeat. "It was all for nothing," she whispered. She left the crater and walked amongst the Assassins and Nomads, bowing her head to them in thanks.

Savannah silently watched them bend their knees to the Crown and knew what she must do.

It was the only way now.

She reached in her coat pocket for the small parcel she'd carefully tucked into the corner. Once she unwrapped it, she pulled the top off the vial and tied the small bottle securely to her belt. Then she calculated the time in history she had to hit. She recalled the date she'd learned from the Crevlin in the Berian dungeon, and added the time elapsed since that day.

Visualizing the date and the hill at Deadman's Knob, Savannah touched the small flower that the old Time Warden had given her back in the Bubbling Pit when she ran The Gauntlet.

She only had a second to jam the top back on the vial before the Oasis winked out of sight.

CHAPTER FORTY-SIX

THE VALLEY OF THE PIPERS

*A*fter three days of marking time in the Wetlands, Jayden appeared with the news they'd been waiting for, "I've received word that General Grogan reached the Moaning Pass six hours ago. We're moving out tonight."

Lilybeth nodded, relieved the anxious wait was over. "My warriors are prepared."

"And the Guardians and Mani are ready, Jayden," said Gladofin.

"Then let's go. No lights ... we move by moonlight only."

The big cats went first, stalking silently through the wheat fields and forests until they reached the first village. They circled the houses, then crouched on the outskirts, ready to pounce on any escaping Crevlin.

The Hawks and mounted Ice Elves followed, hovering over the houses while the Berian soldiers went in with the Guardians. With a population of twelve hundred, the outlying village was small, and it didn't take long to find the place deserted except for a group of women and children in the town hall.

The women stood stiffly in a row to shield the babies, eyeing them warily when Lilybeth and Gladofin entered the room.

"We're friends," Lilybeth called out, moving into the light so they could see her. "Where are all the other people?"

A gray-haired woman stepped forward, relief on her face. "Our village was attacked by an army of Crow shifters two turns of the moons ago. The birds appeared one evening in the streets and changed into soldiers. No one knew who they were or why they came, but we soon learned they were cold-blooded killers. Those who resisted had their throats cut, and the remaining able-bodied folks were forced to harvest the crops and the market gardens. The enemy ate the food in our homes and slaughtered half our herds."

"Where are the invaders now?" asked Gladofin.

"Yesterday, something must have happened because they loaded the wagons and rushed off. They took our people, tied them behind the wagons." She wiped away tears with her sleeve. "My two sons are with them."

Lilybeth patted her arm. "We'll get them back. We'll leave guards, but we must go on."

"Thank you. We'll get the babies fed and into bed."

Gladofin signaled to an Ice Elf. "Four of your squad stay to guard these people."

"Yes, Countess. Prince Jayden sent me to tell you that we move out in five minutes."

"We'll be ready."

As soon as they reached the village gates, Jayden called a halt. "I suspect we'll find all four villages with the same story. The Crevlin will make their stand at Wynfield."

"Why have they given up the territory in the south?" asked Gladofin. "They wouldn't have known we were coming."

"I think it's an obvious answer," said Jayden. "Borrentine needs all the soldiers he can get. He's sustained heavy losses so far, and because he's only been able to dribble his soldiers in, most are still stuck in the past. With the armies of Rand on his doorstep, he must be sweating on the Gateway opening. He has his bombs, but his army is outnumbered."

"That makes sense," said Lilybeth. "They're taking all the stores to the capital."

Jayden looked to the sky. "We've only five hours before dawn. I'll go with half the Elves, the Bears and the Tigers to check on the other villages. Gladofin, you take the Guardians, the rest of the Mani, two squads of my Ice Elves under Captain Leena, and the Berian soldiers, and fly to the outskirts of Wynfield. Half the Hawks will accompany you. We'll be there by dawn if we don't run into trouble.

Gladofin nodded. "We'll get going. Everything now rests on the Covenant of Queens completing their task." When Jayden's expression tightened, she said softly. "Ollie will be fine, Jay."

He grunted. "I hope so. My wife acts as though she's invincible, but her magic will be useless against their bombs."

"Pela has complete faith in the Weyfire Assassins, and the Commander isn't one to exaggerate," Gladofin assured him.

†

A mile from the city, they halted by the river in woodlands thick enough to hide the soldiers and the horses. The Wyn was a slow-moving river, meandering from the Northern Ranges, through Wynfield, then down the valley and spreading into the Wetlands bordering the Sea of Mists. It also afforded a way into the city without being seen. Since the scouts reported no activity in the southern parts of the city, they guessed Winston's supposition was correct. Borrentine had his army facing north to defend the city from General Grogan's army.

After picketing the horses in the trees, Leena set up guard posts, and they settled down to wait. Chaffing at the forced inactivity after two hours, Lilybeth picked up her sword and said quietly, "I'm going to have a look around." Before Gladofin could protest, she padded quickly into the trees.

After a search of the shadowy places in the small woods, she returned much happier. "There's no sign of anyone," she announced. "No Wolves either. Where would they be hiding?"

"Since we haven't seen one since we left the Wetlands, I'd guess they stayed in the Great Northern Forests to join the enemy when the final battle begins," said Gladofin. "Borrentine must be confident the Gateway won't be closed, or he would have ordered them to come."

"One less thing to worry about," muttered Leena.

Gladofin pursed her lips. "Maybe, but I can't help worrying he has some surprises we don't know about."

"No use beating ourselves up about it. We'll face it when the time comes. Borrentine must surely prepare the Oasis for an invasion today — the third moon is nearly in place," Lilybeth said calmly, though she had a feeling Gladofin could be right. Borrentine was an astute commander and didn't come all this way to lose the war again.

The words were no more out of her mouth when a fanfare of trumpets sounded in the north. The long blasts reverberated down the valley and were sure to set the enemy's nerves on edge.

"It's begun," said Gladofin. "The Queens must be at the Oasis." She searched the night sky. "Where is Jayden? We must move before the Rand army is within range of their bombs."

"I've been thinking about that," said Lilybeth. "My troops can follow the river to the outer city and enter via the sewers. We'll be in a position to inflict damage while you attack from the air."

"Don't be ridiculous, Lilybeth. You've no defense against the Guardian's magic."

"You forget I've seen Borrentine in action. He's powerful, and even if he can't beat you, he'll tie you up so you can't use your magic." Lilybeth waved to her troop leader, who ran over immediately. "Get our warriors ready for action, Captain. We move out in five minutes. Camouflage mode, please. We're sneaking in."

"Yes, Ma'am."

Ignoring Gladofin's frown, she donned a dark cape from her saddle pack, then took out a pot of black ointment and plastered it over her hands and face.

"We're ready, Ma'am," came a whisper from the shadows.

Gladofin grasped her arm and said urgently. "Wait, Beth. If you must go, put this on." She took off the pearl necklace and held it out. "The ancient magic can't touch me now, but it can hurt *you*. That foul Black Wraith could be with the enemy, and she's vowed to kill you." When Lilybeth hesitated, she added, "Please don't argue."

She took it reluctantly, more to appease Gladofin than fear for her own safety. "Okay, love, if only to stop you worrying. Be safe," she murmured and took off into the trees in a silent run.

They hugged the tree line on the bank of the river to within sight of the city outskirts before she signaled a halt and dropped low to take stock of the surroundings. "The sewerage outlets should be here somewhere," she whispered. "Be careful from here on. They'll have guards posted somewhere."

A moment later, two men carrying lamps appeared from a flight of stairs that led to a pathway along the riverbank. When one called out something, the other trotted down to the water's edge, peered up and down the river, then shook his head. They turned and headed back up the steps. Lilybeth hadn't understood the language, but she presumed it was only a routine inspection, for there had been nothing urgent in their movements.

Once she was sure they were well out of sight, she dashed across to the wall, her troops following at her heels. They hugged the bricks, moving along the shadows until she caught the whiff of sewerage ahead, and in the dark, she nearly stumbled into a stream of water running out of a hole in the wall. She peered inside, expecting a grate at the entrance. There wasn't one — the outlet was open, but the smell was so atrocious she had to steel herself to enter the tunnel. Once they were far enough inside, she took out a light crystal, pointing it into the gloom. The sewerage tunnel was old; the walls were stained black with age, the air moist with condensation and the water was sludge. They silently moved through, ignoring the smell, the floating debris, and the scurrying rats.

When she judged she was far enough into the city, Lilybeth found an exit passage, and called a halt at the bottom. She climbed the rusty ladder to the top, and after pausing for a minute to listen, tentatively pushed up the grate far enough to peer over the rim. The shaft came out into a deserted cobblestoned street in between two warehouses. Silently slipping the grate to the side, she climbed out, then gestured to her squad to follow. Without wasting any time, she led them on a trot through the streets.

Three blocks further on, two guards rounded the corner in front of them. Lilybeth acted quickly, pushing the point of her blade through the front soldier's chest while her captain sliced the other's throat. After the Crevlin disintegrated into Crows, she tossed the dead birds into a dark recess.

When past the industrial part of the city, she was puzzled to find the residential streets also empty. As they moved along in the shadows, she realized why there were no soldiers — battle cries began to resonate in the north like thunder peals without end. General Grogan had started the assault. Lilybeth knew at any moment the Magical armies would attack from the south, and she searched for a way to help. Hearing a rumble in the next street, she peeped around the wall to see two soldiers coming out of a building, pushing a loaded wheelbarrow.

Once the way was clear, she whispered, "Five soldiers can come with me, Captain. The others stay here with you in the shadows."

Without another word, she led them to the door, pushed it open, and stepped inside. The room was lit by wall lamps, making it easy to see the piles of round black balls that took up over half the space. She picked one up to examine it, finding it was small enough to fit into her hand. It was a round casing with a long wick protruding from a plug at the top.

"Their bombs," she whispered. "If we could light a few, it should blow the lot up."

Abruptly, a voice echoed outside, and the door was pushed open. The nearest Berian slammed the hilt of her sword into the back of the first one's head, while the other soldier was met with Lilybeth's sword. After they collapsed on the ground, she searched a body for something to light the bombs. When she spied a small pot containing a lump of glowing coal attached to the belt, she pulled it off and held it up with a grin. "Here's how they light it. Three of you take one bomb each, and when I count to three, set the wicks alight. Then as soon as I say go, throw them into the pile and run for your lives."

Immediately the wicks began to sizzle, she called out, *"Go!"* and they bolted out the door. When they reached the others, Lilybeth yelled, "Everyone run."

The rest of the troop, catching the urgency, dashed after them. They had just reached the corner of the next street when there was an enormous explosion, followed by a cloud of black smoke billowing into the sky.

Lilybeth lurched as the city shook, vainly trying to keep her footing before she sprawled onto the cobblestones. Then they all fell as a blast of hot air ripped down the street, taking everything before it. Lilybeth turned to see the buildings at the far end of the street were blown apart, but fortunately, the houses their end were still standing, though the wood was starting to burn.

After crawling to her feet, she grinned down at her squad. "Let's go back and leave the rest to the armies. We've done our bit."

CHAPTER FORTY-SEVEN

THE CREVLIN CITY

*S*avannah sped backward in time.

For a period that she could only measure in heartbeats, she moved through the darkness, feeling every throb of her pulse in her temple and hearing every beat of her heart in her ears. As she gained speed, the years raced by faster: a week became a year, a century, five hundred years, a millennium. She spun through the very fabric of time until the darkness became light, and when the universe as she knew it shuddered, she swam between the stars.

She had no idea how long she'd been traveling, but this was entirely different from passing through the portal from Earth. It was mesmerizing. As she floated in the heavens, she reached out to try to touch the stars, marveling at their beauty.

But then the world seemed to shift on its axis, becoming an off-kilter version of the Rand she'd left. The sky became gray, autumn became winter, and the landscape covered in dying trees and frozen rivers. Massive beasts roamed the plains while Skeldachs sailed the skies.

The next instant, she was in a narrow laneway with closed doors on either side. Taking a moment to catch her breath, she huddled against the wall as people passed by, but they ignored her, all hurrying in the same direction. Pulling her cloak around her body to hide herself as much as to ward off the cold, she joined the crowd heading toward the tall tower in the distance. The street led into a large marketplace, where, surprisingly, there were food stalls with a selection of fruits, vegetables, and bread. Meat and game birds hung under the awnings, the cold air keeping them from spoiling. Though the people were very thin, it was not the hollow, sad place she envisaged.

Savannah ducked off into a side street to head for the hill in the northern section for a better view of the countryside. The few people on the track were all going down, and no one gave her a second glance. At the top was a paved area, where a marble statue of a king surrounded by hunting dogs stood in the center. It was set up as a lookout, with seating and railing for visitors to admire the view of the countryside on three sides. To the south, she could make out the Great Elken Lake and the Snakefish River winding like a giant serpent into the distance, while in the east, herds of enormous animals filled a plain. The city was overflowing with people, and in the west, camps stretched as far as the eye could see — it looked like the entire population of the Southern Lands was lined up for a mass exodus.

Surprisingly, though this alien landscape was bleak, little snow was left, and a tinge of green tinted the land on the flats as if a long winter was nearly at an end. Although the people seemed gaunt, presumably from famine, she wondered why they wanted to migrate if the land was regenerating. Then she put it out of her mind as she studied a huge palace dominating the inner city. It was as regal as Arcadia's Palace and the grounds as extensive. From her vantage point, she could make out that the people gathered there were finely dressed.

Lastly, Savannah turned her attention to the tower that soared over the city. It was a seven-sided shape, the base the size of the Gateway at the Oasis. It looked like a chimney but with a closed cap, and she presumed it was in this structure the people were turned into shape-shifting Crows, then propelled through time. Recalling the crack in the ground when she was here last, the way was down, not up.

She couldn't even hazard a guess why they had to go through the Realm of the Dead, nor could she understand how they were turned into Crows. Extremely powerful magic was needed to do something like that, and from her experience with Borrentine, she doubted he possessed that ability. The Black Wraith was far more likely to have hatched the time-travel scheme, and Savannah had no doubt the specter would prove to be her greatest nemesis. Considering what she had come here to do, Savannah thanked her lucky stars the black thing was still in the future.

After one last look around to get her bearings, she made her way to the square with the tower. She climbed the long staircase and with her head down, sidled around the milling crowd to peep through the door. The inside was a maze of colors almost too bright for the naked eye. The walls vibrated, the air pulsated, and a pungent smell hung in the air. She recognized the odor immediately — the same she'd smelt on the Black Wraith. It wasn't the smell of the dead, but a rancid burnt-tar stench even worse than the Wind Howler's black magic. That Demon's stink had been foul enough and remnants still remained where she'd killed it in the canyon.

"Hurry up. You're holding up the line," a strident voice echoed from behind.

Savannah hastily stepped sideways to let the man past — the last thing she wanted was to be caught in there and turned into a Crow. She studied the crowd, finding she'd been in a line of soldiers. Borrentine was moving his army through first. When she retreated against the wall to plan her next move, she heard a commotion in the square at the bottom of the steps. As soon as she saw who it was, she slipped around the corner of the tower out of sight.

His face like thunder, Borrentine strode into the square and gestured to a soldier. "Get them out, Captain," he ordered. "I'll have to reset it to take the other route."

"But we have three men halfway through the process, sir."

Borrentine bared his teeth and swore. "I don't give a tinker's damn. If you don't get them out, they'll be caught in the Realm of the Dead. Those wretched Queens closed the first exit door."

The captain hastily saluted, "Yes, sir."

"And get everyone off the platform," snapped Borrentine. "Everyone within range could be fried by the magic."

There was a rush to vacate the tower at this warning. The captain returned with three men who had wings in place of their arms.

Borrentine eyed them closely. "Once I'm finished, put them in first. The short wait shouldn't compromise the process," he said then bounded up the steps.

As soon as he reached the top, Savannah stepped out

from the shadows. "That's far enough, Borrentine. The Gateway remains closed."

He stopped abruptly, staring at her in disbelief. "Savannah. How did you get here?" He narrowed his eyes. "You're a Time Walker?"

"No, I'm not. How I came here is my secret, but why I'm here is not. I intend to put an end to this once and for all. The future is *our* land, *our* time. You cannot slaughter a race of people to make room for those from the past."

"Pah! You know nothing. We'll die if we stay."

"Your time is now. Whatever's in the future for you, it must happen here. You can't change your destiny at the expense of others."

He glared at her with hatred. "You're from another world, Savannah. Your loyalties lie there, not in Rand. Go back to where you came from … it's not your fight."

"Oh, but it is. My lineage is from Rand too, Borrentine. Didn't you know that?"

He frowned. "How is that possible? You're only here because you found the medallion and put it on."

"I've learned in this world that magic is never random. I was meant to find it because I'm a descendant of Elsbeth."

His eyes widened. "She had a child?"

"Twins." She regarded him thoughtfully. "You didn't know?"

"She didn't tell me," he said furiously.

Savannah stared at him, digesting his words. If he had expected to be told, Borrentine was probably the father of her twins. She hadn't foreseen that.

He must have regretted his response, for his expression turned ugly. "Enough. It's time I put you in your place."

She feigned amusement. "Your magic isn't strong enough."

"I know. But there are other ways to kill," he said, drawing a knife from his belt.

Though Savannah showed little expression, underneath, she burned with anticipation. This was the opportunity she needed. "You can try," she goaded, pulling out her short blade with which she'd practiced so extensively during her training at Falcon's Keep.

His lips peeled back in a diabolical grin. "I can't be killed, Savannah. But *you* can." With a deep growl, he lunged forward, sweeping the knife in an arc.

She ducked, then turned slightly to the side to make herself a smaller target as her Elite Guard instructor, Rhiannon had shown her. He was considerably taller, but Pela had taught her that being smaller had some advantages. She weaved, parried, then ducked low and nicked his side, drawing the first blood.

Infuriated, he jabbed at her with the blade and swung

his other fist savagely at the same time. She danced backward, though not fast enough. The punch caught her in the right kidney, knocking the breath out of her. For a second she saw stars, then rallied and kneed him in the groin. He bellowed, then eyeing her warily, stepped back.

They circled, looking for openings, and for the next five minutes, they thrust and parried. But as time wore on, Borrentine, being stronger, began to get the upper hand. Savannah knew if she didn't do something soon, she might never get the opportunity she sought. She waited patiently, then when she swung at him and he bounced backward, she pretended to slip. As soon as she fell to one knee, she reached for the Dagger of Yorn in her boot.

Now she was down, Borrentine grasped the advantage, stepping forward to deliver the final blow. As he loomed over her with his arm extended, she jabbed the Dagger into his thigh. It was only a flesh wound, normally something he would have brushed off, but not this time. Stopping his swing mid-air, he stared down at his leg.

His face turned purple, then deathly pale. "What have you done to me?" he wheezed out.

Savannah pulled out the blade and said sadly, "I've stabbed you with the Dagger of Yorn, Borrentine. But it gives me no joy to kill my ancestor."

He frowned, desperately trying to get out the words, "Why do you …"

Then his voice drifted away as spittle frothed out of his mouth, and then he was dead.

At the sound of clattering, she looked around to see a band of soldiers running up the stairs. Their raised swords were enough to galvanize her into action. She leaped to her feet and conjured up a ball of fire in her hand. "If you come one step closer, I'll blast you off this platform," she warned.

They halted abruptly, fear reflected in their faces at the sight of magic.

"Everyone get out of the square immediately," she called out, then added, "If you don't, you'll be killed."

The warning, combined with her display of magic, was enough to shock the crowd. They rushed to the exits en masse, though the soldiers were harder to budge. She sizzled out a stream of magic fire in the air and said firmly, "Take your King's body and leave. You have three minutes."

They darted forward, hoisted Borrentine up and carried him off.

With no doubt in her mind, Savannah walked to the edge of the square and turned to face the heptagon tower. She lifted her arms, summoning up the power within her, feeling it rise in a rush and saturate every cell in her body.

With a scream, she unleashed the Death Vale.

The tower exploded with an enormous bang, bricks shooting into the sky as the structure burst into pieces. She clapped both hands over her ears to block out the noise. She was too late: her ears were ringing, her head spinning, and she was so woozy that she felt as if she was going to pass out. Aware she had only moments to get out of the place before the soldiers returned, she tried to concentrate.

Somewhere in her befuddled brain, she remembered Cassine saying the moons aligned the day before winter. She added another day to be sure, then she struggled to think of a safe house. Knowing the Wraith would be out for vengeance, she doubted in this depleted state she'd have a hope against it. After a moment straining for an idea, a place popped into her head. She visualized the library at Falcon's Keep, said the date, and touched the Keeper of Time's flower from the Bubbling Pit.

CHAPTER FORTY-EIGHT

THE VALLEY OF THE PIPERS

*A*n explosion shattered the dawn.

Startled, Tamasin whirled to look to the east. In the direction of Wynfield, smoke jetted into the sky, and at the rate it was increasing, the city had to be on fire.

Shading her eyes to peer into the distance, Pela regarded the smoke intently. "General Grogan must have begun his assault. I wonder what caused that enormous bang."

"Whatever it was," said Tamasin, "it was mighty powerful."

Pela didn't reply, distracted by the approach of the head Assassin. He bowed, then said quietly, "We'll take our leave, Commander. There's no need for payment this time."

Pela looked at the hard man in surprise. "You earned the money. We wouldn't have succeeded without your help, and your Guild has lost many men."

No longer inscrutable, he made a wry face. "We live in this world too, something we've conveniently forgotten. We bent our knee to the Imperial Queen, and until this war is over, we'll fight for the Imperial Crown." After saluting Valeria, he glanced slyly back at Pela. "The Chosen One's a brave woman and smart as well, Commander. You're lucky she picked you for her mate."

Without further words, he led his men in a jog toward the oasis, and they faded into the trees.

Tamasin hid a smile at the expression on Pela's face. Her cheeks spotted red, Pela made a huffing sound. "Call the horses to get everyone out of here. Take the Queens somewhere safe, Tam, though close enough if they're needed. Savannah and I will join the troops." She glanced around. "Where the hell has she gone off to now?"

Tamasin said quickly, "I'll ask Malkia to call her."

When the reply came back immediately, she relayed it with some misgivings. "She doesn't answer, and Sunflower's still there."

Pela blinked at her, as though not quite sure what it meant. "Has anyone seen Savannah?" she called out to the assembled women.

"She couldn't have gone far," said Valeria. "Perhaps she walked to the water."

Before Pela could reply, a flash of light lit up the desert, followed by a sucking sound like air drawn into a vacuum. When Tamasin spun around, the Time Gateway, or what had been left of the heptagon crater, had vanished. Smooth sand lay where it had been, without a mark to indicate the hole had ever existed.

Bewildered, Tamasin stared at the spot. "Why do you think it disappeared now and not when you closed it, Val?"

"It must take time to go, I suppose." She looked hopeful. "Perhaps this means —" The words died in Valeria's throat when out of nowhere, an eerie scream echoed across the desert, "Nooooooooooo,"

The dawn became night again, and a savage wind began to howl, nearly blowing them off their feet. Shivering, Tamasin glanced at the sky. A black cloud swirled above them, and she could sense the malice in the air. "I'll killllll herrrrrrrrr," the wind moaned and then, as quickly as it had appeared, it withdrew, leaving an eerie green light in its wake. Seconds later, the sun was shining again like nothing had happened.

Her face pale, Pela threw Tamasin an uneasy glance. "What in the Goddess's name was that weird thing? And where is Savannah?"

Tamasin shook her head. "I've no idea." She looked

over at the Enchantress. "Can you catch any of Savannah's thoughts, Reagan?"

Reagan, clearly shaken by the foul wind, said in a low voice as if loud sounds might bring it back, "She can block me out completely. I can only sense her presence. She isn't in the Oasis."

When a flutter of wings sounded overhead signaling the arrival of the horses, they all looked relieved.

"If she's not in the Oasis, then it's no use hanging around here," Pela said gruffly. "I'll do a sweep of the desert … she most likely went off with the Nomads. She's too used to going off on her own," she grumbled, then roamed her eyes over the area. "This place makes me uneasy."

†

As soon as the horses touched down in General Grogan's base camp, Tamasin pulled Sunflower over to a tethering post and tied her securely. She'd spent a full five minutes persuading the mare to leave the Oasis and had lost patience with her. In the heat of the moment, Sunflower had even tried to bite Tamasin, earning the defiant horse a hard slap on the rump.

"Stay here until I come to fetch you," she ordered, "If you're not at this post when I come back, there'll be trouble."

When Sunflower reacted to this by flattening her ears and baring her teeth, Tamasin just shook her head. Savannah was letting the horse get away with far too much.

When she returned, still cranky, Valeria chuckled. "Having trouble with the little mare, Mistress of Horses?"

"I swear that horse tries my patience to the limit," she grumbled. "Savannah spoils her."

"Nonsense. She loves Savannah and is intensely loyal. That's a trait to be admired. She's worried like the rest of us."

"I know, Val, but she still lacks discipline," she replied, and kissed her on the cheek. "I'm going to the battlefront. Stay here until you hear the all-clear trumpet call, then come down."

"Be careful. That Black Wraith will be lurking somewhere."

From her vantage point above Wynfield, Tamasin could see flames devouring the lines of wooden houses in the southern quarter. With the fire behind them, the Magical army attacking them from the air, and Grogan's soldiers on the outskirts of the city, the Crevlin were in disarray. For some reason, their cata-pults weren't throwing any more bombs, which left the ground army an unimpeded march into the city.

The Black Wraith was nowhere in sight, nor was

Borrentine. When the ground troops were within yards of the enemy stronghold, and with the Ice Elves' barrage of arrows raining down on them, a sharp cry echoed in the Crevlin's ranks. The enemy immediately morphed into Crows and began a mass retreat to the west. As they desperately fluttered into the air, the flocks of Hawks swooped down, plucking them out of the sky before they reached the city outskirts.

When, minutes later, the final trumpet call reverberated over the city to signal the end of the battle, Tamasin flew down to join Pela on the portico at the entrance of the Palace. It was a large building, far less ostentatious than those of the wealthier Realms in central Rand, but it had plenty of open space surrounding it. General Grogan rode through the ranks of his army and dismounted in front of them in the courtyard. Though he looked tired, he held himself ramrod straight when he saluted Pela. "The battle has been won, Commander."

Pela straightened as she accepted the salute. "Thank you, General. Many losses?"

He permitted himself to smile. "Minimal. Whoever blew up their arsenal should get a promotion. A lot of lives were saved. Once they lost their advantage with the bombs, it was all over for them. Their force wasn't as large as we anticipated."

"Borrentine had lost too many in the last battle."

Grogan nodded. He flicked a glance at Tamasin. "I take it by their retreat that the Imperial Queen succeeded in closing the Time Gateway, Consort."

"She did, General," Tamasin said, not mentioning the second gate. They'd face that hurdle if it eventuated — the troops deserved to celebrate this victory.

"Borrentine disappeared a while ago and never came back," said Grogan. "He's a slippery fellow, but I didn't think he'd abandon his troops."

"Maybe he knew it was a war he couldn't win and cut his losses," said Pela. "He'll be back in his own time now."

Grogan looked over at the burning houses. "With their long march here, my troops have had little sleep. I'd better organize a squad to contain that fire so they can rest."

As soon as he left, Tamasin strode off to search for the Magical army. When she found Jayden with his Elves, she could see from their sober expressions something serious had happened. "Where's the Countess?" she asked quickly.

Jayden pointed solemnly to the ballroom. "She's in there with the wounded."

Tamasin swallowed in alarm. "She's hurt?"

"Not her. But Lilybeth is missing. She's very upset and didn't want us in there."

"I'll talk to her, Jayden," she said and hurried to the

door, dreading what she was going to find. Tamasin always hated this part of a battle, the aftermath when the air was filled with the screams of the wounded and dying, and they had to count their dead.

The room was so crowded with the injured and healers that she initially failed to see the Countess. Then she caught a glimpse of her on the far side of the room, searching through the bodies. Tamasin hurried over and touched her arm. "Who are you looking for, Glad?" she asked softly.

Her face scrunched up in agony, Gladofin let out a long breath like a painful sob. "We can't find Lilybeth or any of her squad. We're sure it was them who blew up the Crevlin's bombs. They must have been caught in the explosion."

"Hey," said Tamasin, touching her arm reassuringly. "Lilybeth's a smart woman. She knows her way around a battlefield and wouldn't get caught in a blast she knew was coming."

"Then where is she?"

"I imagine somewhere away from the fire. She probably headed to the river. How did she get into the city?"

Gladofin pressed her lips together. "Through the sewers. I hated that she went."

"She didn't ride?"

"No."

Tamasin forced a smile. "There you go then. They

534 | COVENANT OF QUEENS

probably went back to the horses, and that would take time."

Gladofin blinked at her. "You think so? Maybe that is possible. I'll get Jayden to send someone to look," she said with renewed vigor and hurried off to find him.

Tamasin trailed after her, worried she'd given her false hope. But she needn't have been concerned. As they stepped out the front door, Banner carrying a soot-covered Lilybeth, her uniform streaked with grime and missing a sleeve, came into land. As soon as she dismounted, she grinned broadly and ran up the steps.

Her lip quivering, Gladofin hugged her fiercely and said with a voice thick with emotion, "Never give me a fright like that again, Beth."

"Hey. I had it under control. You should have seen those little suckers go off." She clapped her hands elatedly and called out, "Boom! I …" She stopped abruptly at the look on Gladofin's face. "I'm sorry, Glad. I'll have to get used to someone worrying about me."

Tamasin looked on amused. Lilybeth's single days had come to an end.

Then she turned as a roar went up, and Valeria appeared overhead. Marigold floated down into a perfect landing, then stood still while Tamasin helped her Queen dismount. When the soldiers, including the Magical Folk, bent their knees, Tamasin brushed away an emotional tear in an unconscious gesture. Though Valeria accepted the homage regally as the Crown's right, Tamasin could see underneath that she was touched.

Tamasin watched her proudly, knowing it had been a stressful day for everyone, especially her wife. It must have taken enormous willpower to ignore the Wraith while she concentrated on absorbing the immense power of the Covenant. To hold and channel it would have been almost overwhelming. She was going to need comfort tonight.

Tamasin glanced across at Pela. Standing in the background, she looked strained. They locked glances, and Tamasin's unspoken thought reflected in Pela's eyes.

Savannah could be dead.

CHAPTER FORTY-NINE

FALCON'S KEEP

Savannah opened her eyes gingerly, relieved her ears were no longer ringing.

"At last you're awake."

Savannah looked around to see the elderly librarian on the chair beside the bed. "How long have I been asleep, Glenda?"

"Two days, Savannah. I came home from lunch to find you unconscious on the floor."

"That long," she exclaimed. "Has the sun been blocked out yet?"

"Yesterday. It was a little frightening, for the sky was so black it was the first time the stars shone in the sky."

"I would have loved to see it," Savannah said, then added anxiously. "Does anyone else know I'm here?"

"No. By the state you were in when I found you, I guessed you needed a hiding place. Am I correct?"

"You are. There's someone after me and I can't be found. Not yet anyhow."

"You are quite safe here until you decide to leave." Glenda put down her book and tilted her head to study her. "Tell me why you came here of all places?"

"It seemed the logical place to hide. No one would think to look for me here. Hidden in plain sight..." Savannah gazed around the room. "This is where you sleep. I didn't mean to take your bed."

"I've another in the next room. It's quite comfortable," Glenda said and stood up. "Use the washroom and the privy while I fetch you something to eat and drink. You must be starving."

Back to her old self after the meal, Savannah joined her in the reading room but as she watched the old librarian potter about, she couldn't help feeling she'd come to the library for a reason. Her sixth sense had twitched when Glenda had asked why she'd chosen here to hide. She'd replied it was the logical place, but on further recollection, it hadn't been quite like that. The thought had just popped into her head. She froze. Or had someone planted the thought?

Damnit! When had she become so suspicious of everything? Crafty old Ronja had made her a paranoid mess.

But try as she might, she couldn't shake the feeling she'd come here for a reason. There was a secret to ferret out, and in a library, it would most likely be a book. She shrugged — no time like the present to start. "Who looked after the library before you, Glenda?" she asked.

"Another former Elite Guard."

"Have all the librarians been Guards?"

"Yes. We're a specialized school."

"But not authorities on history," murmured Savannah. "Mistress Moira trains librarians to staff the public libraries."

Glenda frowned. "What are you getting at, Savannah?"

"I'm curious. Being so well-stocked, I guess this library warrants a full-time librarian. But why? The recruits only come to study physical maneuvers and these books can be put anywhere. The librarians are soldiers, not academics." Savannah gave her a disarming smile. "I imagine you are an exception."

"That's how it's always been. What's your point?"

"If I wanted to hide an important book, I'd put it here. It's a legitimate but obscure library that few frequent, in a tough training school in the middle of the most forbidding place on Rand." She raised her eyebrows at Glenda. "You must have had a fit when I turned up and wanted to access the archives."

"You're being fanciful," said Glenda, though this time, her smile was missing. "I enjoyed your company and welcomed you."

"And I liked being here with you as well. Nevertheless, I think this library was put here for a reason. To hide a book, and if there is such a book, may I see it, please? I have a feeling it will explain a lot of things that have been puzzling me."

Glenda's eyes widened. "If there is a secret book," she whispered, "why would I show it to you?"

"Because I wouldn't ask if it wasn't important," Savannah replied patiently. "There's something or someone out there that's going to wreak havoc on the world if I don't stop them. I must know what I'm up against."

"There is a book," said Glenda cautiously.

"What is it?" asked Savannah, tamping down her excitement.

"The Register of Births, Deaths, and Marriages."

Savannah frowned, deflated. "Why is that so important?"

"Because it's the record of the very ancient world."

"Oh! I see."

"Exactly. It dates back long before Iona. Imagine what would happen if the people learned Iona was flesh and blood." She chewed her lip for a long moment, then straightened her shoulders. "Swear on the sacred medallion, Savannah, that you'll never mention this to anyone, and you may see the book."

Savannah was so excited that she leaped up and hugged her. "Thank you, Glenda, for trusting me. I promise, on the medallion, I'll keep the secret."

"I hope you find what you're seeking, my girl," said Glenda quietly. "Some secrets are never meant to be revealed."

"I know. But I must understand the past if I'm going to fulfill my destiny in the future."

Glenda looked at her oddly. "You speak in riddles, Savannah, but I have always sensed there is more to you than meets the eye. So much more than a bearer of the medallion. Set up a stand, and I'll bring you the book. But be careful; it's fragile."

"Just one more question," Savannah said quickly. "Who owns the Keep?"

"The Imperial Queen, of course."

When Glenda bustled off, Savannah pursed her lips. That'd be right — Valeria had more secrets than rabbits in a warren.

Savannah pushed back her chair and rubbed her smarting eyes. The writing was so faint and spidery that she'd had to use the magnifying glass, but it had been worth taking time to decipher the entries. It proved to be a treasure trove of bloodlines.

Iona was only one in a long line of Queens in ancient Rand and was married to Prince Dazorak. Because he died in his late thirties, Savannah presumed he lost his life in the War of Creation. Iona gave birth to twins — a girl and a boy, Una and Colan.

Una went on to be the next Imperial Queen, but when Savannah saw Colan's family tree, she knew she'd hit the jackpot. He married a woman from the Southern Lands, and they also had twins — two girls, Ronja and Hola.

At twenty-five, Ronja moved to the Magical Lands and married a female Mani, but there were no details of the kind of shapeshifting abilities she possessed. At this point, Ronja's family tree became sketchy — the Magical Folk probably didn't enter every birth — but they did record one. A girl. Their place of residence was Amarim.

Meanwhile, Hola married a Prince from the Southern Lands. They had four sons; Borrentine was twenty generations further down the ancestral line of the first son. His place of residence was recorded as Crevlinia.

And an interesting fact emerged: the Ancient Magical Houses like the Sirens of Sunhaven were already well established by the time of Iona's reign. Savannah frowned, trying to think. It was called the War of Creation but was that merely a convenient way for the Imperial Queens to explain the battle. She left that one in the too-hard basket, then called out to Glenda that she had finished.

As she carefully picked up the book, Glenda asked, "Did you find what you were looking for, Savannah?"

She nodded. "I did, thanks." She didn't offer any more information, nor, to her credit, did Glenda ask. When she went off to put the book away, Savannah settled down to try to put things into perspective.

She jotted down the facts she knew.

She had inherited a potpourri of magic, which meant her ancestor possessed many magical forms. Borrentine was a Time Walker, and though he'd possessed great power, she sensed he hadn't been a magical being. He hated them too much. And Hola couldn't have passed on the *Mind* Walker gene.

So logically, because Savannah was a *Mind* Walker, Borrentine couldn't have been the father of Elsbeth's children.

Ronja married a woman, so she couldn't have had sons. But even if someone in her lineage had had a son, he wouldn't have been a *Time* Walker, because Ronja couldn't have passed on that gene.

Savannah toyed with the idea of the father of Elsbeth's children being Prince Dazorak, but she dismissed it. When Iona had looked at her from the tapestry, she had said with love, "You are so like him, dear one." No woman would say that about a husband she despised.

But she would have said it about a son she loved.

That left only one person who could be the father. Colan, the son of Iona and the father of Ronja and Hola.

It was time for a frank talk with Grandmother.

As soon as Glenda returned, Savannah feigned exhaustion and retired to the bedroom. She shut her eyes and called with her mind, *"Grandmother, are you there?"*

"I am, Savannah. Where have you been? I lost track of you."

Savannah frowned. *"What do you mean?"*

"You moved out of this plane of existence, away from the threads."

"You didn't see me destroy the Crevlin Time Tower back in time?"

"You did what? How is that possible?" For once, Ronja sounded off-kilter.

"I used the flower the Keeper of Time gave me. Now I want answers, and I'm in no mood to banter, Grandmother," she said sternly.

"I will answer them now, girl. You are ready. The last threads joining our times were broken when you made your own journey, and the old ways have passed into history.

When I die shortly, you will inherit my mantle. What do you wish to know?"

Suddenly, Savannah felt like crying. Ronja had become dear to her, and she would miss her dreadfully. *"Take me somewhere where we can be together to talk, please, Grandmother,"* she said in a small voice.

As soon as she spoke, the air swirled, transporting her to an oak tree in a field of daffodils. The old lady sat under the tree and patted the ground. "Sit here, little one."

Savannah leaned over to kiss her cheek. "It's better when I can see you."

Tears sparkled on the lids of the blind eyes. "I know. Ask your questions, but some I may not answer."

"Why not?" asked Savannah curiously.

"Because you must have earned the right to know. You won't fully appreciate or understand the knowledge otherwise."

"Huh! You're tough," said Savannah, then took a big breath. "Is your father, Colan, the father of Elsbeth's twins?"

The opaque eyes widened. "You worked that out. Well done. When my mother died young, he began to time travel."

"Are you a magical being as well as a Time Walker? I know you're the first Guardian, so I suspect you must be."

"Yes, I inherited a lot of my father's magic."

Savannah continued, "But Hola didn't. She's a Time Walker but nothing else, that's why she resents the Magical Folk. Her magic comes from the demon world. Am I right?"

"You are very astute," Ronja said approvingly.

Savannah chuckled. "Not really, I smelt it on her. Borrentine, too, had the stench of black magic, but his wasn't so bad."

"Had?"

"I killed him with the Dagger of Yorn when I destroyed the Time Tower in the Crevlin City."

The aged hand shot out, grasping her arm in a tight grip. "You must be ready, Savannah. Hola won't rest until she kills you now … you have wiped out her bloodline."

"I know," Savannah said, feeling a wave of anxiety. "I've learned the most important things in Rand are bloodlines and magic. I'll be waiting for her." She went on chidingly, "You've played a dangerous game keeping me in the dark about Hola, Grandmother. Why didn't you tell me right from the beginning that Hola was behind everything. When she first appeared in the Prophecy Tower, you even told her about the next invasion as if she didn't know. And then assured me not once but twice that she was harmless and just a meddler."

"I lied to protect you, Savannah. Hola's magic can't touch you, but she has other ways to kill. She controls the darkest black magic from the very pit of the demon world. You are strong enough to fight her now that you've come into your full power. You wouldn't have had a hope against her before."

"Is she a demon like Agatha?"

"No, far worse."

"Oh!" squeaked Savannah, not being able to visualize anything worse than Silverthorne Witch Agatha's demon form.

"Just remember when you meet her that she plays mind games."

Savannah swallowed "Okay, I'll be on my guard. Now, I have something else that I'd like to know. Why did Iona and Dazorak fight?"

Ronja turned to stare at her with her sightless eyes. "You have a theory?"

"It was a power struggle, I suppose. He coveted the throne." Then Savannah had a thought. "Or perhaps, considering their son was magical, maybe it was because Iona was magical and he wasn't."

"I'll leave you to work that one out yourself, Savannah. It is a little more complicated."

"Before you go, Grandmother, could you tell me why the Crevlin disappeared. If it was a famine, some would have survived. It looked like the land was regenerating when I was there."

"Come, hold my hand, and I will show you."

As soon as Savannah clasped her hand, the scene changed, and they were riding a winged horse above the Southern Lands. Ronja pointed a bony finger to the south at the Bolderdore Mountains. "A day ago, there was an enormous eruption in the Southern Ice Ocean. Watch."

As Savannah concentrated on the mountains, something appeared on the top. At first, it was hard to make out, but soon she recognized it as a wave of biblical proportions heading toward the Southern Lands. The tsunami rushed over the mountains, spreading right across the flat southern continent, freezing everything living when it hit. The following three waves cemented their doom, leaving every inch of the land a frozen wasteland. Nothing could have survived except for the few Skeldachs who managed to elude the Black Eagle Hawks and burrow into the Isle of Misery.

Savannah gaped at the destruction. It had been cataclysmic.

In retrospect, she realized that signs had been there to indicate the sea had come inland; the seashells at The Blushing Bear, and the fossilized seahorse she'd found on Deadman's Knob. It also explained why the pioneers left it so long to resettle the land — they waited for the rains over time to dilute the salt in the soil enough to grow crops.

She felt enormous pity for the people but suffered little guilt for stopping their time travelling. It was a fate they could have prevented if they had been on better terms with the people from the north.

CHAPTER FIFTY

The following morning, Savannah knew she couldn't wait any longer. Even though she would have preferred leaving it a few more days to be off Hola's radar, her silence was hurting those she loved. Pela must be searching everywhere, and Sunflower would be frantic.

Time to let them know she was here. Concentrating hard, she sent out a mind message.

"Are you there, Sunflower?"

There was no answer, so she tried Malkia. When he didn't reply, she sent out a random message. *"Is anyone there?"*

After another try without an answer, she cursed. The horses must be too far away, and she'd have to master her talent if she was going to be a Mind Walker. She was hopeless at it.

Pressing her fingers to her temples, she shut her eyes and projected the thought with the help of magic, *"Can anyone hear me?"*

This time, an answer came faintly as if from a long distance. *"Where are you, Savannah?"*

"At the library at Falcon's Keep. Is that you, Tamasin?"

"Yes, I... do ..." the voice began, but then it faded away.

Though the disconnection left Savannah frustrated to grasp the concept, she looked on the bright side. Now Tamasin knew she was alive, she would pass on the message. All Savannah had to do was to see the Commander of the Keep about lending her a horse. In the meantime, she'd have some breakfast with Glenda since there was no rush.

They'd just finished the meal when there was a loud knock on the door.

Glenda rose and gathered up the plates. "You get it while I wash these up."

When Savannah opened the door, her heart leaped into her mouth. Pela was standing on the threshold, staring at her under lowered brows. When Savannah flashed her a warm smile and leaned forward to hug her, Pela brushed past her irritably. Hurt, she trailed after her.

As soon as Savannah stepped into the room, Pela whirled around. "Do you even care what you put people through, Savannah?" she snapped.

Savannah's lip trembled. Pela was more than pissed off this time, she looked furious. "That's not fair, Pel. I did what I had to. I destroyed their Time Tower ... the Crevlin won't be coming here again."

Instead of placating her, it seemed to incense her even more. Her hands bunched into fists as she shook with rage. "You bring grief to everything you touch. That mare of yours savagely bit off Tamasin's fingers, and Valeria had to put her down."

At the words, a lump in Savannah's throat threatened to choke her. She brushed away a tear, trying to grapple with her grief. Beautiful Sunflower was dead. The words knifed through her heart, leaving her barely able to whisper the word, "Nooo."

Pela's eyes were cold, reflecting no love or sympathy. "And you caused her death. You're not worth anything to anyone on Rand, especially me. You are an interloper, a harpy. You suck people dry and then throw them away." Pela gripped her face in her fingers. "Remember when you're lonely in your bed at night, Savannah, that you weren't woman enough to keep me. You were a poor excuse for a lover."

Savannah wiped her eyes with her sleeve. She felt

her hopes and happiness collapsing. Pela didn't want her. "You can't mean that," she cried.

"Yes. I. Do," Pela grated out. She grabbed a fistful of Savannah's shirt and slammed her against the wall. Savannah winced but held off with her magic. Even though Pela's behavior was beyond frightening, she wouldn't be provoked into using her magic against someone she loved.

"Stop it, Pela. I love you."

"Rubbish, you love no one but yourself. You don't give a damn about anyone."

She slammed her against the wall again. "Kill yourself. That's the only way you can serve the people of Rand. Die and the medallion can be passed on to someone worthy to wear it. With your death, there will be hope for the future. Your perverted magic has infected the world."

Bereft, Savannah's emotions plunged to a place where the deprivation was so dark that she was beyond comfort. Was there any reason to go on?

"Commander. What are you doing?" Glenda's voice rang out from the kitchen doorway.

Pela dropped Savannah and spun around. "Who in the Goddess's name are you?" she snarled.

Glenda squeaked, "What do you mean? You gave me the librarian position."

Savannah blinked, her mind in such an agonizing

mess that it took a moment to absorb the words. Then through all the turmoil, she remembered Grandmother's warning, *"She plays mind games."*

Oh crap, she'd been so stupid.

Pela went still, then she darted a look at Savannah and saw the dawning recognition on her face. When Glenda went to speak again, she snapped, "Hold your tongue or I will cut it out."

Glenda paled, then ran back to the kitchen.

Savannah backed away, readying her magic. "So you found me, Hola. I should have realized it was you. Pela would never behave like that."

A cackle exploded. "What do you mean Hola, stupid girl? I thought you were smarter than that."

Her body began to shrink, her skin turned old, and her face changed. When the metamorphous was complete, Ronja stood looking at her, though she was no longer blind. "Oh, Savannah, you've been so naïve."

Savannah blanched. It had been Ronja all along, manipulating her every step of the way. "You were responsible for everything, Grandmother?" she asked incredulously.

"Of course. And you were so gullible. Finding the medallion for me and bringing it back to Rand. Elsbeth knew I wanted to kill her, and she disappeared where I couldn't find her."

"Why did you want to kill her?"

Ronja sneered. "She was my father's whore. I was his heir."

Savannah stared at her. A giant piece of the puzzle fell into place. Colan had married a woman from the Southern Lands and settled there. He was the Crevlin King; another child could have been a Time Walker and a contender for the throne. All this suffering was about one woman's lust for power.

"I know Conan was your father and my ancestor. I also know you went to Amarim to live, Ronja," she murmured.

Anger blazed in the old lady's eyes. "How would you know, Savannah? It was over three thousand years ago."

"You have no idea what I've learned. You said yourself the threads are gone." She glared at her. "I know this woman in front of me isn't Ronja. It's you, Hola. And I hate that your father is my ancestor."

"Bah," she snarled, then the air about her began to shiver until Ronja disintegrated and Hola stood in her place.

But this time, she wasn't old but looked like a horrifying version of a Banshee from a book of Irish folklore. She was as ugly as sin, the face of pure evil.

But the black eyes were the same, the windows to her bitter soul. As Hola stared at her in hatred, Savannah could see in their depths there would be no mercy. "Since you have wiped out my bloodline, I will make sure that all you hold dear is destroyed. You have no idea what dark times are."

"That's a load of rubbish, and you know it," snapped Savannah. "Your people were doomed by an act of nature. If you hadn't been so hungry for power and were at odds with the rest of Rand, they would have given the Crevlin a safe place to escape the tsunami. As for Borrentine, he tried to kill me, so deserved everything he got."

Hola clenched her hands into fists. "For his death, I'm going to make you suffer."

"And you know how to inflict great pain, don't you," Savannah stated flatly. "You've caused enough on this world. After your first attempt at bringing your people through time failed, you systematically went out to destroy all the magic in Rand. You loathed magic because you inherited none except the ability to walk through time, and you hated Ronja because she got it all. You started on the ancient houses of Rand first, urging the sorcerers to bring the demons through to destroy them. Then you organized the Mystic Wars and subsequent banishment of the Magical Folk to the Forgotten Realms. What did you offer the Witches and Wizards, Hola?"

Hola sneered. "They wanted more power, so I gave them black magic." Her eyes blazed with hatred at

Savannah. "You haven't understood anything, girl. I inherited magic, Grandfather Dazorak's black magic."

Savannah stared at her. "He created the demons," she whispered in horror.

Hola shrugged. "He wanted an army, so he made one. Now, enough talk … prepare to die."

She shot out threads from her fingertips which Savannah met with her own.

Magic tangled together, tightening, snarling into knots.

Hola dropped her hands, exclaiming, "You have become powerful. There are other ways to kill."

With a wave of her fingers, a sword appeared in her hand. Savannah sprang back warily, searching for something to ward her off. As Hola lunged at her with the sword, she grasped a chair to shield the blow. When the blade sliced through the wood like butter, she knew she was in trouble. The weapon had magical qualities. After the next two swipes barely missed, Savannah knew she had only one hope. As she ducked the next thrust, she reached for the Dagger in her boot. But she doubted whether she'd have a chance to use it. Hola's cold eyes stared down at her, her arm poised to deliver the fatal blow.

Suddenly, a cry, "Get out of my library, witch," echoed through the room. Glenda burst through the kitchen door, brandishing a sword in both hands.

Twisting quickly at the sound, Hola, with a flick of her wrist, threw a magic bolt at her. As it pierced her upper torso, the old librarian screamed in pain. She clutched at the widening bloodstain on her shirt, desperately trying to staunch the flow.

Rage surged within Savannah. Grasping the opportunity Glenda had given her, she sank the Dagger of Yorn into Hola's belly.

Hola grunted, swatting at it with her hand. As she attempted to raise her weapon with the other, she stiffened with a gasp. She looked incredulously at the Dagger still in her abdomen and then at Savannah. "What have you done to me?" she whimpered.

"I've killed you, Hola. Now your line is truly gone. And good riddance."

Her eyes filled with fury, Hola moved her mouth but failed to utter any sound. Her body began to shrink until only the black eyes were left. Finally, they too disappeared into a pile of dust. The powerful stench of black magic wafted into the air, then drifted out the window.

Savannah ran over to Glenda who lay sprawled awkwardly in death. She sank onto the floor beside the dead woman, and as Savannah keened out her grief, the ghastly events of the morning closed in on her. She lay down next to Glenda, closed her eyes, and willed sleep to come.

┼

"Savannah, wake up."

She groggily opened her eyes to find Pela kneeling beside her. "Pela," she cried. Clutching her around the waist, Savannah promptly burst into tears.

"Hey, love, it'll be fine," murmured Pela, her face a mask of concern. "What happened here?"

"It was ... sniff ... Hola. She killed Glenda."

Pela looked around fearfully. "Where is the bitchy witch now?"

Savannah mustered up a smile. "I killed her."

"Good for you," said Pela. She hugged Savannah tightly. "I'll fetch someone to collect Glenda's body."

Bereft, Savannah reached over to stroke the old librarian's hair. "Glenda was a dear friend and a brave woman, Pel. She sacrificed her life to save me. She would have known she had no chance against magic, yet she didn't hesitate. When Hola was about to strike the fatal blow, Glenda rushed at her with a sword. It gave me time to stab Hola with the Dagger."

"She'll be buried with full military honors and her sacrifice recorded. She was an excellent trainer in her younger years," Pela assured her. "Elite Guards prize courage and the Keep will give her a worthy send-off."

"She deserves one."

Pela's face clouded. "Where did you disappear to,

Savannah? We feared the worst. There's worrying news... we haven't found the second Gateway. Rand is preparing for a full-scale war but we have no idea where the enemy is amassing its forces."

Savannah tried to smile, though it felt more like a grimace. The recent events were too raw. "There'll be no war. I went back in time, killed Borrentine and destroyed their Time Gateway."

As she proceeded to tell her story, Pela's face was a mask of emotions. When she finished, she didn't say a word, simply pulled Savannah into a tight hug.

They sat there for a long minute, content in each other's arms. After giving her a gentle kiss, Pela said quietly. "You did well, love. I'm proud of you. Now, I'd better see to Glenda, and while I do that, there's a certain horse who has been frantically waiting for news. She's outside in the common."

"Valeria didn't kill her?" she asked, fighting a fresh bout of tears.

Pela stared. "What did that bitch Hola tell you? Come on, the fresh air will do you a world of good." She pressed lips to hers in another lingering kiss. "I love you, Savannah. And always will."

She took her hand, and when they walked out into the sunlight, Savannah's world spun back on an even keel. All was well. After a last smile at Pela, she ran across the common to meet the little horse galloping to meet her.

She threw her arms around the silky neck and projected softly, *"I couldn't take you with me, Sweetie. Not this time. I went back to the past."*

"I was worried sick, Savannah. I couldn't find you."

"I know. I'm sorry. Now I'm back, I'll take you to visit the Blue Fjords in their Valley. We're due for a holiday together."

Sunflower gave a happy snicker. *"And bring a bag of apples."*

CHAPTER FIFTY-ONE

THE AMARIM PALACE

The Amarim valley was picture perfect; snow that had coated the north white had melted with the coming of spring, leaving the countryside a flowering wonderland. Thousands of animals had come to the valley to watch their Countess marry Queen Lilybeth, and the gardens were full of Mani.

The wedding ceremony was held on the front porch of the Palace to allow the Magical Folk a view, while guests from the Royal Houses were seated in the front courtyard. Savannah clutched Pela's hand as she watched the happy couple take their vows under a floral arch. The hoop was packed with pink and white blooms, while masses of flowers and lanterns decorated the marble floor either side. With the splendid white

Palace as the backdrop, it seemed to Savannah like something out of a fairytale.

The brides looked beautiful and so completely in love that she choked back a tear. She wiped her eyes, conscious Pela's eyes were on her. Savannah smiled at her ruefully. Lord, she'd faced the worst demons without flinching, yet here she was wallowing in sentimentality.

Pela squeezed her hand fondly and whispered, "You're an old softy, love."

"I know. Can't help it," she murmured.

When the celebrant, an old woman with yellow hair and bright green eyes, called out, "You may kiss the bride," loud clapping resounded over the courtyard and gardens.

As everyone rose to congratulate the newly-weds, Savannah noted none of the Royal Houses were missing — since this was Olivine's first official function, they'd all be dying to get a glimpse of the Amarim Palace. As the happy couple wandered among the guests, Savannah, knowing Pela's aversion to formal gatherings, clasped her hand. "Come on. Let's go up to our room until it's time for the banquet."

Once upstairs, they settled against the balcony rail to watch the sun set over the Forgotten Realms. When Savannah leaned her head on Pela's shoulder, Pela's arm drifted around her waist and she whispered, "I'd be happy to stay here all night."

"I know," said Savannah, "but I'm afraid our absence will be noticed. We'll slip in quietly, and maybe after a suitable time, we can quietly go off to bed."

"Huh! I know you love these things, especially the dancing."

Savannah laughed, then pulled her head down for a soft kiss. "I do. You'll have to put up with it tonight. And we'll have to do it all again when they have a celebration at Beria." She looked back at the valley and said wistfully. "The brides looked lovely."

"I'd liked to have heard the conversation when Gladofin told Lilybeth she had to wear a wedding gown," said Pela with a chuckle.

"The tailored gown was very regal and suited her," said Savannah. "I imagine the old Berian Palace will get a facelift as soon as the Countess takes up residence."

Pela nodded. "Lilybeth won't have a say. Not that she'll object … she thinks the sun shines out of Gladofin."

At the sound of a horn, Savannah pushed away from the balcony and took her arm. "Time to go. That's the call to come to the banquet hall."

After they walked down the central staircase, Savannah pulled her into a shadowy recess under the steps. "We'll wait here until all the Royals are seated, then come in with the rest," she whispered.

The newly wedded couple came first, then as befitting their rank, the Imperial Queen on the arm of her Consort, followed by the Amarim Queen and Consort. Fern and Jezzine came next, trailed by the rest of the royals. It was decked out splendidly for the occasion. Olivine had spared no expense for the wedding and the banquet, and in the gardens, there was a feast for the Mani.

As the less important folk filed through the door, she tugged at Pela's arm. "Time to go."

Their attempt to enter unnoticed proved useless. The crowd parted to let them through, and a burst of applause resounded around the room. Olivine indicated two chairs near the head of the table. "Come Commander and Chosen One, sit here as befitting honored guests."

"So much for your *let's slip in unnoticed*," mumbled Pela in her ear.

Savannah took the offered chair, pleased to see Luna and Floris next to her. A pretty young Elite Guard sat on the other side of Pela, blushing as she threw her a timid glance.

Pela bowed at her. "We haven't met."

"Gosh, Commander, this is an honor. I'm Maybeth, Queen Lilybeth's daughter."

Savannah discreetly studied the girl as Pela responded, "I heard you were at Falcon's Keep. You have big shoes to fill. Your mother is a fine warrior."

Savannah nearly rolled her eyes. So much for Pela making the girl feel at ease. She needn't have worried, for Maybeth smiled and said cheerily, "She is. Few are as proficient as her with the sword, but she's not much at knife throwing. I can beat her there."

A glimmer of a smile flitted on Pela's lips. "Then you'll have to show me sometime. Now, tell me about your training. I miss the Keep."

Savannah tuned out, turning to Luna who was talking to Eric across the table. He looked so smart in his new formal clothes that the hair on his face didn't seem unusual. Reagan stroked his hand with her thumb while she nodded to Savannah. She didn't look at Pela, but being Reagan, Savannah knew perfectly well she would be roaming around the minds at the table. She wouldn't be able to help herself, though after the debacle with Pela, she'd pick a softer target.

Suddenly, Floris tilted her head to regard Reagan closely. "I am a strong Empath, Mistress Reagan. I can feel your presence in my mind. What do you see?"

Reagan had the grace to blush. "You are a true innocent, and they are rare. I apologize for intruding."

Floris reached over the table to take her hand. "I read emotions. You're helping my people, but it's taking a toll on you. You cannot absorb all their grief and pain without help. If you come to me tomorrow, I will teach you how to separate your emotions from your patients' anguish."

Reagan blinked at her in surprise, then said in a low voice, "Thank you, Floris. I would appreciate your help." When she caught Savannah watching their interaction, Reagan made a wry face. "I've been quietly, but firmly put in my place," she murmured.

Savannah chuckled. "That you have, Mistress Enchantress."

A moment later, the master of ceremonies thumped his staff to announce Olivine, who stood to welcome the guests, and the banquet commenced.

Six courses later, they moved into the main hall for the entertainment. Savannah roamed around, catching up with everyone.

When she reached the Arcadian Queen, Fern took her hand and whispered, "We have some exciting news."

"Oh?"

"We're going to have a baby." She smiled at Jezzine, who looked blooming. "The Daughters of the Sacred Temple performed the ritual ten weeks ago. Jezz wanted to carry our first child."

"That's wonderful," said Savannah, happy for them both. They would make such loving parents.

"Mia can't wait to have a sister," Jezzine said, teary-eyed. "I'm the luckiest woman in Rand."

Savannah smiled at her fondly. "I think you're both lucky. I see Gladofin beckoning, so I'll see you two later."

"Hi, Countess, you look gorgeous."

Gladofin smiled. "You always know the right thing to say, Savannah. I haven't had a chance to thank you for what you did for us all."

"I spent the winter with Pela in the Bramble Hawk village. We needed a break together." She stopped and eyed the green pearl necklace. Her magic was rising to its call. "That's an interesting necklace. Where did it come from?"

"I can sense it's responding to you," said Gladofin, studying her keenly. "It's from a race of Sea Nymphs."

"May I touch it?"

When Gladofin nodded, she stretched out a finger. As soon as the tip hit a pearl, an image of a beautiful coral island filled with people flashed into Savannah's mind. She smiled at Gladofin. "The Island's very beautiful," she whispered.

"I think they'll be pleased to meet you, Savannah. Now, Tamasin approaches and she looks like she wants a word with you. I'll catch up later."

Savannah turned to greet her. "Hey, Tam," she said. "You look smashing in that coat."

Tamasin gave a little snort. "Huh! Valeria spent a fortune on it, and the thing makes me look like a peacock. She wants to talk to you ... she's out on the balcony. She hasn't seen you since the Valley of the Pipers."

"I was with Pela in her village. She had duties to attend to." She looked at Tamasin wistfully. "It's been over a year since you brought me through the portal. So much has happened that it feels like a lifetime."

Tamasin squeezed her hand. "I know. Lord knows what would have happened to this world if I hadn't found you. Pela is lucky you came, but I have no idea how you managed to tame her."

Savannah chuckled. "I haven't tamed her. I won her heart." She stood up. "I'd better go to Valeria. She doesn't like waiting." She didn't tell Tamasin that after reading the book at Falcon's Keep, she'd deliberately avoided Valeria — she'd been too annoyed with the Imperial Queens and their dangerous secrets.

Valeria was sitting in a side alcove off the balcony and looked up when she approached. She pointed to the seat opposite. "Sit down, Savannah. I've been wanting to thank you for your heroics. Rand owes you a debt. You're a fine Chosen One."

Savannah sat down tentatively and replied quietly, "Thank you, Your Majesty."

Valeria eyed her speculatively. "I've been waiting for you to come to Iona to see me."

"I took time off to be with Pela. The war was hard on us both. Was there anything specific you wanted to see me about, Ma'am?"

"Why did you go to the library at Falcon's Keep?"

"I wanted a place Hola wouldn't find me after I destroyed the Crevlin Time Tower."

Valeria raised her eyebrows. "You never do anything unless for a good reason, Savannah. Rand has plenty of places to hide out. What were you looking for in the library?"

"What was there to search for, Ma'am?"

"Don't play with me, girl," snapped Valeria.

"You know perfectly well what I went there to find, Your Majesty. You put it there," retorted Savannah, her temper rising.

Valeria paled. "You read it?" she whispered.

"Yes, I did. It solved many puzzles, and I know why you went to such lengths to hide the book. Iona was an Imperial Queen whose disastrous marriage nearly brought down the Imperial line. Her Consort, Prince Dazorak created a demon army to take her throne, and she only just averted ruin by defeating him in battle. And what did the next Imperial Queens do? To save face, they perpetuated a myth that it was the Battle of

Creation, thus venerating Iona as a Goddess. After Dazorak was killed, I suspect Iona banished the demon hordes to another dimension."

Valeria pursed her lips. "You're right, of course. Once the battle was recorded in history, we had no option but to continue the legend. Iona didn't have the power to kill all the demons born from the black magic, so she sent them off Rand into another plane of existence. How did you kill Hola, Savannah? Nothing on Rand can destroy the very ancient black magic she possessed, not even the Death Vale. It's different from demon magic."

"Iona made a safeguard for the future world should that magic ever surface again. She had the Dagger of Yorn forged, the weapon, I suspect, she used to kill Dazorak."

"I've never heard of it," said Valeria, then her eyes narrowed. "You have come a long way as the Chosen One, which creates a dilemma for me. What am I going to do with you? You know too many secrets."

Savannah looked her straight in the eye. "You're not going to do a thing, Queen Valeria. I am as much a pawn in all this as you. Iona's son, Colan, was the father of Elsbeth's children. By some quirk of nature, I inherited all his magic except the ability to time travel." She stopped as a thought hit. "Maybe Iona did create something: the Magical Folk. Then she infused their genes into Colan. But we'll never know that for sure."

"So you're a descendant of Colan. That explains a lot," said Valeria thoughtfully. "But you're still the Chosen One and bound to protect the Crown."

"Which I will continue to do," replied Savannah. She looked slyly at Valeria. "With me as your bodyguard and Pela as your Imperial Commander, you will be very well protected."

A reluctant smile crept over Valeria's face. "That I will, Chosen One. Now, I'd better find Tamasin before she takes off her coat. It cost me a fortune."

As soon as Valeria left the alcove, Savannah closed her eyes. She hadn't heard from Ronja for a while, which was a little worrying.

"Grandmother. Are you there?"

"Yes, my child, but my life is fading away."

Alarmed, Savannah quickly called out, *"Take me to you."*

Immediately, the world tilted, and she was beside the old woman under the oak tree. She was lying on a bed of flower petals, a small, sad smile on her face. Savannah knelt beside her, took the thin hand, and gently rested her head on her chest. "I don't want you to go, Grandmother."

Ronja stroked her hair soothingly. "My time has come to leave this world, my sweet Savannah. I have lived for over a hundred and fifty years; much longer than my beloved Claudia."

"Your wife?"

"My wife, my lover, my best friend. We did very well together."

"You had children, Grandmother?"

"Two girls. They are beside my bed with their children, keeping vigil," she whispered, then smiled at Savannah. "You are as precious to me as my blood. You'll make a fine Mind Walker."

"I am not much good at it," moaned Savannah.

A soft laugh came. "Don't be so impatient. You must crawl before you can walk. Since few people will be able to hear you outright, you must use your magic to get your message across. Channel it through something."

"You're the voice in the medallion," Savannah exclaimed.

"Yes. It's a perfect medium to mind speak. As well, Dreamers are very receptive through their dreams."

"Just one thing I can't understand, Grandmother. If I can't *time* walk, how do you and I move through time."

"Ah, it's an illusion, Savannah. We are projecting our minds, not our bodies to another place. It just feels like we are there."

"I have so many questions. What exactly is the role of a Mind Walker? Do I have the ability for a purpose?"

"You have a very important role to play. Mind Walkers have the responsibility to protect Rand. You'll know when you need to help and guide … it's an inbuilt instinct."

"So something will tell me when I have to interfere?" asked Savannah.

The old lady sighed. "More or less, But I prefer to call it *help*."

"Hmmm. You didn't by any chance send me a task today?"

"No, Savannah. I have already passed on the mantle. Why?"

"The Sea Nymphs spoke to me through the Sacred Pearls. Something evil will be coming to Rand next year."

The bony hand reached out to take hers. "Your first task, child. But, I'm sorry, I won't be around to help. I'm so very tired now."

A wave of hopelessness rushed through Savannah when the old lady closed her eyes. "Grandmother, I'm not ready to say goodbye," she choked out.

"It's time for me to go, my sweet girl."

The oak tree began to sway, its leaves fluttering off into the wind like the years into eternity. One by one they floated away as Ronja's life-force petered out. She sank into unconsciousness, then her breathing became labored until finally, she disappeared. And then

Savannah was back in the alcove, tears trickling down her cheeks. With an effort, she pulled herself together — this was a celebration, not the time to grieve. That could come later in a quiet place.

Savannah walked to the railing and looked over the gardens where the Magical Folk celebrated. She recognized many she'd met in her travels: the Mani from the Milky Mountain, the Willow Dryads, the Tigers, the Deer, the Bears, and in amongst them, Winston with his arms around two pretty Faeries. A moment later, the Golden Unicorn from the Enchantress's castle saw her and whinnied loudly. At the sound, the Magical Folk turned toward her, then, all together, bowed deeply to her.

Manoak appeared in the sky and dipped his wings, closely followed by his Queen, Snow Pine, then Hyacinth, Malkia, and Marigold. Sunflower came last, giving an extra theatrical twirl before soaring back into the sky.

"There you are, love," Pela's voice echoed in her ear. She wrapped her arms around her tightly. "I was wondering where you disappeared to."

Savannah sank back into the warm embrace. "I'm just getting some fresh air."

Pela ghosted a kiss on her neck. "We're going to have a good life together, Savannah Cole."

"We will, Pela, Queen of the Bramble Hawks."

†

End of Book 3

†

I hope you enjoyed *Covenant of Queens*. I'd appreciate if you left a review at the Amazon site.

Printed in Great Britain
by Amazon